IN
W✗MEN
WE TRUST

IN
~~WO~~MEN
WE TRUST

A Novel

N.H. SAKHIA

ACROBAT BOOKS

New York

PUBLISHED BY ACROBAT BOOKS

A division of Acrobat Publishing Group, Inc.

747 Third Avenue, Suite 200 New York, New York 10017

Book Cover and Interior design by Najdan Mancic

ISBN 978-1-7354535-2-1 (Paperback)

ISBN 978-1-7354535-0-7 (Hardcover)

ISBN 978-1-7354535-1-4 (E-book)

Library of Congress Control Number: 2020918956

*To my family
and anyone who has
faced injustice*

PROLOGUE

WHILE THIS BOOK is a work of fiction, it was inspired by real-life events which came to light only when a courageous woman took a stand and was supported by the lawyers, journalists, and society in general who stood with her in very testing times.

The Universal Declaration of Human Rights in its preamble states "whereas recognition of the inherent dignity and of the equal and inalienable rights of all members of the human family is the foundation of freedom, justice, and peace in the world, whereas disregard and contempt for human rights have resulted in *barbarous acts* which have *outraged the conscience of mankind.*"

Unfortunately, the conscience of mankind is very selective in getting outraged.

In human rights treaties, states bear the primary burden of responsibility for protecting and encouraging human rights. This doesn't mean that members of civil society don't also have a responsibility to prevent human rights violations. It is a shared responsibility of all to protect the rights of the entire humanity. Violations occur all the time, but they should always be called out.

The author of this book is an Attorney at Law and can be reached at **SakhiaLawGroup.com**, should someone need to explore possibilities of asserting their human rights under the law.

ONE

B ADRI'S EYES OPENED suddenly. Darkness. A void deeper than any black, starless night engulfed her. Eyes wide open she stared into an indiscernible place of blurred, bluish-black. She squinted and blinked several times, hoping to detect something, anything.

Nothing.

Her stomach sickened with an indescribable primal fear. The darkness lengthened and then shortened like dancing shadows, teasing. Disoriented by the lack of a horizon, which even the inkiest night usually provided, she felt propelled away from earth, from reality, dizzying her steps. Lost in thought and without much balance she felt a feather-light breeze graze her face tousling her hair ever so gently, reminding her that she's alive. Reaching towards it was a natural reaction and it was the first comfort in what seemed like a very long while. She leaned her thin bruised shoulder against a rough damp surface, needing support, praying for something to hold her steadily. She could barely hear the dreamy voice coming from somewhere close, echoing, calling her name. She knew it wasn't real but chose to accept it as Mimi Jan's soft whisper. The word she heard was: *Noor*, meaning moonlight. *Noor* was also another name for *Badri*, and it was a name used only by her grandmother, the love that Badri felt for her was unworldly. Mimi Jan loved short words, and it rolled easily off her tongue in a way that "Badri" never could. Her voice felt as close as it sounded, coming from somewhere in those dancing shadows, and Badri sensed it right alongside her.

"Mimi Jan," Badri whispered back, twisting around rapidly, in desperation. "Where are you? Why can't I see you?"

"I'm right here, just as I always will be...never far." Mimi Jan whispered back.

Badri continued to twist and turn quickly but was still unable to see the phantom voice.

"Look up my Noor." Mimi Jan laughed from above. Badri's eyes dilated wide from the darkness, narrowed instantly at the sight before her.

"Mimi," she whispered in awe.

"How are you my dear - my Noor?" Mimi Jan asked with the familiar compassion that in the past had soothed her.

"The truth, Mimi Jan, is that I'm in unbearable pain." Badri's voice was barely audible, and her eyes glistening and burning. She was unable to lie to her grandmother, even though her instinct was to smoothly erase any hints of indignity or malevolence to spare her grandmother from any weighted concern, but now the truth prevailed, although she was confessing to a spirit, a ghost. To Badri, she was real.

"It will pass, my Noor, you must believe that you *need* to believe." She whispered.

"Will it?" Badri sobbed softly, extending her hand, wishing she would grab it, willing it to happen. She could feel Mimi Jan clutching her wrist as she used to. A bittersweet feeling overwhelmed her and she fought to contain it and prevent it from slipping away. She would hold on at all costs. Her memory of her beloved grandmother was at this time all she had.

"I'm wounded Mimi Jan." Her agony so deep she struggled to find the words, and each breath greatly painful. "These vicious animals have destroyed me; they've broken me Mimi Jan."

"Noor, it's true, these monsters have violated you, they have beaten you terribly, and they have attempted to break you, but there is one thing they will not be able to do. They will never succeed in taking away your pride. Don't worry my dear Noor, you'll see what happens to them, stay strong. *Allah* is with you."

She kept sobbing, the pain insufferable, nearly to the point where she wasn't lucid. Mimi Jan's voice called out, "come here my dear Noor, come to me."

Badri felt lifted, as though she was floating toward her grandmother's loving arms as they pulled her close. She could feel Mimi Jan kiss her forehead as she used to, and in that moment, in the perpetual night, she began to heal. She became aware of something other than torment coursing through her, where there ran blood there now ran fire. Her newly born strength gave her a reason to fight, and dread began to be replaced with vigilance.

Her growing courage however couldn't stop the flow of relentless tears that seemed to be coming from someone other than herself, she could feel them running down her cheeks, but she could not feel herself crying. Every move she made hurt in new ways, and so she held onto Mimi Jan even tighter knowing that at any moment she might slip away and disappear back into the shadows. She pleaded with her to stay, "I won't let you go. I won't, I can't."

Mimi Jan cradled her as she would an infant, and ran her fingers through her tangled and matted hair hoping to soothe her. Badri's rapid breathing slowed, and she began to feel a sense of tranquility as she recalled her grandmother's words of kindness: "your face glows more than the moon because Allah made you extra beautiful."

"It's a curse Mimi Jan, my face has never brought me happiness." Badri blamed her beauty for the extreme violations she just endured and for the hopelessness that now ensnared her.

11

"Don't say that my child," Mimi Jan retorted. "*Allah is Jameel*. HE is beautiful, and he made everything beautiful, and you, he made you extra beautiful. Always be grateful, always be thankful."

"I am thankful Mimi Jan, but look what's happened to me. These animals might have spared me if I didn't look this way."

Badri, despite her words, knew that animals will be savage in a wasteland as easily as in a paradise, but she also needed to know that there would be an end to this brutality and unjust treatment.

"They are beasts, Noor," Mimi Jan said. "Pretty face or not, they will attack."

Images flashed in front of her closed eyes, images nearly as painful as her physical hurts: vicious creatures in the form of human beings attacking her. She tried keeping count, but it was intolerable, so many of them taking turns violating her, laughing cruelly while devouring her, destroying her, ripping her to pieces.

 Badri relived the caustic moments of last night, the night she had lost her honor, the night she had felt worse than a beaten animal, just a soulless body gratifying their unbound lust and urges and base fantasies. She knew that she needed to stop the incessant flow of flashbacks because it was pointless, and she knew that it was possible that she might never again feel cleansed or pure. Badri knew that she, like many others alike, would have to learn to extinguish hope and quietly accept the inevitable.

She sat in a state of quasi hypnosis, gazing into thin air, streaks of tears staining her face, remembering a story her grandmother used to tell her, a bedtime story providing solace, the story that would allow her to temporarily escape. Folklore about the beautiful *Lake Saiful Muluk*. It was a tale about dreams of beauty and love, about how a child's heart is pure and unconditional and an adult's heart is tainted and conditional and easier to corrupt. Badri needed to comprehend this to be able to understand why people are so cruel, so barbaric. Maybe it would tell her that in the end evil doesn't win, that may be good, will triumph, that maybe it's alright to have hope.

She kept staring straight ahead, barely blinking, transfixed by the memory of her talks with Mimi Jan about fairytale-like love. How will good be able to prevail when an adult's love is transactional? Did these brutal beings feel love? Do they love only if they get something in return? The battle between good and evil is never ceasing. "The purest form of love is to love without expectations, and usually only the very young can do that." She recalled Mimi Jan's true words, holding onto whatever voice she could.

Badri began crying once again, or so she thought until she realized she had actually never stopped, not for a moment, shedding tears from a pool as deep and wide as the vast sky. She craned her head up into empty space, willing the appearance of her grandmother's face, willing it to look down upon her, and gently kiss her cheeks. She in return kissed the air softly almost tasting Mimi Jan's invisible tears. Tears, blood, and pain—that was who she was now.

"Mimi Jan please tell me the story. Please Mimi Jan just once more." Badri pleaded, and not sure if her grandmother was still beside her, or if she was fading away.

"I'm still here my Noor, and I remember how this tale brought you comfort, and how you would have dreams of love and all things joyful." Her voice was slightly softer than before. "You were so little and so lovely. You still are. I loved the way you used to beg me with your tiny hands, your lovely eyes, and your sweet voice."

"Did I make you happy Mimi Jan?" Badri asked, wishing she was still that small child safe in her grandmother's arms, in the warmth of the summer sun, ignorant of the ways of the world they live within.

"Of course you did Badri. You were the only person who brought me joy." Mimi Jan's voice was paling. "Every parent hopes for a sweet little girl like you."

"Why is that Mimi Jan? Why do parents wish that their children remain small?" Badri was grasping at anything so that she could keep her grandmother close, anything to keep all the darkness around her at bay.

"A baby's love is pure Badri. Purity in love does not, it cannot belong to adults."

"Not even me?" Badri asked, knowing the answer.

"No my dear, not even you."

"How can you say that Mimi Jan!" Badri turned her head and wrapped her arms around her frail body. She wondered if that meant that she was no longer loved. "Mimi Jan how can you say that?" She asked again.

"Because it's the sad truth my Noor. A child's love is pure and unconditional, but the love in an adult's heart is tainted with other things...it is impure. It is easier to corrupt." Mimi Jan paused for effect. "An adult's love is transactional; they love only if they get something in return." Badri stayed silent, she knew this already but needed to hear Mimi Jan's voice and wisdom. "Occasionally an adult will expect and accept love in return of love, but usually they want something else. The purest form of love is to love without expectation, and usually only the very young can do that."

"Mimi Jan, please tell me the story now." Badri herself was beginning to tire, to weaken. "I am ready." Her eyes closed, and Mimi Jan began.

It was a tale from long ago when mountains were not this tall and clouds were not this high. When trees were not so old, and flowers never shed their petals. It was a time when humans and animals lived together. There was no war and there was no hunger. There was no fear; there was only peace.

The idyllic world changed. Slowly and gradually the people in this world changed. They stopped wanting to live with animals, in fact, they stopped wanting to live with other humans. As time passed, the same people who used to take care of one another, would not want to so much as look at each other. And worse, this peaceful world came to an end. One man paid a very high price for this, he paid dearly.

This man was the great, great, great, great-grandson of Joseph, and Joseph was the most handsome man to walk the earth. Nobody before him, nobody in his time, and nobody after him could match his charm, beauty, or strength. But just like all others, he was a mere mortal and time caught up with him. He grew old and weak but never lost his charm or kindness. No one knew his age, but it was said that he lived a very long life. He had many children, but none of them inherited the charm and beauty that God only gave to him.

Joseph became very, very old, and very sick and he wasn't long for this life. He was on his deathbed and people had many questions. They could not imagine a world without him. One thing everybody kept asking was: who would inherit his looks and charm? Would these things die with him? None of the children nor his grandchildren possessed his wonderful attributes, they were nothing like him. The people were concerned about losing Joseph forever if there wasn't anyone to take his place, at least then, he could live on through that person.

Joseph, being the gracious and kindhearted man that he was, wanted to reassure the people and put them at ease. He called for a blacksmith to come to his bedside, and he whispered something in his ears. The blacksmith nodded and said that he would return in three days. All those around him wanted to know this big secret, but the blacksmith kept quiet. He left with plans to return in three days, not knowing that when he returned, Joseph would no longer be alive. When he returned, Joseph's children and grandchildren demanded answers. What was the secret?

The blacksmith said nothing, not a word; just waved in front of them, two round cast iron embossing seals. The people clamored around pushed and shoved peering and craning their necks over the shoulders of others, trying to see, but they did not understand what they saw. Joseph's family asked what the iron seals meant. He reminded them about their desire to know about Joseph's inheritance, and so at that moment, he presented them with the iron seals. They still did not understand, and so the blacksmith asked them to bring him a piece of paper and ink. He said he had something to show them, and that then they would know. They gave him the paper and ink, and the blacksmith dipped the seals in ink and pressed them onto the paper. After he lifted the seals from the paper, they could see two faces: the face of a handsome young man on one side, and the face of a fairy on the other. Then the blacksmith explained it.

The face of the man was the person who would one day inherit Joseph's charm. It would take a long time for this man to come into the world, and into their lineage, and after a long journey, he would fall in love with the fairy from the other seal. The search for the fairy would take years, and then they would marry. This marriage would only come to pass after a great struggle, and after much bravery and sacrifice on the part of the man. Once he married the fairy, he would be granted all of Joseph's beauty and charm, and stay that way forever. They would make their home in the middle of a lake surrounded by very high, snow-capped mountains, which would be covered with very tall trees. They would never grow old and they would have many children, and those children would be the most beautiful and courageous of all children.

That is what the blacksmith told Joseph's family.

They stared at him fascinated, but taken aback. They wanted to know where he had heard such a story, and the blacksmith told them that he'd heard it from Joseph. One child was doubtful, another was unconvinced, and some were skeptical and blamed Joseph's exhaustion, claiming that he wasn't of sound mind and didn't know what he was saying. The blacksmith told them that they could believe him and take the seals, or he could throw the seals in a ditch and walk away. It was their choice and he had done his part.

"Mimi Jan what happened to the seals?" Badri needing as much detail as possible. Anything to keep her away from her bruised bones and fear.

"The seals were misplaced and eventually nobody believed they ever existed, and so they became a myth. A family legend, but it didn't stop people from searching. Many generations passed but there was always someone who believed in the story."

One day after many, many years, a boy found the mysterious seals, he was familiar with the tale of Joseph. He polished the mysterious seals until they shined, and then he showed them off to anyone and everyone. This boy was well-liked, and over time many asked him where he found the seals. The boy said he couldn't remember, and the more he tried to remember, the more confused he became. So then, it was believed to be divine intervention. The boy's name was Saif ul Muluk, and because of his regal beauty and elegance, he became known as Prince Saif ul Muluk, meaning "guardian of the land." He showed off the seals to all, and the famous tale of Joseph became alive once again. They asked him if he was pleased with the face of the fairy. He told them that he was, that in fact, he was already in love with her, but that he would only search for her if he knew where to look. A pious man in the crowd named Dervish came forward and asked Prince Saif ul Muluk if he was serious about finding the fairy He said he was. He said that he wanted the whole story to come true, he said he has known about this tale his whole life, and now that he has become the center of it all he has a burning desire to find her and complete this story and live the life of his dreams.

Dervish told him to get ready for a great journey. He would need to head east for at least a thousand nights going toward the Malaka Parbat ---the queen of the mountains. There he would see a beautiful lake at the foot of the mountain range, and it's there that he needs to wait for the Fairy. It was known that she liked to swim in the lake upon occasion. Once he found her he would have to hide her wings to prohibit her from flying away, and that soon enough her anger would cease and she would fall in love with him, and they would live happily ever after.

It was a challenging journey, full of peril, but that didn't stop him. He kept going never discouraged and after a thousand days and a thousand nights he finally came to a lake which looked like paradise. He waited at this lake at the foot of the mountain range for her to arrive.

"Noor, the legend has it that he waited twelve lunar years and that each year that passed, as the boy grew into a man, he became more and more handsome. He never gave up hope. It was said that the divine forces of the universe brought her to life and then to him." Badri stayed silent, waiting for more.

One day, Prince Saif ul Muluk saw her walking to the lake to swim, in the company of several of her friends. He couldn't take his eyes off her, he was mesmerized by her beauty and composure. He watched her from behind a large tree. At first, she didn't notice him, but when she did she was unhappy that he had been watching her without her consent. But soon she forgave him. The following day, he took her wings and hid them, and told her that she could have them back if she would agree to stay with him at the lake for three days and three nights. He decided to call her Jamala, meaning beautiful. The fairy stayed for the agreed-upon three days and three nights, and then asked for her wings and told Prince Saif that she was leaving. He asked why and asked if she enjoyed her time with him, and she said yes. He wouldn't give up, he refused to simply accept her answer, and so he asked her why she was leaving. She told him that she wasn't free and that her soul was captive. That the Safaid Deou; the "White Beast" was her captor and that she wasn't allowed to go anywhere without his permission. Prince Saif told her that he would free her from this

19

beast, but the fairy told him that it's not possible, that the only way she can ever be free is if the beast is dead. The Beast however was very strong and unnaturally powerful and he would not be easily defeated. Prince Saif was determined to find a way to free his love, he couldn't bear her tears and sadness. He searched for ways to weaken the beast, and one day, the fairy's friend told him that she'd heard that the evil beast's soul was hidden in some type of talisman, and if the talisman was destroyed, the beast would become weak enough to be killed. And so, the search for the talisman began, and Prince Saif succeeded in finding it and destroyed it.

After a long battle and great struggle, he was at last able to kill the beast. Finally, after conquering even more obstacles, and another suitor called the White Giant, Prince Saif ul Muluk married his beloved fairy and Joseph's words came true. They lived in a cave in the middle of the lake, at the foot of the snow-capped mountains covered by trees, they never aged, and they had many children. Saif and the fairy lived happily for eternity.

Mimi Jan paused. Badri's eyes were shut.

"Sweet dreams my child," she whispered in her ear. "May Allah be with you in these difficult times, and may you have peace in your heart."

Badri was finally fast asleep. Mimi Jan began to fade away into the dark shadows, there was nothing else she could do except hope that her prayers were heard, and that faith was restored. While traveling away from Badri, she turned around and she saw her beloved Noor. Her clothes were ripped, she was covered in bruises and dried blood and she was lying asleep but not defeated on the damp dirt floor.

As she floated higher up, she could see the shabby house, the dirt road, and the small town where Badri had lived her whole life. Mimi Jan's ascent continued, higher and higher, until the earth was just a mere speck.

~

Badri's moments of sleep ended abruptly when a loud bang shocked her out of her dream state. Her heart pounded so heavily she feared it might be heard, her burning dry eyes opened wide riveted on the door, her mouth slightly agape. After a seeming eternity, she blinked and swallowed and recognized her surroundings. She was in the same dimly lit room where she had lost consciousness and had erased any trace of her life as she had known it.

Mimi Jan's visit in her dreams was surreal, she knew that but she could still feel her grandmother's healing kisses on her forehead and she could still hear her soft voice telling the tale of *Prince Saif ul Muluk*. "I will free your soul from this beast," she remembered hearing. Surprisingly she felt no pain. Not even when someone reached down to grab her arms and yanked her up. Not even when they shoved her, pulled her by her hair, and elbowed her in the ribs forcing her to stand. She heard the sounds of someone getting slapped. *Where was her Prince Saif from the fairytale? Where was her Prince Saif?* Her left cheek burned. She opened her swollen eyes to find several men surrounding her. The last thing she remembered was a fist coming towards her face.

TWO

MULLAH AZIZ WAS a short, portly man in his fifties. He had a long beard, with few strands of grey and white sprinkled throughout. He was in the habit of touching his nose all the time while talking, even in his sleep. And talk in the sleep he did; mostly cursing and muttering, using profanity that was filthy to its core, words which he would never use while awake, or, at least, outside his home.

The inside of the home was another story.

He believed in totality that a man's house is his castle where standard social rules didn't apply. When in his own house, if he wanted to shout, he would shout. If he wanted to curse, he would curse; if he wanted to hit his child, he would hit him. If he wanted to mistreat his wife, he would; that included the taking of physical pleasure from her, which he so often desired, and she so often resisted. It made absolutely no difference to him as long as his desires were fulfilled.

They lived in a small apartment-like structure, inside a big mosque, located in a small town named Hayatabad. The Pakistan Air Force Base was the biggest commercial complex nearby. Other than that, the town's economy depended on agriculture, and most of the land was owned and controlled by three families. A mafia of sorts. Of these three, Sardar Timur Barlas was the biggest landowner and by far the most influential.

The region was known for its fertile land and hospitable people. Everybody knew everybody and even in the rare case that they didn't, they knew him – the renowned Mullah Aziz. He was, in his opinion, a celebrity.

He was the Imam of the largest mosque in this small town, a practical deity in a town sprinkled with small homes and shops. This vast and expansive green-tiled structure with giant white minarets and green dome was his castle as well as the center of the town's activities. As the Imam of this grand mosque, Mullah Aziz occupied a central place in the religious life of the people of this town. His was the only mosque that could hold Friday's congregational prayers, as it was the largest and Friday congregation was required–at least according to the belief of the town people–to be held in the biggest mosque in the city. Mullah Aziz reveled in the glory of his magnanimous reputation. An essential part of the Friday prayers was the *Khutba*, the religious sermon delivered before the start of the prayer, attendance to which was considered mandatory and during which any worldly activity was considered a grievous error, religiously prohibited, and an inexcusable sin. Everyone from the city and areas surrounding the city was familiar with Mullah Aziz and the firebrand sermons he delivered every Friday. In the last ten years, he had never failed to appear for the Friday's congregational early afternoon prayers, no matter what.

In the beginning, people ridiculed him for his outlandish utterings, some even openly questioned his radical ideas and what they called "hate-filled" speech. However, over the years he noticed that people tended to agree with him more frequently. He noticed, too, a softening of criticism; which naturally comes with a sort of, beginning of acceptance. After that, he saw more quiet acquiescence and finally, quite a sizeable following. He felt that his words were reaching the right ears and found it was mostly the youngsters who were befriending him, and willingly obeying him while the older generation was not as enthusiastic about his brand of religion. They were still a bit resistant, or, hesitant rather. Due to this hesitance, which was viewed as questioning, he chose to brand them as followers of infidels despite the fact that many of them were his childhood friends. In his opinion, they had been led astray by the unholy freedoms that 'others' espoused and had no interest in returning to a truly correct way of life, to make sacrifices for what was right.

In his opinion, those people were too soft, too timid, and too unholy to be trusted with the treasure of the religion they had inherited from their forefathers; without, the understanding of what it actually meant to be religious. He often branded them the "lost generation of the great religion," which in his view demanded that the message should be spread and enforced using *all* means possible; means including force and violence, if and when necessary. As to the question of when the violence becomes necessary—in his opinion, it was subject to circumstance and situation, and no hard and fast rules applied.

As time passed and he faced less resistance and criticism, the more his conviction grew in the truth of the message he was spreading. The more impassioned he spoke, the greater his following grew. As his following increased, so did his power over the people who formed his audience. He was convinced that he was on the right path and that he had divine help behind his stance.

At first, it was only small shopkeepers, farmers, and the chronically unemployed who would follow his teachings, then the composition of his audience started to gradually change. Over the years, he began noticing that more individuals wearing various types and colors of military-type uniforms were listening to him and following him. These uniformed men would come to the mosque, listen to his sermons, and then leave quietly, barely noticed. At first, he thought that he was being watched, observed; it wasn't at all uncommon.

This went on for several months. During these months the number of uniformed individuals coming to listen to his sermons kept growing. His concern increased and unfortunately because he was the only person with real authority and power over the congregation; he didn't have the luxury to seek advice or counsel from anyone else, without revealing his anxiety about this issue. A man of his stature couldn't be known to have doubts and fears. So he kept quiet but didn't stop guessing and worrying.

He had started keeping a hidden journal in which he described and sketched out to the best of his ability, each uniformed person as well as observations about any person who appeared to be an unknown. While these records were not perfect, he did the best he could. Documentation was a "just in case" measure; if something were to happen to him, it was better than nothing. A form of insurance.

Then came a day when things changed.

One Friday there was an unusually large presence of uniformed men during the congregational afternoon prayer. Among the visitors, there appeared to be someone high ranking, a tall dark man with a curvy north pointing mustache, wearing gold-rimmed designer sunglasses which complemented his slender face perfectly. The insignia on his shoulders was a clear and imposing sign of his rank, additionally, it was obvious that all others deferred to him. Mullah Aziz became increasingly suspicious. After prayers, he went into his apartment and as always, and not so politely, asked his wife to serve him lunch. She was halfway through when there was a persistent knock on the door. Mullah Aziz's son, Rauf, answered the door, spoke with the visitor, and then came running back in.

"Baba, there are *Faujis* at the door! They're in uniform asking for you." Rauf was referring to the uniformed soldiers knocking on the door.

He froze for what seemed like endless moments. His mind went blank as he stared at his son with an apprehensive expression, he was speechless.

"Baba, what's going on? Why are these *Faujis* here? Are they going to take you away?!" His son's blunt approach obliterated any chance of hopeful thinking. Instead, in that instant, without knowing it, Rauf foreshadowed all of his father's fearful thoughts. Now he thought that maybe they were here to take him away! Everyone knew the stories about people being picked up by uniformed men: taken from their houses, their workplaces, or simply from the streets, never to be seen or heard back from again. Sometimes people would just disappear at the hands of "random" men in civilian clothes.

"Shut up, you stupid ass," Mullah Aziz loudly snapped at his son, demonstrating his utter lack of ability to control himself while he inadvertently rubbed the side of his nose.

"I am just asking," the boy retorted, "Why are you calling me names?"

"Do you have any sense of appropriateness? You simply don't know what to say, and when!" He shoved the boy with his left hand and went past him to the door.

"Paro," he shouted his wife's nickname. "Come here."

She came running from the kitchen without hesitation, her face was red from the hot cooking fire and her hands were covered with flour. She opened her mouth to say something but Mullah Aziz didn't, and wouldn't, wait for her question.

"There are some armed men at the door," he whispered in a hushed and panicked tone. "I don't know what they want from me, but if they take me away and I don't come back in the next three hours, call Turab and let him know."

"Who…who is Turab?" Paro was clearly worried and perplexed. Her husband kept so many secrets and for the most part, she was glad and quite relieved; but now, her curiosity was piqued and she wondered who this Turab person was. How would they even know how to reach him?

"He's the journalist I've told you about numerous times! He's the newspaper writer who reports on TV news shows." Mullah Aziz didn't bother hiding his agitation and his disapproval of his wife's ignorance. "I've told you about him so many times. Why is it that you can't seem to remember?"

"I'll remember," Rauf said from behind his mother.

"Good, his number's in my diary."

"I know," the boy replied. Mullah Aziz looked at him, sharply. Rauf had seen his diary and apparently had gone through it. He was about to embark upon another tirade when he was interrupted by another knock at the door. His son's offenses would have to wait.

"Oh God, I'm doomed," Mullah Aziz mumbled and walked hastily towards the door. Paro and Rauf followed closely behind him. The knocking was soft but it was persistent and Aziz saw that as reassuring; they most likely would have barged right in if it was bad news. Instead, they knocked in a civilized manner. That was a sign of respect. They meant no harm. He repeated those words like a mantra; civilized...respect...no harm... he needed to believe them. He opened the door. Two armed, uniformed men stood there and he recognized them immediately from the mosque.

"Mullah Aziz," one of them spoke, quietly but firmly. "Our Captain wishes to speak to you, please come with us."

"Where to?" Aziz was able to summon up enough courage to ask.

"You'll see," the other man extended his arm to the left. "Not too far from here." Mullah Aziz turned around to look at his wife's panic-stricken face which was partially hidden by the kitchen curtain. He shifted his eyes towards his son who appeared absolutely indifferent.

"Please take a walk with us," the first man said. "The Captain has been waiting for a while now."

"When will I be back?"

"Shortly," they both said in unison. "It won't take too long."

Paro was expeditiously reciting Qur'anic verses in whispers. She was about to bless him when he walked away. She started to follow him but one of the uniformed men stepped directly in front of her gesturing her to stop. She was frightened enough to forget that men outside of her family were seeing her face. She was uncovered. The man refused to move, he was blocking her, glaring at her with indignity. She saw her husband walking away from her in the escort of two uniformed men. They made a left turn some two hundred feet away and disappeared.

"Rauf, call Turab. Call him immediately," Paro said frantically.

"But Baba said to call Turab only if he's gone for at least three hours. It hasn't even been a quarter of an hour!"

"There's no reason to wait, Rauf, call him immediately!" Paro was filled with dread, these men were not properly identified and she was concerned for her husband's safety, despite his bullish temperament and the regular onslaught of insults. "Okay fine, whatever you say," Rauf murmured. He went into his father's small office found the diary, opened it, and picked up the phone.

One man walked ahead of Mullah Aziz and the other followed behind him. They walked out of the short and narrow street, which led them to the main open road adjacent to the ample cornfields. There were three black SUVs, idling on the side of the road, humming engines disturbing the silence that otherwise blanketed the surroundings. The left rear door of the middle SUV swung open, and the man walking in front of Mullah Aziz, turned around and motioned for him to get in.

He looked around, his substantial stomach was in knots and he reluctantly stepped inside the vehicle with tinted windows. The man in the middle row was now recognizable: gold-rimmed sunglasses hid his eyes, and his face was masked by clouds of fragrant smoke billowing up from the cigar which hung slyly from the side of his mouth. Aziz knew who he was. The door shut immediately after he stepped into the car, even before he was seated, and the convoy started moving slowly at a quiet crawling pace.

"Sorry to disturb you like this, Maulana," the Captain spoke in a polite yet commanding tone. "We don't mean any disrespect." He seemed somewhat amicable, his face was passive and he was softly smiling, but by the time he completed that sentence the smile was gone, and his once passive face steeled.

"Well that's a relief," muttered Mullah Aziz

"We've been listening to your sermons," the Captain said after few moments of silence.

"I never say anything to disparage the government or the armed forces." Mullah Aziz was careful about whom he criticized.

"We know this," the Captain smiled, "and we appreciate it." The Mullah wasn't sure how to respond to the compliment so he kept quiet and waited for the Captain to continue. "In fact, we very much appreciate what you do say in your sermons. We like your message and we think that it's essential that it reaches as many people as possible."

Mullah Aziz remained quiet since he wasn't sure where this conversation was headed.

"You know, Maulana, I think people like you, who are gifted with noble ideas and the ability to convey those ideas effectively, should consider it a duty to enlighten these dumb people."

"Dumb people? What do you mean?" He was genuinely surprised by this description as well as the overall flagrancy, he'd underestimated the Captain and was unprepared for the blunt response.

"Yes, dumb, stupid, and ignorant people. I can go on. They're all over the place. They are all around us. They're everywhere. Haven't you noticed?"

"Truthfully I'm not sure," Mullah Aziz responded, still unclear as to where this conversation was going and apprehensive about choosing a position.

"You mean to say that you haven't noticed that the people around you are clueless and ignorant?"

"Well yes, there are people, lots of them, in fact, most of them around me are clueless and ignorant. But dumb? I am not sure if they are dumb and I prefer to not label them as such."

"If they aren't dumb, then how do you explain their continued and constant state of ignorance?"

"They are simply clueless, uneducated people. They were never given an opportunity to better themselves academically which is a different thing entirely." Mullah Aziz felt an urge to defend his community, he pictured them sitting in the mosque, listening to him with such intent and admiration that it made him feel atypically protective.

"Oh, the same old excuse," the Captain said dismissively. "Lack of resources, lack of opportunities, it's all bullshit."

"Well it very well may be an old excuse, but it's true. The government doesn't do much to help these people." Mullah Aziz was still unwilling to give up his ground.

"Well, it doesn't take too much effort to gain some knowledge on your own. Anyone can learn."

"I try to do the best I can to educate them, to enlighten them."

"And you think the government doesn't do that? You seem to think that the government doesn't do much at all for the people? Isn't that what you just said?"

"It isn't my intention to disrespect government workers, they're only doing their job." Mullah Aziz's discomfort heightened, he knew that his opinion or the slightest criticism might very well land him in some type of trouble, it was well known that those that voiced "negative thoughts" paid a high toll. Powerful men such as this Captain would casually talk to people like Mullah Aziz, on various unrelated topics to gain some insight. They were cagey and their goal was usually to ensnare and punish. Their trusting remarks would willingly open up and share their deepest thoughts and their best kept secrets, under the false impression that they were reaching a receptive– and especially, influential and resourceful–audience. However, later, they would discover that they were being played for fools all along and that they'd walked right into a trap. Mullah Aziz wouldn't be so easy to catch.

He decided it best to quickly change his position. "Captain on second thought, you are absolutely correct when you say that people are dumb, and yes, indeed, they can easily learn if they are willing to put in a degree of effort. There's nothing the government can do to better them if they are content within their misguided worlds. If being the way they are, suffices, then, honestly, what can be done?!"

The Captain stared at him for a minute too long with apparent indifference. His razor-thin lips closed abruptly and his stern face formed a cold, false smile.

"How rapidly you change your mind." There was more than a hint of derision in his tone.

"Well I'm flexible," Mullah Aziz responded. "Besides if one is wrong, one shouldn't shy away from owning it. Acceptance or admission of the fault has to happen before any type of correction can take place."

"That is true in principle. But in principle only. The way you flipped tells me that it was not because I was able to convince you to abandon your position, but instead, it tells me that there's something else going on in your mind. What is it, Aziz?"

Avoiding response, he shifted his eyes away from the Captain and looked through the black tinted window, in the tension-filled silence, the Captain's probing gaze felt like a branding on his neck.

"Maulana, please look at me when we are conversing, I know that there is absolutely nothing interesting going on outside."

"I'm sorry Captain." Mullah Aziz shifted his gaze.

"Here's the thing," he said, pulling another cigar from his front pocket. The uniformed soldier in the front passenger seat jumped to attention and took the half-smoked cigar away with one hand, while he formally offered "a light" to the Captain with his other hand. The cigar was lit in seconds and soon the Captain was once again puffing thick clouds of aromatic smoke from his nostrils "we have soldiers in our units who are confused about their duties toward our country and towards our religion. They do fight when ordered, but there is a sense of unease among them about fighting people who look like them, act like them, and share the same beliefs. Confusion in the mind of a fighting machine is detrimental, it's a weakness that cannot be afforded. It can be fatal. Not for the enemy but for their own side. Wouldn't you agree?"

Mullah Aziz didn't realize that this was a question to which the Captain was expecting an answer. It wasn't rhetorical and he seemed to be having delayed reactions to any and all of his questions and comments. The Captain repeated, "Wouldn't you agree?"

"Huh…yes, I suppose."

"Are you clear about your thoughts on this war which is going on next door?"

"You mean in Afghanistan?"

"Yes in Afghanistan, in Waziristan and also in FATA generally," the Captain responded, with deep-rooted spite in his tone.

"Yes, I am clear, *Alhamdulillah*," Mullah Aziz said with conviction.

"So do you think we are doing right by our brothers who are fighting the foreign occupiers? Is this the best we can do for them?" The Captain looked directly into his eyes. Mullah Aziz started to say something but suddenly the weight of the question hit him like a ton of bricks. He paused to carefully collect his thoughts, his answer would determine his fate in a way, the Captain would likely categorize him based on that response. Either sympathetic to the occupiers or against those who were fighting the occupiers. Either way, the consequences could be profound.

"Well, do you have an opinion? You said that your mind was clear and that you had no doubts, so you should be able to answer me fairly quickly."

"I think the occupiers must be defeated." Mullah Aziz said.

"That was not my question." The Captain cracked a slight smile. "I want to know if you think that justice is being served.

"Tell me what *you* are doing with your brothers in this war Captain? Your brothers who are your soldiers." Mullah Aziz asked. "Are you helping them or hurting them? Are you fighting with them against the occupiers, or are you fighting against them alongside the occupiers?"

The Captain didn't say a word, he just smiled - all-knowing. He looked away for a brief moment, sucked on the cigar, blew out a thick cloud of smoke, then looked into the Mullah's eyes and softly whispered, "you know full well that the official policy is to side with the foreign invaders."

"I know the official policy. I am asking you about your actions. What exactly is your role in this war?" Mullah Aziz had a feeling that the Captain wasn't quite on board with the official policy and he definitely didn't like being challenged, however, being a soldier, he was bound by discipline and wasn't quite ready to share his personal views so easily.

"My personal views are never a priority," the Captain said with careful consideration, measuring his response before uttering each word.

"Well, then how can my views be a priority, or even relevant?" Mullah Aziz took his cue from the Captain's response. The SUV was becoming thick with cigar smoke and his throat was tightening.

"Very clever." The Captain burst into laughter. "But I think I know where you stand. You chose your words wisely; by not saying that you oppose the official policy, but you did not say you support it, either. You're beating around the bush, and, I understand why you would do that. I fully understand that."

Mullah Aziz remained quiet, studying the Captain's facial expressions, hand gestures, and general body language.

"Now, let's say that there are enough people in the force who form an opinion. And that opinion is, let's say, an expression of new ideas. They dump the old thinking and propose their desire to change policy. In fact, they offer a new way out of this mess, and that new way is also welcomed by others, but not just welcomed, it's embraced. In that case, our personal views will not conflict with the official policy. Do you know why?"

"Yes. Because, the official policy would have changed," Mullah Aziz responded. "Widespread change of opinion in the fighting machine's mind will force this change in the official policy. Is that what you are suggesting?"

"Exactly," the Captain said, hitting his thigh with his open, wide palm. "It's like the old saying; you kill one man; you are a murderer. Kill millions, you are a conqueror. Kill them all, and you are God."

Mullah Aziz smiled for the first time since he was escorted away from his home. The tense feeling, he had earlier suddenly evaporated. He began to feel a connection with the Captain, he actually thought he might even like him.

"At this time, let's just try to be the conqueror and not God." The Captain sounded enthusiastic. "Except that we won't kill people, we'll just change their views and their outlook."

"How do you propose to do that?"

"I have a plan and in due time I'll share it with you. But for now, our chat will suffice, really... I just wanted to understand what you're thinking, where you stand. Luckily, Aziz, I believe that I'm fond of you. I like what I've heard here today, but, I'm still going to put you under surveillance. As you probably know, we'll do a thorough background check on you, and then I'll approach you again with the specifics of my plan; if all goes well that is. In the interim, I'll keep you abreast of your duties and our expectations."

Mullah Aziz found himself nodding his head meekly, like an idiot, as though somebody else was controlling the movement of his head, like a puppet. He was both surprised and disgusted by his own submissive behavior.

"I think I've spent enough time with you today, wouldn't you say?" The Captain said with a smile. This time, the smile didn't appear fake or forced. Mullah Aziz believed that he was seeing a genuine facial expression for the first time during the brief and unexpected encounter, not that it made a bit of difference, the mystery behind this whole affair still deserved some worry.

"I didn't keep track of time." Mullah Aziz looked at his wristwatch toying with it, tapping it restlessly.

"Doesn't matter how much time was spent. What matters is what was achieved in that time."

Mullah Aziz, the puppet, once again found himself nodding.

"You'll be dropped back home," the Captain said, patting the driver's shoulder. The driver glanced back at the Captain, the Captain nodded. He pulled the vehicle to the side of the road and within seconds, the sound of heavy boots thumping on the ground neared. Somebody was running towards the SUV. Mullah Aziz looked through the back windshield and saw the third vehicle in the convoy parked behind theirs with passenger-side doors open.

"And Maulana," the Captain stared at his face again. "It would be wise to keep our conversation confidential."

"Of course, that goes without saying."

"If something comes to your attention, anything at all, contact me." He reached into his jacket and pulled out a heavy stock matte black card with nothing on it except a white embossed number. "Between you and me." Mullah Aziz nodded and pocketed the card.

"Now that we're in agreement, my men will take you back home," the Captain said, his tone dismissive. He puffed another huge cloud of smoke, mouth closed and through his nostrils, and shifted his eyes to the front. Before Mullah Aziz could say anything, the soldier from the vehicle behind them, opened the door and ushered him out of the car directing him to the third vehicle. He got into that SUV, while the Captain got into the first SUV and drove away in the opposite direction-a shell game. If the enemy can't find you, they can't kill you.

The ride back home was quiet, the rhythmic sound of the wheels on the pavement was hypnotic, soothing after the jarring experience. He was dropped off near the mosque, he walked with urgency through the large prayer hall, crossed the courtyard, and entered his apartment. Once the door closed behind him he exhaled. At that exact moment, Paro came running.

"What did they want from you?!" she asked with genuine concern.

"They just wanted to talk."

"About what?"

"Nothing specific." His mind was racing, backtracking, he was trying to decipher the meaning behind it all. He had no interest in engaging in any type of conversation with his wife, who frankly was just getting in his way. He ignored her, and then Rauf came out, so much for privacy.

"I called Turab as you requested and he's on his way.," Rauf declared.

"Why did you call him so quickly?" Aziz was worried that Turab would question him relentlessly about this encounter, really grill him. Which is of course what he wanted earlier, but now that he was unable to answer him and literally sworn to secrecy, he knew he had a problem. Skirting the questions would only make Turab suspicious, yet at the same time, he desperately wanted his help. This was a conundrum, and he had absolutely no idea what he should do.

"I told you to call him, only, if I didn't return in three hours."

"I told him to call Turab," Paro spoke with fear in her voice. "I did! We didn't know where they took you."

"Oh, my God! You are such an unbelievable idiot! Can you not follow the simplest of instructions?! Rauf!" He growled. "Call him now and let him know that I'm back, and tell him there's no need for him to come, tell him your stupidity got the better of you, and for God's sake apologize for inconveniencing him."

"Yes, Baba," Rauf replied and went inside to make the call.

"You! Go and make me tea and bring something to eat." Aziz barked at his wife. She looked at him with deep-rooted disgust but as always she dutifully walked back towards the kitchen, head down.

"Stupid woman," Mullah Aziz mumbled to himself, picked up the *hookah* sitting on the floor next to the wall, and started sucking on the long pipe. Rauf was calling Turab on speaker. He shifted his eyes between the phone screen and the tiny window through which he was able to see the indoor courtyard where his father sat on a broken wooden chair sucking on the hookah pipe. His concern apparent, Rauf was used to seeing his father agitated, but not usually worried, and that in turn worried him.

Turab's phone kept ringing but there was no answer. He was either deliberately avoiding Rauf's call or he was on the move. The network coverage was terrible and completely unreliable, especially while one was on the road traveling. At first Mullah, Aziz didn't notice Rauf through the window, but eventually, that sense that he always relied on kicked in and sure enough he saw him staring, directly at him.

"Did you tell him not to come?" Aziz shouted when their eyes met.

"I am trying, Baba. He is not answering," Rauf shouted back.

"God damn it," Aziz barked. "What a moron you are, a real son of an ass."

Rauf couldn't help but laugh out loud.

"What the hell are you laughing at, you idiot?"

"Think about it, you just called me the son of an ass Baba!" Rauf baited his father. He found Aziz's rants amusing and quite enjoyed winding him up.

"Shut the fuck up," Aziz retorted. "Stop this idiot Turab from coming here."

"I'm trying Baba," Rauf said with a smirk, "But looks like he is either avoiding my call, or he's already on the way."

Rauf saw his mother enter the courtyard holding a dinner tray carrying a carefully placed cup of tea, and a plate with snacks. She pulled a chair from the side, set it in front of Aziz, and put the tray on the chair.

"Be careful," Aziz held the back of the chair. "One leg is loose. The tray may fall down with the chair."

"You remind me every single time. Why don't you buy a coffee table?" Paro asked, annoyed.

"I will soon. Don't worry," Aziz replied.

"You've been saying that for months."

"Don't pick on me over a stupid table," Aziz warned her. "And if you want it so much, why don't you ask your brother to give one to you? He has plenty of money, yet he never seems to help his sister. What a miser."

"God, you are so useless!" Paro responded, with frustration. "You're the man of the house, yet, you keep preaching about other people and how they care or don't care for their family. Why don't you start practicing what you preach?"

"I know what to preach and what to practice." Aziz stood up, furious. "Don't try to educate me. Do you understand?"

"You're hopeless," Paro almost gave up. "Just hopeless. I don't know why I keep thinking that you'll do even half of what you keep telling these poor people in the mosque to do."

"Okay, that's enough! Shut up now," Mullah Aziz dismissed her comment. "Now, listen carefully. Rauf, you come here too and listen to what I have to tell you. Come here." Rauf sauntered in and they all stood in the middle of the room.

"Now listen," Aziz stated, in whispers, "these soldiers who came today, they want my help on a special project. Do not tell anyone about them. Do not mention a word to Turab and do not, I repeat, do not, tell him that they came to see me."

"But I already told him," Rauf responded. "He asked me why we were rushing him here so I told him about these men who showed up unannounced."

"Oh, I see." Mullah Aziz realized the foolishness of his previous instructions. "What exactly did you say to him?"

"We just told him what we saw," Paro said scornfully. "Turns out you got off easy. Too bad they weren't harder on you."

It took Aziz a few moments to realize what his wife just said. "What, you wanted them to do me harm?"

Paro just threw her arms up in frustration, knowing better than to expect her husband to be reasonable but still somehow hoping that he might be. "I don't want to talk about it anymore," she said, walking back to the kitchen.

"Good. That's exactly what you should do. Not talk about it. Don't talk about it to anyone. Not even to Turab when he comes over. I'll do all the talking do you understand? There's no need to tell him any more than what he already knows. Do you two understand? Have I made myself clear?"

Paro was gone and his son stood in the middle of the room nodding his head. Mullah Aziz shot a sharp glance at him before reaching for the teacup.

Rauf gingerly reached for the hot *samosa* sitting on the plate in front of his father, the smell was tantalizing and mouthwatering. He'd always loved the warm, crispy ground beef triangular snacks, especially with his mother's heavenly homemade hot sauce. Apparently, he had inherited this passion for the samosa from his father, who liked them more than anything Paro ever cooked, he cherished them. However, due to the cost of meat, such a luxury was a rarity, and his father, as always, got the first pick. He had to resort to stealing and shamelessly snatched them from his father's plate which would result in an anticipated bellowing outburst. This time was no exception. The moment Rauf extended his hand towards the plate, Mullah Aziz slapped his wrist.

"Stop stealing from my plate."

"She never makes me samosa."

"Yeah, well that's because food costs money and you don't bring any money into this house. That's why."

"Yes but you always say it is good to share. Sharing food brings *barakah*. It brings blessings. Allah's bounty multiplies when it is shared."

"Well, there are exceptions." Mullah Aziz couldn't come up with a better excuse. He was trying to greedily shield the snack plate and take a sip of tea at the same time, the hot and spicy mixture on his tongue was one of his favorite combinations. That little cocktail tasted heavenly; he guarded it with intent.

"Can't you give me at least one? You have so many." Rauf was unable to move his eyes from the plate.

"No, I cannot. I'm very hungry; starving actually, even all of these aren't going to suffice."

"Okay," Rauf said thoughtfully. "So for you, even these aren't enough and I'm just asking for one. Are you saying that you cannot spare even one samosa for me??"

"I told you, meat is very expensive. When you earn some money you can have as many as you want."

"Well, I want one from your plate now." Rauf was adamant. "In fact, I want half of what you have on your plate. I want at least two pieces."

"You are not getting any," Aziz responded, barely containing his anger. "Now go away."

"Okay, fine! I'll go away but I'm going to talk to Turab and I will tell him everything that happened today. Your secret isn't safe with me anymore." Mullah Aziz couldn't believe what he was hearing. He stared in dumbfounded silence at Rauf for some time, so shocked and enraged by his son's audacity that he couldn't even speak, he couldn't believe that his son was behaving like this.

"You, filthy little bastard. You're going to blackmail me now? You would do this to your own father?" How had things so shifted against him so quickly?

"You leave me no choice."

"You aren't my son," Aziz screamed at the top of his lungs. "A bastard like you couldn't have come from my loins."

Rauf was indifferent to the insults Aziz was hurling; he was busy eating the samosa he had plucked off of his father's plate. He finished it and wiped his mouth, which was now open wide with a cat-ate- the-canary grin. His eyes were twinkling with a sense of victory.

"What's going on here? Why are you so angry?" Paro heard Aziz screaming and came running from the kitchen.

"Be honest, Paro! I want the truth. Tell me if he really is my son." Mullah Aziz threw the plate at Rauf and shouted again, not phasing Rauf, who giggled as the plate landed on his chest. He didn't care about any potential injury or mess, his one and only goal was to catch the snacks before they had the chance to land on the dirty and dusty floor.

"Are you out of your mind, Aziz?" This time it was Paro who shouted. "Are you saying that he is from another man?" She thought she was immune to his inflammatory remarks, but this was too much.

"I cannot believe my son would act this way, with his own father. I wish he'd never been born. I would have been better off childless." Mullah Aziz realized the gravity of the accusation against his wife but he lacked control and couldn't contain his wild frustration. Rauf was oddly dispassionate about any of it; all he cared about was his full tummy and licking any excess crumbs from his fingers.

"Look…look at him. He either cannot hear us or he doesn't care," Aziz shouted, looking at his wife and pointing his finger towards Rauf.

Paro was about to say something when there was a loud, impatient knock on the front door. They all froze. Aziz looked at Rauf and Paro, and they in turn watched him looking for a command or a directive from their fearless leader.

"This must be Turab," Mullah Aziz started walking towards the door. "Remember what I said. I'll do all the talking, all of it. I need you both to keep your mouths shut."

"I'm not promising that. I'm quite sure that you remember that I told you that I plan on telling Turab what I saw." Rauf said.

"But Rauf, you had the samosa you wanted. Why would you do that to your father? Your family?" Aziz was now beyond feeling annoyed.

"Yeah, I had the samosa," Rauf replied. "But I had to take it from you, I had to steal it from you because you didn't and wouldn't offer it to me, your son. So there is no deal."

Aziz stared at him for a long moment, his eyes bulging with fury. Before he could say another word, there was another barrage of loud knocking on the door; he spun on his heels and beelined it towards the door. Paro and Rauf stood quietly; disapprovingly; avoiding eye contact.

Mullah Aziz opened the door. His guess was correct: standing outside was Turab.

THREE

GUL DIDN'T HAVE a complete picture in his head or perfect memory of the precise moment when he lost the innocence of childhood, but the transition from innocence to adolescence was so very clear to him, and the impact was monumental. While he clearly remembered that day, all of the events didn't register fully in his mind. It was a bit hazy, and too far out of his realm to really comprehend.

His memory of that afternoon triggered a surge of uncomfortable emotions, he distinctly remembered how he felt that day as it was so very different from anything he had ever experienced before. The blood rush, the hot flashes on his face, the strange pleasure his body felt, and a racing heartbeat. He felt changed. A turning point. He thought he was meeting himself for the first time: totally unfamiliar yet very welcomed.

For several years Gul had regularly accompanied Zara Bibi, his mother, and sometimes his elder sister Badri Jamala, to the Haveli, the large estate owned by Sardar Timur Barlas and the biggest house in their small town. His mother was one of the numerous housekeepers on staff, and his father Shams was a *mazareh*, a peasant who worked on the land also owned by Sardar Timur Barlas.

That day, the servants were scattered all throughout the vast estate. They were in each room cleaning, in the kitchen cooking, they were gardening and trimming hedges, they were seeing to the horses, polishing cars in the extravagant fleet - and the list went on and on. The great contingent of servants consisted of men, women, children, and even some eunuchs.

It was rumored that the eunuchs were intact young boys when they began working for Sardar Timur Barlas. Those who behaved inappropriately paid for their misdeed by losing the essence of their male being. It was so horrifying to think about, that Gul avoided being around them. Seeing them was sickening.

He thought back on the day that his life changed. His mother brought him to the Haveli just as she had many times prior, except this time the house was being prepared for a grand festivity, one of many, so his mother was required to arrive earlier than usual. Since Gul was still in a quasi-sleep state, Zara Bibi brought him to a small staff room outside the main house.

"You can sleep here all you want, okay my dear boy?" She hugged him adoringly, almost as if he was the small child she still thought him to be, before laying him down on the clean but torn and faded blanket she had brought with her from home.

"Yes, I understand," he remembered saying, without asking what he was supposed to do upon waking. His mother kissed him on both cheeks and left the room, closing the door behind her while throwing a long loving smile his way. The dizziness he was in morphed into a deep sleep almost instantly.

He didn't know what time it was when he woke up; although, he remembered feeling disoriented and ravenous. The small room was quiet and empty. He stepped outside and welcomed the intense heat of the sun-baked ground, already bone dry and cracked. He could feel it penetrate the thin soles of his flimsy canvas shoes. A familiar sensation. Braving the scorching glare, he looked towards the grand entrance door of the Haveli and decided to embark upon a quest for water and food. He was apprehensive about entering the house, but hunger and thirst drove him; that and naiveté.

He had been in the main house many times but never alone, only alongside his mother, and he was concerned about finding his way. Even with his mother guiding him he would still get lost, the house was a sprawling structure of endless corridors and magnificent rooms. Ideal for hide and seek a favorite in this maze of wonder and excess. That particular afternoon things turned out a little differently. That day sudden and unpredicted adolescence was thrust upon him, and from that moment on, nothing would ever be as it was.

He pushed open the heavy and palatial mahogany door with great difficulty, opening it just enough for his long slender frame to slide through. Once inside he stood by the door for a few moments scanning the foyer and any other room he could see into from that distance. Strangely there was nobody around. He looked both ways again, and after some deliberation and a little courage, he decided to go left. He took about fifteen steps and stopped.

"Not this way," he murmured to himself. "I'm going in the wrong direction. Come on Gul hurry up! The kitchen is on the other side!" He stopped muttering to himself and started walking, turned around, stopped again, and stood in place, and calmly thought for a bit before taking hasty purposeful strides. He found himself passing through several living rooms, and sitting rooms, and reading rooms, and eventually reached the much sought after kitchen. On the way, he'd spotted several maids all engaged in their daily chores but he didn't see his mother amongst them. Not at all concerned about it, he continued his forward march. There was a hole burning through his stomach that was getting larger by the second.

His eyes gleamed when he saw that the kitchen was devoid of any worker or family member. He could have whatever and as much as he wanted without questions. The smell of food which had been cooked hours ago still lingered in the air only enhancing his appetite.

There was a double refrigerator at the far end of the kitchen, and he saw several pots and pans haphazardly sitting on the stovetop and the long stone countertop. At one end, there was a stack of clean plates with a tray holding silverware. The sink was full of dirty dishes and crumbs were scattered all over the floor. The kitchen appeared as though at one point during the day it became mayhem, and stayed that way.

He walked towards the industrial size stove, looked inside, and found a large pot of ground beef cooked in fragrant spices. He loved this dish, it was his absolute favorite. He picked up a large serving spoon and greedily dug in collecting a little mountain of stew when he heard footsteps approaching. Someone wearing hard plastic shoes was shuffling his way.

Gul panicked, and for a reason unbeknownst to him, felt the need to hide immediately. He tossed the food back in the pot, and dropped the spoon in the sink–all very quietly–and briskly rushed toward the pantry door. Once inside, he shut the door without a sound. He stood close to the wall, practically pancaked flat to it, and pressed his ear to the door. All he could hear was his own racing heartbeat thumping uncontrollably.

The shuffling footsteps were closing in and it sounded as if they were right beside the pantry door. Someone was in the kitchen. All he could hear were those footsteps that were now a little lighter and slower. Whoever it was seemed to be stopping and moving around, not at all like the steps of someone who might be rushing. Gul gingerly opened the door, very slightly, just enough to peek through. He could see a light shadow moving around, but then they moved right past the pantry door and that was when he saw the face. He recognized the face but didn't know his name. He was one of the eunuchs who attended to the needs of the women of the house. Gul had seen him talking to his mother over the course of time and got the feeling that she didn't particularly like him.

He found himself breathing irregularly. He shut the door quietly and stood in the dark, firmly holding the doorknob as if he could keep the door from being opened. He was unable to control his racing heart and he couldn't seem to get any air. Then he heard someone else entering the kitchen.

"Chaman, what are you doing here?" He heard a female voice addressing the eunuch. He could sense a false annoyance in her voice.

"I'm hungry."

"You're always hungry," the woman said jokingly. "You sure eat a hell of a lot."

"I eat for fun. You know why? Because I can't fuck, so eating is the only fun thing for me to do."

The woman started giggling.

"Yeah," Chaman said. "If I could fuck, I wouldn't eat this much. I would be busy fucking."

"How do you know?" the woman asked, hardly suppressing her laughter. "How can you be so sure?"

"I'm not," Chaman said with his loud trademark clap. Gul could imagine the sudden movement of Chaman's hips and his raised hands going in the direction opposite of the pelvic jerk which would usually accompany the rhythmic clap. He had seen this before. "But if I could fuck, I would have less time for eating. If I could fuck, I am absolutely sure that I would find more fun and pleasure in fucking than eating. Who wouldn't?"

"And why can't you?" the woman asked, her tone reflecting with what sounded to Gul like some kind of malicious joy.

"Why can't I what?" Chaman asked, even though it seemed that he knew exactly what she was asking.

"Fuck." Gul flinched. Hearing a female use such a word made him feel uncomfortable.

"You know why," Chaman said with despair. "You've seen my handicap."

Another burst of laughter. Gul wondered if this was true, had the woman actually looked upon him, there?

"It's not a joke, okay?" Chaman was now furious. His voice was raised and even higher in pitch than usual. "You don't know what it's like to feel so violated, and suffer through such a loss."

The laughter stopped abruptly. "I can imagine," the woman said in a heavy tone. "It's a grave loss and a very harsh punishment indeed."

Gul waited for a response but apparently, Chaman had decided to stay quiet.

"Who did this to you, and why?" the woman asked after a long pause. This time she sounded serious.

"You know who did it."

Gul heard a whisper from the woman's mouth, but could not understand the words she uttered. He pressed his ear to the door even harder. His hunger forgotten.

"As to why," Chaman started speaking again after a brief pause, "I don't know for sure. But whatever I may have done, the punishment was not proportional. It's inhumane."

"How can you say that you don't know what you did?" the woman asked again, apparently not believing Chaman's claim of ignorance.

"Believe me," Chaman said with a depressed tone and his trademark clap. "I don't know why I was mutilated like this."

An uneasy silence hung in the air for what seemed like an infinite amount of time, and Gul thought they were gone. He had decided to come out of the pantry just when he heard the distinct jingle of bangle bracelets crashing into each other. He could picture the woman sensuously waving her forearm in the air, bracelets clinking and clanking. Gul wasn't sure who she was, but his imagination was more than ready to supply an erotic image.

"So, how was it?" The woman asked. She sounded mischievous and horny at the same time.

"What?" Chaman asked. Gul detected confusion in his tone. Apparently, he wasn't expecting such a question.

"The thing they took away from you." Once again she burst into laughter. "I mean, your lost manhood? How was it?"

"You are such a bitch," Chaman shouted, once again clapping in his trademark style, arms, and pelvis going in opposite directions.

"Come on, tell me."

"I can't," Chaman said, flatly refusing to entertain her request. "I won't."

"Oh, so you can, but you don't want to," the woman said, still snickering. A barrage of questions followed. "Why? Were you not proud of yourself? Were you not the type of man who could brag about himself? Were you not a man? Not man enough to talk about it?"

"Shut up," Chaman sounded bothered and slightly piqued. The female–Gul was still uncertain who she was–kept laughing in low voice. She sounded genuinely pleased.

"Why are you getting so upset? I thought men like to talk about it."

"Yeah, men who have it do like to talk about it. But I don't." He paused for a second "Besides, why are you even asking? You'll get married soon and then all your questions will be answered."

"That's different," she said. "He'll be my husband and you're my friend. With him, it will be a duty. With you it's fun."

"You are such a *kanjri*." Suddenly Chaman laughed out loud. "You're a dirty slut. A real whore."

The woman kept laughing. Gul found this awkward but also very exciting. His heart was still racing. But no longer out of fear. He couldn't identify his feelings, they were foreign to him, and he'd never been privy to this type of conversation before, it felt forbidden. He stood very close to the door, fearing that if his ear was not stuck to the door, he might miss something.

"You want to see it?" Gul heard Chaman ask.

"What, you still have it?"

"No. I don't have it. But I have pictures." His voice nostalgic, yet exhilarated.

"Really, you took pictures of yourself?"

"No. I didn't. Someone else took the pictures," Chaman dismissed the disgusting idea of a selfie.

"Who? Who took your pictures?"

"I can't tell you. I can't…I won't." Chaman was almost humming a childish teasing rhythm.

"Tell me. I won't give up until you tell me."

"Do you want to see the pictures or not?"

"Yes, I do."

"Then stop asking me questions. If you don't stop, I won't show you the pictures. That's the deal. Got it??"

"Yes-got it, now show me the pictures."

"Alright, here they are." Gul couldn't see a thing from the thin opening in the door. Chaman and the woman had moved away. Gul was dead silent, trying to listen-of course he wasn't in Chaman's position, so he couldn't really judge, but, he sure did find it strange to carry that kind of picture in a back pocket.

"Hmm…" The woman. She seemed somewhat pleased with something.

"You like the picture?" Chaman asked.

"Yes, the picture is good," the woman replied casually. "But looks like you were not the man I thought you were."

"What the fuck do you mean?"

The woman laughed a strange laugh, and Chaman began to clap.

"Even for a man, it seems you were…" The woman's voice trailed off.

"I was what?"

"Never mind, I don't want to say anything." The woman now sounded genuinely concerned about offending Chaman but somehow, Gul didn't think that was the case.

"No, go ahead, say it. I want to hear it."

She was apparently not moved by Chaman's insistence. No reply.

"Come on, say it. Tell me what you were going to say. I want to hear it. Damn it, I demand it. You must tell me what you thought of me." Clearly disturbed and anger escalating.

"You're not going to like it."

"I'm not liking it now, either," Chaman retorted. "You must tell me. Come on, say what you were going to say."

"Okay, I think you were inadequate."

Gul heard Chaman gasp. He didn't utter a word but his gasp was indicative of the hurt he felt. For a moment Gul stopped breathing. He feared the woman's comment would invite a violent or deeply emotional response, and as if on cue he heard Chaman start to sob. Gul again tried to peek through the narrow opening, holding the door slightly open.

"See I told you, you'd get hurt, but you insisted. Don't blame me."

"Still, you did think of me as inadequate." Chaman's voice was hoarse and somewhat high pitched, almost screeching. "Maybe you didn't want to say it, but you actually thought I was not enough of a man. I feel so insulted and hurt."

"Why does it matter now?" the woman said in a matter of fact tone. Gul heard Chaman gasp again, then silence for a while.

"Shhhh... Quiet," Gul heard the woman say. She sounded panicked. "Be quiet. Someone is coming."

"Go in, go in," he heard Chaman respond, sounding equally panicked-go in where? and why? But then he realized, Chaman must have been referring to the pantry; although, he couldn't make sense of it all. Why all the hiding and whispering? There wasn't any time to think. Gul instinctively stepped away from the door, looked around, and found a hiding spot behind a large cupboard. The light in the pantry was dim so he might still be unseen. He felt his heart racing. From behind the cupboard, he could see the pantry door, which opened. The woman and Chaman stepped inside.

He recognized the woman instantly: Farah, one of Sardar's daughters, soon to be married. He had always liked her and had always had a type of inexplicable attraction to her; he had never been subject to this unidentifiable feeling for anyone else. She was different from her sisters, she appeared to be less submissive, instead, she was candid and straightforward, fearless. Whenever Gul had encountered her within the past few years he felt her dark probing and piercing eyes on him. Always warmly and almost coquettishly smiling whenever they crossed paths, but he never found the courage to speak to her. Seeing her this afternoon, in this situation with Chaman, was unnerving. Both of them were standing close to the door in the shadows, and they were standing very close.

"Move, move." Gul heard Chaman's urgent, forceful whispers.

"Move where?"

"Away from the door, find a spot inside," Chaman responded, gesturing her to move quickly. Farah realized the urgency and stepped away from the door. Chaman followed her.

Maybe he wasn't seeing clearly, but then Gul realized that he was in actuality seeing exactly what he thought he wasn't seeing. Chaman was holding her in a tight embrace, he was kissing and caressing her. Farah didn't resist his advances, welcoming him, she held him in her arms. Gul saw her grip on Chaman tightening and heard her moan. Gul wondered what was happening. Now that they were safe from others' eyes, they seemed to feel safe reveling in intimacy.

"If only you were still a man." Farah's low whisper was loud enough for Gul to hear. He could feel the blood rushing in his arteries, his temples were pounding, and sweat was dripping from his forehead which he tried to wipe with his equally damp palms. He forced himself to look away but found himself staring at them again almost immediately. He couldn't control his curiosity or his reaction. He kept turning his head to look away, but could not resist looking back again and again. His own heavy breathing seemed to drown out the even louder and labored breaths he could hear them taking. They must be very distracted, he realized, not to know he was there.

"God, I miss the touch of a woman," Chaman whispered back. "And yes, if only I was a man still, I would have done things to you, you cannot even imagine."

Farah's low laughter was filled now with what sounded like true pleasure.

"You are doing very well for whatever you are now," Gul heard her say, between bursts of seductive sighs.

"Good for what? I cannot really complete what I started," Chaman suddenly released Farah from his embrace.

"Don't stop now. Don't let go of me," Farah, gasping, sounded like a fish out of the water, and looked rather like one as she tried to grab Chaman, who was inching as quickly away from her as he could. She reached out to try and comfort him. At least, that was how it appeared to Gul.

"Oh, God," Chaman suddenly started sobbing. "What have they done to me? What have they done?"

Farah pulled her hand back and watched him quietly. Chaman's sobs were growing loud and intense.

"Be quiet, why do you have to be so loud?"

Chaman kept sobbing, getting ever louder. Farah grabbed him and wrapped her arm around his neck. She was using her other hand to cover his mouth. Chaman tried to break free but she wouldn't release him.

"Let me go," Chaman demanded, still sobbing.

"I won't," Farah was furious. "You need to finish what you started."

"I can't, you know I cannot do that," Chaman said, sounding completely defeated.

"Find another way." Farah was not willing to give up.

"No...I can't. You need to let me go." Chaman forced himself out of Farah's grip. He staggered and almost fell. Instinctively, Farah grabbed his arm and tried to pull him up, but he was too heavy for her and kept falling. Gul heard a heavy thud and a shrill scream. From the sound of it, Gul couldn't tell if the scream came from him or her.

The loud knock on the pantry door startled them all. Farah jumped and almost exclaimed again, but covered her mouth in time. She seemed to understand that they were about to be discovered. Chaman was still on the ground, blocking the door.

"Who's in there?" They heard a loud female voice from outside which Gul immediately recognized. It was his mother, knocking and trying to get in.

Gul saw Farah hastily stepping away from the door, coming towards the cupboard. For a moment he thought she had seen him, but then realized she was merely looking for a space to hide. The spot where he was hiding was as good as any. She didn't realize there was a person already there and pushed herself into the space. In the faint light making its way through the pantry door, now partially open, Gul saw a confused look on her face. Then their eyes met. "Gul?" She almost shrieked but was able to control herself. He could hardly breathe. He felt her hands squeezing him, felt her body closer than any girl had ever been, or at least in this way.

"Who's in there?" Gul heard his mother's voice again. He could also see her face peeking through the partially open door.

"It's me, Chaman," Gul heard Chaman say in a weak voice.

"Open the door. Let me in."

"Wait a minute, I fell." He was still trying to get up.

"How? What happened to you? How did you fall? Are you okay?" Gul's mother asked without pause.

Chaman stood up. The door was now wide open. Gul saw his mother come in, her arm was extended, apparently trying to find the light switch. Chaman was trying to pick up the pictures he had dropped on the floor when he fell. Gul heard the click of the switch but there was no light. Apparently, the bulb was out.

"What are you doing here?" Zara Bibi demanded.

"Nothing."

"Really?" Clearly, she didn't believe him. "And what is that– what did you pick up from the floor?"

"Stop asking questions." Chaman sounded agitated. Gul saw him trying to hide the pictures behind his back, holding them between his fingers.

"Let me see." Zara Bibi was insistent. "What are you hiding? Are you stealing something? Are you taking something away from here?"

"I am not stealing anything. Now go away," Chaman shouted.

"I am not going away until you show me what you have in your hands." Zara Bibi was adamant. Chaman tried to leave the pantry, but she blocked his exit.

"You can't force me, okay? It's personal." Chaman was equally resolute. However, from his tone, it was clear there was something strange going on.

"Are you stealing food?"

"Absolutely not," Chaman snapped back. "Why would I steal food? The kitchen is always open and I've never gone hungry." Gul couldn't hear his mother's response, but he knew she was most likely trying to calculate her next move.

"Okay, so you are not stealing. But you're still hiding something. What is it?"

"I told you, it's personal. Now get out of my way," Chaman's tone regained its strength. He pushed her aside and barged his way out. Gul was relieved when he saw his mother leave as well. She closed the pantry door behind her, leaving him and Farah in complete darkness. Gul heard Farah take a deep sigh of relief; however, instead of letting him go she wrapped herself around him. He felt her grip tighten like a boa constrictor around his hips and back.

Without thinking, Gul wrapped his arms around her slight frame. She rested her chin on his shoulder, spreading her hair over his neck, his shoulder, and part of his face. He felt a jolt of pleasure through his entire body. The fragrance coming from her hair made its way into his soul. The scent was intoxicating. He grabbed her hair in his fist, gently yanked her head to the side, and allowed his lips to nibble her earlobe. The sudden and exciting moans from her mouth to his ears felt like heaven.

"How old are you?" she asked. He just heard her voice, not the words.

"What?"

"How old are you?"

"I'm not sure." Gul couldn't think straight. "I'm thirteen. No wait, I think I'm fifteen."

"You don't know your own age?" Farah burst into soft laughter. Her hands were caressing him all over. "You boys never know anything."

"Why do you want to know?" Gul's mouth was dry. His cheeks were burning. He could feel her warm hands all over like hundreds of tentacles. "I don't really want to know. It really doesn't matter," Farah dismissed his question.

"Okay." Gul did not know how else to respond.

"As long as you're a man?" Farah questioned.

"I am a man," Gul said with pride. "Don't I look like one?"

"Maybe, maybe not. You are still too young to be a real man, but that doesn't matter."

"Okay." Once again Gul didn't know what to say.

"As long as you are functional," she giggled in his ears. Gul didn't understand the meaning at first. He felt her hand where he was most warm and sensitive and heard himself moan. He felt the need to stop himself from what was happening, but he couldn't. The urge was too great and powerful. The pleasure was intense. He lost control of himself.

At the same time outside, Chaman was moving fast and Zara Bibi was having a hard time catching up to him, but she was determined not to let him out of her sight.

"Stop following me," Chaman yelled while running to an outside patio without turning to look back at her.

"I won't," she shouted back. "You need to stop. Show me what you're hiding and then I'll stop."

"I told you, it's none of your business," Chaman was truly frustrated. He turned around, waited for her to catch up to him, and then punched her in the face. She fell hard, her cries were loud and painful to hear. He stood there and stared at her waving his closed fist and doing his signature move, almost dancing, he looked almost not human with glazed eyes and spit coming out of his mouth, like a rabid dog.

"You coward, stupid bastard! You hit me. How can you hit a woman!?" She felt warm liquid flowing from her lower lip, down her chin. The back of her hand went up to wipe it off and came back covered with blood. She saw red spots falling on the floor and started shaking uncontrollably.

"Oh my God, I'm bleeding you bastard! I'll see to it that you get punished. You're not getting away with this." She started screaming. Chaman was still circling and bouncing around her, glaring while waving his fists and fingers for no apparent reason. He was out of control, wild with fury.

"You are certainly not a woman! You're a bitch, an old, stupid bitch," he shouted and kept moving in peculiar manic circles around her. Servants came running from all directions as if they'd been hiding behind walls waiting, but there was no way to silence or calm the commotion.

"Zara, you're bleeding! Let me get a bandage." A frantic maid saw the blood dripping and turned around urgently looking for help, while the others all tried to work out what to do next.

"This bastard Chaman stole something from the pantry. I saw him hiding it in his hands, so I questioned him and then he took off and just hit me when I caught up to him." Chaman found everybody staring at him. Questioning glances.

"She's a liar!" Chaman shouted back. "I didn't steal from the kitchen or the pantry. I don't steal!"

"Then show everybody what you were hiding from me," Zara Bibi insisted.

"It's personal," Chaman shouted again.

"See!" Zara Bibi looked around while pointing at Chaman. "He's lying. He's hiding something and he refuses to be forthright about it. He's stealing because he's untrustworthy!"

The peering crowd of local spectators, servants included, started murmuring, whispering. Heads nodded and eyes rolled. Chaman closed his eyes and kept shaking his head in disbelief. Noise from the crowd was getting increasingly louder, and then suddenly it all came to an abrupt halt. Absolute quiet. Sensing something very wrong, Chaman opened his eyes. He saw Sardar Timur's wife, Sarah Khanum, standing in front of him.

"Zara Bibi, what is going on here?" Her eyes were fixed on Chaman while she spoke to Zara Bibi, who stood up and repeated her allegation.

"Is this true? Are you a thief?" Sarah Khanum asked Chaman. Her tone was austere.

"No. I am not a thief. I swear." Chaman could hardly speak. He felt his heart sinking and fear began to replace rage.

"Wasn't the punishment given to you last time enough?"

"I haven't done anything wrong. I swear Sarah Khanum, I swear!"

"Take him to the pantry. Let's see what he was doing there, let's see if anything is missing." She ordered anyone and everyone as she started moving towards the kitchen. Zara Bibi got up and followed her. Two men grabbed Chaman by his arms and dragged him behind them. No one spoke. The only sound that could be heard was the rough dry dirt and the small jagged rocks being dispersed by Chaman's legs and feet as they scraped the ground.

"Chaman, if you want to confess, this is your last chance." Sarah Khanum stood in front of the pantry door, facing the crowd.

"I am not lying, I am not hiding anything, so I have nothing to confess."

"He is a thief and a liar." Zara Bibi was barely able to control her anger. "He won't admit it; he'll never admit it."

Sarah Khanum stared at Chaman for a long time. Their eyes met for a brief moment before Chaman lowered his gaze. She shifted her eyes to Zara Bibi and nodded. The crowd was silent, watching, waiting. Zara Bibi boldly pushed open the door and flicked the light switch on out of habit even though it didn't work just a little while ago. To her surprise, the bulbs worked this time. The pantry was fully lit.

The crowd gasped in utter awe and disbelief at what they all saw through the open door.

FOUR

S ARDAR TIMUR WAS foaming from the mouth, pure
hate resonating. It was scribed all over his grimacing face, his
intimidating frame in battle-ready position. His eyes fixed on Gul while
pointing the loaded Beretta M9 handgun steadily and with purpose at
his head. Gul was desperate for a way out but unable to muster enough
courage to utter a single word, let alone seek forgiveness.

The tall, solidly built man looked around, jet black eyes keenly
scanning everything, and began to pace back and forth, thumping
the ground with his thick-soled boots, like a giant from a folkloric
Lake Saiful Muluk tale. The dust under his feet flew up and around
him like hot steam from a raging furnace seemingly animated. He
held a leash in his left hand. Gul's neck was encircled in a collar
on the other end of that leash and attached through a metal loop.
There were spikes on the inside of the collar that spurred his neck
and if he didn't keep pace, Sardar Timur would tug on the leash in
order to remind him. In the background three ferocious Doberman
Pinschers barked and growled incessantly, trying to break free
from the chains that tied them to steel poles set firmly in the hard
ground. Their keepers were engaged in an unsuccessful struggle
to pacify them.

Farah stood with her mother Sarah Khanum, on the balcony
above, her weakened and trembling legs barely able to support her and

her hands clasped in front of her paralyzing her even further. Her eyes were following Sardar Timur, her father, who avoided eye contact with her. The occasional glances he did throw her way made her flinch. She tried to recall the events of the afternoon. Haphazard images flashed in her mind, impressions, and moments that she couldn't piece together. Everything felt disjointed.

It had all started in the early afternoon hours during her conversation with Chaman. Her curiosity about men and her need to understand them and know more about them—other than the angry and dominant forms of brothers and father—was half satisfied by her association with Chaman. After all, he was a man once, a complete man, perhaps. She knew that going after a man, even Chaman, in the manner she desired was wrong and could land her in trouble, but inquisitiveness and excitement persevered. She had to keep going, she had to test boundaries because that's who she was. She didn't want to wait until she was married only to become subject to the whims of her husband. To perform her required duties. Finding this young boy Gul, in the pantry, in an aroused state was unexpected and an obvious recipe for disaster. Thinking about it now, she realized that she should have stopped to think, and she shouldn't have taken advantage of his excitement for her entertainment.

She didn't expect things to go so wrong so quickly, and she believed that there was a chance that they wouldn't have been discovered at all. The irony that they were caught by Gul's mother could have been comedic if the consequences weren't so drastic. Farah understood that by questioning Chaman, Zara Bibi was following rules and that she was being loyal to her masters, she knew that Zara Bibi couldn't afford to lose her job, but she too, pushed too hard when she confronted Chaman. By forcing the matter, she created a real predicament resulting in what will most likely be a true tragedy.

When the pantry door opened, Chaman and Zara Bibi were the first to see Farah and Gul standing behind the cupboard. They were partially clothed, in an exotic embrace, really excited. The reality of it all was undeniable. Seeing Gul in such a raw state shook his mother to the core, an awful inexplicable feeling of loss and vulnerability passed through her. When she finally realized the absoluteness of the situation, she tried to shut the door, but Chaman kicked and shoved it open, and there they stood, frozen.

"See, she doesn't even watch her own son, yet, she wants to come after me. Me!" Chaman yelled. Farah remembered Chaman shouting, waving his hands. Everyone else was silent. Zara Bibi's face had turned ashen. Farah thought she would say something, either yell at Gul or respond to Chaman but apparently, the intensity of the moment was too much. She was mute, truly without a voice.

There was no stopping Chaman's rants. Zara Bibi's silence infuriated him further and he became increasingly aggressive. He jumped forward and attacked her, slapping her all over her body and working himself into a fit. It's as though he'd gone insane and no one dared to interfere.

Farah remembered Gul covering himself and attempting to shield himself, he seemed so defeated. Watching Chaman slap his mother repeatedly clearly was too overwhelming for him, he was in a situation so alien to all that he'd ever known, that he had no other recourse but to stand, motionless and silent. But then he snapped. Farah heard him shout and saw him run towards Chaman. He charged slamming into him, tackling him, and knocking him to the floor. He then straddled Chaman and wildly attacked him, without control and definitely without forethought. Chaman's cursing and dramatic screams overcame everything else. Muffled shrieks, whispers, and gasps seemed to be coming from every corner and Farah took the opportunity to compose herself while the onlookers focused on the mayhem. She then remembered seeing her mother walk into the kitchen and stop right beside Chaman and Gul. She saw the familiar stick in her mother's hand rising and then she heard it land on Gul's back. She heard his ear-piercing screams. He raised his head and saw Sarah Khanum's face glaring down at him and suddenly he was off Chaman and on the floor back down looking up at her while she continued to strike and whip him. Lashing his chest, his neck, anything she could make contact with. Chaman's yelling had been replaced by Gul's howls.

"What is going on here?" Sarah Khanum's voice was firm and her tone was sharp. Now that some semblance of order had been restored, she demanded answers.

Nobody spoke or made a sound. Even Chaman stayed quiet. Sarah Khanum looked around, waiting for a response from someone, her commanding eyes stopped at Zara Bibi.

"He is your son, correct?" She was pointing towards Gul jabbing him with her stick. "Is he your son?!" She asked again. Zara Bibi couldn't speak. Both hands covered her mouth and she couldn't still her eyes, which darted frantically.

Sarah Khanum waited for a few moments before yelling. "Answer me!"

"Of course he is." Chaman was incapable of staying quiet.

"Shut up." Sarah Khanum turned towards him ferociously. "Do not speak unless I address you. Do you understand?"

"Yes." Chaman retreated.

"One more outburst and you will lose what little you have left." There was muffled, nervous laughter from the crowd. Sarah Khanum chose to ignore it. Chaman looked at them, humiliated.

"Answer me," Sarah Khanum turned to Zara Bibi. "Is this your son?"

"Yes." Barely audible.

"What was he doing in the house, in the kitchen? Shouldn't he be outside, in the guard's room?"

"Yes, yes he should be. That's where I left him in the morning when I came in. I left him sleeping on the *charpoy* in the guard's room."

"Then why is he here, in my house, in my kitchen?"

"I don't know, Khanum. By God, I don't know. I swear I left him in the guard's room when I came this morning. I don't know when he left or why!" The scarf on her head slipped, her hands shaking, she absently moved to fix it almost unaware of her actions as though her hands moved themselves.

"Keep talking."

"I don't know what else to say, that's exactly what happened." Zara Bibi sounded baffled.

"I am asking you why your son was here? Why was he fighting with Chaman? You haven't given me complete answers yet, so keep talking!" Sarah Khanum was barely able to contain her impatience.

"I don't know anything about that, Khanum, I don't know why he was fighting with Chaman. I have no idea what any of this is about, I swear."

Farah remembered seeing her mother turn to Chaman and then back to her. By her facial expression, she knew an unpleasant encounter was on the brink, her mother's final turn was toward Gul demanding an explanation.

Gul was having trouble piecing his words together as he tried to describe the conversation that he'd overheard between Chaman and Farah while he was hiding in the pantry. Uninterrupted thus far, he continued his attempt at a re-enactment and his fear began to dissipate. His newly found confidence resulted in an accelerated speech which became loud and aggressive, and then erratic. Following his story became challenging and he appeared not credible, at least to Sarah Khanum. Farah belonged to the master's family. It was impossible for anyone, let alone Sarah Khanum, to consider for a moment that Gul was innocent and Farah the real culprit.

"So you are saying that you are innocent? That Farah made you do what you did to her? Is that what you are saying?" Gul looked at his mother, then shifted his gaze to Farah and then to Chaman. His eyes quickly surveyed the silent, studying crowd before boldly meeting Sarah Khanum's gaze. Their eyes met for a fraction of a second before he lowered his head and nodded.

"See what happens when you bring young boys in the house" Sarah Khanum stared at Gul for a long while before shifting her eyes towards his mother. "You know what will happen to him now? Don't you?"

Zara Bibi stood there motionless. Her face paling. She raised both her hands up to her face, palms together, attempting to hide the tears as they streamed out between her fingers. She knelt in supplication in front of Sarah Khanum, her eyes barely level with the other woman's expensive Italian designer shoes.

"He is just a child, Khanum. Just an innocent child, please I beg you, have mercy on him. I'll send him away, far away, he will never set foot in this house again." She broke down. Her hands gripped Sarah Khanum's ankles. Then she stood up and ran towards Gul, grabbed him by his shoulder, and shoved him towards Sarah Khanum's feet.

"Don't just stand there! Apologize for what you did! Don't you understand what can happen to you!?" she shouted. Despite her words, Gul just stood there like a silent statue staring in what appeared to be a strangely vacant but defiant way. Sarah Khanum held her stance studying him, and then she looked at his mother.

"You may be sorry but look at your son, he is not. He's not even ashamed." Her voice was void of emotion but by looking at her tightly set mouth and her narrowing eyes, Zara Bibi detected some hint of empathy. She was impossible to read but anything was better than nothing.

"He is sorry Khanum. He is. I promise! And he is ashamed but he is also a child. He doesn't know anything and he does not understand," Zara Bibi pleaded. She knew what could be done to her only son. She also knew that he too realized what could happen to him, but he was in a strange mesmeric state and totally incapable of handling himself correctly. She also knew that her pleadings would fall upon deaf ears and her tears would fall in vain, but as a mother, she had no choice but to try and save her son.

"I don't see any shame in his eyes and I don't see it in his demeanor." Sarah Khanum was glaring at Gul whose gaze was fixated on the ground.

"Please forgive him." Zara Bibi was not willing to give up. "I am asking for my sake. I've served you for so many years. Please forgive him. Please."

Sarah Khanum stood there quietly, seemingly without any concern for the poor woman's ceaseless begging. "You know I can't do that. Forgiveness isn't for me to grant. He can ask for it when Sardar Timur talks to him."

"No... Khanum...no! Please don't tell Sardar Timur, he won't spare my son. He cannot know about this."

"That's not possible and you know that! You know very well that hiding anything from my husband would place me in danger, and Farah as well, and your entire family for that matter. I absolutely cannot hide this from my husband, you know the rules of the world we live in, everybody knows, why would you even ask me for such an inaccessible favor?" Sarah Khanum was firm in her position.

"I don't know, Khanum, I don't know. But I do know that I will lose my son if Sardar Timur knows what happened. He's innocent, Khanum. My boy is innocent. He is just a boy, a stupid boy. I don't know what he was thinking. But have mercy on him please Khanum. He is my only son."

Zara Bibi moved close to Gul and slapped him hard. He didn't react. He just stood there and let her slap him again, and again. Sarah Khanum was still unmoved; her face was void of any expression. She let this go on for a while before summoning two guards, then motioned for them to take Gul away, the other guards stopped his mother from following. Sarah Khanum spun around and then grabbed Farah's hand pulling her away from the kitchen. There was not a single soul in the crowd with the courage to utter a word and they stood there in absolute quietude. Farah remembered Zara Bibi's loud screams, before the silence. Gul, escorted by two guards just walked away resigned, without putting up any fight whatsoever.

Sarah Khanum stopped pulling now that they were out of sight, but even now with this softer hold, she was still able to feel her mother's anger. She tried to free herself, but the grip grew tighter, nails digging, warning her with each attempt. After a third attempt, Sarah Khanum's furious stare caused Farah's heart to skip a beat. She gave in. She simply allowed herself to be taken to her mother's bedroom where she would await her punishment. Despite her calm exterior, her heart raced and she could feel the rhythmic pounding throughout her body. Not that long ago she had experienced stimulation of a totally different nature, which led to this. If only she could take that back and erase time. If only.

She remembered seeing her mother's room and the feeling of trying to dig her heels into the ground in hopes that somehow that extra weight would slow down the process, but also knowing that it would only delay the inevitable. She then remembered hearing the heavy wooden door open in front of her and then being shoved to the floor just before the sound of the door shut behind her with a loud slam. The loud bangs continued forever and she couldn't identify that sound nor could she open her eyes until the slaps on her face and the hits to her head became real. "What the hell were you thinking, getting mixed up with that boy?" Sarah Khanum wasn't in the least bit loud, she didn't need to raise her voice because her tone was by far sufficiently frightening.

Farah couldn't say a word. She didn't even try to defend herself. She just crouched frozen in place while she got brutally battered by her mother.

"Answer me! What the hell were you doing in there with that boy?" Sarah Khanum's hands didn't stop. Farah still was speechless.

"And why was Chaman there? What were you two doing in the kitchen? What was going on? Answer me!"

Farah still didn't speak. A heavy blow to the head caused her to spin and fall flat on the floor. The rug cushioned her fall, but the fibers felt like thin, sharp wires penetrating her skin. Sarah Khanum stopped for a minute and then began to kick her daughter in the ribs and legs for what seemed like an eternity before finally stepping away from her. Farah stayed on the floor moaning and whimpering, warm blood running down her lower lip. She shook her head several times and welcomed the tears as they rolled down her cheeks. She couldn't control them, nor could she regulate the sobbing which seemed to have taken over her body almost as emphatically as her curiosity had earlier.

"If you want to live Farah you need to answer me."

"I'm scared, Khanum," Farah whispered.

"You should be, and……." Sarah Khanum was in deep thought. She left her sentence incomplete.

"Is Baba going to kill me?" She was barely able to make the words audible.

"I don't know Farah, I don't know."

"Khanum, please save me," Farah rose to a kneeling position, took Sarah Khanum's hands, and pleaded. "I don't want to die." Sarah Khanum stared at her daughter, raised both hands, and slapped her on both cheeks. Farah screamed loudly and fell back down on the floor, sobbing uncontrollably once again.

"Stand up," Sarah Khanum waited for a few minutes before pulling her arm. Farah stood up, still crying.

"Now listen carefully. I will do what I can to save you." Sarah Khanum was firm but her voice was anxious and her tone was not encouraging. "But there is a condition."

Farah's face was covered in tears, hand imprints, and nail marks. She wiped her bruised and swollen cheeks stopped breathing and looked at her mother in desperation, eager for a solution.

Sarah Khanum started talking after a brief pause. "First you need to tell me the truth. Do you understand?"

Farah nodded.

"Second, once you tell me the complete truth, I will then tell you what to say to other people. Do you understand what I've just said?"

Another nod.

"Now tell me what happened," said Sarah Khanum. "I want absolute honesty Farah. Do not lie to me and don't leave anything out. Tell me everything that happened in the kitchen and the pantry. I want to hear it all."

Farah started talking. She'd lost track of time and had no idea how long she'd gone on for, but she did remember reliving the whole episode while describing it to her mother. She was barely audible, even to herself. She remembered Sarah Khanum's face as it reddened and then paled, her expressions changing throughout it all. She told her everything, completely and truthfully.

"You should be ashamed of yourself. You're the daughter of Sardar Timur, practically royalty, and you spoke to Chaman like a cheap slut. Looking at those pictures, teasing him. Wasn't there any other way to get information, Farah? You couldn't find a girl to talk to? There are so many working here, they are literally everywhere! You are surrounded by sources! I am beyond disappointed in you. And my dear girl this boy Gul is a real rascal! How dare he touch you like that? The only choice I have now is to turn him into another Chaman."

"He is just a boy, Khanum. I don't blame him, please don't blame Gul."

"Somebody has to accept the blame here Farah and he is the only one who can be blamed! I don't see any way around it."

Farah feeling overpowered by guilt kept looking at her mother who was shaking her head in disbelief.

"I can see that you don't blame him! You think he's innocent and I can't understand why you're defending him. What's wrong with you Farah!? Disgracing your entire family doesn't seem to concern you. Not in the least."

Farah didn't look up, instead, she stared at the ground and focused on the teardrops that landed on the floor. She could feel her mother's piercing stare and the wrath of her disapproval. She had so much to say but she couldn't find a way, she could only manage silence. She had no idea how much time had passed or if her mother was still there, but she finally managed to pick her head up. The room was empty.

She felt her legs buckling, unable to carry her. She threw herself on the bed with whatever strength was left and buried her face in the pillow.

Her thoughts were all over the place and everything was hazy. Farah recalled bits and pieces like the checkered boxes on a chessboard. Little square memories. She heard the door open and then loud footsteps and she was able to deduce that there were at least two people. She could hear her mother's incessant rants; however, it was unclear if they were directed at her or someone else. Then she heard a male voice. Her father Sardar Timur's voice. He sounded enraged. More so than usual. An argument ensued between them and she could hear her mother pleading on her behalf, adamantly trying to prevent him from doing something that she was against. Her mother's attempts failed. Farah remembered being violently shaken and thrown off bed, hitting the floor and having cold water thrown on her face.

She vaguely remembered being hit with a blunt object on her back and her arms. She thought she heard a male voice shouting and a female voice screaming. She had a recollection of someone's hand pulling her head sideways and smashing it repeatedly against the headboard. Then she felt hot streaks running down her eyelids. She felt the warmth of what she now knew was blood, trickling down from her forehead. Hard slaps burning her cheeks. She remembered seeing flashes of light and silhouettes waving in front of her eyes. She thought she heard loud and harsh voices demanding answers to some questions she didn't understand. The ordeal went on...and on. She completely lost sense of time. She remembered being hit all over, severely and mercilessly. After some time, the blows lost their individual character and became one long streak of searing pain. She thought she might have asked for forgiveness but could not remember her own words. Blood and tears kept streaming. Her screams kept filling up the empty space in the room. Yelling between Sarah Khanum and Sardar Timur was never-ending. She passed out. White flashes, dancing in front of her eyes suddenly descended into darkness. Voices echoing in her ears died down.

She had always been afraid of the dark but that day she welcomed it. She let out a sigh of relief and allowed it to cocoon her. Her brain stopped feeling pain and she lost the desire to defend herself.

FIVE

GUL'S MIND WAS like a blank slate. Two guards escorted him out of the kitchen by holding his biceps, their grip was tight, blocking the blood flow in his arms. At first, he felt discomfort, but eventually, it just gave way to numbness.

They dragged him for what seemed like time without end. The faces around him passed quickly like flashcards, some looked away and others stared unblinkingly. Eventually, he found himself in an empty dusty room. The guards were followed by a third man, statuesque with a thick mustache and a long, deep scar on both cheeks and his lower lip. He was dressed in black and wore dark sunglasses. The deep crook in his lower lip exposed his stained, half chipped lower tooth.

The man in black's fingertips dug into Gul's skull as he yanked his head up at an unnatural angle striking him with his free hand. The two guards let go of his arms so that he was dangling like a loose pendulum with his hair caught in his attacker's hands. He could hear them all laughing and mocking him while he hung like a rag doll. The taut skin of his beautiful young forehead pulled and stretched out like a character in an American horror film.

"What the fuck?" the large man blurted out. "He's like a little rat! He's just a kid! What could he have possibly done? Why is Sardar's wife so angry with him?"

"Well this rat's all grown up, he's a man now, a real little beast," one of the two guards said sarcastically. "He was showing off his manhood to Sardar Timur's daughter."

"Oh wow," the large man said feigning sincerity. "So you're a big man now, all grown up and you just couldn't help showing off!"

Gul was still dangling. His feet were off the ground but he could just touch the dirt and stones with his bare toes.

"Maybe we should see how much of a man he really is, while he still is one," the first of the three guards suggested.

"Are you all crazy or are you just stupid?" A commanding voice caused the chuckling to come to a screeching halt and the man in black released Gul letting him fall to the ground with a thud. A large, imposing man stood in the middle of the room commanding attention.

"Don't speak your mind. Don't give suggestions. As a matter of fact, don't speak at all. Your only job is to follow orders, not to make suggestions. Get that into your useless head."

The first guard's face paled. He turned around, looked at Gul on the floor, and kicked him in the stomach. The second guard was motionless and void of expression, and the third guard stood in place, impatiently tapping his right foot while staring at the other two waiting to see who would take the lead.

"You! Get up," the third guard finally barked at Gul who wasn't moving. He reached down, grabbed his arm, and pulled him up. It was like lifting a feather and he couldn't believe the boy had so little fight in him, he was almost sympathetic.

"What are we supposed to do with him?" he asked the second guard.

"I don't know. Sarah Khanum didn't say. She just told us to take him away."

"Okay, so let's keep an eye on him. We'll probably need to teach him some manners, which is what I'm hoping! Nevertheless, it's best to wait for instruction." The third guard walked towards the door. "I'll check with Sardar Timur."

"Tie him to the chair." He turned as he approached the door. "There's a rope in the bathroom. Go get it and I'll wait here." The second guard went inside the bathroom and came back with a thin blue nylon rope. He pushed Gul forcing him to sit in the chair, held him in place, and then tied him up. The third guard walked back from the door to check the rope, nodded his head approvingly, and finally left the room.

⁓

Sarah Khanum saw blood dripping down from Farah's forehead and lost all self-control. She was unable to stop herself from positioning herself between her daughter and her husband. Farah was on the bed, already severely beaten and unconscious. Sarah Khanum was right to be fearful, she knew that there was a good chance that he might kill her. Like most men, she knew being dishonored in this manner was not something Sardar Timur could stomach. He needed to punish Farah in order to salvage his honor, regardless of the consequences. Shifting the blame away from Farah was the only way to save her from her father.

"Step away!" She tried to push him away from Farah. "She'll surely die if you go on like this. Do you really want to kill her? Your own child?"

"Shouldn't I?" Sardar Timur shouted. "Do I have a choice?"

"Yes, you do," Sarah Khanum shouted back. "But you won't understand it. You are too angry right now to understand anything."

Without verbally responding, Sardar Timur tried to reach for Farah again but Sarah Khanum grabbed his hand.

"I will not let you kill my daughter," Sarah Khanum's tone was strong and firm. "You should leave the room now. Immediately. Leave her alone. I will talk to her and let you know exactly what happened. Then you can decide."

Sardar Timur stood still while his wife stared at him, their eyes locking until she shifted her glance to look at Farah who like her father also was unmoving. Sardar Timur stepped towards Sarah Khanum, clutched her head in his hands, looked into her eyes, and then pushed her back.

"Okay. You win. I'm going to spare her for now. But only for now!" Anger and spite dripped from every syllable. Sarah Khanum knew he wasn't done with punishing either her or their daughter. This was just an act of temporary leniency.

"I'll let you do what you want. But remember, I don't forgive easily." He wouldn't give another warning, this was it.

"I know that. You don't need to remind me."

He looked at her with disgust, then looked at Farah for a brief moment and without an ounce of compassion spun around on his heels and then left the room. Shutting the door behind him with a loud bang.

Sarah Khanum closed her eyes. For the first time, two tears oozed out and made their way down her cheeks. She looked at her daughter and moved to sit beside her on the bed. She began stroking her head in hopes of pacifying her, her fingers running through the length of her hair. Farah's body remained still, even as her mother bent down and adoringly kissed her forehead.

"You have put the both of us in a very difficult position Farah. I don't know how I am going to save you." Sarah Khanum whispered in her ear. There was no response.

Sardar Timur opened the metal door of the guard room with a loud thump and entered, holding a long rifle. The guard inside involuntarily jumped to his feet. He was blocking Gul from his view, so Sardar Timur pushed him to the side until he could see the boy who was still tied up in the chair.

"Is this the boy?"

"Yes Sardar Timur. He's the one,"

"How old are you?" Sardar Timur asked Gul.

"Fifteen," Gul could only whisper.

"What is your name?"

"Gul."

"Your mother works here?"

"Yes."

"And your father, does he work for me also?"

Gul heard the question but didn't speak.

"Did you hear my question?" Sardar Timur was now growling.

"Yes." The boy was barely able to nod his head.

"What does he do?" Sardar Timur asked again.

"I don't really know." His tone lacked conviction.

"What's his name?"

"Shams," Gul whispered again, "Shams ud din."

"Who is he?" Sardar Timur questioned the guards surrounding the boy. "Who is Shams?" Two of them shook their heads, shrugged their shoulders. The third guard squinted, and shook his head, looking at the boy, appearing to recall something.

"Is he the one with one eye?" the third guard asked, staring at Gul, who nodded.

"He's one of the peasants Sardar Timur. I think I know who he is, I've seen him many times. He always covers his dead eye with a patch and he has a strange walk. Everybody pokes fun at him."

"Is that the one? Is he your father?" Sardar Timur asked Gul, who once again only nodded. Loud, mocking laughter echoed in the tiny room as all three guards broke into childish hysterics. Sardar Timur glared seemingly disapproving of the sophomoric response. The laughter ceased.

"Go get him for me, right away. In fact, get his whole family and bring them all to the back of the house, including this rascal. Everyone should see the punishment this boy has earned for himself and his family." Sardar Timur motioned the third guard. He nodded and left the room with quick steps.

"And you," Sardar Timur looked at the third guard, "Go get the dogs."

The two guards appeared shocked for a second while Sardar Timur just smiled, grimly. They looked at each other and broke into nervous laughter not sure if this was a fear tactic, or if it was real. Gul looked at all three, puzzled and disheartened.

"Now! Go!" The guard sprinted towards the door, but paused for a moment to turn his head, he looked at Gul's face, exhaled, and then remembering his orders, spun around and once again sprinted out the door. Sardar Timur's stone-cold eyes met Gul's for an instant before he shifted his glance to the other guard, signaling him by nodding his head.

❧

Sardar's men didn't take long to bring Gul's entire family toward the back of his vast compound to the plot of land that housed the canines. His father Shams, his mother Zara Bibi, and his sister Badri

Jamala were brought in. Gul was the last one. He still wore the collar that was attached to a leash through a metal chain loop, a choke collar designed for dog training. The guard passed the handle of the leash to Sardar Timur.

This was meant to be a grand spectacle. An open invitation for all so that they could see firsthand how Sardar Timur dealt with those who betrayed him or disrespected him. The yard filled up quickly as they all watched in both horror and fascination while Sardar Timur paced back and forth, dragging Gul, while rivulets of blood streamed from his neck where the sharp prongs bit into him.

Farah stood with her mother on the balcony overlooking the yard. She looked around frantically trying to find Chaman, and once she did, their eyes met. He held her forceful gaze for a moment before shifting his eyes to the vicious dogs barking in the background. He grinned wickedly.

SIX

T HE TALL MAN in a dark brown suit stood on the left side of the table, holding a cigar in his hand. He appeared to have completely forgotten that it was slowly burning, dropping its ash on the table. He was focused on something through the window on the other side of his office. His young, pretty secretary's eyes were following his gaze to see what he might be looking at, but she didn't see anything interesting, or at least anything worth staring at so keenly.

Her eyes were constantly shifting between the window and the man's face. She desperately wanted to break the awkward quiet. Other than the whirring of the floor fan, the deafening silence was absolute. She couldn't bring herself to produce even a soft cough to get his attention. She kept swallowing nervously and her hand that was gripping the pencil began to cramp. Before long, she finally gave up trying and just stood there with lowered shoulders, resigned.

Suddenly without warning the electricity went out. The floor fan lost momentum and the breeze which had been filling the room thus far, no longer existed, leaving an even deeper stillness.

"God, the power is gone again. I hope the backup system is not still out of order."

"Well I guess we'll find out soon enough." the secretary said, with a not so subtle hint of sarcasm.

"Find Aamir Shah for me," he said, waving his hand dismissively. "I need to see him immediately. If he's home, tell him to come here right away and tell him to bring his US passport. He has to go on a quick two-day trip."

The secretary didn't respond with words, only with a broad, knowing smile. She held eye contact for a few seconds before walking to the door, and as she reached the door, her smile turned into seductive laughter for a reason only she knew. He watched as her hair moved sinuously in the air matching the rhythmic swaying of her hips. He knew her game. Her white dress revealed all and her designer stilettos boldly tapped the marble floors as she strutted away.

The man in the brown suit held the door slightly open in order to keep watching, his eyes stayed glued on her until she reached the far end of the hallway and turned left. He kept staring in her direction for a few curious moments, then let out a deep sigh, stepped back into his office, and closed the door. The cigar in his hands was still scattering ashes everywhere. Finally, he placed it in an ashtray and lowered himself into the large leather chair behind the vast desk. He swiveled and swiveled as he sat in deep thought appreciating the large office full of rare and expensive items that he had collected from his travels.

Rajinder Aggarwal was a media mogul. A very rich, powerful, and surprisingly well-liked individual surrounded by a sea of mentally impoverished, hate-mongering, deeply inept, and dishonest people who bowed down to him because of the money and power his empire brought him. Regardless of how liked he was, there were always those who harbored jealousy. Politicians, bureaucrats, judges, sports and film stars all wanted to be in his good graces, but were also often nettled due to the ongoing string of unflattering stories and dirty secrets he printed, digitally and on paper as well as aired on national TV. It was a continuous affair of love and hate.

Rajinder knew to not let anyone come too close, yet he also knew that he couldn't let them stray too far, it was a delicate balance. He couldn't risk absence for too long, lest they forgot about the "tycoon" Rajinder. He loved the mystery and he'd been playing this game for more than twenty years and considered himself a master. He had powerful friends who could and would turn into foes in an instant, depending on the political and economic climate prevailing at any given time.

The general population had an appetite for news and information, usually sensationalized over subdued. They didn't care about the veracity of the stories they were told, as long as they had something to fill the void of their otherwise miserable, empty lives, and were willing to shell out money for his paper and of course, increase his wealth. Those who couldn't afford the luxury of printed gossip would gather at newsstands that could be found on every corner. As soon as all the papers and magazines hit the street, people circled and craned their necks attempting to read at a distance. Half-truths, ignorance, and an unquenched thirst for knowledge, the perfect combination.

A favorite pastime for those who really had nothing better to do was to read unconfirmed rumors and propagate dramatic, yet baseless conspiracy theories. Rajinder was in the business of supplying that demand. Packaging nonsense as a credible journalistic effort, and then selling it to the receptive public. He was not alone, but he thought himself to be more principled than any of the others alike. He tried to break free many times. For all the moral high ground claimed by the people—who sneered at the politicians and looked down upon them as corrupt parasites—the same righteous people were too eager and willing to sell themselves, their minds, their opinions and their votes for petty things, or even just the empty promises of petty things which would never materialize. Yet the offering of mind and soul to a would-be buyer would continue without any shame or self-awareness.

"If they want to buy garbage, then garbage I shall sell." He would often say when sitting with his friends behind closed doors, indulging himself in verboten pleasures. Nobody seemed to disagree.

"What a bunch of hypocrites," he would say in a condescending tone. "They are the first to sneer and raise their voice at the slightest whiff of corruption."

"Keep milking them," another voice would pitch in, and then there would be laughter, more talk of morality, and more forbidden pleasure which the people would pay for. This would go on for hours. Darkness provided them cover, even from their own prying eyes. Mornings: another story. Moral sermons would follow the nights of pleasure, and the cycle kept repeating itself. His wealth and influence kept growing and so did the number of wealth and influence seekers.

Occasionally there were problems: threats, criminal complaints, civil lawsuits, inquiries into his financial matters, tax notices. State resources would be used to zero in on his professional and financial life, only to force him to engage in breaking other laws. His past, his present, and based on what he could clearly see, his future was filled with all the immoral and corrupt practices he publicly opposed. But, this was the way he knew business could be conducted in this country, or for that matter, any third world country, or even the countries with the so-called strong justice system when they are beholden by the officials whose morality had given way to the corrupt use of legitimate powers bestowed upon them, legally and constitutionally. As long as he could keep claiming the moral high ground, keep his hypocrisy under the rug, and was allowed to keep running his empire making millions, he was content. The way he looked at it was that he was not a hypocrite. He was being forced to act with hypocrisy. In that sense, he was a victim of a society that demanded strict morality from others but was not willing to practice it, either individually or collectively.

He was convinced of his own piousness and held a deep sense of self-righteousness. He made money by preaching what he was not practicing, so the fact that he was at least preaching morality was a testament to his good character, in his mind. Others were not even preaching. In his eyes, since he was good-natured & well-intentioned, some acts of immorality here and there, done grudgingly and without evil intent were not terribly bad. On the contrary, they were a testament to his good nature. He had to struggle within himself to stop feeling bad about what he had to do. Therefore, in his mind, he should be lauded for the hesitation he experienced in the processing of being immoral, not chastised for the acts of immorality. At least he felt bad afterward.

He put the chewed end of the cigar in his mouth and reached for the remote control sitting on the side of the desk. The power came back on and soon enough the room was filled with a newscaster's voice, reading the latest news bulletin, on one of the news networks he owned. The newscaster was a charming young woman with a provocative upper physique. Her name faded in on the lower third of the screen.

"Hello, Arsala Khan." He almost sighed her name. His eyes were bright and his stony face was now decorated with a shining smile.

SEVEN

AMIR SHAH WAS in a deep sleep when the phone rang. He abhorred early morning calls. He was a night owl and days were a painful but necessary passage to the next night. He reached out, picked up the cell phone, looked at the screen and seeing that it was from the office, answered it. Reluctantly. If it was not from the office, he would have ignored it without hesitation.

"Hey, champion," the voice on the other end was perky and jovial. "Did I wake you up?"

"No, sweetheart, you just kept me from sleeping." He yawned. "I mean stopped me from sleeping more."

He heard a giggle. It was sensuous. A sharp tingle ran through his body and he couldn't help but smile.

"What's up?" he asked.

"Highly inappropriate question to ask a woman." Her answer was unexpected and he chuckled. This time her giggle turned into rather flirtatious laughter. Now he was fully awake. "Hang on handsome, Master wants to talk to you," she said.

"What for? I had a meeting with him last night." There was a slight tension in his voice.

"He didn't tell and I didn't ask."

"You are so incredibly docile." It was one of her many attributes.

"Hold on, I'll put you through. Oh, and by the way, he said you should come to the office packed and with your US passport."

"Tell me, where am I going?"

"Again, he didn't tell me and I didn't ask." Her voice was followed by a click. The line was silent for a moment and then Rajinder was on the line.

"Aamir, I am sending you out of the country for an urgent assignment. Come to the office this afternoon, ready to leave." No pleasantries–his usual style. "You'll need your U.S. passport."

"Where am I going?"

"I'll let you know once you're here and I need you here by 1:00 pm. You will leave the country no later than midnight tonight. All right? See you soon." Dead silence on the phone told Aamir that the conversation was over. He stared at the screen for a long moment, then decided to get out of bed and was about to put the phone back on the side table when it started vibrating and ringing again. This time the caller was "unknown." He paused for a moment before answering.

"Are you ready to leave?" An unfamiliar male voice spoke in a very pleasant tone.

"Identify yourself please." Aamir was now hyper-alert, sitting on the bed.

"Why is the introduction necessary?"

"If I don't know you and you won't introduce yourself, then why should I keep talking to you?"

"Good logic." Now there was another male voice coming from the phone speaker.

"So, are we conferencing now? How many people are on the line?"

"Yes we are conferencing, but it will turn into an actual meeting soon. We're coming to see you," the first voice said.

"Who are you and why do you want to see me?"

"You'll be able to tell when you see us," the second voice said. "As to why we want to see you, well you should know, in your line of work, unexpected guests are not that unusual now, are they?"

"Hmm." Aamir let out a long deep breath.

"Thirty minutes," Aamir heard the first man's voice, firmness of which told him it didn't tolerate opposition.

"What happens if I leave before the thirty-minute deadline?" In his heart, he already knew the answer.

"Well, then we will catch up to you," the second voice said. "And in that event, our meeting will not be as civilized as it has the potential to be, understand? For example, at home, I'm sure you will have your servant serve us tea and it can all be quite easy. Elsewhere, that may not be possible."

Aamir kept quiet. He'd heard about these surprise visits by strangers from his colleagues but it was his first experience dealing with such a situation.

"I'm a busy man and have many things to do," Aamir said. "I can't just sit and wait around for you."

"Thirty minutes or less," the first voice said. "We will be with you in thirty minutes or less. We won't make you wait but you cannot leave. Do not leave. Got it?"

"I understand. I'll wait. Thirty minutes is all I have, I don't have more time to spare. Here you go, the stopwatch starts now." Aamir was equally firm in his response. He started the timer on his phone and hung up.

He didn't know who they were for sure, but could certainly take an educated guess. Secret police. Intelligence agencies. Those who had taken it upon themselves to define the national interest and then protect it using any means necessary. It didn't matter to them what the book said, laws were for others to follow. In fact, in their eyes, they were the law. Their motto was 'the *king can do no wrong.*' In their mind, this was equally applicable to '*king's men*' too.

Aamir looked at this wife who was in deep slumber, lying peacefully next to him. She hadn't moved an inch. She was used to his calls at odd times, and his irregular schedule in general, and had trained herself to tune it all out. Sleeping pills were also helpful. He gently ran his fingers through her luscious, shiny flowing hair and then pulled the perfectly trimmed ends close to his mouth, gently kissing them. A satisfied, loving smile emerged for a split second as he slowly let the wondrous silky sections of her hair slip out of his hands.

He jumped out of bed and went into the bathroom. A quick shower and then he put on a black shirt and blue jeans. He always kept an extra set of clothes in a "go" bag for moments like this. While drying his hair, he pushed the call button on the video intercom system installed on the wall to the right of his sink, to talk to Shakir, his live-in assistant. The screen lit up. Shakir accustomed to this and always prepared for anything waited for his orders. Aamir put his finger on his mouth, Shakir nodded in acknowledgment.

Aamir pulled out a sheet of paper from the drawer and started using a marker on it. He wrote a few lines and then showed them to Shakir on the screen. Shakir squinted, read the message, and then nodded again with a smile. Aamir gestured for him to wait, and then looked at his cell phone. Stopwatch showed a twenty-four-minute lapse. He gestured Shakir to remain on standby.

Aamir dialed Rajinder's personal number from his cell phone, and the call was answered immediately. Before he could utter a word, Aamir started talking.

"This is Aamir. I am about to leave. But before I do that, I need to let you know that I may have a tail."

"Okay." There was no surprise on the other end of the line.

90

"I got a call from an unknown number immediately after hanging up with you. There were two men, two voices and they sounded like the "usual." They said that they are on their way and under no circumstances am I to leave the house."

"When are they coming?" His voice was calm.

"They said within thirty minutes, it has been twenty-five already. So they should be arriving any minute now."

"And what do you plan to do?"

"I can't wait for them. Well, I can I suppose, but I won't. I'm leaving right now."

"Okay, come right over. I'll see you shortly." Rajinder said and hung up the phone. Aamir looked into the screen where Shakir's eager face was looking at him, waiting. Aamir gestured for him to leave immediately. Shakir nodded, left the video intercom, and headed towards the door. Soon he disappeared.

The phone rang again, from another unknown number. He smiled and ignored the call. It chimed six times and then stopped. It immediately started ringing again. Aamir ignored it again. The cycle repeated itself four times before Aamir picked up the phone. He was hardly able to contain his smile.

"We told you to wait for us." The speaker clearly vexed.

"I don't take orders from you and I don't work for you."

"You, motherfucker." The second voice was more than heated, far less controlled than the first voice.

Aamir was able to contain his amusement only with some difficulty.

"Mind your language," Aamir said firmly. "You're late and I cannot just sit here and wait for you."

"Watch your tone, buddy. I don't like it. This is not helpful." The first voice was barely able to contain his anger.

"Are you threatening me?"

"I don't need to. You know that. We don't threaten, we just *notify*." It was now the second voice. They were taking turns as if they had scripted the conversation. "Once the notice has been given, sometimes unfortunate things happen, I'll admit that. But for the most part, problems do get solved without anything bad happening to anyone. You should know that. You're in that line of work. Right? Don't you know what can happen?"

"Your thirty minutes are up."

"We're here. Don't leave." This time Aamir heard two voices together. "We're right at the corner in front of your house."

"Sorry, too late, I've already left," Aamir said in a calm voice and looked at the video intercom showing the outside of the house. He saw the main gate open and a car leave in haste. The car windows were tinted and Shakir had his cap and sunglasses on. In this guise, and from a distance, his resemblance to Aamir was close enough.

"You, son of a bitch," the first voice said "I see you leaving. I am right behind you. You should stop immediately."

Aamir heard the sound of tires screeching through the phone and saw a small black Suzuki car zoom by the front of his house. He saw two men in the front seat. They flashed by. Everything outside was being videotaped. He went to his computer and started rewinding the video second by second, frame by frame. There they were, two dark-skinned men with mustaches, wearing white shirts. Suzuki's license plate number was also visible. He took a picture of the screen with his phone, picked up his suitcase, which was always ready for such hurried and unplanned departures, and left the house from the back door. He walked to the main street, hailed a cab, and headed towards the office. Aamir was still connected to the phone call, listening to the cussing and screeching. He had the phone on mute so that he could remain unheard.

The cab was going the same route Shakir had taken. Aamir was in the back seat staring straight ahead. After a few minutes, he could see the black car behind Shakir's car at a distance.

"Take a different route," Aamir tapped on the driver's shoulder.

"But this is the shortest route," the driver said in a puzzled voice.

"That's okay. Take the longer route."

"Whatever you say." The driver was agreeable. "But you'll end up paying more and I really hope that you won't complain or give me any grief about that."

"Don't worry. I won't complain," Aamir said cheerfully. "In fact, there's a handsome tip in it for you."

"Thank you! Sounds great! You've got yourself a deal!" The cab driver sounded thrilled, not surprisingly.

He took the flyover to his left and the cars parted ways. Aamir kept watching the black car for as long as he could before he lost visual on it. The phone call was still connected.

He heard loud horns and commotion. Apparently, they were still trying to intercept Shakir's car. He could picture the look on their faces when they realize that he's not the one on the driver's seat, and he couldn't help but smile. Apparently, his smile turned into a nervous giggle because he heard his own laugh, looked in the rearview mirror, and caught the driver's curious gaze.

"Don't worry" Aamir mouthed silently while pointing towards the Bluetooth device strapped on his ear. The driver nodded and shifted his eyes from the rearview mirror back towards the windshield.

"They're blocking me now," Shakir whispered in the phone.

"Okay. Engage them in a conversation for as long as you can."

"I will."

"Let's see if they figure out the trick we played on them," Aamir said. He was sure they would know immediately that they'd been following the wrong person.

"You bastard, son of a bitch," Aamir heard someone screaming from a distance. There was his answer. It sounded like the first voice he'd heard earlier. "We told you to stay at the house. Why the fuck did you leave?"

"I don't know, what do you mean?" Shakir responded calmly.

"Say that again," the second voice ordered.

"I said, I don't know, what do you mean," Shakir repeated "And who are you anyway?"

Aamir's heart started pounding.

"You sound different." The second voice was now yelling. "Are you Aamir? No, you are not! Who the hell are you?"

"My name is Shakir, why do you think I'm Aamir?"

"He played us." Aamir heard the sound of a punch being thrown, then nothing.

"What an army of fools," Aamir whispered to himself.

"Don't you know who we are?" The first voice was screaming. "How dare you try to trick us?"

"I didn't try to trick you!" Shakir answered. "I swear." Aamir had a faint smile now. He was worried about Shakir but enjoying their distress.

"Shut up." There was the sound of another hit. Aamir heard another scream.

"You know us very well. Even if you don't, your friend Aamir does." This time they were both yelling.

"Yes, I know exactly who you are," Aamir said to himself. "You guys are cocky and absurd, running around, playing spy games. Idiots. Plain and simple. Just idiots." He disconnected the phone.

He had no more patience for stupidity, no more patience for his countrymen, and no more patience for his country spending money on idiots like these. He put the phone in his pocket, leaned back, and stared out of the window. His mind was flying in a million directions.

Traffic around them was congested and slow-moving. He looked at his new Apple Watch and figured it would take another twenty minutes to get to the destination. He felt like closing his eyes but decided it would be best to stay awake and alert, he had no choice. Looking over his shoulder had become second nature and today offered nothing to change that habit.

Rajinder was smoking his third cigar of the day when Aamir finally arrived.

"You're going to Dubai," he said before Aamir could even sit.

"Should I ask why?" Aamir asked casually.

"You just did," his Master said without any emotion. "You are the only French-speaking person on my staff and that is the sole reason why you were selected. Otherwise, the assignment is not particularly special."

"Do I dare ask about the nature of the assignment?" Aamir said in a matter of fact tone, his lips half-open with a smile.

"Once again, you just did." This time Rajinder smiled back. Aamir couldn't tell if it was a genuine smile or a smirk. He had learned over the years not to waste time worrying about the significance of his boss's facial or verbal expressions.

"Enlighten me, please," Aamir said.

"Does the name Arlette Baudis ring a bell?"

"The name sounds familiar," Aamir said, trying to recall where he heard this name.

"Let me save you from mental exertion," Rajinder said, realizing that Aamir was having difficulty remembering her. Aamir couldn't tell if the help was sincere or he was being mocked, most likely mocked. "She is a French news reporter and journalist."

"Ah, yes I remember. She did an interview with our beloved Prime Minister some time ago."

"Correct, so you must remember the near scandal which almost broke as a result of that interview."

"I do remember that, and if my information is correct, the scandal actually did break, didn't it?"

"Well, yes and no. She claimed that what she said was accurate, he claimed that the true meaning of his statements was lost in translation."

"I hope we are talking about the same person," Aamir said with little skepticism in his voice. "She's the reporter who claimed that the Prime Minister offered to buy her a phone in order to stay in touch with him privately. Correct?"

"That is exactly right. So you do remember," Rajinder said, a little laughter sneaking out almost involuntarily.

"And his version was that she was referring to the new iPhone that was coming out, and how she said that she loved iPhone like some women love shoes. He said that he simply offered to buy it for her before the official release of the phone and that it was a friendly gesture and good for business."

"I wonder how could there be such miscommunication between the two."

"That's where you come in Aamir," his boss said in a dry voice, sucking deeply on the cigar.

"Okay, I'm not fully understanding this, what is my role exactly?"

"Well, last time Arlette Baudis brought her own interpreter, she doesn't speak English, and our Prime Minister doesn't speak French. Actually, nobody on the Prime Minister's staff spoke a word of French, and the Prime Minister said that he didn't know how his words were being translated and that the translator must have screwed up. He said that this debacle caused him considerable embarrassment."

"Didn't they clear the translation before writing and publishing the story?"

"For the official version, yes," Rajinder said, dropping cigar ash in the tray. "But the statements made after the interview and off the record were not transcribed. She claimed that is when he offered to buy her a phone so that he could stay in touch with her *privately*, she said that his exact words were: "I want to get naughty with you." He of course denied that and explained that he was just being generous, nothing more.

"Okay, so now he wants to control the translator. And that would be my job."

"Exactly."

"But why even grant her an interview, if he feels that she made up a story like that?"

"Beats me. Maybe he actually did say what she claims he did. Maybe he actually likes her and wants to see her again without appearing interested. Obviously, he can't just simply invite her over for dinner after the accusations she made against him."

"Hmm. Interesting." Aamir couldn't say much. There was a brief pause.

"You are not on the official team. You'll be part of a secret security detail escorting the Prime Minister, a team provided by the Sheik of Dubai as an extra security measure. He's due to arrive in Dubai tomorrow afternoon, and you need to be there today so that you can have face to face time with Sheikh's security force."

"How long do I have to stay there?"

"Won't be for too long. The Prime Minister will be there for three days. He has not yet scheduled a specific time with Arlette. Once this interview is done, you will be able to come back unless..."

Rajinder left his sentence incomplete, puffed some smoke, and laughed a little, with a wink thrown Aamir's way.

"Unless what?" Aamir asked but then immediately realized what was unsaid. "Oh, I see. Unless the Prime Minister does try to schedule a secret rendezvous with Arlette."

"Exactly. In that case, you'll become an investigator on our behalf and you'll need to stay there for as long as required and nail the bastard."

"All right."

"You can stay there for thirty days without a visa. Travel on your U.S. passport. It is still valid, right?"

"Yes. Anything specific she wants to discuss with him?" Aamir asked.

"Oh, the usual bullshit: women's rights, honor killing, gang rapes, etc. The West was upset by the Prime Minister's remarks on this subject in a prior interview with another reporter. She will most likely seek clarification and allow him to adjust his views and maybe even offer an apology, if possible. As if that will happen."

"Okay." Aamir rose from the chair. "I guess I should get going. What time is my flight?"

"Maria will let you know." He had no more use or time for Aamir.

"There is one thing I need taken care of before I leave." Aamir thought of Shakir and related the events of the morning, and gave him the license number from the car.

"Don't worry about Shakir," Rajinder responded with utter confidence. "I'll take care of him. In the meantime, if you can find his location, let me know and I'll make sure he's safe and protected."

Aamir nodded and started dialing Shakir's cell number. The phone rang for several minutes and then the tone died. Nobody picked it up. He tried again. Still no answer.

"Give me his number and I'll have him tracked and picked up. Where did you see him last?"

"Near FTC flyover."

"Okay. You can go ahead. I'll handle this."

Aamir stood up and left the room without hesitation. He did not doubt that Shakir would be taken care of, better than what he could have done. Once out of the room, he turned around and looked through the glass window. Rajinder was busy on the phone, with ashes still dropping from the half-smoked cigar in his left hand.

EIGHT

AZIZ EMBRACED TURAB tightly, his big smile masquerading his true feelings. Turab was an old friend, a good friend. They had known each other for many years and had shared countless circumstances and truth be told, Aziz would feel a bit lost without him. But, he took too many liberties. One such strike against him was his assumption that a lack of enthusiasm equated to a deeper friendship than actually existed. As though a relaxed demeanor meant no forced pretenses. In Aziz's mind, this was a complete misinterpretation, and he couldn't understand why Turab wasn't seemingly able to correctly decipher a cold shoulder or a lack of interest. There were times when Aziz thought that he was feigning ignorance, perhaps using this to his advantage in order to stay embedded in his life. Basically, playing dumb, which would mean that Turab was actually the clever fox he was assumed to be. On second thought that was the most plausible scenario.

Turab released Aziz after an especially long, tight embrace and a few cursory compliments. "Aziz, when Rauf called, he sounded absolutely panicked. I was worried sick throughout my trip. Tell me, what the holy hell is going on?"

"Oh my dear friend, I'm so sorry to have caused you so much angst, my son worries over little things, and truth be told, he tends to overreact" Aziz smiled. "Especially when he's thinking about me. I guess he loves me just a little bit too much, and yet, has a funny way of showing it!" Rauf looked sideways as his father spoke. God. How could Turab not see through this act?

"That must be it," Turab agreed joyfully. "After all, you're his father, his beloved dad."

"Yes, right," Aziz said in a tone that sounded sardonic to Rauf and Paro only. Turab either didn't pick up on it or chose to ignore it. "I am the beloved patriarch. That must be it. That explains it."

"Of course that explains it."

Mullah Aziz nodded, looked first at Rauf, and then at Paro's shadow behind the dirty curtain covering the kitchen entrance. Rauf couldn't quite understand whether he was agreeing or disagreeing with Turab. Paro, standing behind the dirty curtain, was grateful in times like these, for the mandatory headscarf that veiled more than her physical features.

"Salam Turab Lala. Thank you kindly for coming." Paro intervened softly, addressing Turab. She wasn't sure if he was either oblivious to her presence or ignoring it.

"Walaikum Assalam," he responded to Paro, carefully keeping his gaze to the ground, while his face was turned in her direction for just a fraction of a second before immediately turning back towards Aziz.

Aziz glanced towards Paro with a smirk, his eyes wide open, almost bulging out. Rauf couldn't decide if his father was pleased or angry, or both – or maybe neither. It was all too confusing. Aziz kept smiling for no reason. It made Rauf uneasy and Turab, unaware of family dynamics, looked at Rauf, and couldn't help but smile himself.

"Your boy is always smiling, always very happy," Turab complimented Rauf while looking into the Mullah's eyes.

"Right, he is always smiling. *He's a true delight.*"

Rauf saw a sudden change in Turab's expression. He was surprised it had taken so long for Turab to realize the contradiction in Aziz's words and bitter, sarcastic tone. What kind of journalist was he? Why the heck did it take him so long to figure things out? Rauf felt infinitely superior to everyone in the room. His father was a blowhard, Turab was an idiot and his mother was, well, *a woman.*

"Are you disagreeing with me? Is my opinion incorrect?" Turab asked after a brief pause.

"What opinion?" Aziz sounded perplexed.

"My opinion about your son Rauf."

"Oh, no Turab. You're right on the money as they say! This boy here, Rauf Aziz, is a real delight to both his parents, but especially to me." Aziz responded carefully, almost chewing each and every word.

"Okay," Turab said. "I am glad you see it too."

"Oh yes," said Aziz "I see *many* things."

"See, there it is. You did it again. Is there a problem between you two?" Turab kept shifting his eyes from Aziz to Rauf and back. Rauf was quietly staring at the floor, there must have been something of interest ingrained in the wood because his eyes were glued and Aziz had a smirk on his face which he was trying to quell, but couldn't. Turab felt uneasy as if there was something going on that he couldn't quite identify. Why was he called? What was the emergency?

"Rauf, you tell me, is there something going on here?" Turab waved his hand in front of Rauf's face. Rauf looked up for a second, shifted his eyes towards Aziz, and then looked at Turab again and quietly shook his head. Turab looked at Aziz, who was staring at Rauf with his slightly bloodshot, angry eyes.

"There, he said no," Aziz jumped in before Turab could say anything else. "You should be satisfied now. Like I already said, there's no problem."

"Okay," Turab raised his hands and let them fall back as a sign of giving up. Before he could say anything else, *Moazzan's* call for the evening prayer resonated throughout the compound. It was *Asar* time. The mosque's public address system was loud and echoing, and despite its volume, it was soothing. They all heard the *Azan* quietly and offered a short prayer after its completion. The *Azan* preceded the actual *Asar* prayer by fifteen minutes, and the necessary body cleansing in the form of *wadhu* or ablution, was compulsory before they could offer the prayer. Mullah Aziz, in his element, motioned in a nonchalant way, for Turab and Rauf to follow while he walked toward the door which opened into the mosque's courtyard.

"Let's pray and then we can come back and have tea and some snacks," Mullah Aziz announced. He wasn't just addressing Turab, his announcement was also meant for Paro, as an order for her to prepare food and stay put in the kitchen. As soon as she heard Aziz utter those words, Rauf saw her leave her eavesdropping post behind the dirty alcove curtain, and march silently into the actual kitchen space.

"Of course, I'll have the tea ready by the time you're back," Paro said from behind the curtain. "Can you bring some *naan* for dinner?"

Mullah Aziz grunted and walked out the door. Rauf couldn't help but laugh to himself, bringing naan from the corner bakery would mean an additional expense which Mullah Aziz would rather not incur, but could not refuse in front of a guest. He detested spending even a penny over and above the monthly allowance that he doled out to Paro to run the kitchen. Inviting guests, who in Mullah Aziz's view tended to eat too much, was an extra burden that could not be accommodated in the meager grocery budget. Rauf could visualize the fight which surely would ensue once Turab left. Play by play. If Aziz didn't comment after their guests' departure, he would find alternate ways to recover his expenses, which in turn would infuriate Paro, which would result in bitter verbal battles on the first day of the subsequent month. Rauf had been witness to these arguments numerous times, and he was certain this time would be no exception to the display of cheapness Mullah Aziz was so comfortable in showing, in fact actually seemed to revel in.

He just shook his head and kept walking towards the main prayer hall of the mosque, not allowing, what he considered, her insolence, to delay his schedule. He could feel Turab's inquisitive stare. They didn't have to walk for long as their apartment was in the far corner of the mosque compound and once in the shelter of the mosque, he dropped the grin.

Mullah Aziz loved living in that particular location. He considered it a blessing to live so close to the mosque, the house of *Allah*. An additional benefit, besides being the only person who had the distinct honor to live in the house of Allah, was that he wasn't required to pay rent or utilities. No one else besides his family lived there, so the distinction was great. As cheap as he was, he loved the status his living quarters bestowed upon him even more.

The way Aziz looked at it, he had devoted his life to impart religious knowledge to the ignorant people of this town— the least they could do was to take care of his worldly needs. In his eyes, this was a winning situation for all involved.

The crowd for *Asar* prayers was smaller than Friday's congregational prayers, that was the norm. There wasn't a sermon, nor was there a loud recitation of the Holy Quran. The entire prayer offering was over in less than ten minutes. The majority of the people who came to pray rushed out again very quickly, but then there were some people who stayed and stopped to pay their respects to Mullah Aziz.

Rauf always found the conduct of these die-hard followers amusing. They would stand in line in a subservient manner, so as not to offend Mullah Aziz, the almighty pious soul, by their ignorant or disobedient ways reserved for the outside of the mosque. Some of them kissed the back of his hand, holding it respectfully while standing on one knee while the other leg stretched backward. Heads would bow, lips would caress the back of his hand, and some of them would actually start shedding tears as a sign of their disdain and regret for their own worldly activities, which were inconsistent with the teachings of this purely spiritual, unworldly man. They felt that they were constructing hell for themselves in this world and hereafter. Their self- recrimination bordered on hate for themselves and the people surrounding them. In their eyes, Mullah Aziz was the Messiah, walking and talking amongst them. He was deserving of the respect befitting only to someone with his singular mind, soul, character, and actions. So they *almost* worshiped him. At least enough people did, which pleased him.

He was acutely aware of his influence on such souls. He would never miss a chance to calm them, give them hope, and share his pearls of wisdom. He welcomed any opportunity to direct them. In return, all he required was unquestioning loyalty and submission which they were willing to offer. To his credit, Mullah Aziz had never yet misused his influence. He never tried to secure favors for himself, or obtain undue advantages beyond what they could manage. He hadn't yet, taken anything that would endanger their already meager manner of living. He made them feel as though they were doing something truly noble by taking care of him.

He was remorseless about this exploitation and felt that what he offered was unique and precious and therefore, invaluable. *He* was, invaluable. In his mind, they, the ignorant souls, should be thankful that they were the chosen ones given the opportunity to be guided by a higher soul. A soul that had the capacity to free them from eternal condemnation, so they thought. Never mind the fact that he was the one who made them think so, as long as they were happy to do what he demanded of them, which was not much. It was fair and just. In fact, he considered his presence among them as a gift to them from God. He was willing to share himself with these people to please God. Everybody was a winner.

So the rituals continued. Today was no exception. Rauf stood at a distance and watched his father perched atop his very high spiritual pedestal. Turab walked with him and even though none of this was new to him, he was clearly in some type of awe. He had been to the mosque before and had seen this performance many times, nevertheless, he remained a bit dazzled. Impressed with Aziz's ability to lead and dominate more than anything else.

They were out of the main prayer hall. In the foyer, there was a newly placed desk attended by a short stocky man, with a very thick mustache. Next to him, stood two girls beside a small table with a pile of neatly arranged flyers. Mullah Aziz tried to walk past them, but, the short man jumped directly in front of him, blocking him, eagerly extending his hand. Turab was a bit taken aback by this impulsivity, but then saw Aziz extend his hand to reach for the man's shoulder, and shove him aside without stopping or slowing down. The man lost his balance and would have fallen to the ground if Turab hadn't been able to grab his arm. The man's little cap fell to the floor. He released his arm from Turab's grip, and quickly picked up the cap, shook the dust from it, put it back on his head, and walked back towards his desk, undiscouraged. It was all so fast, that Turab couldn't say with certainty, that it had actually happened. The girls standing beside the desk stared in shock, one of them started crying out of fear or concern or naivety. Mullah Aziz kept walking, annoyed by the disturbance, but unphased by his actions. Turab took long fast strides to catch up to Aziz and stand in front of him, mimicking the short man's prior move, he spotted Rauf doing the same.

"What was that?"

"What?" Mullah Aziz stopped and asked, puzzled. He had already forgotten the incident.

"You didn't stop to greet that poor man," Turab said, shocked. "In fact, you shoved him away and almost threw him down to the ground."

"Who, who did I shove away?"

"Don't tell me you don't know what you did to that man!" Turab almost shouted.

"That man, you mean Afridi?" Mullah Aziz acknowledged, dismissively.

"So you do know him. Then why didn't you stop to talk to him, at least to shake his hand?"

"Don't worry about him." Mullah Aziz continued to walk. "He is a traitor and an infidel. I don't care for people like him. We're better off without them."

"Why is he a traitor? What's his story? What are you talking about?" Turab became curious and inquisitive. His journalistic instinct kicking in. Mullah Aziz realized that he had made a mistake by commenting in front of him, he would naturally go after this story, and he would want to dig as deep as he possibly could. Mullah Aziz stopped for a moment, looked into Turab's eyes, nodded, and then suddenly turned around.

"You want to know? Then come with me and I'll show you." He started walking back towards Afridi without waiting for a response. Turab followed. Rauf kept watching from a distance, as usual, surveying.

Afridi saw Mullah Aziz marching towards him aggressively. He suddenly looked guarded, raised his hands, and shouted while looking at the girls. "Stay close to each other. Don't get separated."

Mullah Aziz slammed his fist on the table and shoved the flyers off the table to the floor. "Why are you here? Haven't you been told that you are not welcome here?"

"This is the house of Allah." Afridi kept his composure. "Why do I need anybody's permission to come here?"

"If you come to worship Allah, then you don't need anybody's permission. But what you come here to accomplish, well, that is not permissible. Not by me, not by people of this town, and certainly not by Allah. That is precisely why you aren't welcome here. If I see you here again, with whatever you've brought along, I promise I will have you thrown out."

"With all due respect Maulana, how do you know Allah does not permit what I am doing here?"

"It's my job to decide if what you do is permitted by Allah. I have the knowledge and I have the authority."

Afridi couldn't have challenged him more unwisely, and Mullah Aziz didn't take the challenge to his authority lightly. He was very protective of his position.

"I beg to differ, Mullah Aziz." Afridi was not in the least apologetic, he stood his ground. "I am not doing anything against Allah's command. I am just asking people to send their daughters to school, to educate them."

"What school? What are you going to teach at this school?" Mullah Aziz responded indignantly.

"Knowledge, Maulana, I will give them knowledge."

"What kind of knowledge?"

"What do you mean? Knowledge is knowledge. Isn't it?" Afridi held onto his faint smile. Unwavering. As though he was trying to bait the Mullah, trying to get him to react combatively.

"Don't play these games with me," Mullah Aziz was barely able to contain his anger. "I know who you work for. You are an agent with a foreign agenda and your mission here is to brainwash our girls. Your goal is to turn our girls into agents for your foreign masters too and to teach them the way of life of infidels. Am I correct?"

"No, Maulana, that isn't true. Please don't doubt my intentions. I just want the girls to go to school so they can seek knowledge and learn, knowledge doesn't come with an agenda. You should know this." Afridi remained composed.

"I know, that's why I am saying this to your face. Your appearance and your conduct are amicable and yes, sweet–very sweet indeed. But inside, you are poison. Just poison. And your charm won't work on me or anyone who lives around here. Know this. They will always listen to me more than they will ever listen to you."

"That is exactly why I seek your help, Maulana."

"What makes you think that I'm willing to offer you help?"

"It's just my hope. I think you are a reasonable person, I think you are an understanding person, therefore, I think you'll listen to me. It's logic. I'm sure you know that I am not the only one who wants to educate our children, especially young girls. There are towns close to us where schools for girls are being built, other people are doing it too. They can't be all be wrong."

"Why? Why can't they all be wrong? Just because everybody agrees on something does not necessarily make it right. You are such a fool; you truly are a simpleton. You think that just because everybody has bought into the wrong idea makes it right. Do you have any idea how obtuse you sound?"

"Don't people come to the right decision when everybody's opinion is included in the process?" Afridi tried again.

"That is such a false statement. I think I know where this is coming from. You seem to think that people can make wise decisions when they all get to participate? Wrong. Most people are idiots. They need guidance. They need to be taught what is right and what is wrong, what benefits them, and what hurts them. And people need people like me, to tell them what they should, or should not do. If it wasn't for people like me, people like you would never understand Allah's commands. People like you will never understand how to follow Allah's religion. Get that into your head, once you do, you'll have no room for the nonsense in your life. Do you understand?"

Afridi kept shaking his head, sadly. "You're too stubborn to have an intelligent argument with."

"There is no argument. There is no compromise on Allah's words and commands."

"But what you are saying is not Allah's command. That's what I've been trying to tell you." Afridi wouldn't give up hope that Mullah Aziz might come to some sort of agreement.

"Oh, and you think you can tell me what Allah is saying? Now I have to learn Allah's sayings from people like you? You really cannot be that delusional."

Afridi went quiet. The girls standing together by his side stared at him silently, faces tense with apprehension. Turab was slightly alarmed at just how angry Mullah Aziz had become, this was a side to him that he didn't realize existed. His curiosity was peaked, and bystanders began to probe.

"What's going on?" one of them asked.

"I am just trying to ask you, brothers, to send your girls to school. I have opened up a school just for girls and…" Mullah Aziz raised his hand mid-sentence.

"Stop your ridiculous and traitorous speech. I won't allow it. Take your stuff and your girls and get out of here." He kicked the legs of the table, causing it to fall, papers flew off the surface of the table and scattered everywhere. No one but Afridi moved to gather them back up.

"This is not right, Maulana. I have never disrespected you and there's no reason why you should be treating me this way."

"It is not even your place to disrespect me," Mullah Aziz shouted. "And it is also not your place to be respected. Take your stuff and go away. If I see you here again, I will make you regret it. That is a promise. And don't ever bring girls to the mosque. Their place is at home. You shouldn't parade them outside as cheap advertisement and they're old enough to be covered and kept hidden. Go-now!"

Afridi collected his belongings and left with the girls. Aziz's face reddened as he realized that everybody was staring at him. He motioned them to disburse. Turab looked at him with more regard than usual, this time with perhaps a bit of disquietude.

"They really follow you here."

"You have seen this before, haven't you?"

"Yes."

"Then why are you surprised?" Aziz started walking out.

"Your hold on them is seemingly more firm now than ever."

"You're right, I rarely get challenged now. I am very good at what I do, it's a fact."

"Huh."

"Don't worry about it," Mullah Aziz increased his pace. Turab was having a hard time keeping up with him. "Let's go back home. You should try the tea and samosa."

"Can I have some too?" Rauf asked with a broad smile. Mullah Aziz looked at him pensively and in a dry tone, he replied, "Sure. You can have as many of them as you like."

"Great." The walk to the apartment was short. The air inside was filled with the aroma of freshly fried samosas.

Rauf was all smiles.

NINE

THE CROWD GREW tirelessly, and so did Farah's dread and Sardar Timur's rage and thirst for revenge. More so to avenge his honor rather than any wrongdoing on his daughter's behalf. He paced back and forth and with each round, using the spiked leash, pulled Gul closer, until he was within a few short steps. He suddenly realized the unwelcome proximity and hit him in the stomach. Just because he could, just because he wanted to. Gul collapsed.

His parents stood hands clenched, in a sort of paralysis as a result of the abuse being endured by their only son. The humiliation he felt, they too felt. The physical pain he sustained, also left scars invisible to eyes on their fragile bodies. The fear, there were no words capable of defining it. Seeing their son, their boy, in such a battered state and on a leash, was so outlandish that it was hard to accept. Zara Bibi's cheeks were wet with tears, which didn't even near the sadness which consumed her. She didn't bother wiping them, she could barely feel them.

"What happened Sardar Timur, why is my son on a leash?" Shams was not privy to the recent happenings, he had not yet been informed, therefore, seeing his only son in such condition magnified the trauma. He had been taken off the fields where he worked, by two of Sardar Timur's men, and dragged for half a mile to the Haveli. His screams and pleadings went unanswered.

"Stand up, swine." Sardar Timur grabbed Shams by the throat and forced his face towards Gul. "Are you his father?"

"Yes, yes I am. He is my son Gul. Why is he on a leash?"

"You'll find out soon enough." Sardar Timur hit him on the head with the back of his hand. "Go stand with your wife and daughter."

Shams looked around. He saw Zara Bibi and Badri Jamala standing in a corner, apart from the crowd, both trembling. He looked at his son and ran towards him, but was pushed back by a guard, which such force, that he stumbled to the ground. He picked himself up quickly and ran towards his wife and daughter.

"Zara, what's going on here?" Shams grabbed his wife's shoulder.

"He brought shame on this house. He's brought shame on Sardar Timur."

"And why is she here?" Shams pointed towards Badri. Her face was swollen and bruised, she stood slumped over.

"I don't know. Sardar's men dragged her from home. I don't know why they brought her here. I'm afraid to ask." Zara Bibi could hardly complete her sentence without shivering.

"I won't let anything happen to you, I promise." Zara Bibi hugged Badri tight and whispered in her ears. Badri flinched at the contact, it was too late, and while she did not push her mother away, neither did she lean in to accept the embrace.

She pulled herself out of her mother's arms, looked in her eyes, and whispered back, "I know you will try to protect me, but I'm ready to do anything to save my brother."

Sardar Timur approached them and stood near Badri. His face was void of any expression.

"Is this your daughter?" Shams could hardly nod.

"Yes, Sardar Timur, she is our daughter," Zara Bibi spoke.

"So you have a girl and a boy? You don't have others?"

"No, Sardar. Allah blessed us with two only." This time Shams was able to speak.

"How old is she?"

"Twenty-one, Sardar," Shams responded, looking at Zara, who was trying to hide Badri behind her.

"Hey, *chokri*, stop hiding in your mother's arms. Come here." Badri crept out from behind Zara, looked at Sardar Timur for a brief moment before lowering her eyes, and slowly started moving towards him. Her mother tried to stop her.

"Sardar Timur, she had nothing to do with anything. Please spare her." Zara Bibi knelt at his feet and pleaded. She tried to kiss his boots but he forced his foot from her grasp and shoved her away. She fell, Badri rushed toward her and was about to help her to her feet, when she felt a tight grip around her arm, the guard grabbed her and pulled her away from her mother. Badri's other hand extended to reach once again, for her mother's hand their fingers touching briefly before she felt herself being torn away.

"How do you know that she had nothing to do with anything?" Sardar Timur shouted back.

"She wasn't even here when it all happened. She was at home. Never left home after she came back from school yesterday."

"Let's hear from her," Sardar Timur hissed back and looked at Badri. Sardar Timur looked at Badri, then raised his hand, signaling for quiet. Everyone in the crowd went silent.

"Where were you this afternoon?" he asked harshly.

"Home," Badri replied, barely audible.

"And yesterday you went to school? What school?"

"The girl's school, near the main market." She wasn't sure why Sardar Timur was so surprised. Didn't he know about it?

"How long have you been going there?"

"One year."

"Basheer," Sardar Timur looked over at one of his men. "How come I didn't know about the school?"

"I think she's spinning tales Sardar," Basheer answered. "I don't know of any girls' school near the main market. She's making all of this up."

"Is this true?" Sardar Timur turned to Badri. "Are you lying?"

"No," Badri surprised herself by summoning the courage to contradict him. "I am not lying. I do not lie. I never lie."

"Okay." Sardar Timur pacing slowly around her, still holding the leash which had Gul attached to it.

"And you have been attending this school for one year?" Badri nodded, for the moment distracted from her family drama to a larger concern, she realized she had made a mistake by letting this secret out, now the school and all girls going to the school were in harm's way.

"Who is running the school?"

"I don't know."

"Really? You've been going to the school for a year and you don't know who is running it or teaching there?"

Badri was now too terrified to respond. She couldn't speak, only watch, as he marched closer toward her raising his hand in the menacing way to which she was now accustomed.

"You're lying! I can see it on your face! Come clean. Tell me the truth otherwise you will regret it, and your family will regret it too. Tell me who is running the school!"

"I don't know his full name but we all call him Sir Afridi."

"Did you hear that?" Sardar Timur turned towards his men. "You need to find this man, Afridi. Get him here, in front of me. Do you understand?" He turned back and focused his attention back on Badri.

"What do they teach you there, at the school?"

"Everything that is taught in the boy's school."

"Oh, I see, so he wants to make girls like boys. Do you think you are like boys, equal to men?"

Badri remained quiet. She was positive that he would not like the answer.

"Didn't you hear the question?" His voice almost quivered with anger.

"I did."

"Then give me an answer."

"I don't know if I am equal to a man. But I know what Allah and our religion say. We are all equal. That is in the Quran and also in the books of hadith." Badri was surprised at her own answer, she was surprised by her courage. For a moment, she was not the fearful little creature, second to her brother, a fearful little creature, beaten and bruised. She spoke with deep-rooted conviction.

"Your fearlessness is not acceptable... there should not, and will be no schools in my town, where they teach girls how to be disrespectful to adults, to our culture and to our way of life," Sardar Timur's anger at this new insubordination made his words even more clipped than before.

"You are right, Sardar. These schools are trouble." Basheer found it convenient to agree with the man holding the gun and the leash.

"Yet you closed your eyes and let a girl's school open and run for a year without mentioning it."

"I am sorry, Sardar Timur. I'll take care of this problem. This will not happen again."

"Listen, everyone," Sardar Timur took three steps up on a short flight of stairs leading to a platform by the wall, Gul dragging along next to him. "Whoever is sending his daughter to this school should know that he is inviting trouble. If you want to live in peace, if you love the traditions of our ancestors and if you want to be spared my wrath, you should stop sending your daughter to the school of this Afridi, or others like him. I will not tolerate anyone impacting our collective life, our social norms, and the ways of our ancestors. We have inherited our way of life from our elders, and we are custodians of such traditions. We must practice it the way our elders did, and then pass it on to our future generations. I am your Sardar. It is my duty to keep our traditions alive and to preserve our ways of life. If anyone has a problem with it or wants to change how we live, I want to hear from that person now. Otherwise, stop conspiring. Once more, last chance! Is there anyone here who wants to come forward?"

He surveyed the crowd. Here they were - his subjects, his servants—the same thing, really. Some he paid to work, others he merely owned. Every now and then someone felt the need to challenge his absolute authority. Sardar knew how to deal with them, just as he had seen his elders deal with such rebels.

Their world was made up of masters and servants. This was the world he inherited and the one he intended to leave for his children. No change. No "modernization." The master should order and the servants must obey. It was that simple. Any other way was guaranteed to upset the order and sure to bring chaos. Sardar Timur considered it his divine duty to avoid such chaos at all costs, and such costs were paid by the subjects, not the masters. Any challenge to his authority, to his grip of power, was unpardonable.

He knew it was important to make examples. It kept people in check, the idea was to discourage useless and harmful thinking and to always make it clear that he was in charge at all times. He had made examples in the past and it was time to do it again. He was determined to maintain his control over their bodies, their souls, and their minds.

That was the only way to keep his subjects truly subservient to him and his family.

"Shams," Sardar shouted. "How dare you send your daughter to a school without asking me?"

"I didn't know that she has been going to school. I swear. I don't concern myself with her doings, she's only a girl." Shams told the truth. He was gone every day from early morning until late at night and had no idea what his wife or children did during that time. He frankly wasn't interested in what his children did, they were strangers that shared the same house on occasion. His son, he took an interest in, but the girl, she was somewhat insignificant.

"You did not know where your girl was going?" Sardar Timur sounded surprised and sarcastic at the same time.

"I swear I'm telling you the truth. I didn't know. I swear on the grave of my dead mother, I didn't know." Shams was now on Sardar Timur's feet, shedding tears, begging for mercy.

"What kind of father are you? Your girl stepped outside of your home without your permission. She has been going to school for a year and who knows what else she has been doing. Why is she not married?" He scanned his audience. "Do you see?! This is exactly what I'm talking about! This is what happens when you let the girls slip out of your control. They get ideas in their heads and then who knows what's next?! Shame on you! You shouldn't show your face around here anymore." Sardar Timur rambled on, then bent down, picked up some dirt from the ground, and threw it on Sham's head and face. The dirt mixed with his tears, his face a mask of dry mud.

"Stop crying like a woman." Sardar Timur slapped him. "You are a man. Act like one! Do you even remember how to act like one?"

"You," Sardar Timur now turned to Zara Bibi. "Did you know that your girl was going to school?"

"Yes, I knew Sardar Timur. I knew."

"Did you ever tell Sarah Khanum?"

"I made a mistake. Please forgive me." Zara Bibi was barely audible.

"What did you say?" Sardar Timur shouted. "I couldn't hear you. Show some respect and say that again and speak up."

"I made a mistake. Please forgive me."

"Looks like everyone in your family is making mistakes." Sardar Timur had worked himself into a fury. "And this has been going on for a long time. You clearly had no intention of letting me know about all of your activities. If your son hadn't shown his true colors this would have kept going on. I cannot consider your conduct a mistake, no, you were not mistaken. You did all this on purpose, repeatedly. You wanted to keep me in the dark and you've been hiding things from me. I cannot let you keep insulting me like this. You have insulted me enough and now it's time for you to pay. All of you will pay a very heavy price."

"Have mercy on us Sardar Timur. We have been faithful and devoted workers for so many years."

"And I have paid you all these years. In return, all I asked for was honesty. You defrauded me and I don't tolerate fraud. It's stealing. I'll make an example out of you. A horrific example. Do you understand?"

"We understand Sardar Timur, we understand." Zara Bibi's voice was barely audible; she was fear-stricken. "That is why I'm begging you for mercy. I know that my children aren't bad, I know they have pure souls, I know that they didn't realize what they were doing was wrong if, in fact, they were even doing all this. They are young, young people are always unsure about how to act and how to behave and often make mistakes, but this is how they learn!"

"And who is responsible for their ignorance? You are the mother. Why didn't you teach them what Allah wants them to be? He sent them to your home, not mine. If they were in my home, they would be the masters, but they were sent to your home, so they are servants. It's that simple. And it is your responsibility to teach them, to make them understand their place around here. Make them accept that as Allah's will and Allah's command."

"They don't listen Sardar Timur, they don't listen," Shams intervened.

"You know why?" Sardar Timur shouted back. "Because they get ideas in their heads when they go to these schools. They read books and they forget who they are. That's why they need to stay away from schools, otherwise, they will never listen to you, to me, or anybody. They will do just as they please and that I cannot and will not tolerate. That is why I'm going to punish you and your faithless children. I'll make an example out of all of you."

"You can punish us all you want, Sardar Timur," Zara Bibi begged. "But please spare our children."

"I can do whatever I please. Do you think I'm an unjust man, that I should punish you instead of your children for their sins? Don't worry yourself too much–I'll punish you for what you did wrong. But your children are the real culprits here. I cannot punish you if I spare them. That is not justice."

"We will pay for their sins," Shams spoke out with trembling hands raised and clenched together, seeking forgiveness.

"You don't have the right to decide who forgives them. I have that authority. They have insulted me and they have disobeyed me. You either helped them or turned a blind eye."

"We'll leave this town, Sardar, we will leave this place. Please let us go, if you do, you will never have to see us again."

"Hmm…" Sardar Timur thought for a moment, looked at them carefully, and then turned to Basheer.

"What do you think, Basheer?"

Basheer looked around. The crowd was dead silent. "How do we know that they won't cause trouble in other places?"

"Yes. How do we know that?"

"I assure you, Sardar Timur. If you let us go, we will always pray for you and we will always praise you for your kindness. We will never say a word against you."

"There is no guarantee," Basheer said, clearly dubious. "How do we know that he will keep his word, or that he is even able to keep his word?"

"Yes, I agree," Sardar Timur said. "There is no guarantee that you will do what you just said. Your word is meaningless. You didn't know what your children were doing."

Shams had no answer. He just stood there shaking his head, tears flowing into his beard.

Basheer continued to maximize on his new voice. "If you let him go, Sardar Timur, that will not deter anyone from the same actions or worse. You'll be considered weak."

"Shams, you have to understand," Sardar Timur spoke with a false softness. "I am not a cruel person. I believe in justice. But I also believe in preserving what has been passed on to me by my ancestors. Do you understand what I am saying?"

Shams had no answer. He looked at Zara Bibi and then back at Sardar Timur's face. He in fact did not understand.

"I want justice." Sardar Timur said, after a brief pause. "I am going to let your son speak, but, I will also hear from others who know firsthand what happened. I will not hurt you more than your son has hurt me, or my family. But I cannot just let you and your family move away, or move on without being held accountable for what your son did to me, to my family, and to this whole town. Honor must be restored and the only way to do that is to make sure that justice is served."

"We would never hurt you or your family. How could we? We have always served you, we would never intentionally harm you. We are your faithful servants." Zara Bibi could not stay quiet.

"Whether you meant it or not makes no difference. I'll hear from others who saw what happened, and then I'll decide. Everybody will witness all of this and they will be able to see that you will not be treated unfairly." He was determined to get his way but at the same time, he wanted to appear fair. He didn't want to appear vindictive.

"Gul, do you have anything to say before I let others speak?" Sardar Timur shook the leash. Gul stayed quiet. He was still in shock and unable to form words.

"If you have nothing to say, then, I will hear from all of these people here. Justice will be served one way or another." Sardar Timur was loud, clear, and determined. He was surveying the crowd looking for someone, anyone. His eyes stopped at a familiar face.

"You!" He pointed. "You were there. Gul attacked you, did he not?" Addressing Chaman whose usual grin was replaced by a serious look the moment his eyes met Sardar Timur's.

"Yes sir! He was like an animal, like a filthy vicious dog,"

"Did there seem to be any reason why he attacked you?"

"Because I told his mother to stop bothering me and control her son, this boy Gul. She accused me of stealing from the kitchen which I have never done. Your kitchen is always open for us, you are so generous and there's no reason to steal! Why would I steal from you? I never have and I never will. I told her so, but she refused to listen. She kept nagging me and she dragged me back to the kitchen and to the pantry, and when she opened the door, we saw Gul attacking your daughter. He assaulted her. He was molesting her. It was the most horrible, most shocking scene I have ever witnessed! I don't want to go into details, Sardar Timur, but Gul was all over her, smothering her with his body. She was pushing him away but he just would not stop." Chaman paused for effect.

"I am glad that it was his mother who opened the door because now she cannot deny that her son was caught doing the most horrific thing a servant can do. I don't want to see anything like that happen to anybody, ever again. Even after witnessing all this, his mother continued to nag me. So I got angry, I just lost my mind a little, but I still did not disrespect her. All I said to her was that she needs to control her boy before she accuses others of misdeeds. That's all I said Sardar Timur." He paused again feigning distress.

"And then all of a sudden this wild animal, this shameless, thankless creature, was all over me. He hit me hard. He hit me bad. And his mother, she just stood there letting her son punch me, kick me, and attack me. The whole family is vicious, they are savages. They don't deserve your generosity and kindness, Sardar Timur. I forgive him for what he did to me. But, to attack your daughter? To dishonor her? To dishonor you and your family? I can't imagine a decent person doing anything like that to anybody, let alone his master. I know I certainly would never, ever, do such a thing." Chaman paused one last time to catch his breath after his world-class performance.

Basheer was finding it difficult to control his smile. This fat bastard, this overly perky eunuch was obviously letting his internal venom overcome him and using this as an opportunity to let himself be heard. While his story and its rendition were compelling, it sounded suspiciously biased. He was not an objective narrator nor was he an objective witness. Basheer shifted his eyes from Chaman, surveyed the crowd, and finally looked at Sardar Timur. Their eyes met for a brief moment. Sardar Timur raised his eyebrows and signaled him with his index finger.

"Spare us your commentary, Chaman." Basheer understood his master's wish and made sure to keep things moving along. "Just tell us what actually happened."

"That's what I am telling Sardar Timur," Chaman retorted. "Each and every word is true and correct, I swear."

"We understand that," Basheer spoke with a firm tone and dry voice. "You are adding your comments to the facts, do not give us your opinion. Tell us facts only. Do you understand?"

"I don't understand." Chaman was puzzled. "I am telling the truth. Would you not call it a fact?"

"We understand that you are giving facts, but they are mixed up with your feelings and opinions." Basheer was irritated. This little bastard was either thick-headed or really wicked and playing dumb. Either way, he had to be dealt with sternly. "If you saw him molesting her, just tell us that. Don't tell us how you feel, or whether you would do something like that."

"Yes, I would never do anything like that…I am…" Chaman was about to ramble on again when he saw Basheer raising a long wooden stick in his right hand. He went quiet.

"Get this in your head, you moron," Basheer was now furious. "You are to tell us only what you actually saw! Don't tell us how that makes you feel. Describe what you saw. Only that. Do you understand? If not, I will try another method to make you understand." Chaman went quiet for a long moment. He held his gaze with Basheer for a while then blinked and shifted his eyes towards Sardar Timur.

"Okay. I understand."

"Good. Remember, we've cut you once. Don't think that we will not cut you again, you don't have much left but we can always find something to use our knives on. Understand?"

There was a round of loud laughter that reverberated in the entire area for a very brief moment then suddenly died when the men looked at Sardar Timur. He was not amused at all. An intense expression of resentment flashed on Chaman's face for a moment, quickly replaced by a forced smile and a nod of the head.

"Now, go on," Basheer continued. "Tell us what you saw and only what you saw."

"I was in the pantry looking for something. I forgot to turn the lights on before closing the door, and I fell on the floor. I may have stepped onto something; I don't remember that properly. I think Zara Bibi was in the kitchen at that time and I think she heard me fall and came to help. She noticed that I was trying to hide something from her, which I was. Something personal. She kept insisting that I show her and I told her that it was none of her business and I walked away. She started following me. So I ran and then she started running after me. I tried to warn her that I would get physical with her but she just kept coming at me. I don't know why, but we ended up back at the pantry. When we got to the pantry door, she pushed it open, and then I saw, in fact, we all saw, that Gul was molesting Farah. She was trying to push Gul away but this rabid animal would not let go. He was half-naked and he had torn her clothes, but thank Allah, she was still decent."

"Every word you said is true, right?"

"Yes Sardar Timur, each and every word is true," Chaman replied.

Sardar Timur and Chaman's eyes locked in a gaze for a brief moment. Sardar Timur then looked around, paused briefly at Zara Bibi's face, and then shifted his direction towards Farah.

"What do you have to say?" he asked her without mentioning her name. Sarah Khanum looked at Farah's face and then replied. "I'll tell her side of the story. She is too afraid and traumatized to think or speak straight."

"Ask the people, if they are okay with that," Sardar Timur responded. Sarah Khanum looked around with questioning eyes. Nobody objected or even spoke a word.

"They are fine with it," Basheer interjected.

Sardar Timur motioned for her to speak. She cleared her throat softly and started speaking. She laid the blame squarely on Gul's shoulders. How Farah went into the kitchen and was looking for something in the pantry which is why she was there in the first place, then she saw Chaman and Zara Bibi come in the pantry while arguing over something but she never understood what. She saw Chaman fall down and heard Zara Bibi insisting on being allowed to see what Chaman was hiding. Farah, being young and confused, instead of intervening decided to watch them without revealing her presence. Therefore, she decided to hide behind the cupboard in the pantry, which is when the abuse and molestation began. Gul was already there and found an opportunity to grope her. She resisted but had to do it quietly to keep her presence secret from Chaman and Zara Bibi. She ended up paying a heavy price for her silence. Gul took the opportunity to molest her further. She pleaded and begged for him to stop but he would not listen.

Then suddenly the door was opened with a bang. Gul saw his mother standing in front of the door, and the wild animal in him disappeared slightly. He, however, remained seemingly imperious, not at all ashamed. Instead, he found Chaman to be an easy target and began to attack him. Chaman simply defended himself and Sarah Khanum passed by and intervened. Only then did Gul stop hitting Chaman. Even after that, he was still not remorseful, he still refused to apologize. His mother was also insistent that he was innocent. Worse, she has been pleading for mercy, but not forgiveness."

Sarah Khanum went quiet. Farah's face was a study of incredulity. She tried to open her mouth but Sarah Khanum's stare was enough to break her will. She glanced at Gul for a brief moment and then closed her eyes.

Chaman spoke again. "Sardar Timur, you are the pride of this town. You are the most respectable person, and you have earned this respect. Your family has earned this respect. This little rat has no shame and no remorse and his family is the same. None of them are sorry for what happened. My wish is to see your honor restored, no matter what the cost." Basheer looked at the faces of his fellow guards, all trying hard to contain their amusement at this blatant display of flattery. Chaman's naked expression of vindictiveness towards Gul was too obvious to miss, as was his attempt to curry favor with Timur.

Sardar Timur folded the leash in his hand to pull Gul within a foot of where he stood. He had his head bowed down. The giant man grabbed his hair and pulled his head up.

"This, right now, is the time for you to say whatever it is that you want to say, it's doubtful that you will get another opportunity."

Gul still stayed quiet.

"This is all a lie Sardar Timur!" Zara Bibi could not contain herself.

"You will not talk."

"But you let Farah's mother talk for her. He's my son, it is only fair that I speak for him if he can't. It's also fair that I get the same chance."

"I'm going to call the Panchayat and then you can say what you want in front of them."

"Why the Panchayat Sardar Timur?" Basheer sought clarification, not so much for himself but so that others could hear what he would say next. "You are the Sardar. Gul is a *kammi kameen*, less than dirt, he's a nobody! Your decision should be enough."

Sardar Timur nodded thoughtfully. "So, you think that I shouldn't trust the Panchayat? Or that this matter isn't right for their consideration?"

"I see no reason to take this to them."

"Ask these people. How do they feel about it?"

Basheer turned to the crowd and announced Sardar Timur's wish to refer to this matter to the Panchayat. He also used this opportunity to remind all of his power and authority.

They seemed to be confused and undecided, a bit unsure. Basheer waited for the voices to die down, then turned, appeared pensive, and then took it upon himself to announce the verdict. There was no room for error.

"We all have full faith in your judgment and decision, Sardar."

"Then my decision is to call the Panchayat, I need you to gather them instantly and let them decide this little bastard's fate, not me."

"As you wish, Sardar. I'll do as you command."

He smiled. This approach would make him appear just and fair, it was the diplomatic response. He was mindful of the changing political climate–the Governor and Chief Minister of the province were paying special attention to the dissemination of justice at all levels, especially at the grass-root level. Referring the matter to Panchayat was the safe way to go, in case a cover was needed in the future for the punishment meted out to this family. In his mind, the verdict and punishment were very clear.

He handed the leash to Basheer and disappeared inside the sprawling Haveli, the grand compound was an imposing sign of power and influence that his family had enjoyed for many generations. Sarah Khanum and Farah followed him quietly. Farah, now bruised and deprived of food, glanced at her mother, she was anxious and laden with guilt because of what she had allowed to transpire, but too fearful to do otherwise. Sarah Khanum saw the look and pushed her back into her room, locking the door.

TEN

PARO WAS INDEED a skilled cook. Turab had heard his friend say so before, and today's tea and samosa feast confirmed it. Each bite of the samosa and each sip of tea was pure delight. Rauf couldn't pop them in his mouth quickly enough, while at the same time trying to guard the heavenly hot and crisp snacks sitting on his plate. Turab observed Mullah Aziz's face and demeanor carefully, he didn't seem to appreciate the taste of the food his wife had so dutifully prepared for him, just grimacing and stuffing it in his mouth, gorging himself.

"Your wife is a wonderful cook, isn't she?" Turab couldn't hold back. He had to share his appreciation for the mouthwatering snacks. If he had been permitted to talk to Paro, he would have conveyed his gratitude directly, but she observed strict *purdah*. As the wife of an Imam it was unthinkable for her to interact with another man who was not a *Mehram*, the only males she could interact with were those she could not marry, so her universe of male interaction was limited. Turab did not belong to that culture, that frame of mind which was so small, so narrow. It was an antiquated custom, but here, in this region, it was far from outdated. It was historic, current, and forthcoming. Her interaction with him was out of the question unless it was a life and death situation. Today and here, there was no such emergency so complimenting by way of Aziz and Rauf would have to suffice. Surprise dawned on Aziz's face when he heard the compliment.

"Why shouldn't she be?" he said after a few moments. "She's been cooking all her life."

"Yes, but still, some women aren't "chefs" even if they have been doing it for eternity." Turab wasn't willing to let her skills be dismissed or diminished just because of a timeframe. Was an artist any less skilled if had been practicing his craft for decades?

"Those are the women who don't put their heart into what they do," Aziz countered. "Those are the women who don't take their job seriously."

"Their job?"

"Yes," Aziz responded with a hint of surprise in his voice. "To cook for her man and her family is a woman's job."

"Really?" Turab responded with surprise at this blunt declaration of a woman's duty towards her family. "It's her job? I didn't know that." He was sure that Aziz would not recognize the sarcasm behind his words.

"What?" Aziz sounded shocked at Turab's apparent ignorance. Shocked and chagrined. Tiny pieces of samosa meat flew out of his mouth. "How could you not know this? Didn't you see your mother cook for you and your family?"

"Yes, she did it every day. But I never thought it was her job." Turab forced himself to contain the smile caused by seeing food particles fly out of Aziz's mouth and the absurdity of the situation.

"If she didn't consider it her job then why would she do it every day, at least three times a day?"

"I always thought it was just a tradition or just something she chose to do," Turab responded.

"Well, traditions are based on something. They don't just appear out of thin air. Right?" Mullah Aziz put his empty plate on the wobbly table and wiped his mouth with the back of his hand. He reached for

131

the glass of water and quickly emptied it in his mouth. Turab could see his faintly visible Adam's apple moving up and down with each gulp.

"Okay. So what is this tradition based on?"

"It is based on religion. What else?"

"Is it really a religious duty for a woman to cook for her husband and her family? What religious book says that?" Turab put his empty plate on top of Mullah Aziz's empty plate sitting on the tabletop, hoping to make less work for Paro.

"Well, it can be inferred," Aziz replied after a brief moment of silence. He couldn't come up with a specific religious authority citation, or Turab knew he would be reciting it.

"How?"

"Well, the Quran says men are to provide for their families. It says that the man of the house, must go out, earn and return with sustenance. So it makes perfect sense that the woman has to use whatever the man brings to the house. The actual cooking is the only way to use food."

"And what happens if the woman refuses to cook?" Turab asked.

"Why would she?" Mullah Aziz sounded even more surprised. "Does she not eat? Is she going to let the food supplies rot? Is she not going to feed the children?"

"I am sure she will." Turab struggled to counter the logic behind Aziz's questions. "But my question is, why is it her duty to cook the food, why can't the man do it?"

"Well, the man can do it. I am not saying he cannot. But my question to you is why shouldn't she cook?" Mullah Aziz turned the argument upside down. "If the man is busy outside the house, why would the woman not stay busy inside the house? Does it make sense that the woman just stays home, without any concerns, and still doesn't contribute by doing what she is most fit to do, and, has all the time in the world to do it?"

"My point is, it should be voluntary and not forced. It shouldn't be a requirement. It should be her wish. If she does not wish to cook, she should not be forced to cook. I have a problem with all of this, specifically with the expectation that she has to work as a servant in her own house to please her man and serve her children."

"Okay," Mullah Aziz responded softly after a pause. "So you're saying that the man of the house and children should not expect to have meals on a consistent basis. If the woman of the house feels like cooking one day, they will eat. If she doesn't feel like cooking the next day, they should just stay hungry."

"They can always eat leftovers," Turab said, with less excitement than he had started. He sensed that the argument had gotten away from him.

"What happens if there are no leftovers? Or they run out of leftovers and the woman of the house still does not feel like cooking. What happens then?"

"Well, then, the man can cook."

"So you are suggesting that he should cook before he leaves his house in the morning for work, and then come back home in the middle of the day to cook lunch, and then, go to work again. Then, when he comes back in the evening, no matter how late, he should cook another meal so that the family can have dinner."

"Hmm." Now Turab was really at a loss of words. "Well, maybe the children should cook if they are old enough."

"Very well let's look at that scenario. So the children shouldn't study, instead, they should stay in the kitchen all day. Besides, what happens if all the children in the house are females? Should they still cook or no? Or should it be just boys who should be asked to cook?"

"Children should learn to cook, regardless of their gender. It's a useful skill," Turab said in a weak voice. He knew he was losing the argument, and Aziz would argue far into the night if only to prove his point. There could be a kitchen fire and he would still sit there and tell Turab why he was wrong, as the apartment burned to the ground, while he was still pleading his case.

"Why should the female children cook? Aren't they women? Younger than their mothers correct? But, they are still women. So why is it okay to expect the female child to cook but not the female adult of the house? If your argument is in favor of women, then why should the age matter unless, of course, there is some kind of physical handicap because of it."

Turab went quiet. He had expected Mullah Aziz to burst into a fit of anger and a religious argument. He wasn't expecting such logical answers or more accurately, logical questions on this subject. Apparently, he had given it a lot of thought and was ready to back up his position. He could feel the heat of Aziz's intense gaze.

"Let's extend this argument." Aziz sensed that Turab was out of ideas, and it might be time to go in for the kill. "What about other household chores? Should the woman of the house not clean, not do the laundry, not keep the house in order—should the man be required to do all that as well? Why stop at making him handle just the kitchen, why not all the household duties? Why shouldn't he do it all?"

"He should hire help. A maid perhaps?"

"What if he cannot afford one?"

"That's a valid excuse." Turab conceded.

"So in your opinion, if he can afford a maid, he should hire one for his household, while his perfectly healthy wife should not be expected to do anything, all day, every day?"

"Well, one's wife does other things too. It's not like she has nothing else to do. She has many responsibilities." Turab decided to continue this argument, just to dig more in Aziz's mind.

"Before I talk about that, let me ask you this. The help you think a husband should hire for his wife, should that be a male or a female? You know, for household work."

"Probably female."

"Why? I thought you wanted to let a female be free from the duties and obligations of household work. Hiring another female to do just that would make no sense if one was to follow your logic." Aziz declared in an excited, high pitched voice. Turab stayed quiet. He felt cornered. He looked at Rauf who was done with his samosa and tea and was listening to the conversation with great interest.

"But the maid will earn money by working. Right?" Rauf decided to participate in the conversation.

"Right. The maid would receive pay." Turab found Rauf's argument persuasive and decided to agree with him.

"Ah-ha!" Mullah Aziz hit the tabletop with the tip of his index finger. "So it comes down to money. Paid labor. As long as one is getting paid, one should be ready to do whatever they can."

"Yes. It's all about dignity. If the maid is making money by working, then it makes sense. She chooses to do it. A wife on the other hand is not getting paid for household work, but the man, her husband, expects her to do all the chores."

"That isn't a true statement and actually it's a stupid thing to say. Obviously, you aren't married! The wife is getting paid–maybe not in cash, but if the husband's providing the house, the food, and paying the bills, then the wife is getting paid in kind. Do you think all these things are free? Besides, if the woman earned money, what would she do with that money anyway? Probably pay the bills. The end result is the same. Her money will be used to provide for the services she is getting from her husband for free, isn't she? So the wife is getting paid, just not with actual cash. Like I already said."

Turab looked at Rauf, hoping he would come up with another argument to yet again, counter his father, but he just shrugged and looked away. Turab shifted his eyes towards Mullah Aziz. The smirk on his friend's face had begun to really incense him, his arrogance and smugness were becoming intolerable.

"Oh, and one more thing," Mullah Aziz continued, feeling empowered. "What about the maid working in her own house, should she hire a maid for herself?"

Turab chuckled sheepishly.

"What? You give up?" Mullah Aziz was now ready to declare victory and rub it in his face. "See, people like you have a problem: you don't think properly. You seem to go with the slogans. Liberate woman, allow her to be seen in public by other men, make her happy by paying her some money. Men like you don't understand that a woman is happier and respected if she is protected from other men's prying eyes. Men who will use her for their entertainment, make her think that she is worth something by paying her whatever little they wish. You make the relationship with a woman purely transactional: she gets paid for what she does. When she is unable to fulfill your needs or desires, you'll find another woman. After all, there are so many women who are liberated by the efforts of men like you, isn't it?"

"What you don't understand is that the man who married her doesn't want a transactional type of relationship. He'll be there for her for a very long time, for good times and bad times. If he provides for her and pays all the bills, she should have no problem taking care of the home. That is the division of labor. You are college-educated, you should understand that concept. People should stick to what they do best, for example, Turab, if the man is a good earner he should be allowed to concentrate on that, if a woman is good at household work, she in turn should concentrate on that! And by the way, household work is not trivial, unimportant, or undignified. It is essential. So women and their liberators like you should not consider the housekeeper someone who has been relegated to stay inferior forever. That is a folly and a mark of stupidity."

Turab knew he should say something in response to that truly one-sided speech but he really did not want to say just anything, unless it was something really effective. Luckily, he was spared the exercise and agony. Before he could utter a word, there was a very loud knock on the door.

Mullah Aziz shifted his gaze from Turab to Rauf.

"Get up, you ass. Go see who's knocking on the door. Perhaps another idiot like you is on the other side of the door. Maybe he's here to see you!" Rauf got up lazily and walked toward the door as though he was trudging through a pool of molasses, making it a point to not jump at his father's command. Turab just shrugged, appearing indifferent, and started looking towards the door with expectant eyes.

"I've told these idiots not to bother me between *Asar* and *Maghreb* prayers. But they never listen, ever." Rauf was arguing with someone at the door, and then it swung open. The person on the other side was Afridi.

"You! Why are you here? What do you want?"

"Please give me a few minutes to explain. I'm not here for myself or the girl's school. I am here for Badri and her brother Gul."

"Who?" Mullah Aziz demanded. "I don't know these people. Who are they?"

"Her father works for Sardar Timur, her mother works in the Haveli as a maid and she attends classes at our school."

"So it is about the school after all!"

"Actually no, it isn't." Afridi was trying to catch his breath but was finding it difficult, his forehead was covered with tiny beads of sweat.

"Okay, so what do you need from me?"

"You're the Imam of the mosque and I'm sure that Sardar Timur will listen to you. Please ask him to spare Badri and her brother."

"I know of Sardar Timur; I do not know him personally. What have they done to him, these people you talked about? Who are they, again?'

"Shams works on Sardar Timur's land, and his wife is a maid in the Haveli. Gul and Badri are their children, and Badri is a student at our school, and that is why I am involved!"

"Why is Sardar Timur after them?" Mullah Aziz's interest had piqued at the mention of Sardar Timur's name. After all, he was the local titan. A goliath.

"What I heard from one of Shams' friends who also works in the Haveli is that Gul, Sham's son, was toying around with Sardar Timur's daughter Farah. Sardar Timur wants to punish Shams and his entire family, especially, but very strangely, their daughter Badri who has nothing to do with any of this." Afridi was talking too fast, and it was difficult to understand what he was so desperately trying to convey. "I want you to talk to Sardar Timur to spare Badri. She hasn't done anything wrong, she's an innocent girl and he has unjustly targeted her. If her brother misbehaved with Farah, and I say *if*, then why should Badri pay the price for her brother's alleged misdeeds?"

"You don't seem to know much about what happened. I absolutely cannot just talk to Sardar Timur based on the incomplete information you have. Besides, I don't like you. Why should I entertain your request?"

"I am not asking for this favor for myself. You are the Imam of the mosque here and Shams lives in this town, he probably prays behind you and he's a gentle, kind, loyal man and I thought that you would want to be of help."

"I don't know him but maybe I'll recognize him if I see him. Here's the problem Afridi, if his son has disrespected Sardar Timur's daughter then he should be punished, don't you think?"

"If you talk to Sardar Timur, you will undoubtedly be able to find out more about what happened. He'll most likely call the Panchayat, and I am sure that you will be asked to be a member. I only ask that you are just and fair."

"Why are you so interested in this matter?"

"I told you, Badri attends our school and I don't want to see her getting hurt for what her brother might have done, and I repeat, might have done."

"Shouldn't they just report it to the police? They will make sure that nothing terrible happens to the boy. That's what they're there for after all." Rauf said.

Turab and Mullah Aziz burst into laughter. Afridi chuckled for a second before going quiet.

"What? Why are you laughing? That's what my teacher says in school. If anybody does anything bad to another person, they should go to the police to complain, that the police will make them sorry they were born."

"You are such an idiot. And so is your teacher," Aziz replied. Turab agreed but kept silent. It was not his place to explain it. Rauf needed to understand that what his teacher said was true in principle but not in reality. Police and the court system had no real authority and no real power. In reality, the police force was merely an extension of the private security detail controlled by those like Sardar Timur. In fact, the justice system: courts, judges, and all others working in the courthouses were busy doing everything except serving justice. They were at the disposal of powerful people who could use them for their purposes any time they wished. Punishments could be meted out, but it was not always the same thing as justice.

Like many small communities, villages, and small towns in the area, this town also had an informal justice system utilizing the Panchayat mechanism, which was nothing more than a group of people handpicked by the upper echelon to decide controversial situations, essentially a handy tool for them to spread the culpability for sanctioning criminal punishments to whomever they saw deserving of their wrath and vengeance. If Sardar Timur wanted to punish someone, he would not order the punishment himself, he would assemble a group of people to conduct a *trial* before doling out the predetermined sentence, which usually tended to be harsh for sure.

In the past, Sardar Timur had participated as a member of the Panchayat but now was careful not to include himself in the group. In other locations, when horrifying Panchayat verdicts were reported in the newly liberated media, participants had been named as criminals. There was no point for him to directly participate in such activities, especially when the verdict could be obtained indirectly and the responsibility placed elsewhere.

"Instead of the police, Sardar Timur will let the Panchayat make decisions in this matter," Mullah Aziz said, staring into Rauf's eyes.

"Why not the police, why not the courts?" Rauf was still puzzled.

"Because courts do not deliver speedy justice," Mullah Aziz replied. "They just sit on the cases for years and years and nothing happens. Even if they decide, appeals are filed. Lawyers lie to the judges. Witnesses lie in court and the police force is corrupt, anyway. That's why Panchayat is the way to go if people want true justice." Aziz explained. Turab regarded him with skepticism, the police were often corrupt, yes, but the Panchayat wasn't any better.

Aziz looked around the courtyard and noticed Paro standing right behind the flimsy, ratty kitchen curtain listening to the conversation. Her eavesdropping station. She could see through the gauzy, milky thin fabric that her husband was looking in her direction, she could feel that his stare, his expression she was sure wasn't pleasant, but she refused to be deterred.

"You should try to help this girl if she is innocent," Paro said from behind the curtain. Mullah Aziz was taken aback by her participation in the conversation.

"Don't let other men listen to your voice, it's against Sharia. You do not tell me what to do, I'll see what I can do for this girl because it is the right thing to do. Just be quiet Paro, that's quite enough from you."

She recoiled slowly away from the curtain. Turab out of embarrassment for her, forced himself to look away from her direction.

"How did they catch the rascal?" Mullah Aziz asked, eyes still on the kitchen curtain.

Afridi responded with what he knew about the events at the Haveli, which he had heard from one of the servants, who had also witnessed the whole initial episode. Afridi's tone was one of real concern, and he constantly added commentary to minimize Gul's actions. In his opinion, the whole story was blown out of proportion and pumped up to show to the people of the town how deeply offensive Gul's conduct was if in fact there was any misconduct at all, and how much shame and disrespect, it had caused Sardar Timur. Doing so would help secure the harshest punishment possible, not only so Gul would not repeat the offense, but more importantly, to deter others from perpetrating such actions. Afridi had lived in the town all his life and had heard many horrific accounts of severe and unspeakable forms of punishment given to the servants and their families, inhumane punishment completely out of proportion to the crime. He feared that he had an accurate notion of what was in store for Gul and his sister.

Afridi also feared what might be in store for his school, as well as himself. The Haveli servant had spoken of Sardar Timur's fury when he heard about the school. Somehow he had been unaware of it, which was quite a surprise. He had always assumed that Sardar Timur knew about the school but just tolerated it, that he had taken it as a sign of changing times and changing attitudes. Now he knew with certainty that this was just ignorance on Sardar's part which only heightened his concern about the school becoming a target. If Sardar Timur didn't permit it, the school would be shut down, and if he was fortunate, that was all that would happen. But that was a worry for another day. Today, was about saving Badri.

"Amazing. What was he thinking?" Mullah Aziz said after Afridi was done. "Messing with Sardar's daughter in his own house. These lowly people can never be trusted."

"Aziz, why would you say that?" Turab felt compelled to ask. In the mosque, Mullah Aziz preached equality of men, but what he had just heard sounded like a true belief and not a slip of the tongue. "Who is lowly? Anyone who is a servant? They are automatically not to be trusted? What holy book says that?"

"I didn't mean that he is lowly as a human being," Mullah Aziz said attempting to erase his unfortunate words. "I meant that he is lowly because of the position society has placed him in. I'm just pointing out a fact, I don't mean to disrespect anyone. I tell those who come to my sermons that all men are created equal, and I firmly believe that!"

"I see." Turab reluctantly accepted the explanation. Afridi and Rauf stayed quiet.

"Anyway," Mullah Aziz spoke after a brief pause. "I'm sure that if Sardar Timur decides to call the Panchayat his men will approach me later today after *Maghreb* or *Isha* prayers. That's the usual pattern."

"Do you recommend members?" Turab asked.

142

"Sometimes they seek my recommendation. Other times, they just tell me who the members are and I am expected to go along with their decision."

"How many members are there?" Rauf asked. He was too young to remember many instances of the Panchayat.

"Depends on how serious the crime is."

"How do you recommend someone?" Turab asked. "I mean; how do you decide who to recommend?"

"I know people. I know who to recommend."

"Can you recommend Mother to be in Panchayat?" Rauf asked.

"No, you idiot," Aziz exclaimed, angrily. "This is a job suitable for men only. How can you not know that! What the hell is wrong with you!? Women are too emotional to follow the law blindly, you simply cannot trust a woman in matters of justice. Even the holy books say that the worth of a woman's testimony is half that of a man, you cannot make her a judge. I would never recommend your mother for this purpose."

"Why not? She's very intelligent." Rauf insisted.

"I don't know about that, and how do you even know that? She might be intelligent but she is a woman first."

"Wow," Afridi exclaimed. "You still think like that in this century?"

"What does this century have to do with a woman's role and her place in society?"

"Well, most people are now aware that women are equal to men," Afridi said assertively.

"Just because too many people agree on something doesn't make it right," Mullah Aziz repeated his favorite argument. "Man has been given the upper hand over women by the Almighty himself. Just because people like you who are really not men enough, think they are equal, does not mean that everybody has to accept that."

"I disagree. In my school, I see that young girls are just as intelligent and bright as boys."

"About that school of yours," Aziz suddenly realized he had a perfect opportunity to question Afridi about it. "How old is this girl, Badri?"

"I think she is twenty-one," Afridi tried to remember. He wasn't sure if he'd ever met or seen her.

"Isn't she too old for school?" Turab asked.

"We don't go by age. We let them come in at any age depending on the education they had before. Badri did complete elementary school before she was forced to sit at home in full *purdah*."

"And you encouraged her to abandon purdah?" Mullah Aziz shouted. Rauf jumped. Turab looked alarmed.

"No, I did no such thing. I am just trying to educate our girls, I'm not teaching them to give up their modest ways or defy customs, that isn't our goal."

"It does not matter if you knowingly teach that filth. It comes to them automatically if they start going to school. Schools are bad, a negative influence, especially with people like you running them. And who are the teachers?"

"They are all women," Afridi replied. "I am the only man associated with the school."

"Oh?" Aziz was surprised and a little annoyed to have another objection removed. He wanted an easy answer whether the school and Afridi were bad, or, specifically, wanted answers which tallied with his opinion. "Who are these women teachers? Where did you find them?"

Afridi opened his mouth to respond, but then a disturbing thought halted him. He suddenly realized that his reply could put his much-treasured teachers in jeopardy. It had been quite a feat to recruit these women, and it was due mostly to his wife's efforts. They were able to find women of an appropriate age willing to accept teaching positions, women old enough to remember the town when religious extremism wasn't so prevalent. Back then, people were different. The wars in the 1980s changed everything. Anyone willing to fight was given money and arms. The liberals, the educated, the cultured—mostly those too timid to fight the Russians—were disadvantaged. Power-hungry individuals, religious extremists, and the dregs of society found wealth and security. They would participate in Jihad for brief periods of time and then return as heroes with newfound influence and affluence. They could do whatever they considered just.

In their eyes, an uncovered free woman, in front of a man, was the devil's most lethal weapon. They believed with conviction that she intended to send Holy faithful warriors to hell. Merely looking at a woman, an uncovered free woman, was sufficient enough to undo the religious work they had done and cancel their reservation for a spot in paradise. Therefore, it was an absolute necessity to neutralize this threat. The only way to effect this was to confine that woman behind the walls of the father's house until marriage, and in her husband's house post marriage. A man's control over the woman was absolute.

The women who were a bit older, and who had not been absolutely controlled by their husbands before, were now afraid of their sons, many of whom would vouch their love and respect for them, but not tolerate any infraction from Allah's command, as they understood it, even by their mothers or sisters. In fact, these women, especially those considered younger-looking, beautiful or attractive, were now in exactly that position. They were dominated by their sons instead of their husbands or fathers. It was titanic for these women to overcome this fear of losing whatever freedom they had left. However, they were also witnesses to the terrible injustice done to their daughters, and fortunately for Afridi and the school, some were courageous enough to take up the cause of educating their girls.

The school was in an old abandoned house. The sign outside reading "Sewing and Cooking Institute for Girls." At first, Afridi was not sure how long this facade could hold, how long could they fool the inquisitive, religious fanatics. It was worth the risk in order to instill a certain safety. Surprisingly, it worked. The school went on operating successfully and Afridi finally decided to announce that besides sewing and cooking, the building would also serve as a school for other areas of study. He was always extremely cautious, on high alert really when approaching strangers or discussing the school with people that he didn't know. When the electronic media in the country was liberalized and the cause of girls' education was supported by many prominent people in society, Afridi became emboldened and began distributing flyers in the mosque. He was mainly targeting girls below the age of twelve.

"The teachers? They are from the city," Afridi responded, cautiously.

"Really? They come from the city every day?"

"Well, not all of them come every day." Luckily Afridi was able to come up with a reasonable explanation very quickly. "There is usually only one teacher for each day. We have four teachers and they take turns, you see we are only open four days a week, so each teacher only needs to come in once weekly. We rotate."

"How are you able to pay them?" Mullah Aziz was still suspicious.

"We don't pay them."

"So they work for free?"

"Yes. They do it for the girls." Afridi replied without hesitation. "They believe in the cause. They want to see our girls–their girls–educated."

"I don't believe you. I think you are a foreign agent, and I'm fairly sure that you're taking money from your Western masters and serving them, fulfilling their purpose. You're lying to me and you want to poison our young girls' minds by tarnishing them with ideas. I think these women that you call teachers, are also the paid agents, traitors. You have recruited them and the West is paying them through you. I think that you and all of your people are spies!" Mullah Aziz barraged Afridi with allegations.

Disbelief was written all over Afridi's face, Mullah Aziz's behavior was outrageous. An accusation such as this was a serious matter, and this was the second time Mullah Aziz had raised suspicion. No proof was required in order to convince others that the allegation was true and worse, people were too willing to accept the allegation at face value, especially coming from a person like Mullah Aziz. In Afridi's case, he knew that it would be readily accepted by the lunatics out on the street because the cause that he championed was truly controversial, and mostly because the extremists seemed to believe anything Mullah Aziz told them.

"All of our teachers work for free. They are volunteers. I haven't paid them a dime, ever!" He felt compelled to emphasize this point.

"Oh? No matter, because there is someone financially supporting the school, this I know Afridi. Go ahead, tell me that the West isn't paying you. Tell me..."

"No! They are not! As a matter of fact, Mullah Aziz, there is no money coming in at all. In fact, I use my own money to support the school."

"Really, and where does your personal money come from?"

"It's my personal money, my savings, not that it's any of your business."

In response, Mullah Aziz simply stared at him for a while, then looked around, cleared his throat, and said. "You say you are the only man in the school. All others are women and girls?"

"Yes."

"So you are alone with so many *na-mehram* girls and women, well now that makes me wonder about other things. I'd say that your personal character is really in question."

"How dare you make such an accusation against me!" Afridi was enraged. His face reddened with rage and he waved his small, determined clenched fists in the air. "How dare you!"

"We need to know more about you and your activities." Mullah Aziz ignored Afridi's protest and pointed towards Turab. "This man here, Turab, is a reporter for a newspaper and a TV channel. I'm going to ask him to check on you, perhaps visit your school and find out exactly what have you been doing. About that girl Badri like I said, if Sardar Timur wants to set up a Panchayat his men will most likely approach me later today, after *Maghreb* or *Isha* prayer. It is then that I'll be able to see what needs to be done. If that girl is guilty, I can promise you that I'll make sure that she gets the punishment she deserves. If she is innocent, I will protect her. But you Afridi are on my radar now. I'll dig deep and find out all that you are hiding. I promise."

Before Afridi could respond the air was filled with the *Azan*. The call for *Maghreb* prayer ended their conversation leaving Afridi even more troubled than before, nonetheless, giving Turab the perfect opportunity to question him.

ELEVEN

AAMIR SHAH KEPT watching the aerial map on the screen showing the plane's location. His tension had elevated since leaving the office and stayed that way all the way through airport security clearance. Once seated, he was able to begin to once again breathe freely, his tension lessened. He felt confident that he was safely out until the sight of an Airport Security Force officer entering the plane was enough for his heart to beat twice the normal rate. He was expecting a tap on the shoulder or announcement from the captain or worse. What would happen afterward was all too clear to him since he'd seen it happen before to multiple passengers and had always wondered what was going through their minds in those moments. Today he was experiencing it firsthand. His body temperature increased rapidly and his mouth became bone dry making it impossible to swallow. The perspiration on his forehead began to drip down his face, while the person sitting next to him was wrapped in a synthetic wool blend blanket, shivering from the AC vent blowing cold air above Aamir's head. The security officer passed by his seat and went all the way to the rear of the plane.

His heartbeat began to regulate as the plane smoothly ascended, passing through marshmallow formed clouds was the sign that he was safe. He studiously scrutinized the map on the screen, and for the first time since leaving Pakistani airspace, he felt comfortable enough to resign in his seat and look around.

The cabin was full. He was flying Emirates which was based in the tiny Emirate of Dubai, one of the few international airlines still servicing Karachi. The aerial distance between the two places was merely twelve hundred kilometers, yet the two cities seemed worlds apart.

Karachi, the biggest city in Pakistan and its commercial hub. An infrastructure disaster. A filthy, poorly constructed city and home to over twenty million people. It was best described as a huge unsightly heap of concrete, iron, and trash. Pollution, crowded streets, noisy traffic, lack of basic civic facilities, constant power outages, and lawlessness: those were its noted characteristics, not historical attractions or architectural marvels or anything positive. And then there was the overwhelming population problem.

People in Karachi, even those considered educated, also struggled with serious behavioral problems: respect for law and order was almost non-existent, a lack of civic duty, and a sense of entitlement was prevalent. Interestingly, Dubai was filled with people from Pakistan, but for some reason, in Dubai, their behavior was very different from what one would expect from them in Pakistan. One could see the difference in their attitude and approach from the way they behaved in their adopted country of the United Arab Emirates.

On the other hand, Dubai is known as the most populated and inarguably the most developed of all the Emirates. People traveling on Pakistani passports needed a visa to visit Dubai, but since Aamir was traveling on his U.S. passport he was granted entry for thirty days without any questions. Outside the baggage claim area, he saw a chauffeur holding an iPad with his name and picture. Upon seeing him, the chauffeur greeted Aamir with a warm smile and a slight bow. He was taken to the Armani hotel in Burj Khalifa–the world's tallest building and the first hotel designed by the famed Italian fashion designer Giorgio Armani. The Prime Minister was staying in the same hotel and so was his entourage and the proximity to them already felt stifling.

"There's a message for you," the registration clerk told him while handing over the room key cards. "It is from Arlette Baudis. The message is that she'd like you to join her for a drink in the lounge close to the moving sidewalk around eight pm."

"Okay. Did she leave a phone number?"

"I don't think so, but let me check with my colleague." She turned around and disappeared behind the huge marble wall, but was back within seconds with a head shake and a "no."

"I don't know what she looks like," Aamir said. "I guess I'll have to search for her image online. Don't worry. I'll take care of it."

While walking towards the elevator he saw photographs of the various phases of the construction process of the building, surely a marvel of the modern world, acknowledging the brains and sweat of countless souls. One picture attracted Aamir's attention in particular, the portrait of a man named Fazlur Rahman Khan. Aamir stopped to read the text below his image. The text provided the man's full name, date of birth, and death and praised his revolutionary Tubular Design which, according to the sign, made possible the construction of skyscrapers such as the Sears Tower, John Hancock Center and so many other tall buildings.

Fazlur Rahman Khan's name and image brought Aamir a strange sense of pride and for no apparent rhyme or reason. The engineering genius was born in 1929 in Dhaka, Bengal, then part of United India under British Rule, long before Aamir's birth, and died 1982–more than thirty years ago–yet, Aamir felt a strong connection, but why?

He thought it might be his need to be acknowledged, linked to a positive productive force so to speak. Like so many others from a third world Muslim country, he had deep-rooted self-image issues. He did not want to be viewed only as a Muslim fanatic always ready to die and kill others for some radical agenda. Thanks to extremists, he felt that burden whenever he traveled away from home.

The ride to the room in the high-speed elevator was a thrill in itself, the elevator was claimed to move at ten meters per second. Once in the room, Aamir decided to shower and take a much needed quick nap. He set the alarm for seven p.m. to allow sufficient time to get ready for his meeting with the intriguing French reporter.

Before heading towards the lounge Aamir studied Arlette's pictures online. The woman was in her mid-thirties and had the looks of a movie star, with medium dark hair that was usually styled in an elegant but not fussy manner and almost always appearing expensively clothed. No matter what her profession, she would have attracted male attention, so it was no wonder that the Prime Minister wanted to buy her a phone and attempt to engage her in some sort of relationship. While some would consider the purpose of attempting such a connection obvious, Aamir was not so sure that it was that simple. He had known the Prime Minister for many years now and had met him several times in private, as well as in public settings. He was fairly religious and conservative, married for over forty years, and had adult children and several grandchildren.

When Arlette mentioned the Prime Minister's overtures in one of her stories, she subtly presented him as being struck by her good looks and charming personality. While she did not explicitly state it, her unflattering description was enough to paint him as a drooling pervert which became a major source of embarrassment for him, especially given his carefully constructed image of a right-leaning politician with a religious edge. As a result, Arlette's credentials were canceled and she was de-facto banned from Pakistan and even from events held outside Pakistan where the Prime Minister was to appear. It was surprising in more ways than one that she was here.

Aamir was trying to figure out why the Prime Minister would even engage in such risqué behavior. If he were to jump to the easiest conclusion, the matter was simple: the man apparently had desires. However, Aamir wanted to delve further into this matter, curious to know what the Prime Minister in his sixties would do with a woman in her thirties. A reporter. The answer wasn't very clear. Aamir couldn't picture the Prime Minister seeking any type of physical gratification from Arlette Baudis, a rendezvous between them could be arranged only with great difficulty or kept secret, even if she was a willing participant. Even in the unlikely event that it could be arranged, such interludes could not be more than few and far in between. It didn't make sense for the Prime Minister to jeopardize his political career and good name for something fairly trivial, the risk was far greater than the reward. If he wanted such an arrangement, if he was looking for a companion, he wouldn't have to go far or go through any trouble.

Aamir posed the argument: from the Prime Minister's point of view, that he just wanted a female friend who was open-minded and willing to have frank conversations with him. After all, he was a man of wealth, connections, and international repute. His wife, on the other hand, was a deeply conservative woman who belonged to a rich, traditional rural family from interior Punjab. Aamir had met her and could not imagine her engaging in any intellectually satisfying conversation with her husband. There was no harm in having a friend from the opposite gender, and if Arlette fulfilled his intellectual needs, there should be no objection. Aamir also heard through the grapevine that the Prime Minister was shopping for a biographer. Arlette could have been a candidate, but then, her limited ability to communicate without an interpreter would have been a major impediment. In conclusion, Aamir considered the Prime Minister's actions a very poor expression of frivolity or just not well thought out.

Soft music and clouds of cigar smoke greeted Aamir in the lounge. The aroma was a bit overwhelming but the laughter, talk, and TV cricket commentary provided a sense of life humming with all its energy. Most of the tables were occupied, and the bar was fairly crowded. He finally found a cluster of stools empty at the end of the bar and decided to take one. As soon as he sat down, the bartender appeared with a welcoming face.

"You can order using the tablet in front of you," he pointed to the gadget installed under the glass top of the counter. "Or you can shout the order the old fashioned way."

"I prefer the old fashioned way," Aamir replied with a broad smile. The bartender also showed him that the electronic tablet could be used to communicate with the other guests in the bar as well as order drinks.

"Okay," Aamir was impressed. "That's neat."

"Your first drink is on the house," the bartender continued. "What would you like to start with?"

"Whatever is your special today."

"Be ready to be pleasantly surprised. Would you like regular or virgin?"

"Virgin, please," Aamir did not want alcohol to cloud his judgment when meeting Ms. Baudis.

He took out his smartphone from the jacket's breast pocket and started reading the questions he had written during his flight for his meeting with the Prime Minister. The two-hour flight gave him enough time to focus on the issue at hand and he felt a need to clarify exactly what had happened in Arlette's previous interview with the Prime Minister.

A strong fruity fragrance broke his concentration. An alluring blonde in a black evening dress took the empty stool beside him. Their eyes met for a second and she didn't waste any time to flash a very warm smile. Her facial features were an exotic mixture of beauty, sexuality, and the stealth of a hungry wolf. Aamir wondered what she wanted with him. He was slightly tired and very anxious about his meeting. It had been a long day, and it was far from over.

"Are you a lady of the evening?" Aamir decided to be direct.

"What do you mean?" she asked in broken English. Aamir was disappointed. While an encounter with a prostitute in the lounge was not a complete surprise, he expected that she would at least be on par with the potential client in this seven-star hotel.

Dubai, with an outward appearance of a wealthy place and supposedly an Islamic country, was overrun by sex workers from all over the world. They were the modern 'businesswomen' there on a visa, which came at a hefty price, and which was renewed for them every three months, again at a hefty price.

"You don't speak English?" Aamir asked.

"I do." The accent sounded Eastern European.

"How come you didn't understand my question?" Aamir asked.

"I understood the words, but I don't know what you meant by the lady of the evening."

"Are you a prostitute?'

"No. How dare you think that?" She sounded furious. Aamir was taken aback. Maybe he had jumped to conclusions.

"I am sorry. I'm truly sorry."

"I am a respectable businesswoman." She picked up the glass in front of her and took a big gulp.

"You know, you men are all filthy," she began and turned towards him while almost smashing the glass down on the wooden counter. "It is impossible to walk into a hotel lobby in this damned city without being propositioned. Looks like all of you are on a hunt for a cunt. You are staying in a very expensive hotel, but your mind is in the same gutter as a beggar on the street. You looked like a nice person. I thought you would approach me like a gentleman and treat me the way a lady should be treated. But, forget about it."

Aamir retreated slightly with embarrassment. He realized he should have played along and let her lead the conversation, if she was a working girl like those that roam Dubai, she would have addressed the subject sooner or later. Even those who had been trafficked found it acceptable to sell themselves for a few hours and then enjoy the fruits of their labor during the day or send it to their families in far off lands. With so many lonely men, there was an abundance of harmless clients, mostly family men who were unable to bring their wives to Dubai because they didn't make enough money to qualify for a family visa. In order for these men to be in Dubai, they had to have a job or a business in partnership with a local sheik. Therefore, these women knew that the men they would encounter would be financially secure. The officials knew that men hungry for companionship had to be allowed an outlet, so this system worked well. Therefore, in order to keep everybody happy and calm, turning a blind eye to this practice was a convenient way out for everyone involved. Unfortunately, for those other women, those that weren't involved in this world, being propositioned was a probability. If they rejected such invitations, they were usually not harassed or pursued since there were so many others who were willing participants.

The woman sitting next to Aamir was now staring at the TV straight ahead, decidedly ignoring him. He got up and walked away from her without saying a word. Her expression changed when she realized that he was moving away, but she kept staring straight ahead. Aamir kept looking at her until he had no choice but to turn and walk away. The city was filled with temptation and minefields, often in the same place.

A black Suburban pulled over in front of the impressive side entrance of the Burj Khalifa. Darkened windows on the passenger side slid halfway down and a Caucasian woman's bright blue eyes started peering into the lounge, visible through the glass walls. She saw him walking away from the bar and towards a table.

"Go get him," she said in French to the front passenger seat occupant. He complied without hesitation. Arlette continued to watch. He approached Aamir in the lounge, asking him to come outside with him. She saw them conversing for a few minutes, then her phone rang.

"Does he wants to talk to me before coming out with you?" she asked without waiting for him to explain. He nodded and without uttering a word handed the phone to Aamir.

"Why do I need to come out? Where are we going?"

"Well, hello yourself. If you can come out, we can talk safely."

"Safe talking is possible in the lounge, too. Or we can go to my room."

"Don't make me upset. Just come out and join me." After she said that, Aamir went quiet.

"Should I be worried?" Aamir asked after a few moments.

"You will have fewer reasons to worry if you would just follow my lead." She saw Aamir nod his head and then hand over the phone to her man in the lounge. They started walking towards the door and within a few very short minutes Aamir was in the SUV sitting beside her. She put a finger on her mouth signaling him to stay quiet. The vehicle was in motion immediately and in less than fifteen minutes, they were at the beach. Arlette got out without saying a word and motioned him to follow. He complied. He saw her take off her evening shoes and walk in the sand so he mimicked her actions and soon enough they were walking in the ankle-deep water on the beach, looking like any random couple taking a moonlit stroll.

"Now we can talk," Arlette said, looking deep in his eyes.

"What is all this?" Aamir was perplexed. "Are you afraid of something or someone? Are you trying to intimidate me? This is too dramatic Ms. Baudis and unnecessarily cloak and dagger-ish."

"You really think that, after what happened to you when you left your house in Karachi, you really think these precautions are too dramatic? Aamir didn't respond. He was unpleasantly reminded of those events and wondered how she knew about them.

"The chances are high that you are being observed and I don't want my conversation with you overheard by the wrong people."

"You think I am being spied on?" Aamir was surprised. "Here?"

"It's a possibility," Arlette said. "After what happened to you in Karachi, I know that you are a person of interest, the question is for whom? Who wants you? Is it your local "spy" agency, the police, the competition? The CIA? Whoever they are, it's likely that they are watching you here too, and I have to take precautions. If they are not watching you or listening to you, then there's no harm. But if they are, these so-called theatrics may make a real difference and I'd rather remain shielded."

"Sounds like overkill to me. You appear panicked and a little paranoid truth be told."

"Better safe than sorry Aamir. Anyway, you know your assignment and I hope I don't need to explain what is expected?"

"No. But I do want to know what happened between you and the Prime Minister."

"I wrote a piece about it. Did you not read it?"

"I read your article. You just alluded to a suggestion he made. Did you omit the details on purpose?" Aamir asked with a wink and a smile.

"Yes. That piece was for readers of a certain intellect. For those who can read between the lines. So I guess it served its purpose and still gave him an opportunity to come up with a believable explanation. He's now tainted, but not smeared. It was enough for what he did to me last time."

"What exactly did he do or say to you?"

"Well if you must know he got far too close. He assertively grabbed me and held me in a gripping embrace and tried to touch me inappropriately. I was truly stunned at his behavior. Apparently, he misread my lack of protest as silent consent and then offered to have a private communication channel and then some."

"Did you do or say something to lead him on?"

"No," Arlette Baudis said with a cat-like grin. "But I am a beautiful white woman–a very desirable woman–I know that. I have that effect on men. All men, but especially those coming from third world countries, particularly those with money and power. I'm a trophy for such men. They see me and they desire me. Some of them are quick to pursue, others lack courage but none of them lack the desire to conquer me."

"I am not pursuing you." Aamir felt offended by her condescending attitude. He felt compelled to protest on behalf of 'men from third world countries.'

"You aren't the type," Arlette said dismissively.

"How do you know? Maybe I am." Somehow he found himself now trying to prove to her that he might pursue her when moments ago he had no interest.

"You're not rich and you are not powerful. People like you consider a woman like me out of their league, so they never have the confidence or courage to pursue the likes of me. I travel all over the world and speak to the most powerful men in various countries. People like you, who are powerless and penniless are intimidated by my presence."

"Wow Arlette, you have a big head full of hot air do you know that? I'm trying really hard to restrain myself from using - arrogant - as a word to describe you." Now Aamir was truly vexed. He felt insulted and belittled. "I am not intimidated by you. I don't care how beautiful you are or how well connected you are. I don't give a damn."

The smirk on her face enraged him. He turned around and started walking away from the beach.

"Are you married?" he heard her shouting the question behind him. He paused for a moment and then turned around.

"Why do you ask?" Aamir shouted back. "Shouldn't you know that already?" She shrugged, still smirking. Aamir tried to calm his nerves.

"Ever hit your wife?" she asked.

"No. Never."

"Ever took advantage of her when she was not in the mood or didn't want to come close to you?"

"That is none of your business." Aamir didn't consider this question worthy of an answer.

"So you have," Arlette responded, apparently drawing a 'yes' from Aamir's failure to give a straight answer. "Why do you men do that? Why do you have to force yourself onto your woman? Why do you not respect her wishes?"

"You really don't appreciate the cultural differences between West and East. Your question speaks volumes about your ignorance." Aamir said after a few moments of quiet pondering. She was condescending and irritating, yes, but she was a woman with a voice worth listening to, and a huge audience at her disposal. He thought engaging in an intellectual conversation with her might be beneficial since he had heard this opinion of men like him before. There were countless souls in the West with a certain image of men from his part of the world. Perhaps he could change the image by talking to her.

"There is no cultural difference on a basic human level. Men in your world are taught to disrespect the wishes and desires of others, especially women." She sounded absolutely certain.

"You will have to leave your ego and your opinions behind if you wish to have an honest discussion to learn something new," Aamir said, now standing next to her, facing the sea. She had her back to it.

"Oh? What new thing do I need to learn?"

"You have an unwavering confidence in your opinions, you really need to learn to open your eyes and see other perspectives. You know what you think is right, but you don't consider that you don't know what *others* think is right."

"Okay. Show me your perspective. Teach me exactly what you think it is that I'm lacking." Arlette almost dared him.

"All right. Tell me specifically, why you feel so angry towards men of my background."

"Well, generally you men are pigs, your behavior and demeanor are primal and brutish and you're cruel to women. Especially to your wives. You don't care for her wishes, you don't even allow her to excuse herself from your physical wants and demands. You still consider a woman your property. There are so many women, even in my home country France, who are married to men like you, who feel that they have no say whatsoever when it comes to their own bodies. They get raped by their husbands for the sake of marriage and marital duties–all in the name of religion."

"That is a false impression."

"It's not an impression. It's a reality. It is actually what I have been told firsthand, and it is not false. I've been given accounts of real events occurring all over the world at the hands of men who use religion as an excuse for everything they can- no matter what the woman wants or thinks. My information is not only accurate but correct."

"What we consider a man's right to his wife is what you are labeling rape. There can be no rape in a marriage." Aamir said with conviction in his thoughts, firmness in his tone.

"Oh really? You really think so?"

"Yes, I do. There can be no rape in a marriage," Aamir repeated. "You know why? Because the consent given at the time of making the marital vows is permanent, cannot be revoked, cannot be taken back as long as the marriage is intact. A man's right to his wife is established for as long as marriage does not end or he does not fail in fulfilling *his* marital responsibilities."

"So one mistake made by her and her body is yours to use, it is yours to devour whenever you want?"

"Absolutely not. Nobody has the right to devour anybody. It's the sickness of your mind which considers the legal union of flesh, rape, or an act of devouring."

"What if she is sick? Do you still have the right to gratify yourself by using her?"

"That's a valid excuse. It would be inhumane to put a demand on her which she physically cannot meet," Aamir said. "If there's a valid excuse, she cannot be forced. But at the same time, she cannot

162

flat out refuse without reason, either. The marital contract has to mean something. If the marriage demands no physical contact outside marriage, and yet allows the woman to deny the same thing in the marriage, people will consider staying out of the marriage a better option. All divine religions forbid such conduct."

"Oh, so you have religious permission to engage in such sadistic behavior. I see."

'There is no sadistic behavior in the marital relationship allowed in any religion, you're twisting my words. I didn't say that divine religion allows sadistic behavior or a relationship based on sheer force. All I am saying is, that religion is the source of social morals and one of them is no relations outside marriage. When someone enters into a marital contract, it should either be performed or broken. It's like going to a sporting event and not being allowed to watch it past the middle, or not being given your money back when you've done nothing to deserve the denial of service." Aamir went on, passionate about his beliefs.

Arlette studied his face with keen interest for a moment before asking. "You are a U.S. citizen, correct?"

"Yes."

"And you lived in the U.S. for how long?"

"More than ten years."

"Strange. You've lived there for so long and yet you still have the mentality of a close-minded mullah."

"You're too judgmental," Aamir replied. "Unfortunately your judgment is also clouded by the strength of your sentiments."

"Oh! Now, who is being judgmental?"

"Well, I'm just sharing my observation." He knew he sounded defensive.

"Isn't that what being judgmental is?"

"Enough Arlette! I'm done arguing with you," Aamir raised his hands up in the air before letting them fall back down. "Why did you want to meet me? I was told clearly what I'm expected to do. Do you wish to add anything?"

"Well, we may be working as a team for the next few days. If the Prime Minister does not come up with any suggestions of personal business besides the interview, then our association will be hardly necessary. However, if he decides to rekindle the old flame then we may end up working together for longer than you may have anticipated. If this were to happen, I wanted to get to know you better."

"I am sure the Prime Minister is a wiser man now and in tune with his actions. Hopefully, he'll stay focused on official matters only. I'm fairly sure that he will proceed with the interview and not let other things cloud his judgment."

"Well we shall see, men rarely wise up in these matters. Particularly hunters like your Prime Minister."

"You are not planning to lure him into a trap. Are you?"

"I am not planning anything, anything at all, except for the interview questions. Come, let's go I'll drop you back at the hotel."

"Where are you staying?"

"I'm with my team in the Villa that we've rented," Arlette replied while putting on her shoes.

The ride back was relaxed and comfortable. No words were spoken. The moment they left the beach, a soft chime announced a text message on Aamir's phone, from the Sheik's security chief, letting him know to be ready by nine-thirty a.m. The meeting he had expected that evening, was instead going to take place in his room the next morning.

TWELVE

B Y THE TIME Mullah Aziz, Turab, Rauf, and Afridi arrived in the main prayer hall, the call for prayer was over and the congregation was waiting for the Imam.

Mullah Aziz stood at his designated place and faced the crowd. He repeated the usual instructions for the congregation to form straight lines and stand shoulder to shoulder without any gaps. The mosque was unusually crowded for the *Maghreb* prayer. He made it a point to instruct the congregation to switch their cell phones to silent for any sound prevention while prayer was offered.

In the beginning, his instruction about phones being silenced was not heeded until he encouraged people to shame those whose phones had gone off. Subsequently, any incidences of beeping and ringing during prayer reduced significantly. In the spirit of trying to maintain quiet, he failed to notice new unfamiliar faces.

The obligatory three *rakah* prayer was over in about five minutes. After that, people were encouraged to offer at least two more rakah, not mandatory, but routinely performed by the prophet Mohammad and therefore were considered *Sunnat-e-Moakkada*, as close to obligatory as possible.

The moment Mullah Aziz stood up to offer rakah, he felt a tap on his shoulder. Highly unusual. He turned around and saw a man of significant stature with an intimidating jet black handlebar mustache.

"Salam Maulana," the large man said, without giving Mullah Aziz an opportunity to speak.

"Wal-ae-kum Assalam," Mullah Aziz almost whispered. He was not sure how to react. This was unheard of.

"You need to make an announcement," the man said. It was more like a demand, if not an outright order.

"Now? At this moment? I'm still praying as one can see, so you'll need to wait."

"No. This cannot wait," the man insisted. "This announcement needs to be made before they all start leaving, it needs to be heard by as many *Namazis* as possible, as many followers as possible Mullah Aziz."

"Who are you? What do you want to announce?" Aziz asked in a whisper. He forgot that the clip-on microphone he was wearing on his shirt collar was still active, and the congregation could hear the conversation loud and clear, which caused people who otherwise would have resumed prayers, to stop and watch the two men.

"I work for Sardar Timur," the man told Mullah Aziz. "He needs to call the Panchayat immediately and he wants at least twenty-four men. As you know, the Panchayat must consist of a certain type of person, so I need it announced in the mosque right now so that we can get decent faithful and loyal volunteers."

"What is he calling the Panchayat for?" someone shouted.

"Is this about that boy caught in the Haveli with his daughter?" another asked.

Mullah Aziz took note of the man's reaction, he was surprised. Apparently, the story was spreading fast.

"What have you heard?" Sardar Timur's soldier asked loudly.

"I heard that some boy Gul was caught molesting Sardar Timur's daughter, Farah. I have seen his father, Shams, in the tea shop many times, a very quiet and kind man."

"Do you want to volunteer for Panchayat?" The soldier asked.

"I can't, it's impossible I have to work," he responded.

"Okay, well anyone who volunteers for Panchayat will be paid good money for their time and service. But at this time, I only wanted to announce that we need twenty-four or more people. All necessary information will be provided after prayers to any and all interested in volunteering."

"Who are you?" another person amidst the crowd asked.

"My name is Basheer, and I work for Sardar Timur. I take care of his horses, and his cars, among various other things."

"How come we haven't seen you before?" the first man asked.

"I'm new here. Until last week I was in the city taking care of Sardar Timur's property there. This is my first week here in this town."

"Why do you have to wait for Isha to finish before choosing volunteers, why don't you do it right now?"

"I don't have an answer for you, Mullah Aziz, I'm just following Sardar Timur's orders. He told me to make the announcement immediately after *Maghreb* prayers, and to choose the men after *Isha*."

"Okay," Mullah Aziz decided to intervene. "You heard the man. He's obeying his master's orders and we all should do the same, obey our master's instructions. And right now, the instruction is to complete our *Maghreb* prayer."

While turning around, he happened to lay eyes on the first man who had spoken to Basheer from the crowd and decided to inquire about his source of information regarding the incident.

"Hey, what's your name?" Mullah Aziz pointed his finger towards him.

"Raza," the man replied.

"How did you know about the incident in the Haveli?"

"Why do you ask? Am I not supposed to know? I heard someone talking about it when I was coming to the mosque."

Mullah Aziz stared at him for a long moment before shifting his gaze to Afridi, standing to Raza's right.

"I hope this makes things easier for you," Afridi commented while looking straight at Mullah Aziz.

"What do you mean?" Basheer inquired, looking keenly into Afridi's eyes. "What's he trying to do? What's likely to become easy for him?"

"Nothing."

"Let's finish the prayers and then we can talk," Mullah Aziz said in a dry tone and then turned around and started praying. Sardar Timur's man gave Afridi a suspicious look, turned around, and walked out of the prayer hall. By the time he set his foot out of the hall, Afridi was busy praying.

⌒

The word spread in seconds that a Panchayat was being called and that volunteers were needed, they began pouring into the main prayer hall well before the scheduled *Isha* prayer time. By the time *Azan* was called, the prayer hall was full and the rest of the people were clamoring to gain entrance. Nobody knew exactly how this Panchayat was to be run, but interest was definitely piqued.

The topic wasn't of much significance, what really mattered was: they would get paid. Most of them had heard stories that *if* the Panchayat was willing to listen– really listen–to the person calling for a Panchayat and deliver– really deliver–justice, which was likely to be well received by the person presenting the matter, then good things happened for the Panchayat members. Very good things. Such good things were rare in their lives, so an opportunity like this one, could not be missed. The fact that a Panchayat was being called by the most influential and richest person in town, only raised people's hopes and guaranteed greater participation.

"Looks like too many people want to partake in the serving of justice," Turab murmured sarcastically but was still loud enough to be heard by Rauf and Aziz who walked beside him.

"Right, people here just love to serve justice," Rauf mocked the crowd. "They'll serve if they are paid, if not justice can wait until later." Aziz couldn't contain his smirk and for once he agreed with his son. Basheer walked noiselessly behind them, listening, but keeping silent. It was hard to gauge his thoughts; his face was perfectly impassive.

Isha was the longest of the five obligatory prayers of the day, taking about twenty minutes for the congregation to finish, and during this time, the crowd kept growing.

"As you all know, Sardar Timur has called the Panchayat," Mullah Aziz addressed the crowd using the handheld microphone which allowed him to move around as he spoke, holding court. "He has been dishonored and disrespected by a boy who is the son of two of his employees. I don't have all the details, but from what I know, this boy did a terrible thing to one of Sardar Timur's daughters. Luckily, he was caught in the act and the person catching him was his own mother. Therefore, there is no allegation of false accusation."

"Who is this boy?" someone from the crowd asked. "Who are his parents?"

"I know his name, but I would rather not say," Mullah Aziz replied. "Only Panchayat members will be given full and accurate information so they can consider this matter and handle it with utmost discretion and objectivity."

"Lots of people already know," someone else from the crowd shouted. "It is not a secret. You can say the name."

"Even if everybody knows, I am not going to name names. You should know the customary method of handling these types of issues. You're old enough to have seen Panchayat called many times. Full and authentic information is provided to the selected individuals only, even if there are rumors flying around and even if those rumors are correct."

"It's Gul, isn't it? His father's name is Shams, right?" another person from the crowd declared loudly.

Basheer took the microphone out of Mullah Aziz's hands and shouted angrily, "Shut up, don't say any names or anything else or I will have you thrown out of the mosque."

"Why is he insisting on keeping this information secret?" Turab looked at Rauf, who was standing right next to him and whispered in his ear.

"None of this makes any sense," Rauf shrugged his shoulders and whispered back. "They'll pick only those people who will do what they're told, people who can blindly follow orders. This whole Panchayat thing is just a show. None of this is real, it's all smoke and mirrors. You'll see."

"Wow, you are a bit more in the know than I had imagined," Turab couldn't contain his surprise. The Rauf he was seeing now, was a much different Rauf than the one he had seen before.

"If the boy was caught by his mother red-handed, then why call the Panchayat? Sardar Timur can punish him without their decision. Why doesn't he just punish the boy and be done with it?" another person from the crowd asked.

Basheer spoke up before Mullah Aziz could reply. "Because Sardar Timur wants justice served. He's not seeking revenge, certainly not from a person who is weak and helpless like the boy who is accused of this crime."

Suddenly someone in the crowd loudly chanted a slogan in praise of Sardar Timur. Others began to follow his lead, reminiscent of a cult-like reciting that went on for a few minutes before the Mullah spoke.

"Please, no chants or slogans," Mullah Aziz said after the crowd had gone quiet. "Keep in mind that you are in a place of worship. This is not a political rally. So, please no slogans of any kind."

"This will be a Grand Panchayat," Basheer spoke again. So, that means that there will be twenty-four members. Mullah Aziz will select them. Only those who come to the mosque regularly are eligible. Out of those initially selected, none can be relatives of Sardar Timur or the other family. Sardar Timur has set aside two hundred thousand rupees for each member of Panchayat. This amount can increase if there is a need for it. The money will be given to Mullah Aziz before the selection begins so members can be assured that their compensation is safe with a neutral person. Is that fair?" The crowd stayed quiet for a while before someone shouted out.

"No. It is not fair."

All eyes turned to this person. It was Afridi.

"Why is that?" Basheer asked.

"You said Mullah Aziz will select the members of the Panchayat, and that he also will be the custodian of the funds? Well, that means he is going to decide who he hands out the money to, this is anything but fair. He can also misuse the money to gain influence."

"What's your name?"

"My name is Afridi, Farhan Afridi."

"Afridi. You are the one with the school for girls, I hear. And you don't trust Mullah Aziz, the Imam of the mosque you attend?"

"I trust him. I do trust him. What I don't trust is the idea of too much power in any one hand. Since you are saying Sardar Timur wants justice, it would be in his best interest to ensure that everything is done with the utmost impartiality."

Mullah Aziz stared at Afridi with hostility, smothering his impulse to yell, but he knew that he needed to restrain himself. Any outburst of anger towards Afridi would only prove his point.

"Do you have a suggestion?" Basheer asked after a brief pause.

"Yes. There is a reputable, credible man visiting our town these days. I met him at Mullah Aziz's house today. He's a media person and he's not from here so he will have every reason to remain neutral, he doesn't have anything to gain or lose. I think he should be given one of the two tasks. He can either control the money or have an influence on who gets chosen to be a part of the Panchayat committee."

"Are you going to tell us who this person is and how you know him?"

"I believe his name is Turab and he's standing right there."

The crowd was now looking at Turab, who was stunned by the sudden attention thrown his way.

"You believe his name is Turab?" Basheer asked in a surprised tone. "You don't even know his name and you want to trust him with our money?"

"Well, I don't know him personally. In fact, I just met him today for the first time at Mullah Aziz's home," Afridi replied. "And that's a good thing. That shows that I am not suggesting his name for any other reason. All I want is to keep this whole matter credible and above board. There is this old saying, justice should not only be done, it should also appear to have been done. I think choosing a neutral person to handle the money, will make it appear so."

Basheer looked at Turab prudently and then motioned him to come forward in such a way that Turab felt compelled to do so, as though he didn't have a choice. He felt like a squirrel who had been walking around minding his own business and then finds himself in the talons and teeth of a hawk.

"You're a media person?"

"Yes. I'm a reporter for a newspaper, and also a regular on a TV news show."

"And why are you here?"

"I'm visiting Mullah Aziz," Turab replied. He feared the direction this conversation was going. He glanced at Mullah Aziz noting a mildly panic-stricken expression, a clear signal for Turab not to mention the phone call his son had made.

"Why are you visiting Mullah Aziz?"

"Well, actually I am here to talk to his son, Rauf." Turab pointed towards Rauf. "Mullah Aziz's son who I've known since he was small. It so happens that he's about to graduate high school with top grades and I came here to interview him, take some pictures, talk to his parents, and write a story for my paper. If it's well-received, I may even do a story for the TV show after his graduation, a story about graduates across many regions. A documentary-style piece."

Basheer continued to stare at Turab's face with suspicion. He obviously didn't want to buy the story, but he couldn't find a reason to reject it outright, either.

"Is this true, Rauf?"

"What? I don't know what are you asking."

"I am asking you if this man Turab is telling the truth?" Basheer asked angrily. "Have you known him for a long time and did he come here to talk to you about this graduation story?"

Rauf considered the question for a brief moment before nodding. "Yes," he managed to speak softly. Turab felt the suffocating weight of the cement brick on his chest lift. He inhaled deeply and exhaled as quietly as possible, He threw a glance towards Mullah Aziz who looked equally relieved.

"You said your name is Afridi, right?" Basheer now turned towards Afridi.

"Yes, Farhan Afridi."

"And you met Turab at Mullah Aziz's house?"

"Yes," Afridi replied without hesitation.

"Why were you at Mullah Aziz's house?"

"Well, he is our Imam." Afridi felt that the real answer might land him into trouble which he would rather not invite. "I needed his guidance on a certain religious matter."

"What was the matter?"

"I would rather not say in public, but, if you must know, I can tell you privately."

Basheer stared at Afridi's face for a long time before opening his mouth. "It's all right. You don't have to tell me now, but keep in mind, that I can question you at any time day or night or both. I work for Sardar Timur, you know his position and the way he manages situations, meaning that I have his blessing to handle anything, in any manner that I choose. My intervention is for your benefit, for everyone's benefit."

"Okay, I understand," Afridi found himself nodding in agreement. He was not sure what he had agreed to but it felt appropriate. The last thing he wanted was unnecessary attention, he needed to keep the school protected, especially from anyone who was on Sardar Timur's payroll.

"So," Basheer spoke again. "That's settled. Mullah Aziz will select the members of the Panchayat, Turab will be trusted with the money and you all may volunteer for service. That's why you are gathered here today, correct?"

"Yes," many in the crowd yelled, loudly declaring their intention.

"I am going to let you begin the selection process," Basheer said to Mullah Aziz and stepped back. Mullah Aziz came forward.

"All right." Mullah Aziz motioned them all to calm down. "You all know that this is a heavy burden. It's challenging, risky, and truly difficult. Someone's life is likely to be turned upside down. Each one of you needs to be aware of the gravity of this responsibility before you volunteer. Try to understand what you are getting yourselves into because if you end up delivering injustice, you will be dealt with very severely on the Day of Judgment. Keep that in mind. Do not think only about earning some money and doing whatever is needed, do not have a casual attitude about this, you must think about the impact a casual attitude towards this immensely important duty may have, not just to the individual who was wronged, but also to the society as a whole, for a long time to come."

He took a brief pause, cleared his throat, and resumed.

"In short, what I am saying is, don't accept this responsibility just to make money. Volunteer only if you think you can truly objectively commit yourself, without any prejudice, vengeance, or anything else for that matter. Your only goal should be justice and the delivery of justice the way our creator intended, and our religion teaches. If you feel you're up to the task, raise your hand and I'll speak to each of you individually."

Turab was impressed by Mullah Aziz's oratory and his message. He felt that many would decide against volunteering, so he was stunned when he saw nearly everyone raising hands.

Apparently, they all thought they could rise to the occasion and not be swayed by the temptation of money. He wondered how many people would have volunteered if no money was offered. The question was moot. The crowd knew they would be paid for their service, and they knew who was paying.

Mullah Aziz started counting the raised hands. Basheer looked at him with surprise. "They all have their hands raised. Why are you even counting? You may wish to just want to start asking some basic questions and pick any thirty."

"Why thirty?" Mullah Aziz asked. You said we need twenty-four only."

"Just in case any of the original twenty-four isn't able to serve or something happens to them, we should have backup immediately available."

"Okay."

"You should get started, it's getting late."

Mullah Aziz gave a short nod and looked at the crowd. "Since all of you are volunteering, I am going to ask each of you to recite a specific portion of the Quran. If you cannot recite from memory, you'll be disqualified. Do you understand?"

He didn't wait for a response, instead, he began pointing at individuals signaling for them to come forward. He asked each one to recite specific Ayah from the holy book Quran. Most failed. In the end, out of almost three hundred people, only fifty-two were able to recite some portion of the Quran. The whole process took about two hours, but they succeeded in finding thirty candidates for the Panchayat. Basheer took down each person's name and contact information before allowing them to leave. They were told to be available at short notice for the next few days. By the time they were done, it was well past midnight.

"My men are going to deliver food to your homes as a thank you for staying late, dinner tonight is on Sardar Timur," Basheer said after the last of the thirty candidates left. By this time, the prayer hall was silent and empty except Mullah Aziz, Turab, Rauf, Basheer, and his men.

"Thanks, but that's not necessary," Rauf found it necessary to jump in. "I'm sure that my mother has prepared food for us already."

"Quiet," Mullah Aziz flared up. "Do not disrespect the man by rejecting his gift." Mullah Aziz had no intention of turning down free food.

"What paper do you write for?" Basheer asked Turab.

"I'm with the Globe Media Group, all platforms."

"Hmm. You guys are very vocal against everyone and everything. Very bold."

"Well, it might appear that way, but we believe in honest journalism," Turab replied, uneasy. He was sensing menace in Basheer's tone. As a journalist he was used to being threatened: phone calls, emails, letters, but face to face threats were a rarity. However, in a small town or "territory" such as this one, one had to be especially careful when faced with any threat, a big dog in a small town could do a lot of damage.

"Really? And who decides the nature and level of honesty in journalism?"

"I suppose it is the norms of society. They can be a good indicator of honesty in journalism, or for that matter, all aspects of life. What people want to know and why."

"You people in the media world have claimed a very high moral ground for yourselves without any justification. You think you're right and that everybody else is wrong, on every issue. You insist that society follow you instead of proper and established social values, and you are trying to define those values for all of us. You think just because you have the biggest megaphone, everybody else should just stay quiet and listen to you. Don't you think it's very condescending of you and insulting to the rest of us?" Basheer apparently had strong opinions about the recently freed media in this part of the world. Or his employer did, it was the same thing.

"I'm sorry that you feel that way, journalism is journalism and that's the way it..." Turab began to respond but stopped at the waving of Basheer's invasive opened hand in front of his face.

"You don't have to feel sorry for anything, if you believe that your point of view is right then you should simply say so. People can only be won over by the strength of the argument that you make, not by the justifications you present."

Turab decided that silence was the wisest course of action as the final destination of the argument was clearly an unknown, and most likely a troublesome one, it wasn't in his best interest to continue to debate the media's role and place in society, especially with a guard dog like Basheer who would do anything for his master—the likes of Sardar Timur. He wished he had the courage to confront the man about how much he was paid to speak for his master and what methods he used to win people over to his point of view.

"Now, you will be entrusted with the money for the Panchayat member's service. Do you know what that means?"

"Yes, I do. It means that I keep the money in my custody for now, and after the Panchayat has delivered justice, not injustice, I distribute it among the members."

"Yes, that is correct," Basheer said, toying with the gun he was holding. "You will distribute the money after Panchayat has rendered its decision, but, you can also *use* the money to nudge the Panchayat in the direction you wish them to take."

Turab paused, not sure if he heard correctly, was this a bribe? Was he being bluntly asked to use the money to influence the verdict? He decided to play along. "I'm not sure how to do that."

"I thought you were smart. You should be able to figure it out yourself. Why do I have to spell it out for you?"

"Are you suggesting that I should bribe people?"

"I wouldn't use that word, bribe, it's not a bribe, its money being put toward education. You need to let people know what's right and what's wrong. Sardar Timur is a respectable man, and when someone who feeds off of his generosity decides to threaten or test his honor, they just don't deserve any sympathy. Such a person should be dealt with severely. You're in the media so I have no doubt that you can communicate this effectively, and furthermore, I think you should use your skills to help restore Sardar Timur's honor. Try to make sure that this boy pays for his crime. If you have to use persuasion, then so be it. If you need to use the money to accomplish that goal, well, use the money we are going to trust you with for that purpose. Don't just *spend* the money, *use* it. *Use it wisely.* That's all I am saying. Understood?" Basheer started walking towards the door and by the time he was done with his speech he was through the door. He didn't look back. All three heard the man talk and all felt they knew what he was saying, or more accurately, not saying.

The next day began early with a surprise breakfast delivered to Mullah Aziz's house consisting of traditional *kulcha naan, puri, nihari, haleem, halwa,* and *lassi*. It was accompanied by two large fruit baskets and one large bag full of several new clothes for Mullah Aziz, his family, and Turab. If the purpose was to immerse Mullah Aziz's family in Sardar Timur's generosity, it was a success. He was unable to contain his delight, so much so that in his state of jubilation, he almost forgot how irritating he normally found his son and wife. This morning he didn't yell, he didn't growl and he didn't curse at his wife or his son. He saw Rauf rubbing his saded belly, and yawning from the exhaustion of devouring such a decadent breakfast. By the time they were done consuming the food, it was almost ten-thirty and time to meet the Panchayat members to learn about the incident, Basheer had instructed all the Panchayat candidates to gather in the large hall in the back of the mosque. At eleven sharp, Mullah Aziz was supposed to prepare and motivate them to "deliver justice" and to restore Sardar Timur's honor.

"I need tea with lots of sugar and make it dark, I need caffeine," Aziz told Rauf while burping. He blew out a burst of pungent air from his mouth "Tell your mother to make strong milk tea for all of us we can't afford to be sleepy or unfocused in the *Chopal*."

Rauf was readily agreeable and went inside without uttering a word. He came back after fifteen minutes with three large cups of steaming hot tea. They were now ready to start their day.

When they arrived, there was already a crowd waiting. Turab counted more than sixty people, the thirty who were selected the night before, and then eager spectators. Many people in the town were unemployed and on the lookout for some exciting activity to fill the empty minutes and hours and space in their lives and solitude in their hearts, so this whole event was thrilling, hence, the doubling in size.

"Shouldn't you get rid of all these extra people?" Turab asked Mullah Aziz.

"Why?"

"Because you are going to discuss the conduct of the Panchayat. Basheer or another Sardar Timur soldier will likely present evidence or testimony. If there are additional spectators here they'll get information not meant for them, and start leaking it. Don't you think that might jeopardize the outcome for this poor boy?"

"Ah, you worry too much over trivial matters," Mullah Aziz dismissed Turab's apprehensions. "If this was happening in a court of law, wouldn't there be spectators?"

"In court proceedings, yes, but any meetings before the trial are not open to the public."

"Well, this is not a court of law," Mullah Aziz replied. "This is better than the infidel court of law. The courts in this country still follow the legal procedures of infidels—ones they inherited from the time of British rule. Those rules are designed to delay the delivery of justice. Our system ensures swift delivery of justice, in the Islamic way. The way the Prophet, peace be upon him, and his followers used to. We don't follow the procedures of those infidel courts here. This is the place and time for Sharia law to be implemented, and in Sharia law, we cannot restrict the flow of information. Do you think the Prophet used to shut down the mosque when he was listening to disputes in the Madinah Mosque? No. Of course not!"

Turab was not in agreement. "Once again, this is not the actual trial or Panchayat proceedings. This is a meeting before the matter is actually considered, and I don't think that this should be open to the public. People tend to gossip, spread rumors, and base their decisions on nothing at all, and possibly on incorrect information! It will make it impossible to stay neutral and will ensure that this whole exercise is just a charade."

"I don't want to argue with you on how to conduct this matter Turab," Mullah Aziz dismissed him and moved on. "You're to receive the discussed money today so be prepared. What you get out of it depends on how cooperative you turn out to be, so if I were you, I'd decide carefully."

Mullah Aziz moved with definite and long strides towards the crowd. Turab and Rauf stood back and looked at each other's amazed faces. Rauf shrugged. Turab stared at his friend in disbelief from behind for a short while before following along.

It was time.

THIRTEEN

T HE BIG GREEN sign outside stated *Universal Bank* in white
partially faded letters. However, local people did not need to
read the board to know the name of the bank as it had been there for
so long. It was in a busy commercial area and it handled the financial
accounts of almost all the nearby businesses.

For the last twenty years, the bank had operated out of this
location, neighboring businesses had seen many managers come and
go. Usually, the branch managers were deputed by the head office for
a short period of time, just enough time to get acquainted with the
local business community. The head office preferred to keep certain
information away from the branch managers, they kept their distance,
so short and sweet training was the directive. The senior management
of the bank had been very careful in limiting the tenure of the managers
in this branch and many others like it to prevent personal relationships
from impacting business rules being upheld. However, something out
of the ordinary had happened in the last two years.

Besides being a popular and effective branch manager, Zain Malick
was also the longest-serving head of this branch, now in his third year
at the same location. This longevity allowed him a little bit of a longer
rope, enough to cultivate the personal relationships which were usually
well beyond the normal professional limits. He had developed deep
personal associations with the many business owners in the vicinity,

so much so that he had obtained access to their secret business deals, and secret stashes of cash which they had accumulated and hidden from the tax authorities or parked in charities, and accounts which only existed on paper. He had developed a system where he would help the trusted account holders who needed services beyond what the legal operations limit allowed, and in return, he would accept generous gifts and dutifully share those gifts with some influential people so all could benefit.

While he was very effective in generating gifts and very scrupulous in sharing those gifts, he had also generated other streams of income for himself which he did not share with anyone else in the bank. He did have to share that stream, but only to the extent that it was a necessary expense in keeping the stream flowing. It was not a usual occurrence, but the opportunity to cash in presented itself every so often. Today was one of those days.

The town was abuzz about an event at the Haveli of the most influential person in town. There was a lot of chatter about a boy who had been caught assaulting Sardar Timur's daughter, and the word was out that a Panchayat was being assembled. While the rumor mill was at work in full force, there was no mention of it yet in the only local newspaper, a copy of which was in Zain's hand. He had the paper right in front of his eyes while his other hand held a cup full of steaming dark brown milk tea. He took an occasional sip from the teacup without moving his eyes from the paper.

It was about nine-thirty a.m. and the lobby was empty. The bank usually started to get busy around ten-thirty or so when the shops and small businesses in the surrounding areas started to open for business. The staff of four was busy doing various necessary and unnecessary chores to make the branch look tidy and welcoming for the would-be customers.

The silence was broken. An electronic chime announced the automatic opening of the main door allowing two individuals to enter the branch. One of them was a boy roughly fifteen years of age, the other a grown man, perhaps in his mid-thirties, medium built, average height with a dense black beard. Zain looked at them through the large glass window of his office directly across from the branch entrance door. The boy looked familiar but the man accompanying the boy was a complete stranger. To the best of Zain's recollection, he had never seen this man in the branch or for that matter anywhere in this town. That was noteworthy as it was important for the security of the bank, and also for him, to take notice and remember everyone who visited the bank. Zain never missed an opportunity to seek an introduction with new faces. He flashed a warm smile when their eyes met for a brief moment, the adult customer smiled back and moved towards the teller counter, the boy's face was void of expression and he just followed the man.

Zain was paying attention to their actions while still appearing to be only reading the paper and sipping tea. He saw the teller holding a check which the man had presented, then saw the teller holding it up in the air in front of the bright light, then flipping it front to back. He then moved from behind his desk and starting walking towards Zain's office, which meant it must be a large check, all checks above ten thousand had to be approved for payment by the branch manager.

The teller entered Zain's office and placed the check on his desk. Zain read the amount: four million eight hundred thousand rupees.

"They want cash, and they want small bills."

"Do we have enough cash?"

"We do. But mostly in larger bills. If we give them all the small bills, we will definitely have some trouble for the entirety of the day and we won't be able to meet other customer demands."

"Just tell them we can only give larger bills," Zain suggested.

"I did. But they insist that they want small bills. They said they have to distribute funds to several people."

"Well, then let them know that they have to wait for a while before we can get them the bills they want."

"I did already and they are willing to wait."

"Problem solved. They wait. The boy looks familiar. Who is he?"

"His name is Rauf. He is the son of Mullah Aziz."

"And the man with him?"

"I don't know. I've never seen him." The teller picked the check back up and looked at it again while responding to Zain.

"Let me see the check again please," Zain extended his hand. It was simply a Pay Cash check without any payee named, therefore, any bearer of the check could cash it. The account holder was Sardar Timur, the most influential landlord, and "power player" in town. He wasn't anyone to cross or challenge. Zain looked at the check for several minutes, flipped it over to confirm that it was properly signed in the front by the account holder and in the back by the bearer of the check.

"Does it look like this boy may be in trouble?" Zain asked the teller.

"What do you mean, sir?"

"Remember that incident with Farooq Bukhari?" Zain replied. "Last year he was in the head office and cashed a check for a large amount. He had a person accompanying him, and then later Bukhari told the newspapers that they had kidnapped him, tied a bomb to his leg, and forcibly brought him to the bank to withdraw money from his account. He was forced to withdraw money from his account to pay ransom to his kidnappers. We don't want a similar event repeated in our branch."

"I can't say...that sounds confusing! It's really hard for me to tell."

"You said this boy is Rauf, Mullah Aziz's son? Why would Sardar Timur write a check of such an amount and had it over to this boy? This makes no sense."

"Should I call the police?" the teller asked.

"Not yet, let me make some phone calls. In the meantime, just tell them to wait. Tell them that we are processing their request and that the cash in small bills they want needs to come from our head office." The teller left with a respectful half-bow and gently closed the door behind him. Zain's gaze was fixed on the strange man and the boy as his hand reached for the telephone, tensing with excitement. He dialed a number without looking at the dial pad and waited for his call to be answered.

"There is going to be a lot of juice in one hour. A lot of juice," Zain almost whispered in the mouthpiece of the phone. "Make sure to leave a quarter for the carrier. Do you understand?"

"Yes," someone from the other side answered.

"Good. Don't mess up, I don't want a repeat of last time. I'm serious."

"How many bottles?'

"Four hundred and eighty."

"Okay."

Zain disconnected the call, then immediately started dialing another number. This time his call was to the head office for an extra cash dispatch, he was promised a prompt delivery. He decided it best to inform the teller and the mysterious clients himself, and so he summoned them into his office.

Earlier that day, Rauf had arrived in the Chopal with his father and Turab, he paced impatiently while waiting for Sardar Timur's man, Shujaa, and his entourage. Shujaa handed over a check to Turab in front of the would-be Panchayat members in order to appease, and assure them that the money was real. Mullah Aziz asked Shujaa why he was given a check instead of cash, but Shujaa chose to ignore the question and replied only by suggesting that the check could and should be cashed right away. Mullah Aziz and Turab conferred and decided to cash the check and distribute at least some of it, and it was decided that Rauf should be the one to go to the bank, accompanied by Assef, a new arrival in town.

Rauf had never held a check before, and he'd certainly never cashed one, in fact, he'd never been to a bank in his life. To add stress to the already tense situation he was ill at ease with this stranger, Assef. He'd seen him in the mosque but had never been introduced to him before today.

The trip to the bank was meant to be quick. However, it didn't turn out to be that way. All this was quite surreal. First, they waited in the lobby like sitting ducks, then after what seemed like an eternity they were summoned and led into the branch manager's office.

"Hello, gentlemen! I'm Zain Malick the branch manager, welcome to our bank." Rauf heard the man in the office with a large glass window say as they took seats in front of him. Zain looked at them for a moment expecting them to introduce themselves, but instead, they sat there, silently. Rauf couldn't make sense of the inquisitive look he saw in the branch manager's eyes, he didn't understand why this needed any questioning at all, this was a bank, they must see check-cashing customers all the time, why the special treatment?

"I'm curious to know how you got this check," Zain spoke after a brief pause. "It's for a very large amount and it's from Sardar Timur. What is this money for?"

Rauf was about to answer when Assef placed his big calloused hand over his mouth.

"We can't say, and it's not your concern."

Zain was startled to see this blatant display of authority. He looked at the teller with puzzled eyes, then turned his gaze towards Assef.

"His name is Rauf, Mullah Aziz's son, right?" Zain asked, just to confirm. Assef nodded. "And who are you?"

"My name is Assef," he replied bluntly. "I just moved here from up north."

"And why are you with him?" Zain asked. His suspicion was growing by the second. "What's the relationship?"

"No relationship," Assef replied in a cocky tone. "His father asked me to accompany him to the bank so he can cash the check."

"So the check was given to him?"

"Not really," Assef responded. "It was actually given to Turab."

"Who is Turab?"

"He is a journalist, quite well known and he's here in town visiting Mullah Aziz," Assef replied curtly, getting agitated with this questioning.

"Why would Sardar Timur write a check to a reporter from the city who is just visiting Mullah Aziz and then send you to cash it? It makes no sense."

"Look, you're a bank manager, not a police officer so what's with the interrogation? All you need to do is cash the check, it's your job. The check is properly signed, so stop asking questions that you have no business asking, and please get us our money."

"This is my business, and I think I should call the account holder. That is precisely the right way to do my job." Zain reached for the phone.

"It won't help." Assef forced Zain's hand away from the phone. "Sardar Timur will not answer any of your questions. He has nothing to do with this money once this check is cashed."

"So this is not his signature?" Zain asked pointing towards the check. "Are you saying he didn't sign it?"

"He did," Assef replied. "This is his signature. The check will go through. But if you were to question him about it, he will most likely decline to talk to you."

"And why is that?"

"I cannot answer that question, and if I were to answer the question, I would need to reveal what needs to be kept secret."

Zain looked at him with intense eyes for a long moment, and then let out a deep, loud sigh while rising from his chair.

"Here's what I think," he said. "I think that you have obtained this check improperly, and I'm going to compare the signature on this check with the signature card in our records before executing any transaction. You two stay here. If it so happens that this signature is forged, I'll call the police, and if you try to leave the bank, I will have you arrested. Do you understand?"

"And when the signature is verified?" Assef asked in a calm and calculating tone.

"Then you will get your cash, but I have to act with necessary precautions. Both of you need to stay here," Zain said and then motioned the teller to stay on guard while closing the office door behind him. Rauf heard the loud jingling of keys that alarmed him and he suddenly panicked and began to hyperventilate.

"What is the matter with you?" Assef asked angrily.

"Are we going to be arrested? Is he going to bring us to the police? I don't want to be arrested. Police are so very cruel and I know that they beat people up very severely. I know people who've been arrested and when they've returned some of them were without their hands or legs, and some had their ears cut off. Some cannot walk or talk properly and, I don't want–"

"Shut up! Rauf stop stammering and for God's sake behave like a man! Don't you dare cry like a little girl. Don't even think about it." Assef almost yelled at him.

Rauf started sobbing without any control, he'd lost all composure. Assef slapped him in hopes of shocking him out of this display of total hysteria. Then both heard the keys jingling. The door opened. Zain entered the door with a stern face and started wagging his finger in Assef's face.

"Get up," he commanded.

Assef didn't move. "Why?"

"You're just accompanying this boy, right. He's the one who was given the check right? That's what you said before."

"Yes."

"Well, I need to talk to him alone. So you need to get out of my office."

"I won't let you do that."

"This is my office and you'll do as I say."

"Make me," Assef dared him. Zain stood motionless for a few seconds before reaching for Rauf's hand and dragging him out of the office. By the time Assef realized what was happening, the office door was locked from outside and Rauf was getting pulled by Zain and taken to a windowless room.

"You'd better come clean, how did you get ahold of this check? Is this man forcing you to cash it or did you get it personally from Sardar Timur?"

"Don't call the police on me, for God's sake," Rauf begged. "I don't want to be crippled for the rest of my life."

"Then be honest and truthful with me. Tell me exactly how you got ahold of this check."

Rauf started talking and crying at the same time. Zain looked at him for a few moments and then like Assef, slapped him hard across his face. The crying stopped immediately, but the terror in Rauf's eyes grew more intense. Zain could see that he was at a breaking point.

"I cannot understand you if you cry and talk at the same time, so just talk. Be honest and straight with me. That is the only way I will spare you, otherwise, you leave me no choice but to either give you to the police or take you to Sardar Timur. Either way, you'll be in hell."

Rauf nodded his head and narrated all the related events of the last couple of days. Zain found the whole story far-fetched but may be plausible. Maybe. Once Rauf went quiet, Zain left him in the room to sulk. He paced in the lobby for a while, walking back and forth, again and again, fighting the gnawing feeling that warned him. The teller tried to talk to him but he signaled him to hush waving his hand in an agitated manner. Realizing his grave mistake, he decided to call off the attempt on the "juice" heist and rushed to the phone to dial the number he had used earlier. No answer. He kept trying but after a few failed attempts he began to feel a strong sense of consternation, he had miscalculated. Greed had birthed this newfound complacency. If the money really belonged to Sardar Timur and he was using it for the purpose Rauf described, then robbing Rauf of that money could become very dangerous, very quickly. Just the idea of stealing anything connected to Sardar Timur had his stomach in turmoil. If he was unable to get in touch with his contact it would be impossible to stop the robbery. Despite repeated and increasingly frantic attempts, he wasn't able to contact his source. Zain thought that perhaps today was payday. Today, he thought, he was going to be punished for his sins.

He had to think fast, as much as losing this battle was a real possibility he couldn't just roll over and play dead, he'd come too far. The most viable option at this stage in the game was to keep Rauf and Assef in the branch hidden until close to closing time. At that point, his source would hopefully come to the conclusion that the job was void. No client, no target. Or better yet, he could have the money directly delivered to wherever Rauf was going to take it, but the earliest he could arrange for a courier was later in the evening, and he was sure that sundown was too late. He kept pacing back and forth, calling the number again and again. The teller was observing him with inquisitive eyes full of suspicion.

"Call the head office and check on the status of cash delivery," Zain barked an order to divert the teller's attention. The teller nodded and walked back towards the cash counter where a small line of customers had already begun to form, all the other tellers were running late as usual.

Zain knew he had to think fast and act faster. So far his schemes had proven successful because he made sure that nothing could ever be traced back to him, and he also knew not to target those too powerful or too resourceful, like Sardar Timur. His strategy to target those who were financially strong, but otherwise weak, had always worked well for him, today he broke his own rules.

It had started about two years ago when he was approached by two men who looked respectable but had soon become rather quietly menacing. They told him that they initially wanted to rob the bank and the people in the bank, but then they came up with a better plan: instead of robbing people while they were in the branch, they would rob them outside the branch. Much cleaner and fewer variables could go wrong. They brought him in as their inside man, he was the one who would find the ideal target and orchestrate the heist. Zain would stay in his office and inform them about a withdrawal and hold the customer in the branch by stalling him or her for as long as necessary, then he would let them go once the team was near and in position. In order to minimize the looted customer's likelihood of reporting the crime, they usually took away no more than three-quarters of the cash available on the customer.

They took care to remind the victims that they were being deprived of only a portion of the money in exchange for their silence. They also threatened their safety and told them that they'd do well to keep quiet. Some did not get the message.

At first, Zain was worried that too many incidents like this would trigger an inquiry by the bank itself, if not by the police. The people who recruited him were eventually able to recruit others in positions of higher authority, so now, every robbery which occurred because of the tip given by Zain was shared with higher-ups as well.

This had been going on for a while and so far things were working out just fine. Now Zain was afraid. He'd made a mistake by informing his contacts about this transaction too early, he jumped the gun so to speak. The amount was large and the people presenting the check didn't appear to be worth that type of money, so it was very difficult, if not impossible, to pass up such a large sum. He now grimaced in remorse-haste. He should have realized that there was something out of the ordinary happening, and it would have been wise to have made the necessary inquiries first before tipping the contact.

Suddenly the branch's main door opened and armed uniformed guards walked through holding bags of cash. Zain saw Assef look at the guards and within seconds he was up trying to open the door which was locked from outside. Zain had no choice but to rush over and release him, there wasn't an alternative. Meanwhile, the cashier was busy counting the bills.

In less than fifteen minutes, Assef and Rauf were out of the bank and on the street with a big bag full of cash. Zain watched them through the floor to ceiling glass windows until they were off bank property. He knew what was about to happen and wished he could stop it, but the bell had rung and there was no way for him to un-ring it.

⌒

They left the bank around noon but didn't make it back until well after four. What happened in those hours was a hazy memory. Rauf remembered getting into the car and before getting in, he knew that he had placed the bag full of cash in the trunk. He knew that Assef had checked to make sure that the trunk was properly locked and he recalled sitting in the back seat since the front passenger side seat was occupied by some small, but heavy boxes that Assef didn't want to move. These were facts he could bet on.

Less than five minutes into their departure from the bank, two motorbikes started tailing them. Neither Rauf nor Assef realized what was happening until they saw the bikes flanking their car. One on each side blocking them. Each bike had two riders. Each rider wore a mask. The two rear-seat riders of each bike began knocking on the front windows of the car from each side, one tapping the driver window and the other the passenger window, then motioned Assef to pull over. He hesitated until one of them pointed his gun, he almost lost control of the car narrowly avoiding an electric pole. One of the motorbikes then sped up and maneuvered itself so that it was in front of the car giving them no option but to come to an abrupt stop. All four of them dismounted the two bikes and two walked towards their car with large knives. They sliced the driver's side front tire, opened the door, jiggled open the trunk, picked up the cash-filled bag, opened it, threw some blocks of cash toward Rauf, then put the remainder into their knapsacks and sped off.

Before leaving one of them circled around the car motioning Assef to roll down the window, and told him that they weren't taking all the money because they wanted him to stay quiet. He threatened Assef and told him that if he reported it to the police, he would be followed, deprived of the rest of the money, and worse. It had taken them less than ten minutes to complete the well-executed robbery.

"God damn it," Assef punched the steering wheel. "They took all the money. What are we going to tell the Panchayat?"

"They didn't take all," Rauf replied without thinking. "They threw some towards me."

"How much?"

"I don't know! Why don't you count it?" Rauf shouted back, his nerves were completely shot. Assef got out of the driver's seat and slid in the back seat beside Rauf and started counting.

"We have only one-quarter of what we had drawn from the bank."

Rauf now saw tears in Assef's eyes. "Why are you crying?"

"Don't you understand what will happen to us when we get back? I doubt Sardar Timur or his men will believe us. They're going to think that we are making up the whole robbery story and that we have stolen or hidden the cash. Who knows what will be done to us. Oh, God. Why did I agree to come with you? I should have refused. I should have let your father come to the bank with you. I'm finished. I'm finished! Who knows if they will even let me live! Oh, God. What have I done?"

Rauf hadn't thought of this. First, he thought Assef was overreacting. But then a heavy dose of fear gripped him too. He started shaking and couldn't stop, he had no control over his body. Suddenly his mouth was paper dry and the images in front of his eyes started to get blurry. Drops of sweat on his forehead were streaking down his eyelids. He felt sick to his stomach. "Should we just disappear?"

Assef looked at him in disbelief then shook his head. "No, we can't. We still have this money which we need to deliver to your father and that other guy," he said. "If we disappear they will definitely think we took off with all the money. Besides, they may even think that I kidnapped you since I just moved here! They'll believe anything bad about me. You are a kid who grew up in front of them. They should believe you. Right?"

Rauf thought for a second. "Yes. I think they'll believe me and I'll just tell them exactly what happened." Rauf spoke with renewed confidence. He had grown up among them, well, most of them, and he was the son of the Imam of the mosque. Of course, they would believe him. Why would he lie to them? He wouldn't. Absolutely not!

"I don't know. I really don't. Shit!" Assef was clearly nervous and Rauf's newfound confidence was not comforting him in any way.

"What do you not know?"

"I don't know if they will believe you. Money's a strange thing, Rauf, people don't even believe their own siblings when it comes to money."

Rauf could not discount his doubts. He could only hope that people would believe him, but then again there was always a possibility that they wouldn't. He realized that they had no choice but to return as soon as possible and let them know what happened. The longer they were absent, the more difficult it would become to convince Sardar Timur's men (or for that matter participants in the Panchayat process) that there actually was a robbery, and the money which would otherwise belong to them, was no more.

Assef opened the trunk in a daze, took out the spare tire, and with unsteady hands replaced the slashed one. The only noise to be heard was the deep bass like thumping of their hearts as they drove back in dread. There they all were, waiting in anticipation of riches, when they saw the car approach most of them stood and flocked around it, like black crows waiting to take. Mullah Aziz and Turab shoved through the dense crowd anxious to retrieve the money, indicating to the others to stay behind. Mullah Aziz was the first to speak, starting off with a customary complaint, this time about wasted time. Rauf however didn't waste any time at all as he attempted to get out of the car, tripping over himself, his legs rubbery and weak. He reached for Turab like a lifeboat, grabbed his arm, looked into his father's judging eyes, and told him the whole story.

When Mullah Aziz heard that only one-fourth of the expected amount of money was available he clenched Assef's hands and whispered, barely audible, directly in his ears. Assef's face turned ashen. Rauf was pushed out of the way by Turab and was left standing there holding the bag of cash, until he came back, took it from him, and then moved towards Mullah Aziz.

"Let's give them a little bit of money so they can be mollified and start working towards the task at hand," Turab whispered in Mullah Aziz's ears. Mullah Aziz agreed.

"Listen up everybody," Turab announced. "You'll be paid in three phases: some now in order to get started, more in the midst of the process, and lastly the final payment after the verdict has been carried out. Do not worry! Whoever participates in this Panchayat will get paid! Take the cash. Go home and please come back tomorrow."

Turab started distributing the cash and Mullah Aziz observed, watching the participants' facial expressions and overall body language in the hopes of singling out any potential trouble makers. The initial takers appeared to be happy and thankful for whatever they were being paid. As the line of people waiting to get paid shortened, he relaxed and started breathing normally. It was hard to believe that in the group of thirty diverse people, there wasn't one problematic participant. Then, his fears turned into reality. Like every group, there was bound to be that one, that oddball, and as predicted he surfaced toward the end.

"Maulana Sahib," said an old man as he counted the money and then approached Mullah Aziz. "Is this all we are going to get?"

"No," Turab jumped in the conversation. "As I just said this is the first phase, it's a token of our gratitude, consider it a down payment of sorts. You will get more."

"How much?" the old man asked loudly enough for others to hear.

"I can't say exactly," Turab responded. "It all depends on how much is allocated for this purpose."

"Allocated by whom?" the old man asked again.

"You don't know?"

"How am I supposed to know?" the old man questioned back, sounding equally surprised.

"Were you not in the mosque last night, when Basheer came and spoke to us all?" Mullah Aziz asked.

"Oh, that man. Yes, I was in the mosque. I heard him. Is he from the government? Really?"

Before Mullah Aziz or Turab could respond someone from the crowd shouted out, "Yes. He is from the government." A few of the others nodded and agreed with the shouter.

Turab looked deeply into the old man's eyes and then nodded with a warm, broad smile on his face. This seemed like the best way to handle the situation—go along with what half of them believed anyway.

"Yes, the money is coming from the government," Turab agreed with the old man. "And you know how government works: they are never on time, they are always lagging behind, but eventually we will get the money." The old man made a sound that was either a chuckle or a snicker. Turab could not decide if he was actually pleased or being sarcastic about government inefficiency. The way Turab saw it, he hadn't lied: Sardar Timur was the almighty in this region, so really he was the unofficial government.

The old man walked away seemingly satisfied while putting the cash in his pocket. The next person in the line moved forward with his hand extended. Turab put cash in his hand. He started counting, slowly.

"Can you move to the side and count your money there?" The second man couldn't contain himself and spoke loudly and aggressively in the first man's ear while tapping his shoulder.

"Don't tell me what to do," the first man replied, in a sharp tone.

"Okay. Then I will move to the side." The second man took two steps sideways and one step forward. He was now standing diagonally from Turab with an extended hand. Turab exchanged stares with Mullah Aziz, who gave a faint smile and then put cash on the man's hand.

"What does the government have to do with a shortage of cash?" the second man asked. "Isn't the money coming from this man Shujaa? And he works for Sardar Timur."

"Here he is," Mullah Aziz thought while letting out a deep sigh. "The troublemaker, just when I thought this group was going to be easy to handle. I hope Turab can answer him satisfactorily."

"Well, nothing directly," Turab said in a calm tone.

"What do you mean? You just said that to the other man."

"I mean, there was not enough cash in the bank today, they didn't have what we needed so they have to wait for a transfer of funds. Therefore, we are handing out part of the compensation you should expect for your services."

"When will you pay the rest?"

"Very soon," Turab said, "Don't worry. You will get all of your money in no time at all, every penny as they say!"

"Okay," the man said. "How much will you pay?"

"I'll let you know once Shujaa tells us how much Sardar Timur is planning to pay."

"Okay, if you say so." The man nodded his head, quickly counted the money in his hands, and walked away. Both Turab and Mullah Aziz were relieved, fortunately, the last few people in line didn't ask any questions because they were running out of answers, fast. Once the hall was empty, Mullah Aziz turned to Rauf and Assef.

"We have a problem," he said in a sharp and worried tone. "Both of you caused it. Now you will have to find a way out."

They had no answer except empty stares.

"Now tell us again exactly what happened. Don't leave any detail out. Start from the moment I gave you the check until the time when you came back here. I want every little detail. And you will do it individually. First Rauf and then Assef. Separately," Turab told them, his reporter instinct on alert.

They each narrated the events and then were questioned together. Mullah Aziz and Turab listened without interrupting.

"Did you see the robber's faces?"

"Kind of. They had the masks on though, but we will still be able to recognize them. Their masks were not covering their faces much." both replied.

"Good," Mullah Aziz said in an uncertain tone. He was not certain if this fact was likely to be helpful, but it couldn't hurt, either.

"What are you thinking?" Turab asked.

"We need to inform the police," Mullah Aziz replied.

"No. They were very clear about this. We were told not to communicate with the police," Assef protested.

"The police chief in this town was my student at one time. I'm going to ask him to look into this matter quietly and unofficially," Mullah Aziz replied and moved forward, not interested in their response or comments.

FOURTEEN

B EHZAD KHAN WAS the Station House Officer of the only police station within a sixty-mile radius. The area was remote. With its administrative center in the small town of Ahmadabad, the greater district under his watch was home to about fifty thousand people, and the police force to serve these people was very small and for all intents and purposes impoverished.

He was a proud servant of the country's historically ill-equipped, ill-trained, ill funded but very influential and highly profitable police department. Profitable for those who joined the force and were posted in affluent areas, not something he had experienced in his fifteen years. For the most part, the police department was rife with inefficiencies and corruption, but his station was slightly less corrupt than others. Not because of a lack of desire, but due to a lack of opportunity. The spread of corruption was like water. Just like heavy rains do not cause a flood in all areas, heavy tendencies of corruption did not corrupt everyone in the force. Just as water flows downstream, the spread of corruption mostly occurred in the areas which were populated and more developed, allowing for more possibilities of graft and personal gain.

Places like Ahmedabad were for the most part quiet. Not much happened, and the economic standing of the community was fairly low. But in such places, abuse of power and influence was a problem much greater than corruption. When Behzad Khan joined the force he didn't have any desire to play the dirty game of influence, power, and all things illicit. He wasn't political. His goal was to stay clean and to rise above all things that led to immense gain, illegally. In the initial years of his service with the force, he was transferred to many places in very quick succession, but since he did not jockey or push for a posting in well-endowed, desirable areas, he ended up in Ahmadabad and ended up serving here for the last ten years.

While the police force as a whole was strapped for resources, those who were serving remote areas like Ahmadabad were strikingly starved. In the last eight of ten years, conditions had deteriorated even further. However, due to the shortage of funds, nobody bothered him either and he maintained law and order in his own peculiar way. Behzad Khan was not unhappy, quite the opposite, he was simply content.

There was an obvious shift in the local dynamic that could be attributed to a particular superpower next door flexing its muscles, its mighty military force and accompanying resources were hard to compete with. In order to keep an eye on the cross border movement of undesirable elements, the so-called superpower suggested that local police should be provided additional support and equipment. When the new budgets for police resource allocation came through, it felt as if a floodgate of money had somehow opened. In his fifteen years on the force, he had never seen such a dramatic influx of accessible cash.

The money was not the only difference, with additional resources came the introduction of checks and balances and emphasis on proper resource allocation and accounting of those resources. The superpower was willing to shell out funds but also wanted to ensure that the cow would not be milked unnecessarily and unfairly, which turned out to be a blessing. The physical structure for the police force was built with skill and superb materials and the money allocated for equipment and training was well spent.

And then the political and security situation changed quite fundamentally, apparently, the threat of undesirable elements moved to a different part of the neighboring country. And with that, the focus of the forces keeping an eye on such characters also shifted. Budget cuts were introduced and the ability to purchase additional equipment was no longer an option. The status quo crept back close to what it had been.

Behzad Khan and other officers alike were pleased that this short-lived boom and attention to their town resulted in better infrastructure for the police and armed forces: roads were developed and they were provided with better communication equipment and vehicles, making it easier to provide security services to far off areas with a smaller force. However, the shortage of uniformed men was still an issue. Behzad Khan was reminded of the lack of human resources when he arrived at the Station House every day between noon and one pm.

Aside from two sentries who guarded the entrance, he was never sure who he would find in the building and who would be missing, either out on official business or running personal errands. Today was notably different in that respect. It was about twelve forty in the afternoon when he arrived at the Station House, and the first thing he noticed was the absence of one sentry from the front door, leaving only one to guard the entrance.

"Where is Shahbaz?" Behzad asked the sentry.

"He didn't show up today. I don't know where he is, sir." The sentry shrugged his shoulders without looking at him, staring straight ahead, though not watching anything in particular.

"If he shows up, send him to me immediately."

Once inside, he took his usual tour of the building. There were several offices which were furnished but unused, offices which were being used were mostly empty, as apparently, the officers who used them were out in the field. The detention rooms housed a few individuals locked up for minor criminal infractions. Behzad checked them on the wall of monitors that were prominently positioned in the observation room where two officers were present. The room was required to be staffed constantly. After confirming that everything was under control he headed towards his own office, where his minion saluted him upon first sight.

"Your tea will be ready in two minutes, sir," and he really was back within two minutes with a hot cup of tea. As he was placing the cup on the coaster, the buzzer on the table sounded. The person on the other end told Behzad that he had two visitors, a Mullah Aziz and some news reporter from out of town. Behzad had known Mullah Aziz for a long time, for a brief period he had been an instructor at the police academy. He allowed the visitors in the building.

"Go get Mullah Aziz and his companion from the visitor's lounge." It took less than five minutes for his assistant to return with the visitors.

"We have a problem," Mullah Aziz came to the point right away. "I am not sure if I should discuss this with you as a police officer, or in the context of my personal relationship with you."

"I have to know the problem first before I can agree on either option."

"Okay. Can we do it privately?" Mullah Aziz said, with a brief and pointed look at the lower-ranking man.

"Sure," Behzad signaled the peon to leave. "Go ahead. You have your privacy now. What's on your mind?"

"I am sure you know about the situation at Sardar Timur's Haveli recently," Mullah Aziz began.

"No, actually I do not. What situation are you talking about?" Behzad truly had no idea, which both perplexed and annoyed him.

"Oh, I see, then I have to tell you the background events first before I come to the problem that I'm here to discuss." Mullah Aziz looked at Turab's face for a moment before speaking. Turab nodded.

"Here's what happened," Mullah Aziz cleared his throat and began his soliloquy. He could see that he had Behzad Khan's undivided attention. It took him almost thirty minutes to describe the events at the Haveli, as he knew them, in absolute detail. Behzad did not interrupt even once, listening closely and with keen interest. Turab was impressed with Behzad's ability to listen with true patience and complete attention, especially since Mullah Aziz constantly threw in commentary expressing his own opinion on practically each and every point.

"Is that all?" Behzad asked after Mullah Aziz went quiet. "Are you done with your story?"

"Yes," Mullah Aziz responded. "But it's not a story. It really happened."

"I believe you," Behzad replied. "I am not calling your narrative a fictional story, I simply meant to ask if you are finished telling me all that you'd like to report."

"Okay," Mullah Aziz responded. "Yes. I am done telling you all that I have to say."

"Do you have anything to add?" Behzad asked Turab.

"No," Turab responded. "I think Mullah Aziz has given you all the pertinent information."

"Why *are* you here by the way? What brought you to this nowhere ghost town from your busy life?"

Mullah Aziz felt a pinch in his gut, realizing he had not mentioned his meeting with the Army Captain, and wanted to keep the information shielded, just as the Captain had asked him to do. That was the only reason that Turab was involved in the first place, but surely it was irrelevant information in this matter. He only hoped that Turab wouldn't mention it.

"Well, I've known Mullah Aziz for what seems like an eternity, a long time, and I came to see him and to spend time with the family." Turab was calmly matter of fact and convincing. "No particular reason, just a visit that was long overdue."

"Is that right?" Behzad asked with a curious stare at Mullah Aziz's face.

"That is correct. He visits me from time to time, a good family friend."

"Okay," Behzad said, suspicion still lingering in his tone.

Mullah Aziz and Turab stayed quiet. Behzad stared at them for a brief moment before clearing his throat and spoke again. "You know that holding such Panchayat sessions is illegal."

They remained silent. Turab knew that such sessions were considered a parallel legal system, which was not permissible under the law of the land. But like so many other laws which were routinely violated, the prohibition against Panchayats was never enforced. In a society where people were not willing to obey even the traffic laws, violation of any law was not only possible but actively promoted by powerful people who considered it beneath themselves to follow the law in the first place. They saw their ability to violate the law as an indicator of their social superiority. In such a society, rooting out or trying to abolish a parallel legal system which had its basis in long-held traditions, was next to impossible. In that scenario, even if Mullah Aziz knew about the illegality of the system, he was willing to ignore it.

"And you are sitting here, telling me that you willingly participated in this illegal activity and continue to do so?" Behzad spoke again. His tone was soft but firm and his expression conveyed the message that he was unwilling to tolerate any nonsense.

"I just wanted to give you background information so we can tell you what we need from you," Mullah Aziz answered.

"Slow down we'll get to that in a minute, first I need to hear exactly how you define your role within this Panchayat business? What have you already done?"

"I don't have any so-called role in this and I haven't done anything." Mullah Aziz could not control himself.

"Nothing? You did nothing? Is that right? You really expect me to believe that?"

"It's the truth," Turab said. "Because the actual Panchayat session has not even begun yet."

"When will it begin?" Behzad asked.

"Most likely tomorrow, or if it is delayed again then the day after at the latest." This time Mullah Aziz spoke.

"Okay, well we may end up arresting everybody if there is a verdict resulting in some kind of punishment. You know how sensitive the government is about these Panchayat sessions these days because of…" Behzad left the sentence incomplete.

"Well, I don't know if there will be a verdict," Mullah Aziz said. Turab looked at him with surprise.

"What do you mean?" Behzad spoke with amazement.

"If people don't get the money, they may not even participate in the Panchayat."

"Money?" Behzad asked with a deeper surprise in his tone. "What money?"

Aziz and Turab looked at each other, wondering how this police officer could be so ignorant.

"That's why we are here," Mullah Aziz shifted in his chair. "You see this person Basheer, who works for Sardar Timur, came to the mosque and made an announcement to tell people about the Panchayat.

Several people signed up. Then he told everyone that they would be paid and that he would have the money delivered the next day. Instead of the expected cash, they sent a check, so, I sent my son and another person from the mosque to the bank to cash it. First, the branch manager gave them a little bit of a hard time, he grilled them, apparently, he was sure that they had stolen the check. He then locked them in separate rooms, and questioned my son threatening to hand him over to the police."

"Come to think of it in hindsight it would have been better if he had been delivered to the police," Turab interrupted him.

"Ah yes, maybe," Mullah Aziz looked at Turab's face for a brief moment and then spoke almost in a daze. "That didn't occur to me."

"Anyway go on," Behzad spoke.

"So, he questioned them thoroughly, and when they told him what the money was for, he cashed the check and let them go," Mullah Aziz continued.

"And this money was for Panchayat members, correct?" Behzad Khan reconfirmed.

"Yes," Turab said. "I was put in charge of the money. Sardar's man told me to not just spend it, but to *use it*."

"Okay," Behzad Khan whistled. "Sounds like he wanted you to use the money to manipulate Panchayat

behavior. A straight out bribe."

"Well of course he didn't say it in so many words, but I understood it to mean that I should reward people for a verdict he wanted on behalf of Sardar Timur. So yes, a bribe."

"Okay," Behzad Khan whistled again. "So why do you think that there will be no verdict?"

"Because the money we were going to use for this purpose is gone," Mullah Aziz blurted out. "My son and Assef, the other man I sent with him to the bank, they were robbed when they left the bank with all the cash in their possession. The robbers took all the money except about one-quarter of it. They said they were leaving them with some of it as an incentive to keep their mouths shut, and if they told anybody about the robbery, they would come and take away the rest of the money too and God knows what else."

"So why are you reporting it?" Behzad Khan asked. "Aren't you afraid you may lose the remaining amount also?"

"Well no, because we don't have it anymore," Mullah Aziz said. "We already distributed it to all the Panchayat members."

"Okay, so they must be happy," Behzad Khan said. "I'm sure they will do their part of the bargain, but this does complicate matters."

"Except that they know that what they have received is only a partial payment. They are expecting a lot more. Besides, this other guy Shujaa will want to know who is getting how much and as a result, voting which way. He would figure out that only a percentage of the money has been distributed. He will think that we stole the money and tell Sardar Timur exactly that! We then will face severe consequences. Besides, shouldn't you be interested in arresting them?"

"Well, of course, I'm interested," Behzad replied. "Did your son and that other person, Assef, did they get a good look? Do you think they might be able to recognize them?"

"They might. They wore masks, though," Mullah Aziz replied.

"Why didn't you bring them with you, so they could recount the story?" Behzad Khan asked with curiosity in his tone.

"My son is terrified, he didn't want to come because he thinks that he is being watched and he's too scared to come here."

"And the other person, what did you say his name was, Assef?" Behzad asked.

"Same thing. Besides, I have no control over him. I can't force him to come here."

"You know his address?"

"Yes."

"Good, I am going to need all information pertaining to him, to all things Assef. Tell me this, was the check written on an account with Universal Bank?"

"I think so. I didn't look at the check very carefully."

"Call your son and ask him. In fact, let me talk to him."

Mullah Aziz called home. Rauf answered Behzad's questions, then Behzad terminated the call.

"This is the third robbery of Universal Bank's customers in the last two months," Behzad said thoughtfully.

"Oh, so you think this group is targeting that particular bank?" Turab asked.

"Or they are being encouraged to target the bank customers," Behzad said in a thoughtful voice. "Especially this one particular branch."

"Why this particular branch?"

"You're a reporter. Can you not deduce from my words and my tone what I'm telling you? Or that which I'm not telling?"

Turab's face turned red. "You mean someone from inside the branch is informing the robbers that a customer may be walking out of the branch with lots of cash? An inside man?"

"Now you get it," Behzad said with a smile. Turab couldn't tell if the smile was real or was intended as another insulting gesture.

"If you suspect someone from the branch in cahoots with this crew, then why don't you take action against the culprit? You have the authority and he's a person of interest."

"Yes, I have the authority," Behzad replied curtly. "We are after him— the branch manager Zain Malick. Good thing that you came to report this. Other victims did not do the same but we'd heard rumors about the previous robberies, so, we are already monitoring him."

"Amazing. You just cannot trust anybody with your money these days, or anything else, for that matter."

Turab was in deep thought. It made perfect sense. The branch manager or any other employee who was handling cash for a customer could easily pass on sensitive information about who would be carrying a large amount of currency. The co-conspirators would either have to be somewhere close, to stop and rob the customer or, the customer had to be held back long enough to let the robbers come close to the branch, where they would have the perfect opportunity for the theft. It was exactly what happened with Rauf and Assef, apparently, the branch manager wanted to hold them back long enough so his men could reach the vicinity of the branch, and only then did he allow Rauf and Assef to leave.

"What are you going to do about it now?" Aziz asked Behzad.

"We'll set a trap," he replied. "This will be the easiest way to get the manager to act, and we'll nab everybody at the same time. For that, I am going to use the two of you."

"Us?" Turab asked.

"Yes, you and Mullah Aziz here."

"I really don't feel comfortable doing this," Turab said.

"You don't have a choice. You will either cooperate with me or I will arrest you for illegally facilitating Panchayat sessions."

"You can't arrest us without any evidence," Turab said.

"You have already admitted to the commission of a crime," Behzad said with a smile. He was having fun with Turab's apparent and unexpected naivety. "You admitted your criminal act in front of a police officer, and, I will declare it as an affidavit. That will more than suffice in a court of law. Even if you get off the hook later, it will be enough to have you arrested for now."

They exchanged firm stares for several seconds. Eventually, Turab gave in and looked away. Behzad Khan kept smiling.

FIFTEEN

ZARA BIBI COULDN'T sleep. She kept pacing back and forth in the front courtyard of her tiny mud-brick home. The structure was nothing more than four walls of half-baked bricks made in the local kiln, joined together using substandard mortar which needed constant repair, especially after heavy rain. Bricks would fall off when the rainwater seeped into the mortar, and in long spells of hot dry weather the bricks would chip off. It was a constant struggle to keep the walls standing.

The occupants of this home and others alike didn't really care much, wall or no wall they knew the weather was not their biggest concern. Their well-being resided in the hands of their employer Sardar Timur Barlas. If he was happy with them, they were safe. If he was unhappy, the walls didn't mean much. His men could easily enter and treat them as they pleased. Even if the walls gave a false sense of security it was still home.

Today, home felt like a grave.

Neither her daughter nor her son would return home today. She was hoping for a miracle but knew that was nothing more than wishful thinking. She was hard-pressed to remember having a truly contented day in her entire married life, except maybe the day Gul was born. She was accustomed to bad treatment and understood the illusion of initial kindness. She knew that it was a temporary thing and that it was only a matter of time before that kindness would transform into something darker. This day was especially dark, and the next promised worse.

She had come back from the Haveli after dark with Shams, the previous day. He was crying when they left. On the walk back home, he started questioning her about the day's events, and very soon he came to the conclusion that she was to blame. If she had not taken Gul to the Haveli in the first place, or told him very strictly to not enter the Haveli, all this could have been prevented. He was also enraged with her for allowing Badri to attend school. Everything about their life was in disarray and according to Shams, she was fully at fault.

Today, they both had stayed home all day until night fell. She had prayed *Isha* behind her husband and then they both prayed for their children's safety. She was not sure how they were going to be safe, that word seemed foreign and any attempt seemed futile, but her faith in *Allah* pushed her into submission. After prayer, Shams fell asleep, she could not, it was an impossible feat that felt selfish and sinful, considering where her children were at that exact moment. Sleep wasn't even in the realm of possibility. She continued to recite prayers while impatiently pacing back and forth in the open courtyard, wanting to die.

Suddenly–a loud knock on the door. Her first reaction which was usually correct was fear. She felt prickly chills run from one end of her spine to the other. She shuddered and looked towards Shams who was still fast asleep. She couldn't comprehend how this man, her husband, and father of her children, could find peaceful rest.

The knocking on the door was unforgiving. She hesitated for a moment but realized that she wouldn't be able to prevent them from entering, and really, what more did she have to fear? Nothing worse could happen to her tonight. She opened the door with false bravado and faced the two men standing outside head-on. She heard the soft purring of an automobile engine running at a short distance, and the rays of light from headlights shined brightly in the otherwise deserted street.

She recognized Rahim, but the other stone-faced man wasn't familiar.

"You need to come with us," Rahim commanded in a harsh tone.

"Where? Why?" Zara Bibi asked, realizing the futility of the question after she spoke. They worked for Sardar Timur. They surely would take her to him.

"Don't ask questions. Just do as you are told. Where is Shams? He needs to come with us, too."

The person with Rahim did not wait for a response, he simply entered the house and walked towards the back room where Shams was sleeping. He violently shook Shams by the shoulder, almost throwing him off his bed. The two men pulled him out of the room, practically kicked the both of them out of their tiny hut-like home, and threw them in the black SUV, which impatiently started moving.

On the way to the feared destination, Rahim kept talking to someone on his phone. Zara Bibi heard the name Mullah Aziz several times, although she couldn't hear the person on the other end. From what she heard, she could only gather that Mullah Aziz and his wife were also wanted by Sardar Timur. She couldn't understand what was happening, her mind raced as they pulled up to Sardar Timur's lavish compound surrounded by deep yellow stucco walls and a series of small walkway-pathway gates throughout the perimeter. Rahim mumbled into an intercom at the entrance of the looming iron gates, which opened like magic. On any other night or any other occasion, this would have been an opportunity not to be missed, an invitation to the great sprawling palace of the powerful Sardar Timur. But this time wasn't like any other of her back-breaking working days as a maid. This was the night that her family might be forever gone. Far from a great lavish paradise, it was an executioner's private war zone.

When Shujaa entered the night-filled dimly lit vast sitting room surrounded by open glass doors, he felt an odd sense of tranquility which was harshly contradicted by the turbulence and severity of the moment. He saw the full moon through the open doors, and on the other side of the door was a wide and long balcony, one of many. He saw Sardar Timur walking on that balcony, back and forth. Two servants trailed behind him holding the hookah. Shujaa stood in the middle of the quiet room for a few moments watching, trying to figure out the best moment to interrupt. He saw Sardar Timur suck the smoke through the long pipe. The noise that came from hot water in the base of the hookah, familiar and unmistakable.

Sardar Timur noticed Shujaa moments ago but preferred to always establish an alpha dominance by keeping his men questioning and waiting. Timur's motioning the house servants to leave was Shujaa's cue. He rushed towards the door, shut it tight, and stood quietly waiting for a directive. Finally, after a brief silence, the omnipotent Sardar Timur gestured for him to speak.

"Panchayat is ready Sardar Timur," his tone firm but respectful. "Mullah Aziz is in charge. He understands what we expect him to do."

"And the money?"

"Done."

"Good, let's make an example out of this little rat."

"That's what will happen tomorrow, everybody is ready for that."

"I've sent Basheer to fetch Mullah Aziz and his wife, you'll need to hang around until I'm done with them."

"Why his wife sir?" Shujaa asked.

"You'll see. Now wait outside and stay there. I'll let you know when you are needed again."

Shujaa left the room soundlessly leaving Sardar Timur to stare out at the full moon that he believed belonged only to him, while he planned his next move.

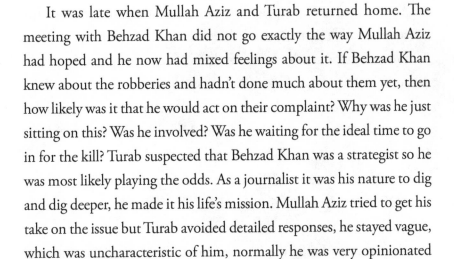

It was late when Mullah Aziz and Turab returned home. The meeting with Behzad Khan did not go exactly the way Mullah Aziz had hoped and he now had mixed feelings about it. If Behzad Khan knew about the robberies and hadn't done much about them yet, then how likely was it that he would act on their complaint? Why was he just sitting on this? Was he involved? Was he waiting for the ideal time to go in for the kill? Turab suspected that Behzad Khan was a strategist so he was most likely playing the odds. As a journalist it was his nature to dig and dig deeper, he made it his life's mission. Mullah Aziz tried to get his take on the issue but Turab avoided detailed responses, he stayed vague, which was uncharacteristic of him, normally he was very opinionated and didn't hesitate to share his thoughts. He wasn't feeling very trusting.

For Turab, this had the potential of a great story, a sizzling scandal perhaps. An influential landlord–someone very close to the Chief Minister of the province–actively involved in running a parallel justice system! Not only that, he was actively trying to influence it by bribing the members. However, Behzad Khan had trapped them, or more accurately, they built the trap themselves and then happily and blindly walked into it.

They had admitted to voluntarily and knowingly helping Sardar Timur to conduct the illegal Panchayat session. They were not simple, illiterate people who could argue a lack of knowledge or understanding about what was going on. In fact, they had admitted their role in helping Sardar Timur break the law to run his own court where he was going to try the accused, and they had bribed the members of the illegal Panchayat to get the desired verdict.

The robbery was an added complication. Now that it had been reported to the police there was no turning back. Even if they had not reported it to the police, they had to let Shujaa know about it. How else would they be able to explain the lack of funds distributed?

Both men were deep in thought when they returned to the mosque. Mullah Aziz noticed three black SUVs waiting, engines humming, just outside the main door of the mosque. *Isha* prayer was over about an hour ago. There was no chance that these SUVs belonged to people gathered to pray. Mullah Aziz recalled his meeting with the army captain in similar vehicles and he suddenly felt sick.

"You look concerned," Turab was watching Mullah Aziz's face.

"Of course I am," Aziz said. Turab heard more than a hint of irritation in his voice.

"These must be Sardar Timur's men," Turab said in a hopeful voice. He didn't want to imagine visitors with worse intent. It was always possible, even if unlikely.

"Let's find out," Aziz parked his pale blue van and walked towards the ominous black vehicles. Turab followed. As Aziz approached the gate of the mosque, he saw the driver's side front door of one of the SUVs open, and a man stepped out. He was in plain clothes, not a uniform. Mullah Aziz sighed with relief. He recognized Basheer.

"Mullah Aziz," the man asked politely but in a firm voice. "You and your wife need to come with us. Sardar Timur wants to see you both."

"Why my wife?" Aziz asked.

"I don't know, not my business. Sardar Timur or Sarah Khanum will explain it all I'm just following orders. We are just here to pick you up, actually, we just arrived and were about to knock on your door but here you are! Why are you out so late at night? Where did you go at this hour?"

Mullah Aziz was not at all ready for this aggressive line of questioning and he knew full well that he wouldn't be able to come up with a convincing answer. Turab thankfully intervened and told Basheer that they were looking at sites for a possible documentary on historical sites and culture. Turab also told him that he was here to hunt, and night time was the ideal time to go around quietly without distraction.

"Go get your wife, please. We need to leave immediately. Sardar Timur does not like to wait for anyone, and this has already taken too long."

"Okay," Mullah Aziz nodded. "Can my friend Turab come with us?"

"Who is he, again?"

"He's a news reporter from the city."

"No, he cannot come. I was told to bring you and your wife only. Nobody else is allowed."

"Don't worry," Turab spoke before Mullah Aziz could utter a word. "Somebody has to stay with Rauf."

"Okay," Aziz said and walked towards his home. Turab followed. Once past the mosque's boundary, they saw a woman standing in front of the door of Mullah Aziz's house, he recognized her as one of the maids who worked in Sardar Timur's Haveli. She had apparently already talked to Paro, because when he entered the small courtyard, Paro was coming out of the bedroom. She was clad in a black burqa, fully covered from head to toe, but still, she turned around and immediately went back into the bedroom when she saw Turab behind Aziz.

Turab had witnessed this behavior many times, not just by Paro but many other women who observed strict purdah. These women behaved as if even the head to toe covering was not enough, but only when in front of men they already knew. When these women went to the bazaar or walked on the street, they had no desire to hide from the strangers all around them. This special treatment was reserved for acquaintances only. Turab smiled to himself but only out of respect, and immediately walked towards the other room. As soon as he disappeared behind the door of the other room, he heard Paro's gentle footsteps walking towards the exit door. She left with the maid and Mullah Aziz. Once Turab and Rauf heard the vehicles drive away they exhaled.

Paro quietly sat next to her husband whose gnawing curiosity prevented him from sitting still, but regardless of his fidgeting, she kept her head turned towards him. Unwavering. Her face wasn't visible, but he knew he would have seen all the signs of panic, eyes full of questions. He could feel it. He leaned forward and asked the driver what was happening, but he didn't reply, feigning an inability to hear. Aziz at that point decided to stay quiet but Paro kept staring at him as if prodding him into speaking. He ignored her by looking straight ahead. She pinched his leg, an easily concealed motion such as a pinch, was the only thing she could get away with without being spotted by Sardar Timur's man in the front seat. He repeated the question to the driver but still failed to get any response. Paro waited for a few minutes, and then impatiently dug her nails into his thigh.

"Stop it," he said in a hushed angry tone. "We'll find out once we are at the Haveli. Why don't you just wait? And don't touch me again. I don't like it." The rest of the drive to the Haveli was silent except for the repetitive sound of the rotating tires. Strong winds jolted the vehicle left to right as it went through the dark narrow roads guided by determined headlights.

They arrived at the compound faster than they might have liked, fear of entering the devil's lair was foremost on their minds, but never voiced. It was their first time inside this Haveli, they waited obediently absorbing all that they noticed from the entry point, to where they now stood in wait and awe at the grandeur. The ornate and substantial iron entrance gate required the efforts of two statuesque guards. Once inside, they found themselves in a room with steps leading to a long, dimly lit corridor with a milky white tile floor, which was spotless and reflected lights of different colors from recessed lights, seeming to part the floor in the middle. The maid walked slightly ahead of them, her footsteps the only sound in the otherwise totally silent space. She impatiently signaled them to keep walking. At the end of the corridor, they took a short flight of stairs leading down and then immediately turned right to enter into a room which in its décor looked like an office. The room was empty.

"Have a seat," the maid said, in a surly tone.

"Will it be long?" Paro asked. "My son is alone at home."

The maid gave Paro a long empty stare, shook her head dismissively, and turned towards Mullah Aziz. "Sardar Timur will come soon," she said to him while ignoring Paro. "Don't bother him with petty details about your home or a child waiting there for you, all alone and miserable. Nobody cares, and he has no time for such trivia."

Before Mullah Aziz could respond, the maid spun around on her heels and left the room. No refreshments were offered.

"Who does she think she is?" Paro muttered.

"Doesn't matter what she thinks of herself," Aziz replied. "One thing's for sure, she doesn't think much of you or even me!"

"This is ridiculous," Paro said. "She thinks she is better than us just because she works in this Haveli."

"Those who are small and shallow inside, make the most noise." He had seen many such characters, people who were insignificant in every sense of the word, suddenly became big-headed and arrogant when they associated with the rich and the powerful merely because they worked for them. Somehow they seemed to think it gave them the same status and sooner or later they started acting as equals to their employers. This maid seemed to be one of those persons.

Before Paro had a chance to respond, the door opened and Sardar Timur entered the room with his wife and daughter trailing behind him, dragging their heels. The wife appeared tired, drained and the daughter chastised. Sardar Timur appeared to be calm and in control.

"You are the person in charge of the Panchayat tomorrow. My daughter will narrate the story and you need to hear the details from both her and my wife. Your wife can ask any questions she wants and she will also act as a witness to ensure that the deposition has been written properly. You both will bear witness to this," Sardar Timur said, in an even tone.

"So your daughter will not go in front of the Panchayat?" Mullah Aziz asked, reluctantly. He wanted to be sure he understood what would happen, or not happen. He also wanted to stay on the good side of this powerful man, a man who could influence his life in so many ways.

"Are you out of your mind?" Sardar Timur's eyes flickered with impatience. "Even the men in our family do not appear in front of a Panchayat as witnesses, and you think I'd allow a woman from this family to do that? Don't you realize that I did not have to go through with this Panchayat business at all? I could have punished this cretin without anybody questioning my authority. It could have all been settled by now. But I want to be fair and just. That's the only reason I'm letting the people of this town decide the fate of this stupid boy and his family. You really think that I would humiliate my family further by exposing them in front of the people I feed and support, so they can decide who is right and who is wrong?" His rising voice finally shouted so loudly that it seemed to keep echoing in their ears.

"Apologies Sardar Timur," Mullah Aziz spoke in a contrite tone. "I didn't mean any disrespect."

"If you don't mean disrespect, then shut up and don't talk foolishly!"

Mullah Aziz instantly lowered his gaze, eyes looking down toward the impeccable gleaming floor, like a punished child. Sardar Timur stood, not budging, in the middle of the room and continued watching him for an extended period of time before turning towards his wife.

"Let Farah speak," he said to Sarah Khanum. "Make sure that Mullah Aziz's wife can listen properly, and that every word Farah says is written, without any deviation from what she says."

"I will Sardar Timur," Sarah Khanum replied obediently. One of the maids who was apparently educated sat on a chair between the two couches and began writing.

Sarah Khanum asked Farah to state her name, then she asked Paro if Farah was loud enough. Paro nodded. Farah then embarked upon her narration of that day's events, the maid writing quickly and almost illegibly trying to keep up with Farah's rapid and agitated speech. Paro attempted to disguise her shocked reaction upon listening to the blow-by-blow, she needed to remain neutral and objective. Once Farah finished recounting, the maid read back the whole story verbatim, once all were in agreement that both the written and spoken words matched, the statement was signed. Farah was escorted out by her mother and the maid. Her duty was done.

"You will receive your copy of the agreed-upon statement as soon as it's signed by the maid who took the dictation." Sardar Timur said once the room was empty of any others. "Just wait here." Then he walked away.

For a short while, Mullah Aziz and Paro were alone in the room.

"Why did they want me here?" Paro asked.

"Isn't it obvious? Use your head!" Aziz said curtly. "They wanted a witness to the statement since I will be the one presenting it to the Panchayat. Obviously, Sardar Timur does not want to allow room for error, he doesn't want anybody to object and state that I'm not a true witness and now you're able to confirm that in fact, I did witness Farah's testimony. Now it's all legal in Sardar Timur's court of law."

Paro nodded and muttered something barely audible.

"What did you say?" Aziz asked.

"Shouldn't the boy be allowed to tell his side of the story? How do we know she is not making things up?" Paro asked.

Aziz didn't respond for a while and then nodded in agreement.

"Why didn't you ask Sardar Timur to bring him here so that he too could tell his side of the story?"

"I don't think he would like that idea," Aziz said after staying quiet for a long moment while considering the question.

Paro didn't respond. Her face expressed her displeasure at her husband's response. They ended up waiting for quite a while before Sardar Timur and the maid returned with two copies of the narrative she had handwritten. She signed them both in front of them and gave them to Sardar Timur, who then passed them on to Mullah Aziz.

"If you want to read these papers before you leave, that would be acceptable," Sardar Timur told them.

"I am sure they are okay," Mullah Aziz replied. Sardar Timur looked at Paro expecting her automatic verbal agreement. She hesitated.

"You know what?" Sardar Timur said. "I think you and your wife both should read it before you leave. Take your time. If you need to stay awhile, then stay. There is no rush. Once you are finished, let the maid know and she'll come and get me."

Before Mullah Aziz could respond to this suggestion, Sardar Timur got up and left the room. The maid bowed until she heard the door shut behind Sardar Timur, then straightened herself and stood there, like a good soldier.

"You couldn't just nod your head." Aziz was agitated that they had to sit and read the papers, and as usual, he found his wife's actions inconvenient. "How difficult was it to just say yes? Now we have to read all this. Who knows when we'll get home?"

Paro stayed quiet. The maid's face was expressionless. They both read the papers, and once finished the maid went to find Sardar Timur. Once back, he asked for assurance that the written statement was exactly what Farah had told them. This time, Mullah Aziz and Paro both agreed. He abhorred Paro's muttering and insisted on a loud, clear, and articulate response. Paro complied, grudgingly.

"You may leave now, you'll be dropped back at your home," Sardar Timur said, dismissing them. They were taken back the way they were brought in.

On the way back, Mullah Aziz recounted the events Farah had described, in his mind. It did appear that Gul might have been trying to take advantage of Farah's presence, but what she had not explained was why she was in the pantry in the first place. It didn't occur to him while he was listening to her story, but now he was convinced that they were not told the complete truth. Something definitely wasn't right.

Farah and Chaman's presence in the pantry together had remained unexplained. But still, Gul's guilt was established by what he did. Farah was in her own home, she could go anywhere in the Haveli and talk to anyone she desired.

Rauf and Turab were pacing and wide awake when Aziz and Paro returned. She immediately went to her back room and Mullah Aziz quietly handed the envelope with the documents to Turab.

"This boy is dead," Turab declared once he was done reading.

"Seems like it." Mullah Aziz agreed.

SIXTEEN

AMIR SPENT THE night reading articles written by and about Arlette. She had worked as a journalist for several years and wrote a column that was syndicated and appeared in several major newspapers and magazines globally. She had a point of view worth listening to, and there were many who followed her, not just in the papers but also on social media. She was particularly interested in the plight of women in general, and in the third world in particular, writing extensively about gender roles, abuse of women as a weapon of war and intimidation, and especially the use of religion to control the free spirit of women everywhere. Both she personally and her work were banned in some of the most conservative monarchies in the Middle East and as a result, she despised Muslims in general but conservative Arabs in particular.

Yet here she was, in Dubai. The glistening, ultra-modern, energetic, and everything-and-anything-goes Dubai. She liked visiting Dubai and had access to the Sheik, who was an interesting mix of traditional Arab culture and Islam with a strong desire for modernization.

Arlette's last interaction with the Pakistani Prime Minister occurred in Dubai a few years before. The soft-spoken, pudgy, and balding Prime Minister had a reputation of surrounding himself with good looking females. In a culture that gave utmost importance to a man's wealth, power, and influence there was no shortage of such women who would be willing to enjoy the good life such a man can offer.

Aamir reread the article about the PM that had caused such a commotion. According to what Arlette wrote, he offered to have a personal friendship with her and also offered to set up a private and confidential communication channel with her. She wrote that she was truly startled to see the head of a foreign government act in such a non-statesman-like manner. At first, she enjoyed the conversation and led him on, but at one point he became too direct so she had no choice but to put a stop to it. When finally, she refused his offer and tried to excuse herself, he asked her to keep the encounter and conversation confidential. At that point, she left him without responding. The whole episode was all too familiar, yet too bizarre for her to digest quickly and respond with any firm commitment.

She reported the incident to her editor and someone heard it and leaked the story to a tabloid. In her home country, the matter was a cause for amusement, but on the Prime Minister's native soil, it became a scandal. Local media printed her pictures with headlines painting her as someone who had a unique influence on the Prime Minister. Her editor received an official statement via diplomatic channels to clarify that he had simply offered to buy her a fancy new electronic gadget and nothing else, the Prime Minister's request for Arlette to keep in touch was simply a friendly gesture between a politician and a journalist, nothing else. Once this clarification was printed, the eruption of anger was contained and the scandal died down even before it could fully mature. Aamir recalled her saying that the Prime Minister's office sent a personal thank you letter, which she tore up and threw in the trash bin after scanning it into her personal files.

While the Prime Minister thanked her for her "discretion," he also officially blacklisted her from coming to Pakistan. That was no hardship to her, according to what she later wrote in her weekly column, as she had no desire to visit Pakistan.

Aamir didn't know what time he finally dozed off. It was a good thing he had a wake-up call scheduled for seven in the morning because he most certainly would have overslept otherwise. He woke in the middle of a dream involving Arlette and as soon as he woke up, he completely forgot the details, only remembering it being especially impactful. It left in him a feeling of thirst and curiosity which he knew would remain unquenched, as though he may never know the truth behind the story. He'd had that feeling many times before, but like those times, the moment passed.

He practically ran out of his bed, ordered room service, and jumped in the shower. All at lightning speed. He had just towel-dried his thick dark brown hair and tied the white towel around his slender tan waist when he heard a knock on the door. At precisely the same moment his phone rang. He answered the phone and at the same time opened the door. The person on the other end of the phone and the people on the other side of the door, both brought him utter surprises.

On the phone was Turab, with whom he had worked at the paper some years ago, but was now with another media group. On the other side of the door was a team of four bullish men in uniform. They didn't wait for an invitation, instead, they barged in and just pushed him to the side roughly. The phone slipped from his hand and dropped on the carpet just under the bed. He wasn't sure if the call was still connected.

"Never open the door without knowing for sure who is on the other side," one of the uniformed men said in a dry voice.

Aamir was stupefied and thrown off guard.

229

"We are the security detail for your nine-thirty meeting." The same man spoke again. "We needed to surprise you, to see how you behave in an unexpected situation. Unfortunately, I must say you have disappointed me."

"Okay, so, now what?"

"You will still be on the team," the man said. "But I needed to assess you to know how to use you. Personally, I don't think you have much to offer."

Before Aamir could respond, there was another knock on the door. This time it was surely room service.

"Don't move," the same man ordered. "I'll open the door, you get ready and we will see you at nine-thirty."

Aamir simply nodded, not really understanding what this man was talking about. The man moved towards the door, opened it, and left with his team. The room server was a small dark-skinned man. He balked at the sight of the four large men and jumped delicately away from the door. Surprisingly, he was able to control the tray held in his hands. Aamir signaled him to come in and put the tray on the table while he picked up the phone from under the bed. He could hear the noise on the other side. The call was still connected.

"Turab, sorry about that. I am with you now," he spoke while watching the server discreetly glide out of the room and close the door behind him.

Turab started with the unnecessary pleasantries for which Aamir didn't have the patience. He asked Turab to come to the point.

"I'm here in Hayatabad, participating in a Panchayat session which is about to start soon. I am certain it is just a façade. This whole thing is illegal and rigged."

"Explain more? How did you get involved? Don't leave out any details." Aamir asked, his curiosity heightened while sitting at his room's dining table, cross-legged still in a white towel, spreading butter on the toast. His phone was on the table with the speaker on so that he could transcribe every detail of Turab's speech.

"What do you want me to do about this?" Aamir asked once he realized Turab was finished speaking.

"I found out that you'll be with the Prime Minister today in the company of international media. Can you bring it to his attention so this can be stopped? Police may not intervene unless it is noticed by the people at the highest level and order a probe. Otherwise, I have a feeling that this episode will have a very bad ending for this boy and possibly his sister."

"I'll see what I can do."

"If you need to convince the Prime Minister, I can send you the audio or video of the Panchayat session, once it begins."

"That will definitely help."

"Ok, Aamir thank you! I'll stay in touch," Turab said, seeming to want to conclude the conversation. "Will call you as soon as I have an update."

"Okay," Aamir agreed and ended the call. He was well aware of the kind of punishments routinely meted out in such Panchayat proceedings, an eye for an eye and a tooth for a tooth was the gist of it. An influential man's honor was more valuable than an ordinary person's life. There was a time when such alleged perpetrators were simply executed. Now, even though their lives were spared, they were made an example of for others by leaving them worse than dead. Death a kinder fate. The perpetrator's family members were made to pay for their sins, especially women. Taking away or harming women of the family to dishonor the perceived criminal men, was more than acceptable common practice. When some victims raised their voices and were able to get the media's attention, the perceived honor of the nation was considered to have been compromised. Such opinions were expressed at the highest level of the government, including the Prime Minister—Aamir knew his views on such issues. He had expressed his low opinion of Panchayat victims during private meetings and had gone so far as saying that they had invited the wrath upon themselves so they could then seek protection in Western countries.

Aamir was not sure that bringing the unfolding story in Hayatabad to the Prime Minister's attention would elicit a helpful response, however, letting Arlette know about it and having her confront the Prime Minister on these events might help bring some encouraging response.

His meeting with the security detail was scheduled for nine-thirty, and it was already eight-thirty. He thought about going through with the meeting first before talking to Arlette but he didn't have the stomach for the wait. Reluctantly, he called her. She picked up the phone and heard the story with interest.

"How reliable is your source?"

"I have known him for many years. I see no reason to not believe him."

"That's not good enough," Arlette was not impressed by the personal reference. "What is the name of the town where this is happening?"

Aamir relayed the requested information.

"I'll get this verified."

"How?"

"I have sources, don't worry about it. I belong to a large news-gathering organization with global reach. A society like yours is not too difficult to buy influence in." The condescension in her voice was all too evident. Aamir felt deeply humiliated and before he could think of an appropriate response, she'd hung up the phone.

The security team came back at the scheduled time but Aamir was finding it almost impossible to concentrate on the agenda. Once they left, he realized he hadn't finished the breakfast he had ordered, the toast on the plate was hard, the scrambled egg was cold. Even so, invigorated by the idea of this new project or story worked up his appetite and he cleaned the plate within minutes.

SEVENTEEN

T HE DAY OF reckoning had arrived. The night before was hell and the day was likely to be even worse. Gul sat on the dirt floor, rubbing his eyes, trying to regain his senses. Badri was lying on the dirt floor, unconscious. Her cheeks were red, her hair filled with dirt, her face was swollen and her clothes were half torn. She had been swimming in and out of awareness throughout the night after being brutalized multiple times, then finally left on her own to die.

Frequent flashes of light popped up in front of her closed eyes, peppered with images. She seemed to have scanned her entire life in an abbreviated period of time, a montage from last night, to the days and nights which passed throughout the years, and then back to the ordeal and trauma of previous nights. She dreamed of days long gone. She remembered the childhood she once had, the first impression she had of herself was the first time she saw her own picture, in which she was holding on to her mother's dress. She visualized herself standing to the side of an improvised swing, it was a swinging crib tied with knots on two metal bars, more like a hammock hanging from tree branches. Mimi Jan stood next to her, looking down fondly at her. There was a baby boy in the crib, wrapped in a warm shawl having his head shaved. His name was Ali. In the picture, she was staring at her mother's face, which was tattooed in a design of pure desperation, evident as she gazed at the little boy. Ali belonged to her mother's younger brother. A baby boy her mother so dearly desired but didn't have.

Badri had never been the recipient of the type of adoration her mother had for this baby boy Ali. The world in which they lived celebrated the male and nurtured him into manhood. She knew that and had no choice but to accept it, be that as it may, she still felt the absence of that warmth and affection. She craved it. Ali would visit their home every now and then with his parents, and those were disturbing days because she knew they'd never last, bittersweet days when her usually melancholy mother couldn't stop smiling. At times she thought it was better to not have joy because when it dissipated, which it would, the despondency was that much greater. She so wished that the boy would stay with them just so she could have better days with her parents. And then her wish came true.

It started with her mother being curiously ill. Her body began to take a different form, and she would refuse to pick her up or let her climb in her lap. The old hunched-back woman who used to come to their house every so often to help started coming more often. One day, her mother told that she was going to spend a few days at Ali's house and while she was at Ali's house, Ali's mother would live in their house in order to help around the house. After several days, Badri was brought back to her home and found another Ali in her mother's lap.

"Who is he?" she remembered asking her mother.

"His name is Gul," she was told. Badri remembered her mother's glowing face and a broad smile at that moment, it was something she hadn't seen in days, if not weeks. "He is your little brother, so that means you're the big sister now, and that also means that you will take care of him when I'm sleeping or not at home. He will be your responsibility."

"Okay," she said, hesitating. She couldn't understand why she didn't feel exuberant the way she did when Ali was around. This was different; all she felt was a lack of joviality.

Sometimes she loved Gul and sometimes she just hated him for all the discomfort he caused her. For the first few months, she was unable to sleep properly, because he would cry all night. Mostly her mother would take care of him, but the crying and all the commotion that went with caring for him was very different from the tranquility she had experienced in their little home thus far. She also noticed that he was sharing all that she used to get from her parents, the most obvious, and most unsettling things were food and love. Ever since Gul had become part of the family, her mother and father both devoted most of their time and attention to him. She didn't feel jealous really, more of a deep ongoing sadness but without knowing the reason for it. Mimi Jan took great care in showing Badri how special she was to her, but once she left her grandmother and returned to her own home, she felt second best once more.

Father would buy new clothes for him first. Mother would feed him first. In cold weather, they would cover him first. All the chores were her responsibility. If he broke things in the house, her mother would just laugh it off. If the two children fought, she would rarely find anyone siding with her.

She was almost seven when he was born. Even at that young age, she could feel the difference in their parents' attitude towards the two of them. At first, it was difficult for her to make the connection, she couldn't quite identify how it was different. But as he grew and time passed the distinction became clear. He was more valued and more cared for than she ever had been. The year he turned three, she turned ten. She suddenly found enough courage in herself to start complaining about these inequalities to her mother and after some time, to her father. Why should a boy be the recipient of more love, care, and attention? Both of them simply said that he was little and needed more of everything, and she really ought to not have any ill feelings towards him. They loved both children equally. She realized that her words were wasted, their actions said otherwise.

Every year the wild monsoon season brought legions of rain. The first few days always brought smiles and sighs of relief. The dust and dirt normally clogging the air would settle from the strong warm winds, and there would be significant relief from the scorching heat caused by that merciless fireball in the sky. People would then start praying for the rain to stop so that the flooding in the dirt streets would dry. It was a very consistent cycle. That year nature decided to ignore all prayers, the rain kept falling and soon enough the dirty streets became filthy canals.

Many of the homes that were made of half-baked bricks and mud collapsed into giant piles of sand and concrete, some of which were better built turned into enormous, flimsy water containers. One day they heard that the gates of the dams had to be opened to bring the level of stored water down, which caused havoc. There were tides over tides of strong waves and currents which swept away everything in the streets. Homes filled with water simply could not resist the strength of the waves caused by the sudden release of thousands and thousands of cubic feet of water gushing down.

Badri remembered seeing giant mechanical birds in the sky. She later learned that they were called helicopters. She saw tall strong men in sand-colored uniforms, soldiers of the Pakistani Army. She remembered seeing some of them holding megaphones making announcements, telling people to climb the tall trees and stay away from the strong water current flowing on the ground until they could be airlifted or until boats could arrive to rescue them. She didn't understand any of this.

She was barely twelve years old and had never climbed a tree, she hadn't a clue what to do and it seemed like a daunting task. Where to begin? What happens if she can't make it to the top? What happens if she falls? She saw her father climbing the tree at great speed with Ali riding on his back and so she asked her mother to carry her. Her mother just kept pulling her arm toward the tree, not helping in the way she needed. She waved for her father to come down and take her to the highest branch, but he didn't come down, he just kept waving his free arm, gesturing for her to keep climbing up, just like her mother.

"I can't climb up, Baba," she screamed.

"Keep trying, you're doing it right. Just keep climbing." Her father said, still waving his arms as if she could not see where he was.

"Give her a hand," she heard her mother yell. Badri's eyes were fixated on her father's face and she saw that he was unwilling to let Gul out of his arms. That it might come down to saving only one child. Badri could see the very real fear in her baby brother's eyes, but regardless of his terror, he extended his small hand offering to pull her up.

"Gul will fall if I climb down," Shams, their father said. Badri didn't quite believe him. He kept on motioning her to climb up. So, that is exactly what she did. She was able to pull herself up just a little, her hand searching for a higher branch, then she got hold of a weak branch, tried to pull herself up and everything turned upside down. She saw the tree moving away from her and then felt a splash of water. She wiped her eyes with the back of her hands and that's when she saw Gul's crying face. He had both hands extended. She raised her hands, hopelessly trying to grasp his when Gul unexpectedly jumped, flying wildly in the air towards her. Their eyes met for a split second and in that instant, she saw something in her little brother's eyes that she had never seen before. She felt connected to him.

Her father jumped after Gul, was able to grab him but both became caught and tangled in the sticks and branches of another fallen tree. Then Gul suddenly slipped and landed right in her arms as they both tried to latch onto the trunk of the fallen tree. Their father then managed to grab them both and drag them to another tree, one that was still standing, and carry them both on his shoulders. Her brother held her hand tightly unable to conceal his big innocent smile while looking at her adoringly.

Badri felt alive. Not only because her pulse was racing and her heart pounding, she felt alive because she saw the true and pure love in Gul's eyes. At that moment, she didn't see the intruder in her home who had taken away everything she had to herself before he arrived: the love and attention she had felt robbed of since he came into her life all appeared to be the right thing now. She now felt she had been offered the love of her brother in exchange for the love from her parents.

If her parents loved Gul more than her, so be it. She couldn't blame him for how they treated her, how they preferred him over her. He didn't demand that. He didn't ask for it. It was the norm in their world, male over female. The stronger gender. She realized that she would have to shift her mindset when it came to family dynamics and if anybody deserved her love and kindness, it was him. After all, he was little, he was helpless. He needed the attention most and she would now be the one to give it to him.

Since that day, Badri loved him fiercely and unconditionally.

Shams was quiet, almost strangely tranquil during the ride, while Zara Bibi in contrast was incapable of that same tranquility. She kept wailing loudly with angry outbursts aimed toward Timur and his family. Shams gently squeezed his wife's ice-cold hand multiple times in an attempt to soothe her but she kept pushing it away.

"You need to shut up," Rahim finally growled.

"Why?" Asked Zara Bibi defiantly.

"Because I said so."

"I don't care."

"Are you crazy?" Shams was terrified. "Be quiet. Do you realize what you are saying?"

"I don't think she does," Rahim said while staring ahead at the road, in a threatening tone. "Looks like everybody in your family needs to learn a lesson."

"What more can you possibly do to me. To us? You've already taken our children. What more can Sardar Timur do? I won't keep quiet, and I will do whatever I please, and feel however I please."

Rahim took a long hard look at Zara Bibi's face, then turned back to look straight through the windshield. The driver looked at his face and smiled. "She's frustrated," he said to Rahim. "Let her make some noise. She'll feel better once she gets over it otherwise she will be too difficult to handle."

Rahim turned around and looked at Zara Bibi again, and turned back. The rest of the ride was seemingly quiet except for the howl-like crying which continued as they entered the Haveli perimeter. They were roughly escorted to the kennel toward the back of the property where Sardar Timur was calmly feeding his pack of sleek Doberman's. They were told to stay put and wait to be addressed. They watched as the trio fought for the pieces of meat that he tossed to them, snarling and viciously growling. Shams and Zara Bibi stood there frozen, fearful that he might release them, and kept watching until he was done. They didn't exhale until the heated canines quieted, sated from their feeding frenzy, and it wasn't until then that Sardar Timur looked in their direction.

"These dogs are very loyal," Sardar Timur spoke. Not quite to them, but at them. "I love them dearly. But if any of them growl at me, I won't think twice before killing it."

No one responded. Sardar Timur looked around at his men and then stared at Shams' face for a few moments. "You should understand Shams that what your son has done to me is much worse than the mere growling of one of my beloved dogs."

"Have mercy on him Sardar Timur, he is just a child." Shams pleaded.

"You've begged me enough for mercy, and it's getting tiring. I have already given you my answer. There will be a punishment. This matter is going to Panchayat shortly."

"I will beg the Panchayat to spare him the punishment," Shams sounded hopeful. "I am sure that they will listen, I'm sure of it because this is unjust!"

"Doesn't really matter now, does it? All this pleading and begging is pointless. The Panchayat will decide his guilt, and all I do is dole out the punishment."

"Then I'll beg the Panchayat to find him innocent. I'll talk to them! Not you!"

"You can forget that!" Sardar Timur replied. Shams heard Sardar's men laughing. "They will not find him innocent. They will never find him innocent because the evidence is beyond compelling. There are too many witnesses and the most important detail is that his own mother, is one of those witnesses! He will be found guilty. That part is settled so don't hope or pray that Panchayat will disregard that."

Sardar Timur cast a long condescending look at Shams waiting and hoping for him to reply if only to give him a reason to continue on his path of narcissistic sadism. Shams didn't or couldn't find his voice, he stared at his son's executioner feeling as though he stepped in quicksand.

"Here is why I wanted to see you tonight. As I said, the Panchayat will decide if your son is guilty or innocent, even though I already know the answer, but they don't decide the punishment, I do. I have already chosen his punishment. Your boy has grown up and I know boys like to play around at this age, but, he decided to play with my family and my honor and that will bring him devastation. I'm going to have him castrated, and I will take him out back and sharpen the knife myself."

"No! Please Sardar Timur, NO!" Zara Bibi couldn't contain herself, she lunged at him with the intent of grabbing his arms but she lacked the strength and fell to her knees on the hard dirt and rocky ground. "Please! He's our only boy and I cannot have any more children. You will kill our name if my boy is harmed this way. Please, I beg you, please don't do it."

"If you play with fire, you get burnt." Sardar Timur replied. "However, there is one way out."

"What is it? What's the way out? Please tell us and we will do anything to save our boy and save our name."

Zara Bibi nodded. Sardar Timur looked at them both, a long silent stare. He then started speaking very slowly enunciating each word carefully.

"You will give your daughter to my men for three nights," Sardar Timur said. "They will not beat her, but they will avenge my honor with everybody's knowledge."

"Oh no," Zara Bibi fell on her knees. "Fear Allah Sardar Timur, fear Allah. My daughter is innocent. How could you even ask for something like this? This will kill her. This will kill us all."

"How could your son violate my daughter? Should he not feel the fear? Should you not right the wrong he did to me and my family? I am not the one who created this situation. He is. I have always been there for my servants, my people. I have cared for all of you. Always. Is this how I should be repaid. No. But I do not seek revenge. I only seek justice. An eye for an eye. That is Allah's way of justice."

"But my daughter is innocent," Shams begged.

"So was my daughter."

"Allah also tells us to forgive," Zara Bibi pleaded. "Please forgive my children. I'm asking you again. I promise we'll leave this town and you will never see us again."

"I cannot and will not allow that to happen. If I let you leave without punishment, then I cannot stop somebody else in the future from doing the same thing, or even worse. You can leave after the punishment, but not before, or without it. That is final."

"Give us one chance Sardar Timur. What if we admit in front of everybody that my son was guilty? We'll tell them that you are letting us leave."

"Don't argue with me. Just take the opportunity I'm giving you." Sardar Timur was dismissive. "Tell me who you wish to present for punishment. I'll permit you to talk to your children, but after that, I need a decision before the Panchayat's verdict."

"We can't do this Sardar Timur, we just cannot do this," Shams said and Zara Bibi crawled, still on the ground, towards Sardar Timur, grabbed his feet, and hitting her forehead on the dirt. Shams followed her. Rahim moved forward with his men, grabbed Shams and Zara Bibi, and dragged them away.

"If you don't choose—I will," Sardar Timur said, then he raised his hand high. Basheer and his men stopped dragging Shams and his wife.

"I will tell you this," Sardar Timur said thoughtfully. "If you don't decide, then I will punish them both. Now go and talk to your children. You'll be showing them mercy if you choose one over the other, otherwise, they both will suffer. If you choose one of them at least the other will be spared."

They couldn't respond, they were incapable of speaking. It was so horrid that it was beyond words. This was pure evil. Shams looked at his wife, who was covering her mouth in disbelief, her eyes were closed but tears were streaming. Her forehead and hair were covered with mud, she looked like a person who had completely lost her mind, which in fact, she had.

Sardar Timur turned around and walked away. Rahim and his men pushed them both past the dog house, behind thick tall bushes to a small shed where two men stood on guard. Rahim gestured for them to open it and let Shams and Zara Bibi pass through. They did so very cautiously and tried to adjust their eyes to the almost pitch black dark room. The room was like a grave, and it smelled of sweat, blood, and nothing wholesome.

"Before I turn on the lights and let you talk to your children, remember what Sardar Timur said. You will do them a kindness if you select one of them to present for punishment. If you don't, then you will end up hurting them both."

Rahim waited for a few seconds, expecting some response to his warning, which never came. The loud bang of the door shutting behind him announced his departure. As soon as the door was shut, the lights came on. Shrieks of relief and joy from both Badri and Gul greeted them, for a few moments they gathered in an embrace, almost forgetting their predicament. Zara Bibi suddenly pushed Gul away and began to slap him. He took a step back and stood there with his head held low. His mother kept hitting as she sobbed, then suddenly broke down and fell on her knees.

Shams held his daughter's face in both hands. He had always treated her as the lesser of his children and now he was about to ask her for the ultimate sacrifice. More than the ultimate sacrifice. He was about to ask her for her honor. For the first time, Shams found it difficult to prefer Gul over her. Favoring his son had always come naturally to him, it was all he knew, but now he couldn't bear it. Choosing Gul over her right now felt wrong and unnatural and he wanted more than anything to spare her. He stared at her silently. Guilt and remorse consuming him.

Her beautiful face gradually faded and blurred in his tear-filled gaze.

EIGHTEEN

R ASHID WAS ALL smiles this morning, walking and whistling a tune on his way to the bank. It was his fifth anniversary as a bank employee, and if history was any guide he was sure to receive a sizeable raise in salary, maybe even a promotion. His hopes were not unjustified. He was a consistently hard worker who had earned a certain appreciation from all his colleagues and bank customers alike and the fact that the bank was doing well, only confirmed his theory.

Unlike other banks in the area, this one did not have a set schedule for employee evaluation. Instead, each employee was evaluated on their performance upon year completion, or his or her hiring anniversary date. Today was Rashid's, and each year to date he'd been given a raise. His previous manager had been exceptionally cooperative and generous, however, he'd since retired and was no longer at the bank. Zain Malick was now the boss.

Rashid was called into Zain Malick's office late morning. In addition to Zain, a representative of the Human Resources Department was present. He introduced himself as Razik. Zain gestured for Rashid to be seated.

"Happy anniversary," Razik said with a warm smile. Zain's face was impassive.

"Thanks," Rashid smiled back.

"I guess there is no need to tell you why you are here," Razik was keen to get started with the business at hand. Rashid nodded his head, crossed his legs twice, and placed his fidgety hands in his lap, hoping that his eagerness was concealed. He didn't want to appear too needy or desperate.

"As you know, for the past two years you've been getting great performance reviews, accompanied by generous salary increases, usually the third straight year of a positive performance review is rewarded with a promotion."

"Great," Rashid couldn't stop himself from blurting out. "Does that mean I'm getting promoted?"

Razik looked at Zain while changing his position in his chair. Suddenly the mood shifted. Rashid followed his gaze and glanced at Zain Malick who was sitting rigidly and still impassive.

"Unfortunately no," Razik spoke softly but firmly after clearing his throat. "You didn't qualify for the promotion this year."

Rashid felt his heart sinking. He digested the news for a few seconds and then was overcome with anger. He looked up, his eyes meeting Zain's.

"Why is that? Why didn't I qualify for the promotion? Did I get a bad performance review?"

"Here," Razik produced a couple of sheets from the leather folder he was holding and slid it toward him. "You should read the material in these papers. This is your formal performance review."

Rashid picked up the papers, glanced over them quickly, and then threw them on the table towards Zain. The words meant nothing.

"What did I do differently this year? What was it that displeased my manager? Last year he was very satisfied with my work, why is he not happy with me this year when the last two years he was satisfied, especially when there's been no change in my performance?"

"Each manager evaluates according to his own experience with the employee for the particular year under review," Razik said politely.

"Okay, so it is *how* the manager evaluates my performance, not the performance itself," Rashid immediately replied. "The problem is not necessarily my actual performance. The real problem is how it has been evaluated."

"Well," Razik replied. "That may be partly true, but you have to understand that you have more experience under your belt now. You are expected to show more in terms of capacity and performance as well as the assumption of responsibilities."

"I think I have shown that in my work."

"That is for your manager to judge."

"You know what," Rashid's temper flared, he jumped up and started wagging his finger in Zain's face. "You're a pig. You've never liked me, ever. Now you want to punish me. I'll show you bad performance, you'll see how a bad employee behaves! Get ready for some nasty action."

"Rashid, please don't get emotional. Please stop threatening," Razik stood up as well. "This is not good for your career."

"What career? He has already made up his mind about me. He's already done plenty of damage. Two straight years of excellent reviews all wiped away. What's the point!?"

"You still have an opportunity to correct your situation." Razik tried to calm him. "You can make this right and have a wonderful career with the bank. This is just one year. You have many years ahead of you in this organization. This is about what is good for your long term career with us."

"He! He is not good for my career!" said Rashid with disgust. He spat on Zain's table. "I'm leaving now and taking the rest of the day off, suddenly I'm not feeling too well."

He didn't wait for a response, instead, he spun around and left the office. Razik glanced at Zain Malick's face. He shrugged and kept sitting in the large, comfortable leather chair.

Rashid burst furiously through the front doors of the branch, his once passive face now radiated animosity. He literally felt his blood boil and rush through his veins. He kick-started his motorbike and got on it without any particular direction in mind, he just needed to run. Fast. He didn't go far. Hunger got the better of him and he regretfully made the decision to just acquiesce, and stop at his usual lunch place: a dirty, old restaurant – for lack of a better way to describe the joint – with good food at even better prices.

It was too early for the lunch crowd so he stormed in, still raging, and seated himself. The waiter came rushing to the table with an old beat-up aluminum pitcher. Old, beat-up metal glasses were already on the table, tied to a chain hooked to the wooden leg of the table. When he came to the restaurant for the very first time and saw the glasses tied to the chain, he asked the owner about it and was told that people were in the habit of stealing them, not for value, just for fun, for the thrill. After losing too many glasses they started protecting their property but were very generous with the length of the chain so that their customers had no trouble gulping water from the protected utensils.

It was too early for lunch dishes so he ordered the traditional breakfast, consisting of *paratha* – the traditional double-fried wheat bread – with thick sweet milk cream and a hot cup of milk tea. He thought about ordering fried eggs also but decided against it. He didn't want to spend too much money on this one meal, especially since he didn't know where his next paycheck was coming from.

He couldn't risk it. No eggs. Food came to the table very quickly; the speed of service here was something he'd always admired. He immediately started devouring the blessings on his plate, but he neglected to notice the person who had taken the opposite chair at his table.

"Food is good here, isn't it?" Suddenly he heard a voice and picked up his head with shock.

"Don't mind me," the man in the opposite chair said politely. "Finish your food and don't rush. Take your time."

"Who are you?" asked Rashid swallowing a large piece of bread with a sip of hot milk tea.

"Oh don't worry I'll introduce myself, but first enjoy your breakfast," the man said even more politely this time.

"Listen," said Rashid while breaking another piece of bread. "I've had a bad day as it is and you are annoying me, so either tell me who you are and what you want or get up and leave before I lose my cool."

"Whoa," the man blurted out with a shocked expression on his face. "Keep your cool. Don't lose it. You'll need it."

"Okay, looks like you are difficult to reason with. I think I should ask the waiter to remove you from my table." Rashid looked around, spotted the waiter, and snapped his fingers.

"That won't be necessary, besides the waiter won't help you at all. Let me show you."

Without turning to face the waiter, he simply raised his fist up in the air. The waiter, who had started walking toward their table suddenly stopped. A smug smile slowly emerged on the man's face.

"He's not walking towards us now, is he?" he asked.

Rashid quickly glanced at the waiter who was intently watching the man's fist and lightly shook his head.

"Now watch," the man used the other hand's finger to point towards his raised fist. Rashid's eyes followed. He saw the fist rotate ninety degrees. The waiter turned around and walked away.

"Is he gone?" Laughter was clearly audible in the man's tone. Rashid shook his head.

"Alright, I get it," said Rashid. "Who are you and why are you at my table?"

"I work for the police."

"What's your name?"

"I have no name; I have no face. None of those details concern you."

"What do you want?"

"I'll tell you what I want. But that's the discussion we'll have after you have answered a few questions."

"Okay. Go ahead." He was sure the man would not take no for an answer. It was best if he at least pretended to go along. His interest was piqued anyway, and with no other place to go to, he thought he might just see where this conversation led.

"You work for the Universal Bank, right?"

"Why ask? You already know that."

"It's always good to confirm and verify everything. Things are bound to change. Sometimes that change occurs gradually, sometimes suddenly. Therefore, I make it a point to confirm my information."

"Huh," Rashid said to himself quietly in his head. Things did change for him this morning. How true! In a way, they changed all the time, but the change he was expecting today never materialized, instead he was sitting in this God-forsaken restaurant in the middle of the day talking to a crazy stranger.

"Looks like you agree with me, that's why you are quiet. Otherwise, you would have said something."

251

"You said you work for the police?" Rashid ignored the comment and asked the question popping in his head. "Why are you interested in me?"

"Well, I am not really interested in you. My interest is in your manager. What's his name…Ah. I remember, Zain Malick, right?"

"Yes, his name is Zain Malick. But why are you interested in him?"

"You'll know soon enough. Right now I need to ask you a few questions."

"You're interested in him, but your questions are for me?"

"Well, for the time being, yes," said the man. "But they are about him. You must have noticed that his behavior is more than often strange and that there are too many unexplained events that occur around him."

"I'm not sure, what do you mean?"

"If you haven't noticed, then let me spell it out for you. In the last few months, there have been several robberies around your branch. Clients that go to make sizeable cash withdrawals seem to always have a problem getting their money in a timely manner, the reason for this is because your manager keeps them at the branch for an unusually long time. When the said client finally gets his or her money, and they leave the branch, they get robbed. Just like that! Somehow, someone knows who's carrying large quantities of cash. Now, this has been reported to the police consistently over the last several months. Have you not noticed any of this?"

Rashid suddenly had an epiphany. His hand stopped mid-air and crumbs began to drop from his hand and plummet down on the dirty wooden table. "Oh my God," he said. "I never saw this before now. You're right! There have been a few instances! Come to think about it some clients even came back to the branch to report the theft and share their awful stories. How did I forget this?"

"Looks like it just never occurred to you to make a connection, why should it?" the man said carefully observing his face.

"Not until now," Rashid replied and put the food in his mouth. He carefully wiped his hands on the yellowing napkin sitting on the side of the plate. "Wow! I mean it's so obvious now, how could I have missed this?"

"Don't beat yourself up about it. Now you see that there is an actual pattern."

"Yes. Definitely." Rashid said. "I've noticed recently that there is something strange in Zain's behavior."

"Can you elaborate?"

"I mean, usually he's very calm and composed, even unnaturally calm when facing a deadline or something like that. But now that I think about it, looking back he would act strangely any time a large cash withdrawal was in process. Sometimes he would call the client into his office and talk to them at length. Sometimes such conversations, from a distance, seemed pleasant and other times they would clearly become confrontational. Hard to miss! Now I get that he was trying to keep them in the branch for longer than necessary. He'd always excuse himself in the middle of the conversation and go to the locker room. I could hear him talking on the phone while in the locker room. I didn't think much about this then, but now I do not doubt that there was definitely a pattern."

"And so when the client leaves the bank, does the robbery occur fairly soon after that? Is that what you've observed?"

"Pretty much."

"Okay, so you did observe in a way, you just didn't actually see it," said the man sitting across from him in a philosophical tone. The grin on his face had disappeared.

"Why are you discussing all this with me anyway? I have nothing to do with whatever Zain may have done."

"I know," said the man. "I know that your hands are clean and that is exactly why I am talking to you."

"Can you explain please?"

"Yes," said the man. "You see, you are clean. You know this, I know this, and most importantly, he knows it."

"What do you mean?"

"It means that you can help us trap him so that we can catch him in the act."

"How can I help you trap him!?" asked Rashid. "What the hell can I do?"

"It should be very easy. What you need to do is let him know that you're on to him. If he panics and starts watching you or tries to create distance between the two of you, then you will tell him that you are willing to stay quiet if he agrees to share the spoils with you. My feeling is that in the beginning, he will resist the idea. You'll need to keep on pushing. You need to make him realize that bringing you onboard is in his best interest and that your share is just the cost of doing business. You will also tell him that if he attempts to cheat you or if he refuses to bring you onboard, you will not only go to the police but also to Sardar Timur, and you'll let him know that he made a big mistake stealing Sardar Timur's money. He knows that Sardar Timur will not hesitate to make an example out of him."

"Sardar Timur's money?" Rashid asked.

"Oh, you don't know. The latest robbery was the Sardar Timur theft. The two people who withdrew money from Sardar Timur's account on his behalf were robbed by four men on two motorcycles. You remember the other day, don't you? Rauf Aziz came to your branch with a man named Assef."

"Yes, I remember them," Rashid acknowledged. "Do they work for Sardar Timur?"

"In a way, yes," said the man. "I'm not at liberty to tell you what kind of work exactly, but they were in the branch to cash a check which Sardar Timur wrote to them. We believe that Zain blackmailed them or at least tried to. They didn't budge, cashed the check, and left, and guess what happened to them once they were out of the branch?"

"They got robbed?"

"Exactly, just how I told you!" the man hit his flat palm on the table like a hammer. The plates on the table bobbled and then landed back in their place with a loud clang. "That is exactly what happened. They got robbed. These criminals took three-quarters of the cash. They left one fourth with the victims and told them to stay quiet otherwise they will lose the remaining one fourth and then some."

"Oh, so they bought their silence with one-fourth of the loot."

"Now you are getting it," said the man. "I'm telling you this so you can negotiate your cut based on what he keeps for himself. One-fourth of the loot."

"Why one fourth? What happens to the rest?"

"I don't know exactly if it is always one fourth, but some money is always left untouched. They want to make sure that the victim has an incentive to stay quiet. One fourth may still be quite a significant amount and they might not want to report it to the authorities because it will raise questions they might not want to answer."

"Wow." Numbers started flashing in Rashid's head. "That means he is minting serious amounts of money."

"Yes indeed," said the man. "But this enterprise is about to come to an end and you'll help us finish it."

"Do I have to?"

"I'm not *requesting*."

"Oh." Rashid felt that his threatening tone was uncalled for. This man had chosen the perfect day to share this story with him and he had every reason to help put a spoke in Zain's wheel. He wondered if this was a coincidence. Maybe they'd been watching him all along and pounced when they saw an opening. Why this man chose today to approach Rashid was of no significance, what mattered was that he was going to cooperate. It just happened to be that today was ideal because all he could think about was revenge.

There was nothing to worry about if he cooperated with them. After all, Zain was a criminal. His behavior so far had been pretty consistent, but things could change any time. Rashid just had to be reasonable in his approach. Maybe he could play both sides. Maybe he could get the most out of Zain by letting him know that his secret was out. Not only could he convince Zain to share the spoils of his criminal enterprise, but he could also force him to change his annual report and give him the salary bump and promotion he so eagerly desired.

"Are you threatening me?" Rashid asked. He wanted to see how badly this could turn out in case something went wrong. The quickest route to knowing was to pretend to defy this "order."

"You can call it whatever you want," the man said in a dismissive tone. He was now puffing on a *Bidi*. The intense aroma of the locally made leafy cigarette was sharp and overwhelming. He puffed several bellows of smoke in quick succession in Rashid's face. He waved his hand in the air trying to disperse the thick smoke from attacking his nostrils.

"Look here Rashid, I am simply presenting an opportunity for you to work with the law. If you don't take this offer, then we have to assume that you are somehow involved. The investigation will open up to include you and you will become a target along with your boss."

"That is not true though! I had no idea about any of this!" Rashid defended himself. "You know that perfectly well."

"Maybe I'm wrong," the man sucked the Bidi very deeply. The glow on the other end of the *bidi* turned from orange to red. "I can be wrong. And when I realize I am wrong, I am willing to correct myself. After all, I am a custodian of the law. I hope you realize this."

Rashid took a deep sigh and melted into his chair, defeated.

"Very well, you win. I'll help you nail the bastard."

"Good," the man rubbed the red glow of the Bidi in the aluminum ashtray and showed Rashid a big broad smile. "Glad to have you on our team."

Rashid listened intently as the man talked him through the plan over the next several minutes, while occasionally nodding his head in understanding. Once he was finished, the man stood up, threw some money on the table, and turned around.

"Just a minute," suddenly Rashid remembered something.

"What?" the man asked.

"You never told me your name."

"Because I don't want you to know my name." The man smiled again and walked away.

NINETEEN

THE PRIME MINISTER was to meet not only reporters but also a group of expatriate Pakistanis who had agreed to invest in their homeland. With chronic power outages, a slowing of industrial growth, and increased dependence on imported goods, and in order to generate employment for the swelling youth population it was necessary for the economy to get a jolt. The Prime Minister had called on overseas Pakistanis to come to the rescue of the motherland and that is precisely what this group of expatriate Pakistanis wanted to do.

However, years of bitter experience had taught them that simply taking one's hard-earned life savings back to the country to invest in small businesses or real estate was not always productive or safe. Too many of them had been defrauded, so this group had set up a formal investment conference, during which they planned to get commitments for the safety of their investment before pledging any funds.

The event was to begin at nine in the morning and the conference hall was already at capacity with potential investors. International media representatives were present, ready with cameras, lights, microphones, and everything necessary for their work. Aamir was with the security team, in plain clothes, unarmed and free to roam around.

In keeping with the tradition of late starts and late endings, the event was running almost an hour behind when Aamir saw Arlette walking towards him, looking stern. In the morning light he could still see no flaw, her face and clothing looked professional and reputable, he couldn't detect any hint of deceit, or weakness. He could not imagine how the Prime Minister could have thought it acceptable to make an overture to her.

She asked him if he had any news about the Prime Minister who had yet to arrive. Something between a smirk and a grin appeared on her face as she told him that the Prime Minister's plane was stuck in Jeddah because the airline had not arranged sufficient fuel.

"You are kidding, right? His plane is unable to fly because they don't have fuel?"

"That's the word I'm getting from my sources."

"I don't believe you,"

"You can check your own sources," Arlette responded in a dismissive tone. "I'm going to go back with my team, I'm sure he will show up eventually."

Aamir stared at her in disbelief as she walked away and disappeared into the crowd. He quickly walked out of the main hallway into the lobby until he found a quiet place to call their media group's source in Jeddah. What he found out was truly incredible. Arlette was right. The problem was that the fuel was to be provided by a local vendor who had not been paid outstanding dues by the airline, and he took the opportunity to make sure the debt was paid and then some. While the payment was arranged, the Prime Minister's plane had to wait. Aamir shook his head as he terminated the call.

"Embarrassing, isn't it?" He heard Arlette's voice just before feeling her hand tap on his shoulder. He glared at her, annoyed to have been startled. Annoyed that she had been correct.

"Are you following me, listening in on my conversations?"

"I have to keep my eyes and ears open. After all, I am in the business of gathering news. It's not always noble and elegant and sometimes you have to stoop low."

"I suppose," Aamir replied. "Yes, it is embarrassing. The national airline–the only airline of the country–is unable or unwilling to pay its bills and the country's leader is sitting on the tarmac arranging to foot the bill."

"He'll be here soon enough; I am absolutely positive that the Saudis are keen to get him out of their country." Arlette glanced at him pityingly and left.

He stood a bit bewildered before being approached by another member of the security detail asking about the Prime Minister, accompanied by a guard from the United Arab Emirates. As the host country, they had the run of the event. Aamir's comfort level about speaking freely in front of this unknown wasn't high, so he chose the route of feigned ignorance.

"You don't know?" the guard asked with haughty sarcasm. "I thought you work for a media group. You should be more resourceful."

"I honestly don't know what are you talking about!" Aamir continued with his charade. The UAE guard repeated the tale and made sure to mention that everyone was talking about it. Aamir asked how it came to be that everyone knew. The guard didn't know the answer to that but could say with certainty that the potential investors were getting nervous and becoming understandably annoyed. Some were thinking of leaving, some were insulted, most were doubting the wisdom of investing in such a country where the leader had to bargain like a man in the street just to get from one place to another.

"I don't believe this," Aamir said, pretty much involuntarily.

"Yeah," said the guard. "Tell me about it. How could a country be so broke that it cannot pay its fuel vendors?"

"No, I meant, how did this information spread so quickly?"

"Beats me," said the guard and walked away. The other security detail member left with him. Some help he had been!

Aamir looked around. People were walking past each other, chatting, some whispering in each other's ears. Nothing unusual. However, for some reason, he was sure that everybody must be talking about the Prime Minister's situation. He decided to take a walk and try to overhear what he could. He didn't have to walk too far before he came across a party of well-dressed but poor-mannered, loud men. One appeared clearly upset and was nearly yelling at another man, who stood across from him in an apologetic posture.

"You work for the consulate here, right?"

"Yes, sir."

"Your office arranged this conference and promised us that the Prime Minister would give us the assurance that our investments will be safe and now he is not even here on time. Why do these politicians think they can set up schedules and then completely disregard them?

"Sir, I assure you, he will be here shortly. Let's not bring politics into this issue."

"I am not bringing politics into this matter. This is purely business. If he cannot be trusted to keep his promise of simply being here on time, then how can we trust him with our money? And we hear that he may not be able to fly out for several hours. Is that true?"

"I really don't know, sir. I cannot comment on rumors and speculation."

"I feel like we should just walk out of this conference. But we will wait only because I really want to give him an earful."

"I appreciate your patience, sir. Remember you are not investing your money back home for the Prime Minister, you are doing it for your country, sir."

"Don't try to play with our emotions and sentiments for the homeland." The man grew even more upset. "The Prime Minister will not face the friendly crowd he was expecting. You should let him know that he ought to be prepared for an unpleasant conversation. He'd better be ready."

"I will let him know, sir," the man said, bowing down slightly to show respect, and walked away. Aamir saw the other men shaking heads in disbelief. He decided to walk around some more and see if he could get a sense of the mood of the crowd. The general feeling was anger and disgust, a feeling that the Prime Minister had shown them disrespect both by being late and then by the attempt of the consular staff to hide the reason.

A consensus finally emerged that the investors would wait for the Prime Minister, no matter how late his arrival. Aamir walked around and heard all sorts of unkind remarks regarding the politicians of the home country, and the general state of affairs. Everyone believed in their own expertise in crisis management, everyone was highly opinionated and willing to offer all kinds of untested solutions. Aamir saw Arlette coming towards him with the usual smirk on her face. She seemed energized and enthused, probably due to chaos.

"Your Prime Minister is not alone in the league of stupid souls," she said. Aamir didn't care to ask her to elaborate, whatever she meant wasn't supposed to be flattering.

"Each and every person carrying an unwarranted idea of his own knowledge is eager to talk about matters they simply don't know about as if they carry a badge made of self-importance which entitles them to do so."

"Whatever," Aamir said, making a hand gesture.

Arlette burst into laughter. "Are you doing the *'whatever'* dance for me? You look silly."

"What do you want me to say? I am sure everyone has ideas about how to make our country better. They deserve to be applauded for their concern, not ridiculed by people like you."

"Well, it doesn't bother me if they have mediocre solutions to offer and if others are willing to listen to them and agree with them. It's not my homeland; not my problem. You are the one who should be concerned."

"If you don't care, then why do you keep bothering me with your sarcastic remarks?"

"I didn't say I don't enjoy sharing my opinion about all this."

"I really don't have time for this nonsense," Aamir replied and tried to turn around and walk away. Arlette grabbed his arm and forced him to spin back.

"This is not nonsense, and you should learn how to handle tough criticism."

"I have no desire to learn any such thing," Aamir freed his arm from her grip. "Especially from a person like you who is absurdly opinionated and unyielding in her views, which are mostly wrong and based on improper assumptions."

"Fine," Arlette stepped back. "Be a cry-baby. You don't have to listen to me. But I will not shut up and I can assure you that I will continue to speak my mind."

Aamir didn't respond but he didn't walk away either. He wasn't sure if there was any other person he really wanted to talk to, Arlette was unnerving but still maybe the most compelling person here.

"What?" Arlette questioned him with interest in her eyes. She saw the hesitation in his eyes. "You don't want to walk away?"

Aamir stood silent for a long moment.

"Any word on the Panchayat in Hayatabad?" Arlette asked after a brief moment of silence. Aamir checked his phone, no text or missing calls. He shook his head and raised his gaze to look at her.

"I hope you have an update before the Prime Minister arrives. I want to question him on this. I hated his latest views on the rape issue. If anything happens to this poor woman in Hayatabad, I will not go easy on him, I can promise that."

"I'll keep checking and let you know as soon as I hear something," Aamir said and started dialing Turab's number. He tried multiple times but there was no answer, and finally settled for sending a text. When he looked up Arlette was gone. He exhaled a deep sigh of relief and walked towards the coffee table, the lure of caffeine too overwhelming to resist.

⁓

While the Consular staff was trying to convince people that the Prime Minister was on his way and the rumors of his plane stuck at the tarmac at Jeddah Airport were just that: mere rumors, cell phones, and other mobile devices started buzzing and clicking. The last straw was the news report on the TV monitors showing live news coverage from Jeddah. It became impossible to continue with their denials and eventually they gave up. The crowd told the staff that they would wait for the Prime Minister until the very last moment that the venue was available, all they needed was truth and honesty.

After several hours of delay, it was announced that the Prime Minister's plane had landed at the Dubai airport and that he was on his way.

In the meantime, Aamir had been able to finally reach Turab. The details were alarming and filled them both with a sense of desperate urgency. It appeared that the Panchayat was about to go into session very soon, perhaps the very next morning. Such proceedings didn't last too long, especially when the verdict was unofficially determined and all that remained was going through the motions. The punishment was extremely swift with no appeals to be concerned with. Within twenty-four hours it could all be over. If the innocent victims of the process were to be saved, it had to be done right away. It was very unlikely that local authorities would move quickly or decisively unless the orders came from high above.

He informed Arlette of the situation. She immediately sent a preliminary report to her editor who they hoped would begin working on it immediately.

"He will approve your reporting of this story, right? Arlette, tell me that he will do something."

"Well, we'll see. Hopefully, he will pay attention to the urgency of the situation. If he doesn't, I know a way around it. I have my charm and I have my areas of influence and believe me I'll use whatever means I have at my disposal in order to see that some good comes out of this trip."

"Well, maybe that will be the only good this evening will produce because I'm not sure if the investment conference is going to get very far," Aamir said with a deep sigh.

"We shall see." Arlette smiled and looked at him in her usual condescending manner.

The usual commotion accompanied the announcement of the Prime Minister's arrival. He was brought into the hall immediately, and in the haste of his arrival, the event organizers forgot that he should have been escorted to a back room and then brought to the stage, rather than passing through the angry crowd. He was apparently oblivious to or didn't care about the inconvenience he had caused everyone, smiling and waving as always. Aamir was amazed at the lack of empathy or awareness. He looked around and saw several unwelcoming faces. People openly and loudly expressed their opinion of being made to wait.

Once everyone was settled down, the usual and expected monotony began. Thankfully, organizers kept the introductory speakers in check and it didn't take long for the Prime Minister to take the podium. He started delivering the speech without a moment of anymore wasted time.

"Any further update?" Aamir heard Arlette's whisper in his ear with her hand on his shoulder. He checked the phone and there was none.

"I am about to go full speed on the Prime Minister in a few minutes. I am the third in a row of reporters who will be able to ask questions," she said. "Let me know if you hear anything new from your sources."

"Okay," Aamir replied. "I will." She patted his shoulder and walked back to her seat.

"This should be interesting," Aamir thought while looking around the room. People had mostly settled down and the conversation normalized, aggression lessened. He kept his phone on vibrate mode and close at hand so he didn't miss a message or call.

Finally, Arlette's name was called and she was handed the microphone. Aamir thought he saw a slight unease on the Prime Minister's face when he heard her name.

"Prime Minister, my name is Arlette Baudis. I am from France," she said in French. "I will speak to you through an interpreter."

"I know you, Arlette," the Prime Minister tried to sound indifferent. "Before you ask the question, I need to make sure that my interpreter is also available."

Aamir saw whispers between the Prime Minister and his secretary. There were some hand gestures, Aamir saw some security officers move across the stage. Then he felt a hand on his shoulder. He turned around.

"You know French?" a man in UAE police uniform was asking the question.

"Yes."

"You need to come with me."

"Okay." He was escorted to the stage. He briefly exchanged glances with Arlette. She smiled and nodded as he was seated next to the Prime Minister. They went through the protocol of confirming that the questions would be repeated back so there would be no misunderstandings or ambiguity. "Yes, Prime Minister," Aamir said respectfully. "I will do that. I will make sure there is no ambiguity."

"Good," The Prime Minister whispered in Aamir's ear in a happy tone. "I appreciate that. I have to be extra careful with this woman. She is an opportunistic bitch. I have German shepherd dogs but she is even more fearsome. A vicious French bitch." Aamir could not help but laugh. Good thing, the microphone was cold.

"Excuse me, Prime Minister," Arlette said out loud. "May I ask the question?"

Her translator spoke. Then Aamir spoke to confirm if the question asked was understood properly. This tedious process took the edge off the question. The words were translated but the tone was lost. Aamir immediately felt that Arlette was not happy about the loss of tonal sharpness. He looked at the Prime Minister. The grin on his face reflected a sense of conquest.

"Prime Minister, there is a real concern about women's issues in your country," Arlette posed her question. "We are hearing reports that women are used as objects of revenge or as a form of punishment. This has happened in the past and there are even reports that it is going on right now. All this despite your government's assurance that such practices will be stopped forcibly."

The Prime Minister kept nodding his head while listening to the translation of the questions. He had a fake smile on his face and a taunting expression in his eyes. Aamir could see anger slowly appearing on Arlette's face.

"What a long question." Finally, the Prime Minister spoke after the completely and properly translated question was presented to him. By now he had switched on the microphone in front of him. "Can you please keep your questions short to the point and not vague or cryptic? I am not sure what you mean by women being used as objects of revenge or as forms of punishment. What exactly are you referring to?"

"I mean if a man commits a crime, a woman in his family ends up being punished by the alternate justice system, which itself is illegal, under the judicial system of your country."

"First of all, this impression is false," the Prime Minister replied after the usual translation routine was over. "Women are not being targeted unfairly in exchange for punishing the culprit if any such thing is even happening. Second, please know that a woman's honor in our traditional society is essentially the honor of the man of the house, more like the honor of the whole family. *Sometimes it is more effective to punish the man by damaging his honor rather than hurting him physically.* Either way, the idea is to punish the culprit so they will not repeat themselves and others will be deterred. Trust me, the real punishment is still for the man who committed the crime, not for the woman. Just like if a man is forced to part with his money or possessions as a penalty, the punishment is still to the man—the owner of the money— and not to the money or property itself."

"This is outrageous!" Arlette almost shouted in anger and disbelief. "Money and physical belongings are property. When you make the man pay for his crime through money, you are punishing the man. But females of the household are not his property. You cannot compare punishment to these women to monetary punishment. That is punishment to the woman and not the man of her family!"

"That's for the family and then the community to decide," the Prime Minister replied. "Crimes are judged according to community standards and so are punishments."

"That makes no sense."

"It should. Let me explain. In many Western societies, people live together and have families together but never actually marry each other. This would have been frowned upon in the same Western countries three, four, or five decades ago. Before that, the children of such unions would have been labeled bastards and would never get rid of this label. But all that sounds strange now. You know why? Because society has changed. Its perception of right and wrong has changed. I will give you another example. Even in the West, prostitution is considered immoral. However, in the West, there are countries where prostitution is legal. In other words, a woman can be objectified and can be taken advantage of if money can be paid and she is willing to be taken advantage of in exchange for money."

"I am not sure about the relevance of all these examples to the question I asked."

"I am saying that in your eyes a man can be punished only when *he* is subjected to a physical or financial penalty," the Prime Minister tried to clarify. "That is your perception of punishment. But that is not the perception of the society in which the man is being punished through exacting punishment on the woman of his family. Just like an honorable woman's perception of honor is different from what a whore or a call girl will consider honor. There was a time in the West when a black man lusting for a white woman would be castrated or killed. Now there are black men for whom white women are willing to do anything and society accepts it."

269

"Your society is punishing females for the crimes committed by their male relatives. That is not right," Arlette insisted.

"Punishment is still being meted out to the man of the family. Sometimes it is direct. At other times it is indirect—through his family's women."

"How can you say that the physical abuse a woman is made to suffer can actually be considered punishment to the man of the house? How is the blood she's spilling or her broken bones affecting him rather than the person suffering them?"

"Once again, since you do not live in that society, there's no way that you can comprehend the concept of indirect punishment."

"How about the fact that when such women are back at home, they face physical and emotional torture at the hands of their own family members on top of the illegal punishment imposed upon them?"

"Well, the law takes its own course if there is any criminal activity or physical torture."

"Is that so? Can you say for sure that the law does come to the rescue of all such victims?"

"How can I, or any elected official, say that the law *always* comes to the rescue of a hundred percent of the victims? Even in the West, the delivery of justice is not without its shortfalls. In fact, sometimes even the officers of the court end up delivering grave injustice. Haven't you heard of convicts winning their freedom after many, many years just because juries convicted them based on insufficient or corrupted evidence, presented by overzealous prosecutors, and now the DNA tests exonerate them. So, if you are asking me whether the justice system in my country is completely foolproof, I cannot, and I will not make this claim. But we do all we can and trust me, the justice system works. And where it does not work, we are trying to improve it."

"What about emotional torture or social boycott?" Arlette was still not satisfied.

"The law can only intervene where there is a criminal act going on. It cannot intervene in people's private lives," the Prime Minister replied with an air of certainty which was intolerably pompous.

"If such women have no recourse and they turn to other countries for protection, will you support that?"

"You mean applying for asylum and such?" The Prime Minister asked.

"Yes," Arlette replied.

"I cannot support that," the Prime Minister's temper suddenly flared, his voice now shaking with anger. "You have to understand. This is against our national honor. The West is very keen on siding with women, especially those who portray themselves as victims. I tell you this, the majority of such stories are just fabricated lies. These women claim rape and assault just so they can gain sympathy and secure asylum and whatnot. I simply cannot support these kinds of activities."

One of the organizers, a tall man in a well-tailored suit, found it appropriate to intervene at that moment.

"Ms. Baudis, may I remind you and all your colleagues that this is a press conference, not a debate. I would suggest you take a seat now and let others have an opportunity to seek answers from the Prime Minister."

"But he has not answered my question."

"I think he has answered your questions the way he wanted to answer," the tall man replied. "You may not like it or find it unsatisfactory, but we have to move on now."

"I see." Arlette reluctantly sat down. Her heated eyes briefly met with Aamir's. He saw her getting a piece of paper out of her purse and start writing on it. She then folded the paper and gave it to one of the stage assistants. After passing through a few hands, the note eventually reached Aamir. It was written in French, she wanted to let the Prime Minister know about the incident unfolding in Hayatabad.

Aamir looked up from the note and saw the Prime Minister staring at him, questioning, so Aamir translated the note in English and pushed it in his direction. After a few more questions a note from the Prime Minister's assistant was dropped in front of Aamir with instructions to translate it into French, to be given to Arlette. The missive assured that notice had been taken of the incident in Hayatabad. Aamir translated it and it eventually saw it end up in Arlette's hands. She sat there for a few moments staring at the note, then suddenly she rose and left, as though the rest of the press conference was of no interest to her. Aamir's eyes subtly continued to follow her until she exited the main hall and disappeared.

TWENTY

THE MORNING SUN above Hayatabad appeared abnormally bloody, the sky was an ominous brew of the very red sun and very dark clouds which seemed to be trying to clutch the bright star and drown it in darkness.

The Haveli was abnormally quiet, almost somber, none of the usual greetings, jokes, complaints, instead every face was serious and everyone was deep in thought. Fear of the unknown prevailing. While they were not allowed to go near the Panchayat hall, their ears were turned towards its walls. Unlike the flimsy mud and wood of their own homes, the hall was made of thick, well-built walls. Nothing could be heard through the imposing hard structure but it sure didn't curb the impulse to try.

Basheer and his men escorted Shams and Zara Bibi into the hall, while Gul and Badri were paraded in front of the entire Panchayat gathering. There were mutterings at the sight of Badri's bruised and cut limbs and upper body which was visible through her tattered clothing.

The proceedings began with Paro walking to the witness chair. Since she was outside the home, she was covered from head to toe. Even the two eye holes in her burqa had nets sewn over them. With the heat, and stress of the occasion, she could hardly breathe. Mullah Aziz was seated nearby. He had felt her quivering hand against his elbow as he walked her to the seat, and knew from experience that she would be nervously rolling her dry tongue across her chapped lips. He felt as if she had tried several times to talk to him but was unable to speak.

"I know you are nervous," Mullah Aziz whispered in her ear in an unusually polite tone. "Don't worry, I'm here. I know exactly what you have to say, word for word. I've read Farah's affidavit too so if you find that you are unable to speak, I'll take over."

Paro was extremely relieved. She exhaled deeply and then retreated once more into herself and the odd bittersweet comfort of the burqa that allowed her to hide. It had been a lifetime ago since her husband spoke to her in a kind manner. She was so accustomed to his constant yelling and battery of insults that this gesture made him seem like a stranger. She wondered if she was seeing a new version of her husband, or if the stubborn grouchy Mullah Aziz was his true self and this was just a convenient act of encouragement. She pressed his hand, then let go.

"I hope they let me," said Aziz after a brief moment, disturbing Paro's train of thought. "After all, there was a reason they brought you to hear what Farah had to say, they must want to hear from you, not just from me."

Once again Paro clenched her husband's hand for a brief moment and then again suddenly let it go. She was finding this kindness unreal, like a scary dream which could become a nightmare if she did not open her eyes. She was finding it hard to fight the distraction this unexpected closeness brought her. She wanted to concentrate on Farah's narrative so she tried to shut her husband out of her mind. She sat in her witness chair and waited.

Everyone settled in. The noise gradually died when Sardar Timur entered, they all fell silent. Turab looked around, made sure that no one was watching him. So far he was in the clear and he chose to see it as a good sign. The night before he had painstakingly sewn his phone in his jacket pocket so it would stay in a fixed spot, then removed the button and cut a larger hole to align it with the camera lens. He had made sure that the phone was fully charged. Now he tapped the pocket to activate it. He sighed with relief to hear the soft sound announcing that the recording was on. He was determined to stay still so that the video would be clear and not shaky or blurry.

As Sardar Timur took his place, he nodded his head to those trying to catch his attention and cast his gaze towards Mullah Aziz, who in turn nodded in acknowledgment. Shujaa was by his side. It was the beginning.

Mullah Aziz simply cleared his throat and the hall quieted.

"You all know why you are here. A man's honor has been attacked. Not just any man, a kind man. A just man. He is an honorable man, a man who is the leader of this community, who has watched over us and protected us. Kept us warm from the cold in so many ways. And even if this wasn't the case, even if he was just some nobody, his honor is still worthy of protection. Not only was his honor destroyed, but it also happened in his own house. His home. No one broke in and did this, it wasn't a stranger. The attacker was not someone unknown. The attacker was someone who owes his life and his sustenance to this man. This man now seeks justice from you all gathered here. Yes, he is powerful. He could have punished the attacker himself. The attack took place in his house, and he had the right to defend his honor by eliminating the attacker right then and there. But he has chosen to let you—the wise men of the community—decide the attacker's fate. Now, you all should understand, you are here to deliver justice, not to exact vengeance. Do you all understand the difference? Do you all understand your duty? If anyone amongst you feels they do not understand their duty on any level, please raise your hand. There is no shame in this, only in continuing in ignorance."

Mullah Aziz paused for a moment. He looked around. All Panchayat members were listening intently. No one raised a hand. He waited for a few more moments. Still, no hands were raised.

"All right. Now I will tell you how this process will move forward. If you have any questions, please do not ask while I am explaining the process because your questions may get answered before I am done. If not, I will entertain all questions before we actually start the proceedings, and I will answer them to your satisfaction. Is that clear?"

"Yes," the crowd replied.

"I can't tell just by voice if everybody is clear. Let me see a show of hands. Please raise your hand if I am not making myself clear," Aziz asked and looked around for a few moments. No hand went up.

"Fine." Aziz nodded his head and spoke in a satisfactory tone. "First we will hear from the accuser. That is Sardar Timur's daughter, Farah. Sardar Timur demands that his daughter not be presented to this gathering. Therefore, my wife will read her statement, both my wife and I have heard it directly from Farah's mouth. We can testify that each word in this statement is a direct quote from her. Her statement was transcribed verbatim and you will hear it from my wife just the way Farah said it. After that we will let the accused speak, he's here and he can say whatever he wishes to say without limitation. You can question him about his statement after he is done, and after that, we will hear from the witnesses. There are two witnesses: Chaman and Zara Bibi. Chaman is a eunuch who works in the Haveli. He has access to all areas of the Haveli. Zara Bibi is also a worker at the Haveli. She works there as a maid and has been an employee for many years. She is also the mother of the accused. You will be able to question both of them after their testimony.

"Once you hear all the testimony and all of your questions are answered, you will decide if the accused is guilty of the crime he has been alleged to have committed. When you decide that guilt has been proven, then you will confirm the punishment. As you know, the honor of a man can only be restored when the guilty suffer the same way he did. An eye for an eye and a tooth for a tooth is the law of retaliation, all sacred books, religions, and systems demand that. We demand that too as a community and so the punishment will come from the Panchayat and the community both. As you can understand, an attack against the honor of a female cannot be avenged by punishing the male perpetrator in the same way, therefore, the proposed punishment for this boy is castration. In this way, the community can be ensured that he cannot repeat his actions, and is in keeping with the traditions practiced by this community. It will also save the community as a whole from a predator such as the accused."

Mullah Aziz paused for a moment to take a sip of water, and to observe. He had given them an abundance of information, a lot to digest. The air in the hall was close and warm, oppressive. As the water slaked his thirst, he looked around taking stock of the crowd, his eyes landing on Turab. He was surprised to see an expression of intense trepidation. He wondered for a moment why Turab was so affected by the proceedings—had he not taken it seriously before? No matter. Turab wasn't a concern, he couldn't change the course of events, or control everybody's reactions. He continued his speech.

"However, as you all know, Sardar Timur is a kind and generous man. He knows that the accused is the only son and that his parents cannot have any more children. Castrating their only male child will stop his family line. Therefore, Sardar Timur has generously offered the parents of the accused a choice. If their son is convicted by this Panchayat, they can either let the boy be punished as I have described or, if they want to save their bloodline, they can offer the girl, their daughter, for punishment. But that question will come later, of course, when the guilt of the accused has been established."

As Mullah Aziz paused, the men craned their necks, looked around, and started muttering among themselves. Turab was puzzled by this very real feeling of doom, it was unfamiliar. This whole episode was unfamiliar. What he had been listening to wasn't unexpected or new, but to hear it all in such finite terms made it real. The catastrophic events that this family would endure were now more vivid, tangible. Before he had only *known*, now–he *felt*.

In addition to this mounting distress, he was deeply concerned about Mullah Aziz. The words he had just spoken and the direction he had given could be used as evidence of his culpability, should this matter become widely known. And that was exactly what was likely to happen once the audio, video, and still images of the proceedings were released. Turab had a sinking certainty that what Mullah Aziz was saying would be considered as evidence of his willing and active participation in this apparently illegal proceeding. If the sentence was hard – and in all likelihood, it was going to be hard–there was no escape for this family, and once the punishment was meted out, a horrific crime would have been committed. His recordings as well as his testimony were likely to be the source of any evidence used in a prosecution. As far as his own role and guilt were concerned, he might qualify for leniency due to his cooperation and efforts to bring the crime to the light of day. Turab knew that when Mullah Aziz discovered he was the source of this evidence, their friendship would be no more.

Turab started to doubt the wisdom of recording the proceedings. Would he really stand to gain anything? There was no benefit that he could see and many bad things that could happen. He didn't understand why he felt so personally affronted by the fates of these people. Gul, his parents, the daughter. Unfortunately, this was not the first, nor would it be the last time this kind of thing happened, so many families just like this one had suffered at the hands of Sardar Timur and people like him. And Sardar Timur was not a unique or uncommon type of character in this society, not a particularly special villain. He was the standard for a character such as himself. And people like Shams and his family were not out of the ordinary, either. This was the normal order of things here. Even if he was able to save one family now–then what? These events were bound to repeat themselves countless times. Families suffering this fate might be different in small ways–perhaps a son was taller or the daughter homely–but there was no doubt in his mind that there would be other families in a similar or worse situation sooner or later. So why should he risk his life and risk his friendship with Mullah Aziz? Even if he were to go through it, there was no guarantee that any action would save Gul or his sister.

He was about to turn off the recording, but then a voice distracted him. It was an old man in white robes using a thick tree branch as a cane.

"If the victim herself is not here to state her complaint, then how can we question her, how can we know that we are hearing is the truth?"

There was sudden quiet in response to the question, the quiet before a storm that was guaranteed to strike. Was the old man suggesting that Farah should be brought before the Panchayat for questioning, hadn't he heard the reason why she was not present? It wasn't the Panchayat's place to question Sardar Timur's daughter.

Mullah Aziz could feel the heat on his face, and the sweat that started to appear merely from the glare burning from Sardar Timur's eyes. He purposely avoided looking in that direction.

"As I said before, my wife and I heard it from Farah in her house, and in the presence of her father, and what you are about to hear is exactly what she said. A blow by blow recount of the horrid episode."

"How do you know?" asked the old man.

"As I said, I was there when the victim told her story," Mullah Aziz repeated, his displeasure at being questioned clearly evident.

"No, you misunderstood me." The old man was unwilling to let up. "I am sure you or your wife will tell the story correctly, the way you heard it. But how do you know what she told you was accurate and true? She may have misrepresented herself."

"Old man," Shujaa could not stop himself. "Are you saying she is a liar?"

There was absolute silence in the hall. Turab could hear his heart thumping uncontrollably, afraid that the old man had condemned himself before he could even judge another person. He turned toward the man, hoping the phone's camera would catch his image clearly and that sound was sharp enough for others to understand.

"I am just saying that it would be helpful if we can question her, and confirm the truth completely before we condemn this family," the old man replied.

Turab was utterly surprised at the confident posture with which this old man stood there questioning authority in such a bold manner. He could not recall this man asking any questions in his previous encounters with Shujaa, Mullah Aziz, or himself, nor did he remember seeing this man stand up to ask questions any other time. He wondered about his motives for speaking up now.

"You should not concern yourself with unnecessary worries," Shujaa's advice sounded more like a threat.

"How can I not?"

"When her statement is read out loud you will know all that you need to know. So stop arguing about this matter. Enough!" Shujaa said in an angry tone and motioned the man to sit down. He didn't budge.

"Have a seat," Sardar Timur intervened after a few moments of awkward silence. "We'll come and talk to you privately in a minute."

The man sat down with some flying hand gestures and muttering under his breath. There was a slow rise of noise in the hall as people started talking among themselves. Turab's eyes shifted uneasily around. Suddenly he felt a tap on his shoulder, he turned around and saw Shujaa standing behind him, gesturing for Turab to follow him. Turab complied, trying not to appear as reluctant as he felt. They walked out, passed the exit door, and found themselves in the glaring sun. As uneasy as he felt in Shujaa's presence, he was glad to escape the hall. The heat beating down on him was preferable to the tension inside.

"Did you give him the money?" Shujaa asked.

Turab suddenly felt his heart drop like a rock, he'd been hoping to avoid any questioning about funds. By now each member of the Panchayat was supposed to have been fully paid the money owed to them. Instead, they had been paid only a fraction.

"Yes," Turab swallowed hard before answering. He was not sure what else to say.

"Was he told the purpose of the cash?"

"Not in so many words, but the reason behind it was made abundantly clear."

"How?" Shujaa asked

"Well, we were very subtle. We told them all that the money was in appreciation for their services and that they were expected to side with the victim. We also reminded them that the Sardar Timur was the one paying for their services, and if the services delivered the desired and just result, then everyone would benefit."

"Did he argue with you or Mullah Aziz?"

"Not with me, I don't know about Mullah Aziz. He did not mention anyone being difficult."

"Okay," Shujaa almost spoke to himself. "I wonder why he is trying to make trouble."

"Maybe he wants more money."

"Yeah, that's always possible. I think I should talk to him."

Turab had the urge to stop him from approaching the old man to warn him that inciting the man further might be a bad idea. But he couldn't decide what to say, so he said nothing. He was worried that the secret would escape, and Shujaa would discover that the money was not entirely utilized as intended, even though he had very sound justification for the non-distribution. Mullah Aziz hoped that the money which had been distributed among the Panchayat members would be considered enough for now and they will fulfill their 'civic' duty. If Shujaa spoke to the old man and found out how much had actually been distributed, it would lead to questions. The two facts that the money had disappeared and that it had been kept a secret from Sardar Timur could have horrific consequences beyond the expected outcome of the trial. Turab kept his head down, his mind going back and forth. There seemed to be no safe solution.

He almost didn't register the silence now surrounding him. He didn't hear Shujaa's voice for several seconds. He looked up and saw him walking away back into the hall. He followed, reluctantly. He wanted to yell his name and somehow stop him but he couldn't utter a word. More than that, he didn't want to go inside and witness whatever unpleasant events were sure to take place.

He dragged himself back in and rested against a wall. There seemed to be an odd pause in the proceedings. Seeing the crowd, the family, and feeling the strain of the occasion became intolerable. Suddenly he felt his knees melting, unable to hold him, he began to collapse, just as he was about to fall he felt a hand on his shoulder. Mullah Aziz was holding him up by his shoulders peering at him closely.

"What's wrong with you?"

"Did you tell Shujaa about the money?" Turab asked.

Mullah's Aziz's face paled and he shook his head.

"Did you tell Sardar Timur when you met last night?" Turab's words were less a question than a statement of hope. The answer this time was the same, which killed all his hopes.

"Who is this old man?" Turab continued after a few moments of silence. "He's causing serious trouble, my friend. Shujaa was asking me if we had distributed the money according to the plan. He was wondering, and couldn't fathom why this man was raising risky questions and attempting to disrupt this session when he was paid and should understand what is expected of him. Why is he being so defiant?"

"I really don't know," Mullah Aziz whispered, distressed.

"I'm afraid that Shujaa will ask him how much he has been paid and when he finds out, we'll be questioned. You should have told Sardar Timur about the robbery."

"I'll tell him right now," Mullah Aziz said. They both looked over at Sardar Timur and much to their surprise and discomfort, they noticed that he was actually watching them, studying them.

"You better do it now," Turab said, grimly. Mullah Aziz nodded and walked away.

Turab's eyes surveyed the hall. Most of the Panchayat members were scattered around in small groups, talking amongst themselves.

Gul and Badri were just staring, eyes vacant. Gul was silent and seemed almost resigned, but his sister seemed to be not there at all. She was disassociating. Zara Bibi and Shams stood in a corner with their heads down petrified. Turab saw Shujaa talking to the old man and tried to prepare himself for the inevitable altercation. The old man didn't appear intimidated by Shujaa's threatening stance, and seemed unmoved by the two men standing next to him, each carrying an AK-103 assault rifle, a popular handheld Russian made weapon which was widely available in these areas following the Afghan war against the Russian invasion of 1979.

Turab watched Shujaa's face shift from angry to enraged in seconds as his hand gestures grew more intense. His gestures becoming erratic and hostile. With each antagonistic gesture, Turab felt a kick in his gut. Shujaa spun his head toward Turab and held his gaze for what seemed like painfully long pounding moments.

"Here comes trouble," Turab thought. He didn't think he had said it aloud but he wasn't certain. Within seconds, Shujaa was walking toward him in haste. Turab had an urge to turn around and run but stood there frozen and stuck in cement watching him yell uproariously while in forward motion.

"What have you done with the money?"

"Mullah Aziz is talking to Sardar Timur about it," Turab, much to his surprise managed to utter a response.

"So this old man is right," Shujaa said, shaking his head. "You didn't distribute the money given to you for this exact purpose. Are you really that stupid? Do you think you can steal money from Sardar Timur and get away with it? Is that what you think? You think you can do something this mindless and hope to stay alive?"

"No, I am not stupid, nor am I mindless" Turab could hardly speak. "Nobody here is either of those things."

"Where is the money? What did you do with it?"

"That's what Mullah Aziz is telling Sardar Timur," Turab's voice was shaking with fear. "If you want answers go talk to them, not me."

Shujaa stood there for a moment while his eyes followed the direction of Turab's finger. He saw Mullah Aziz rapidly approaching Sardar Timur. The Panchayat members were still oblivious to the events unfolding around them.

"Keep an eye on him," Shujaa directed his men who were now surrounding Turab. "Don't let him out of your sight, not for a second."

The armed guards obediently positioned themselves around Turab, he could feel their unyielding stares permeating him. Shujaa advanced towards his boss who was now fully engaged in a seemingly confrontational exchange with Mullah Aziz.

Turab's head was spinning, not really able to logically decipher the events happening around him, and not really able to believe that this was happening. He remembered Mullah Aziz seeing Shujaa, then Mullah Aziz turning around, and then the conversation between them. He kept replaying the sequence of events. Mullah Aziz appeared defiant in the beginning, then seemed to humble rapidly.

Turab saw Sardar Timur rising from his seat and remembered hearing him address the crowd, telling them to leave for the day and come back the next morning.

Shujaa and Mullah Aziz did not move. Turab wanted to walk out but was held back by the guards surrounding him. Once the hall was empty, Shujaa ordered his men to bring Turab in, shoving him towards the now seated, Sardar Timur. Out of the corner of his eye, he caught sight of Rauf being escorted into the hall clearly terrified but holding his head held high. Almost defiantly.

"You went to get the money from the bank?' Turab heard Sardar Timur speak to Rauf, who nodded.

"Who went with you?"

Rauf told him about Assef and narrated the sequence of events.

"Mullah Aziz, who is this man your son is referencing? Who is this man that you sent to the bank with Rauf? How well do you know him?" Sardar Timur took a moment to pause after his brief interrogation.

"I know him because he prays at my mosque, he's always behaved correctly and he carries himself with dignity." Mullah Aziz's voice lacked confidence. His forehead glistened with little beads of sweat.

"How long have you known him?"

"Not too long," Mullah Aziz replied reluctantly.

"How long exactly? How long is not too long!" Sardar Timur paused once again, for effect. "Answer me. How long has he been attending this mosque, your mosque?"

"Six months perhaps, not more than eight months."

"How well do you know him?" Sardar Timur's voice quieted but was brimming with anger, his eyes glazed with ferocity.

"Not too well," Mullah Aziz replied. "I know that he moved here with his mother and that she died two months ago. He has no other family here."

"And yet you trusted him with your son and my money?" Sardar Timur shouted. "How can you be so stupid!?"

Mullah Aziz was incapable of responding, he became aphonic. Humiliated. Turab looked at Rauf who was expressionless. In a different situation, on a different day, Turab believed the Rauf he'd come to know, might have audibly chuckled at such a remark.

"Do you know where he lives?" Shujaa asked. Mullah Aziz nodded.

"Go get him," Sardar Said ordered Shujaa.

"There is one more thing," Turab found himself talking involuntarily. All eyes turned towards him.

286

"There is this bank manager, Zain Malick," Turab spoke reluctantly.

"What about him?" Shujaa asked. Turab told him about their meeting with the police officer and the other robberies. Sardar Timur kept listening, remaining quiet for a bit until Turab completed his explanation.

"Should I bring him too?" Shujaa asked Sardar Timur.

"No," Sardar Timur spoke carefully. "His absence will be noticed at the bank if you bring him here. I don't want to raise any concerns. Just keep an eye on him."

"Okay," Shujaa agreed.

"You three will stay confined in your home from this point on until I release you. You aren't going anywhere. You will not talk to anyone. My men will take you back and will keep an eye on you, do not try to dodge them. You will face severe consequences if you try to flee. Do you understand?"

Turab and Rauf nodded in agreement, Mullah Aziz stood motionless, still voiceless. Sardar Timur stood up and walked out of the hall. Shujaa looked at Mullah Aziz, cocked his head, and motioned him to move. Turab and Rauf followed.

TWENTY ONE

RASHID SPENT THE entire night rehearsing the decided confrontation with his boss. He played out multiple scenarios quite theatrically. The morning was approaching fast and he needed to be prepared for any outcome. At nine a.m. sharp, almost as though he was dreaming, he walked through the bank's front doors, burst into Zain Malick's office, slammed the door behind him, and took a chair without permission. The cigarette in his mouth dangled low for effect and dropped ashes onto Zain Malick's glass desk. The newly confident Rashid exhaled thick circles of smoke, puffing and smiling as the pungent smog floated towards his boss's face, a newfangled sign of blatant disrespect. Zain Malick jumped up out of his chair and undeniably annoyed started yelling, demanding to know what the hell he thought he was doing.

"Shut up and listen," Rashid said, relishing the power.

"What the hell?" Zain Malick was furious. This was gross insubordination. He was a moment away from calling security. "How dare you! Who the hell are you to tell me to shut me up? I'll fire you in an instant!"

"Try that, you stupid bastard, and you will surely rot in jail for years to come."

"What are you talking about?"

"Your scheme is up," Rashid, still in a dream-like trance watched this new version of himself like an out-of-body experience. He tossed his cigarette butt in Zain Malick's face for effect and watched as a collage of grey and white ashes littered his boss's expensive European suit. "From now on, you need to share the robbery proceeds with me. Do you understand?"

There was silence, a long pause. A very, very long pause indeed.

"Did you hear what I just said?"

Zain Malick did not respond. The shock on his face was just as wonderful a delight as he had imagined. Rashid thought about taking a picture and preserving the moment.

"I heard you, but I don't know what the hell you're talking about. What are you babbling about you little idiot, what robbery?"

"Really? You don't know what I am talking about? How do you explain this sudden change in your tone? Why are you so timid and meek all of a sudden?"

Rashid found the long moments of Zain Malick's silence very amusing and enjoyable. "Your silence is very telling. You should be screaming by now like the maniac you always are, but instead, you're not. You are absolutely quiet and I believe very frightened. As you should be. So my dear manager, who's the idiot now?"

"What do you want?"

"Ah. Now we're talking." Rashid lit another cigarette.

"You know you cannot smoke here," Zain Malick was unable to stop himself from trying to control Rashid.

"Stop me if you must." Rashid dared. Zain just shrugged.

"Good, just as I thought," Rashid smiled. "Now you know how to behave with me. I am not just your subordinate; I am also the person who's privy to your secret. Your dirty little criminal enterprise. Think of me more as a partner."

"Again, what do you want?"

"First, I want my promotion."

"That will be difficult," Zain Malick said. "I just did your evaluation as you know, and I cannot change my assessment of your performance this soon."

"Not my problem, you need to find a way to do that."

There was a long exchange of angry stares which ended in Zain Malick giving in. "Let me see what I can do. What else?"

Rashid told him that he expected half of his proceeds, and was rebuffed.

"Half?" Zain Malick asked angrily. "I don't get to keep all of the loot, you idiot, I only get some of it!"

"How much do you get to keep?"

"It depends."

"Depends on what?"

Khan explained that on some occasions he received less than half if his cohorts felt it was an especially risky or difficult job. As he spoke, he wiped his forehead with a wet handkerchief from the breast pocket of his jacket. Rashid had never seen him use one before. He was clearly nervous.

"How difficult can it be? You hand over the money to the customer, call your people, they intercept the customer. Which part of this is difficult?"

"You don't understand," Zain Malick kept wiping his forehead. "I don't argue with these people, ever. Not ever. If they say it was a difficult operation, I simply accept that. I do not want trouble and I do not challenge them. The way I look at it, I'm getting more than a decent amount of money, money that I didn't have before for simply passing on information. They do all the dirty work, they take the bigger risk, I do not. So, I'm happy with what I get."

"Okay," said Rashid thoughtfully, nodding his head. He found the argument compelling.

"Besides, there is nothing to connect me to this arrangement," Zain Malick continued. "If they get caught, they're on their own. They cannot involve me."

"Why not? I'm sure that they can blame you without any qualms whatsoever. How can you be sure that they don't have any proof of your involvement?"

"I am sure the police will want them to have some kind of evidence before they come knocking on my door," said Zain Malick.

Rashid wanted to respond but decided to stay quiet. How could this man be so stupid? It was more than possible, actually, it was probable, that his accomplices were recording his phone calls. Even if they were not, just the allegation would be evidence enough for the bank management to remove him from his position. He could be put under surveillance. In fact, he was under surveillance right now, that's what Rashid was doing at that very moment.

"You poor bastard," Rashid said to himself, looking at Zain Malick's face which was showing clear signs of distress. He thought very briefly about having mercy on the guy and telling him the real story. He hadn't been that bad of a boss. But the idea flickered out almost immediately. There was no benefit in doing so, and he had every reason to continue on this path. He also remembered the bad performance evaluation that Zain Malick had given him. No mercy.

"And keep in mind, don't you even think about cheating me. I want my share, fair, and square. I want to know the exact amount of your cut and I want half of it. Now, if you even think that you will be able to hide the real figure from me, well let's just say, you shouldn't even try. I have my ways and I'll know. I won't tolerate it. Are we clear?"

Zain Malick just nodded his head and didn't utter a word. Rashid kept going since he was doing so well and demanded to know the names and numbers of the accomplices, but Zain Malick could not comply since he did not have their names, and the numbers changed constantly. Rashid pushed back but Zain Malick said that if he demanded that information they would surely become suspicious. It wasn't wise to raise any questions.

Rashid thought for a long moment. There really wasn't much for him to gain by knowing the identity of the actual gang, and there was definitely a lot to lose. He decided to let it go.

"Okay, I hear you, but remember, no games."

"I understand," Zain Malick whispered, and finally relaxed in the big leather chair behind his desk, not feeling as powerful as he once did.

Rashid smiled, tapped the table twice in quick succession with the large stone ring on the second finger of his right hand, and stood up slowly. He thought about making another sarcastic remark, decided against it, and left the office just as casually as he'd breezed in only minutes ago. Zain Malick just sat in his chair staring at an invisible object up toward the ceiling.

Behzad Khan was expecting a busy day. Every Wednesday like clockwork he held his own version of a round table, a debrief with all of the known criminals in town. They were gathered and sat in separate secured cells at the station waiting for their turn to tell all. They were Behzad Khan's criminal informants; his 'C. I's. The focus was to get solid intelligence and to gain insight about criminal ongoings, or on anything that was being planned in his jurisdiction. As with any business, these C. I's were very sensitive about turf, preserving territory was paramount. They were the best source of information.

From time to time they would snitch on each other, and he'd use that to play favorites, and to buy loyalties, and to instill fear in those who would fall on his wrong side. He kept them guessing. The ones who ran afoul would later become favorites, others would feel his wrath, positions would change. Constantly. Taking sides and changing them randomly was a tactic passed onto him from his ancestors who had served under the colonial powers, divide and rule was a time tested policy. If the colonial powers of yesteryears could rule large parts of the world by pitting one group against another, the same could be–and was–done on a micro-level. It was incredibly effective. He did not find any other policy capable of yielding this level of success. The system had worked wonderfully for many years.

He arrived early as always and the group of criminal informants was already placed in separate cells. Behzad Khan walked past the row of cells, scanned all the faces, pointed to two men, and then walked into his office, his secretary following him. He motioned the two identified men to come forward, and the sentry guarding the holding cell let the two men out and two guards escorted them to Behzad's office. As he seated himself, they stood in front of his large desk. The chairs normally available for guests were purposely removed each Wednesday, to remind the criminals of their place.

"Who is robbing Universal Bank's customers?" Behzad Khan didn't care for irrelevant small talk.

The two men heard the question and exchanged inquisitive gazes.

"So you don't know?" They agreed that was so. He asked if they had any knowledge of the robberies, and one man denied knowing anything, "You know nothing at all?"

One of them was still shaking his head, the other was squinting, hesitating.

"So then you know something?"

"I heard about it," stuttered the man.

"What did you hear?"

The man then told Behzad Khan that he heard there were people from out of town getting rich targeting the customers of one specific bank, customers who had withdrawn large sums of cash. It was always on the way out of the bank, no one arriving at the bank to make a deposit ever had a problem. Behzad Khan pressured the man for more information, but the man claimed to know nothing else.

"You are so useless," Behzad Khan was dismissive. "I want you to find out." The man agreed of course since he didn't have the option of refusing.

Behzad Khan glared at him for a moment too long and then motioned for both men to leave. His assistant moved towards the door to let another person in when the phone rang. The assistant answered the phone, listened for a few moments, then spoke to Behzad.

"It's Shujaa, from Sardar Timur's Haveli. He wants to see you,"

"Tell him he can come tomorrow morning."

"He is insisting that you go to the Haveli and see him today, right now."

"Let me talk to him," he said. The assistant handed over the phone.

"I cannot see you until tomorrow," Behzad Khan greeted him, his tone cold.

"This is urgent," Shujaa insisted. "I need you here immediately."

"Shujaa, I am not your servant. If it is truly urgent, I'll see you today but you need to come to me."

"You are a public servant. Your job is to serve the public and I am a member of the public."

"I have no problem serving you, but you are not the only one who needs to be served. I need to be where the government has appointed me to serve."

"Stop being so stubborn," Shujaa said. "You aren't helping yourself."

"I've stuck to my principles all my life," he was not persuaded. "I will serve with dignity and be treated with respect. You are welcome to visit me today, at any time. I'll see you whenever you arrive even if I am tied up with something else. Ok? That's a promise Shujaa, or you can tell me right now over the phone."

Behzad Khan heard the call disconnect. He handed the receiver back to his assistant.

"I'm sure he will be here shortly," the assistant said. He knew that Behzad Khan did not like to be dictated to or willing to tolerate any challenge to his authority, but Shujaa was Sardar Timur's trusted deputy, and Sardar Timur was an influential man.

"I'm quite sure that he will." Behzad Khan's voice was devoid of expression. "Let him in when he shows up, but only him, not his entourage – if he brings one along."

"Okay, sir. I will make sure that he is the only one who gets through."

"No actually," Behzad Khan said suddenly. "Let's have some fun with him."

"What do you mean?" asked the assistant.

"I want this jackass to learn some manners," his tone was now full of spite. "If he shows up, don't let him cross the boundary wall immediately, let him stand and wait, he'll need to be cleared like everyone else. Once he's been let in seat him and tell him that I'm out, that I had to take care of some urgent issue, and that you'll radio me so that I can come back quickly since it's him– an important man of this community–who is visiting us. So, you'll do just that in front of him and ask me to come back quickly. But I won't. We'll let the wretch wait for a little bit and have a little fun. You okay with that, or should I ask someone else?"

The assistant just smiled and nodded. "Okay, sir. Should I bring in the next person from the crowd?"

"Yes," he answered and the assistant complied.

The next few hours went by quickly. He was able to talk to all the criminals brought in that day by lunchtime. He had two officers take notes of names, dates, and significant criminal events in the area under his jurisdiction. Instead of planting informants among criminals, the business of recruiting criminals for the force on an informal basis had turned out to be very productive. More efficient, too.

An hour into this routine, he was informed that Shujaa had arrived and had been seated in the small conference room just outside his office. There were surveillance cameras installed all over the building, and the conference room was no exception. Behzad Khan was able to see the live feed on a screen in his office. Shujaa was not alone. Two men accompanied him as he anticipated and they were getting restless, pacing back and forth and checking the clock on the wall. He found Shujaa's anger which was escalating by the second very amusing.

"I have always hated this bastard," one officer said out loud, laughing.

"Me too," said the second officer, looking over at Behzad Khan. His eyes were glued to the screen, which was displaying very clear images of the conference room.

"What an ass," said Behzad Khan. "He's self-important and he's a complete idiot. His ego is immense and it's only because he works for Sardar Timur. He obviously doesn't realize that he can be replaced in a minute, and most likely will be, but he belongs to a common breed and these people who get close to the rich and all mighty, think they are just that! They live with that illusion until their masters, without warning, pull the plug."

"Should I serve them tea?" one officer asked, clearly mockingly.

He could not contain his laughter. For a brief moment, the entire room shook with the loud bursts of laughter which went around for a few moments before finally dying down.

"Bring him in," Behzad Khan finally said.

"Yes, sir," his assistant said while walking towards the door. Behzad Khan gestured the officers to take two of the three chairs neatly placed across from him. He asked them to leave the middle chair empty.

"Don't say a word unless I tell you to," Behzad Khan instructed them. "Even if he talks to either of you, let me speak. If I want you to say something, I will ask you to respond. During this time, I want both of you to simply stare at his face. I want him to feel really uncomfortable."

"Yes sir," both of them said almost together.

"Let the fun begin," he said and stared at the door expectantly, trying to suppress his grin.

The ride back to the mosque from Panchayat hall was distressing. They had spent the entire day in confinement of sorts before being dismissed and sent back to the mosque. Paro had been transported back to her apartment. Turab was more concerned about himself than Mullah Aziz or Rauf. They both lived there, they were known in the community. If something were to happen to them, it would be noticed and possibly even be an effective deterrent for any negative actions. Turab's situation was different, he was a stranger in this place and bad things could happen to strangers without any consequences. He was unsure if Sardar Timur intended to deal with him in a harmful way. He wasn't sure about his intent at all. He was a journalist, and sooner or later his absence would be apparent and would invite speculation regarding his last known location, might prevent anything untoward from happening. Then again, it might not. These parts of the world had their own set of rules.

In addition to his concern for his physical safety, he was worried about his job. He'd left in a hurry after getting Rauf's call, and suddenly disappearing from work without explanation or approval could create problems. With so many thoughts circulating in his head, the ride back to the mosque went faster than he expected. No one had spoken since they entered the vehicle.

"Go in, and don't leave your place until tomorrow morning," the driver said in an insulting tone. Mullah Aziz was unaccustomed to being spoken to in such a manner, he opened his mouth to complain, but Turab quickly squeezed his hand in an attempt to warn him. They exchanged blank stares and stepped out of the SUV. Two guards followed them to the boundaries of the mosque, nearly marching them directly to Mullah Aziz's dwelling. As soon as Turab and Mullah Aziz crossed the threshold, they closed the door behind them and exhaled.

"Are they going to stay there with their weapons out all night?" Rauf asked nervously.

"I don't know, they very well might!" Mullah Aziz replied. "Let me check. I'll look through the peephole; you check through the window." They watched in unnerving silence, waiting, praying for them to leave.

"Looks like they aren't moving, I'm fairly sure that they're planning to stay the whole night. They're glued to us."

Turab felt the anxiety engulfing him suddenly lift. He was relieved to have the decision of whether or not to flee in the night made for him. Now, knowing that leaving wasn't possible he felt an odd sense of tranquility.

There was a knock on the kitchen wall and Paro's slipper covered feet appeared behind the flimsy kitchen curtain.

"Go talk to your mother," Mullah Aziz pointed Rauf towards the kitchen. "I'm sure she's worried sick. Go tell her what happened today after she was sent home from the Panchayat session. Go!" Rauf almost ran into the kitchen. Mullah Aziz and Turab walked towards the room where they normally conversed and sat down.

"Turab my friend, this really isn't good," Mullah Aziz said in a low-pitched voice devoid of his usual arrogance. He was just about slumped over in his chair. "Sardar Timur is a vindictive man. He never forgives. If he's convinced that we have taken his money, or somehow crossed him, then he will make life hell for us. That's a promise."

"But we haven't crossed him, and we haven't stolen from him," Turab said.

"It doesn't matter," Mullah Aziz said. "All that matter is what he believes. If Timur convinces himself of our guilt – right or wrong– then he will not forgive us."

"I told you not to trust this Assef guy we should have gone to the bank ourselves. How could you trust someone you barely knew with so much money?! Who knows what his involvement is in this whole affair. Maybe he works for Sardar Timur and was spying on us to see what we would do, a test of sorts."

Mullah Aziz gave him a sharp stare for a long moment before breaking his silence.

"I don't like your tone. What the hell are you implying? Do you think I sent Assef to the bank knowing what would happen? Or even worse, are you saying I am involved in the robbery?"

"No!" Turab snapped back. "I did not say any of that. It didn't even cross my mind! Why are you being so defensive?"

"Get your mind straight, "Mullah Aziz stood up and shouted out loud. "How can you even think that? How can you accuse me of being involved in the robbery?"

"I didn't think anything of the sort until you brought it up." Turab was unwilling to back down.

"Get out of my house!" Mullah Aziz yelled. "You cannot be in my house and insult me like this. Get out!"

"How can he leave, Baba?" They turned at Rauf's voice who was standing right by the door. "Sardar Timur's men are stationed outside. They won't let anybody leave. Where would Uncle Turab go?"

"I don't give a damn where he goes and he's not your uncle!" Mullah Aziz replied.

"But he can't go outside. He literally cannot place his foot outside our door. Don't you remember?"

Mullah Aziz gave his son a sharp look, held his gaze for a long moment then turned towards Turab.

"Stop being so stupid. Why would I get involved in a robbery scheme and put my own son in harm's way? Besides, if I wanted the money, I could have just kept it."

"Well," Turab spoke back reluctantly. "We all know keeping Sardar Timur's money without his permission would not have been easy or even possible. But I am sorry, I didn't mean to accuse you. I don't know why I did. I didn't mean it the way it sounded, nor did I mean to insult you."

"Okay," Mullah Aziz said after a long awkward silence, and as he started walking out of the room he turned to Rauf. "Tell your mother I'm hungry and I want to eat, I'm sure you two can use some food as well."

Rauf nodded his head and obediently left the room right behind his father. Turab was left standing alone in the middle of the room.

"You need to assess your situation carefully, boss," Turab said to himself while checking the phone in his breast pocket. He felt the warmth, it was heating up because of continual use. He took the phone out and turned it off after making sure that the recording so far was safe. He was alleviated that Sardar Timur's men hadn't frisked him. To say that they wouldn't have reacted well to his recording the proceedings was an understatement. The consequence could have been fatal. Now he had to work out his next move, he needed to decide what to do with the recording. Of course, he wanted to use it to protect that poor boy Gul, the sister, and parents, but he also needed to protect himself.

His mind was spinning with different ideas, fears, and plans.

When he had received Rauf's phone call and rushed to Mullah Aziz's home, he had no idea what he was getting himself into. Events since that moment were full of surprises and uncertainties with no end in sight.

He had the means to send the recording to Aamir, and by extension, the Prime Minister. That surely would result in meaningful action to stop this atrocity from being committed. But then what? The rigid, barbaric mentality of Sardar Timur and other people like him was not going to change just because people like Turab and Aamir were able to stop one such incident. One incident. Turab felt hopeless, the futility of it all was real. How would one little achievement even count when compared to the number of so many similar incidents occurring daily? It would be one tiny shooting star in the night sky, barely noticeable and quickly gone.

His dark train of thought was interrupted when he heard snapping fingers, followed by the sight of Rauf's face. He hadn't noticed the boy sneak into the room.

"Uncle Turab," he heard Rauf almost whisper. "Food is ready; do you want to join us?"

"Sure," Turab said with a diffident smile. He had always made fun of people who would become so engrossed in their thoughts that they become oblivious to their surroundings. He always considered that a sign of aging. Now, apparently, he was aging. Or perhaps his theory was wrong all along. Perhaps all of "these other people" had more on their minds than he could have ever imagined.

The little wobbly table was surrounded by three similarly broken and scuffed chairs. The comforting aroma of freshly cooked food invaded the room and his appetite returned temporarily displacing the fear. The three men sat and ate in the blissful absence of noise, Mullah Aziz was deep in thought, Rauf was uncharacteristically serious and Turab was still trying to chart his future course of action.

Mullah Aziz suddenly spoke. "I'm not sure if I want to conduct the Panchayat proceedings any longer. I think tomorrow, I'll tell Sardar Timur that I can't go on, that I'm going to bow out." He appeared to be perhaps talking to himself without realizing that everyone could hear.

"I hope you don't think that this is your way out of this money issue," Turab cautioned him.

"What is he going to do? He cannot make me pay. I don't have any money. Besides, I did not steal the money from Sardar Timur. Other people with no connection to me stole it. That's the truth."

"As you said before," Turab countered, "Truth does not matter. It's the perception in Sardar Timur's mind which can save or ruin our lives and that of those around us."

Mullah Aziz went quiet for a long moment, staring at Rauf. The boy was busy eating, not realizing that he was the focus of his father's thoughtful stares and fear.

"See if your mother has made more *chapatti*," Mullah Aziz spoke, realizing his plate was empty.

"Okay," Rauf nodded while speaking and respectfully stood up dutifully. Turab found his behavior odd. He hadn't behaved in such a submissive way during this visit. Rather the opposite.

"Looks like he's feeling guilty or responsible for what happened with the money. Normally he's not this docile." Turab said.

"Yes. Truth be told I'm very worried about him. He is incredibly frustrating most of the time, but he's my child. My first, and the only living son I have. I don't want to see him getting hurt. I really think I should get him out of here and soon, and I'll try to get you out as well. Turab, I think that you might need to take him with you, I think that's a favor I might need and I know it's a very big one indeed. His escaping Sardar Timur's wrath is the most important thing right now for me."

"Are you sure you want to do this?" Turab could not stop himself from asking the question, which sounded unnecessary as soon as he uttered the words.

"Yes," Mullah Aziz nodded. "I am sure."

"Wouldn't that be like admitting guilt?"

"Admission or not, it doesn't matter," Mullah Aziz said. "There is no guarantee that Sardar Timur will not come after me. If Rauf is away at least I'll have the satisfaction of saving him."

Turab studied his face, he seemed defeated, and he very well might be. Mullah Aziz was humbled in that moment; the usual imperious expressions absent. Simply put, he was terror-stricken.

The conversation came to a screeching halt when Rauf came back into the room. He too appeared more quieted, and the real gravity of the situation hadn't yet struck. His father was about to bring him down to earth fast and hard.

"Rauf, this is the deal. Turab and I have agreed that he must leave and that he has to take you with him. The reality is that you may not be able to come back home for a very long time. I don't know how long, but long enough to ensure safety." Rauf's face paled, he looked suddenly ashen. He'd never been away from home, from his family. This was an unexpected gargantuan jolt.

"How will we do that? I don't understand Baba?" he asked. "Sardar Timur's men are standing outside and I don't think they plan on just letting us go, and even if they do, what will I do on my own without you?!"

"I think I can arrange something, please calm down." Mullah Aziz said thoughtfully.

"How Baba!?" Rauf asked.

"Remember the people who came to see me the other day, when you called Turab to come over here?"

"Yes, how could I forget," Rauf and Turab both said almost together. Nothing had been normal since.

"That man, the Army Captain gave me his cell number," Aziz said. "He told me that I can call him anytime, for anything. He promised that he will help me in any way that he possibly can. I think I'll put his words to the test and see what his willingness is to follow through on his commitment."

"What Captain?" Turab asked. "What are you talking about?"

"You'll see," Mullah Aziz said with a newfound calm.

"Who the hell are you talking about Mullah Aziz?" Turab demanded. "Come to think of it, I remember that's what Rauf told me when he called me. In all the excitement I've forgotten the whole reason I came to be here. That's right. Rauf, you said some people showed up and took your father away and you wanted my help. But when I came here, your father was here safe and sound. So tell me, what the hell is going on here? Who came to see you? Who is this Captain?"

Mullah Aziz was staring at the ceiling, muttering. The hum of his voice was audible but they could not decipher the actual words.

"Tell him, Mullah Aziz," a female voice filled the room. All three men appeared shocked by the sound, at the unexpected intercession that Paro decided to make. She was standing behind the closed door, out in the foyer, clearly unable to contain her anxiety, and appeared desperate to know what was going on and perhaps influence what was about to happen. This was her son that he was about to send away. She had a right to know.

Mullah Aziz remained quiet. Turab was surprised to see that he did not immediately and sneeringly reject Paro's suggestion, a quite uncharacteristic suppression of his customary attitude toward his wife. In his mind, she was always wrong and any suggestions coming from her were bound to be rejected, after all, she was just a woman. The lesser of the two genders.

"The Captain demanded complete secrecy and I gave him my word." Mullah Aziz's weak tone was demonstrative of his very real struggle. He knew that he had to find a way to gain some strength if he was going to come out of this unscathed.

"You are in danger, " Paro continued. "I am in danger. We all are in danger. I am sure he would understand that you had no choice."

"But I do," Mullah Aziz replied. "I do have a choice."

"Really? You think you have a choice? What choice do you have?" Paro asked. Her tone was unexpectedly commanding.

"I don't know," Mullah Aziz stayed quiet for a moment before shrugging and acknowledging that he really had no choice. Sardar Timur's men were on guard outside. He was effectively a prisoner in his own house, his friend and his family were essentially hostages. In

Sardar Timur's eyes, he had either cheated him out of money or was irresponsible and stupid. If he was able to get the Panchayat to deliver the sentence Sardar wanted, the members of the Panchayat would want their money. He didn't have it. Sardar could give more money to satisfy the Panchayat members, but the stolen money would still be considered his responsibility and Sardar Timur would want it back. Repayment of some type, the *"some"* is what concerned him. Sardar Timur was not a man that forgave error.

The worst outcome would be if the Panchayat somehow did not deliver the expected and desired sentence simply because the money had not been paid. Sardar Timur would then not have the money, nor the outcome he wanted, and the culprit would go unpunished. All this would fall on his shoulders. This would surely incense him and drive his anger and thirst for revenge. There was no telling what would happen to his family and Turab. It really all boiled down to degrees of evil.

Finally, Mullah Aziz made up his mind. "All right. I'll let you in on the meeting, then you'll understand who I'm talking about. I sure hope this Captain comes to my rescue because it will benefit you and Rauf for sure, and I'll see if he can arrange for my protection as well."

"Okay," Turab was fully attentive.

Mullah Aziz spent the next several minutes narrating the events of the other day and his conversation with the Captain.

"Are you serious?! That's really something Mullah Aziz, my friend." Turab could not contain his surprise once he'd finished with his story. "All this was going on and you just sat on it. You didn't even give me a hint. I didn't realize that you were this deep."

"Are you going to complain about what I didn't do? Or will you start appreciating what I just did? I broke my promise to the Captain.

Now I must ask you to promise that you will not share this story with anyone else."

"I am a reporter and an accomplished journalist. I cover war zones, I cover real-life events, I cover the news. It's what I do." Turab said. "It's my job to share stories with others."

"I told you off the record!" Mullah Aziz was agitated by Turab's lack of appreciation for his concern and trepidation. The Captain, like Sardar Timur, was not a man to cross and Mullah Aziz was caught in the crosshairs.

"You didn't say that before telling me the story," Turab snapped back.

"I am telling you now. You will not report this story! The only reason I told you, is to help you understand that the help I am going to seek is from this Army Captain, and for your benefit. Without knowledge of this whole story, you wouldn't trust him."

Turab went silent for a moment. All eyes were fixed on him. After a long awkward silence, he relented. "Okay, I agree, I'll remain silent on this part of the story. Tell me, what kind of help do you expect to get from him?"

"I'm not sure what to ask him exactly," Aziz said. "As I said, I just want my son to be safe, and I don't want any harm coming your way, either. You were just a bystander, a friend trying to help me and my family. You came here because my son called you. Otherwise, you would probably be comfortable at home, without worry." His face was grim. He went phone in hand to the other room. No one followed.

Turab found Mullah Aziz's concern about his safety touching, a rare thing. For once he came across as a sympathetic and caring person. Turab felt strangled by this feeling of unease at the idea of leaving Mullah Aziz and his wife in peril, he wasn't sure if he could actually allow himself to walk, while his friend remained imprisoned with a future which was uncertain at best.

TWENTY TWO

T HE PRESS CONFERENCE continued until after
midnight. The Prime Minister's assistant told Aamir that he
would need to remain after the conference as the Prime Minister wanted
to invite him for a late dinner with the rest of his entourage, and after
that, he was requested to stay even later for a private conversation. This
was an offer Aamir wanted to refuse but could not, something in the
messenger's demeanor told him that declining was not an option, and
in fact, the man gave him strangely hostile looks as he delivered the
invitation. Aamir felt an unusually heightened sense of disquiet as he
agreed to the plan.

The dinner was lavish as expected, taking place in a sumptuous
and obviously very expensive venue. The Prime Minister had invited
a select group of people, most of them accompanied to the dinner by
their wives. Those who were single were provided company by their
host. All guests were required to leave their cell phones at coat check,
no recording devices were allowed, and all were sworn to secrecy.
Standard procedure.

Aamir knew many of the guests by face. Politicians, businessmen
who benefited immensely by their association with the Prime Minister
and his party, billions and billions in the shape of government
contracts, and bureaucrats with cushy sinecures essential to grease
the government machinery. He knew that, in this respect, all countries

were the same, all governments were the same. Aamir, being a U.S. citizen, had business relationships with media persons in Washington and elsewhere in the U.S., as well as Brussels, China, India, and many other parts of the world.

In his mind, there was nothing wrong with these two components of society cozying up to each other as long as there were fair rules of engagement, strictly followed. The Prime Minister's government did not believe in subtle niceties, and the result was a marked difference in the success and stature of different businesses and the business leaders personally. Those close to the Prime Minister were surprisingly successful in their businesses. Others were less fortunate. Much less fortunate. Tonight, the invitees included only the wealthiest and highly successful individuals.

Aamir looked around, listening. He felt that he was sitting on a rich pile of dirt where he could dig as much as he wanted and would end up with stories for eternity. His mind was swimming laps in an infinity pool by the end of the last course.

"I hope we can speak freely in here," a business tycoon, whose success was almost entirely the result of abundant blessings from the Prime Minister, said loudly, obnoxiously, as if he had more secrets than anyone to keep. "I hope these walls have no ears. Right, Prime Minister?"

"Here, here!" Some other guests jumped in before the Prime Minister could answer. They were eager to display their status by the information they wanted to be kept private. Aamir assessed the look on the Prime Minister's face, and it spurred on a feeling of foreboding, a storm to come. His stomach became unsettled, a deep hollowness in his gut that from experience had never led him astray. He knew that the Prime Minister appeared most relaxed and pleased when he was on the verge of something disruptive.

"For the most part, yes," the Prime Minister said, trying to contain his smug look from underneath his bristly mustache.

"What do you mean for the most part? Are we being listened to, or spied on?" the first man asked.

"Not quite spied on," the Prime Minister said. "But we may have a guest who has, shall we say, very sharp ears and an even sharper pen. You may have to worry about him a little. Not much. Just a little bit."

"Who?! Do we have somebody here from the bloody media?" one of them shouted.

"You guessed right." The Prime Minister's assistant spoke. "We have one such person here. But I won't name him. I'll let you identify him; it will be most entertaining."

"This is really unfair and unacceptable" another person from the crowd shouted out. "We absolutely cannot speak freely if we know that there's a snitch on the guest list. You should tell us who he is or escort him out. How the bloody hell did he get in anyway?"

"We'll get rid of him," the assistant said. "But let's have some fun first."

"How is that? How do we do that?'

"Let's make this the game of the night, tonight's show. Let's catch the bastard together. You can all guess and check out people around you and eventually, sooner rather than later, you will identify the vermin."

Suddenly there was an uncomfortable silence in the room. It lingered and taunted for a few uneasy moments before finally giving into loud chatter. People were studying the faces around them, like sharks scenting blood. Aamir knew it was a matter of seconds.

"You look familiar," eventually one person pointed a finger at him. "I think you were a host of some cheap news show a while ago. Weren't you? You must be the hack."

Now Aamir with certainty was the focus of everyone's attention. The words came out of his mouth involuntarily.

"Yes."

"My," the Prime Minister's assistant spoke, insincere amazement oozing from his voice. "It didn't take long. Amazing."

"Why is he here?" another person asked, his tone was demanding and agitated.

"The Prime Minister invited me." Aamir decided to stand up to the crowd. "His assistant told me that the Prime Minister would like to have a word with me after dinner."

The crowd wanted to know why.

"His presence here at the conference was suspect." the Prime Minister's assistant replied. "He slipped out of the country after dodging our security officials, we saw him here skulking about and naturally it sparked our curiosity. It was agreed that it would be prudent to bring him here, in front of all of you, and question him in order to prevent catastrophe. Call it damage control."

"Yes, prudent is an understatement, that makes perfect sense. So, here he is, in front of us all. What now?" Aamir was not surprised, but still appalled that these supposed Turks of industry didn't see through these cheap lies and blatant manipulations. How quickly they jumped all riddled with greed.

"Well, now we grill him," the assistant said. "Everyone's welcome to ask any questions that come to mind, interrogate him if you will. I know a lot of us, or most of us, have a real beef with his tabloid media group, and now is your opportunity to give him a taste of his own medicine. Call it a gift from the Prime Minister."

"Yes, that is correct! Don't let him go!" someone shouted out. "These bastards think that only they are the guardians of democracy and everything decent. They think they are the angels and that everybody else is dirty and corrupt. I would love to kick some ass today."

Aamir's initial unease was now growing into full-blown apprehension. He began to think that he actually might be at risk. The crowd was angry—maybe not with him personally, but certainly with what they thought he represented: the journalists and news anchors with wildly popular talk shows on the country's fairly new electronic media.

Political talk shows with politicians, journalists, and army generals advertised as distinguished guests went on, only to be mocked. These programs had become increasingly popular and were now an influential public relations force, a modern-day genie out of the bottle. In many cases, the lines between good-faith reporting and outright, malicious fabrication were blurred or not at all present.

It was true that many of his journalist friends felt they had to take part in the 'gotcha' game. While he did not agree with their approach, Aamir understood the dilemma they faced, journalists and news anchors who were balanced and moderate, were ranked lowest in viewership numbers and ratings. People wanted to see behind closed doors. They wanted to watch secrets being revealed, or tune in as scandals unfold, they enjoyed and thrived on chaos. Somber news and serious voices were not as provocative or enticing. Since the media in this conservative country could not use sexualized images and stories to gain ratings and earnings, they used sacrilege and false publicity to do so. When it was argued that to do this was socially irresponsible, the default response was that it was economically irresponsible not to do these things. The argument was that this was the only way, otherwise, jobs would be lost, businesses would fail, and the country would fall into even a worse state.

Aamir could speak to this to the crowd around him, but only if they allowed it. He had a strong feeling this would not be the case, no matter how convincing his arguments might be. He knew how bad it looked, but he couldn't stop constantly shifting, like a runner about to sprint, his eyes scanning the room for the nearest exit. One of the Prime Minister's guards loudly asked him if he was looking for an escape route, which caused the ripples of ridicule, insults, and laughter to grow even louder. Voices demanded that he should not be allowed to leave.

He had never faced a situation like this. Involuntarily his hands were patting the pockets of his jacket and trousers, only to realize that he did not have his phone. He found himself staring at his trembling hands. The sudden realization that he could be facing an imminent danger to his physical well-being, life, and liberty sent sharp, cold chills through his body. It was a real possibility especially since he was an unwanted commodity in his country. Journalists were known to disappear.

Two guards magically appeared on each side and held Aamir by his arms, as a third guard stood in front of him facing the crowd, blocking him in. Aamir could only see the back of his head and his profile. He was unfamiliar. It didn't matter if he knew them or not. What mattered was who signed their paycheck.

"Gentlemen, we are all angry right now," Aamir heard the man say with his hand extended backward and a finger pointing towards Aamir. "Please allow my men to do their job and to question him privately."

Aamir heard the murmurs spreading across the room only to be shattered by a sharp toned, shrill, female voice. She objected to the plan, and many agreed.

"Don't worry, we'll question him," the guard said. "Let us handle this, it's what we do. Please go and enjoy yourselves, let the party continue as it was before this interruption."

They were silent for a long moment, not responsive through gesture or voice. The guards didn't wait any longer, they pushed Aamir towards the exit door and dragged him away. He remembered hearing insults and booing behind him, but didn't bother to turn around to see the faces. There was no need for it. One face was just like another. They were all of the same mind. Cut from the same cloth.

He was brought to a small room outside the banquet hall, shoved through the door, and forced to sit on a small wooden chair.

"Give me the claim check for your jacket." Aamir saw a hand extended towards him while he heard the stern voice. He complied quietly. Within a few minutes, his jacket was thrown at his face. He caught it before it fell to the ground. He stood up, put it on, then checked the pocket.

"My phone is missing. I need it."

"Walk to the exit. We will get it for you." The two men pulled him from the chair and shoved him toward the door to the outside. The moment he stepped past the door, he heard someone shout his name. He turned around and saw a phone thrown at him, almost hitting him in the face. Remarkably even with frayed nerves, he was able to catch it. He hurriedly put it in his pocket, walked off the hotel grounds, and was almost run over by a cab. He motioned to the driver.

"Where do you want to go?" the Filipino cabbie asked.

"Burj," Aamir startled himself by shouting the name very loudly, still unstrung from his experience. The cabbie looked at his reflection in the rearview mirror with some suspicion, he knew how he looked, but Aamir was too afraid to notice or care about the driver's reaction. The car went into motion and Aamir threw his head on the back of the seat, exhaling a long and deep sigh of relief.

The ride to the hotel and subsequent elevator ride to his floor, followed by a quick walk to the room, was delightfully uneventful. He locked the door behind him immediately. Without turning the lights on, he threw himself on the bed surprising himself when he realized that rapid breathing was his own. Eyes closed, he tried to calm himself.

This was the second incident within one week where he'd found himself terrorized by government power players and so-called heavy hitters. Tonight's incident was shocking even in light of what he had seen done to other journalists. Being threatened by mysterious people presumably working for the government's secret agencies was not uncommon, but being subjected to such harassment at a private party hosted by the Prime Minister himself, was atypical and in his mind, daunting. If the Prime Minister could orchestrate this and carry it out directly, he must feel quite omnipotent and unassailable. What did that mean for the rule of law in his home country, or even in foreign lands, at the hands of custodians of the law of his country? No wonder he and his colleagues were said to be working in one of the most dangerous countries for journalists.

Aamir knew that the message couldn't be clearer. No more snooping. But the more important issue, or question, was why? Was it known that he had meetings with Arlette, or that his boss was not the biggest supporter of the Prime Minister? He sighed. It didn't really matter. The point was clear: stay away.

After a long dark moment of feeling the dregs of defeat, he slowly opened his eyes. The room was completely covered in a wallpaper of shadows except for the soft, safe glow of the night lamp. He noticed the red blinking light on the hotel phone sitting on the night table, indicating that he had messages waiting. At first, he was hesitant to retrieve them but curiosity won over fear. He played the recordings. One message was from Arlette and another from Turab, both referenced urgent, unanswered calls to his cell phone. He retrieved the cell phone from his pocket and checked the call log: two missed calls from Arlette and ten missed calls from Turab, and several voicemails as well. Turab's persistent efforts to reach him were startling and he called back without hesitation. The call was answered almost before the first ring had ended.

"God, I have been trying to reach you for hours! Where the hell have you been?"

"What do you need?" Aamir decided to ignore his question. They could discuss his evening some other time.

"I'm in big trouble and need your help," Turab said and without pausing, narrated the day's events. Despite his dazed condition, Aamir was able to absorb the severity of the situation. He didn't say much as Turab spoke, just the occasional "Uh-huh" as the story was told.

"I don't know what to do," Turab sounded genuinely concerned. "I want to save this boy and myself, but I don't want to leave Mullah Aziz and his wife behind."

"Let me check with Arlette and I'll call you back," Aamir said, starting to consider possible options.

"No!" Turab almost yelled in the phone. "Please don't hang up, I'm staying on the phone. You can talk to anybody you wish but put me on hold, please Aamir don't hang up. Stay with me."

"Very well stay put," Aamir said as he gently put the cell phone down, face-up, on the bed. He called Arlette from the hotel room phone. She was on the way, promising to join him without any delay.

"Can you send the video?" Aamir asked Turab.

"I'll try," Turab replied. "It's a large file. I am not sure if the internet connection here will let me do it."

"Can you separate the audio from the video and send just the audio first?"

"Let me try." Aamir heard him putting the phone down as he placed him on hold.

"Dammit, I'm still trying." Turab's voice came through after a long pause. At the same moment, there was a demanding knock on the door. Aamir looked through the magnified peephole and saw Arlette's troubled expression peering directly back at him. He let her in as he spoke to Turab.

"Keep trying, I'll stay with you," Aamir said out loud. "I am going to mute from my side. You won't hear my voice but I'll hear yours, I am going to stay with you, I won't leave you Turab. Once you are done, just give me a shout out."

"Okay, understood." he heard Turab's voice from the other side and then pressed the mute button on his phone. Arlette had remained quiet during this time.

"Thanks for coming," Aamir addressed her. "I had a terrible time with the Prime Minister. Unbelievable! Shocking! Please forgive me if I rant on and on, but I'm still really worked up and I have to tell somebody, I'm trusting you, Arlette. I can't keep this bottled up."

"Okay," Arlette said. "Tell me what happened. I'm all ears." Aamir opened his mouth but before he could speak, Arlette interrupted. "Wait a minute. Let me record it."

"Why?"

"I'll tell you later," Arlette said and pressed the recording button on her phone. Aamir started speaking. He sounded feeble and perplexed initially, but by the time he was done, he was enraged. Arlette held him in a tight embrace in hopes of pacifying him, she needed him clear and functioning, not falling apart. Fortunately, the simple human interaction renewed him, knowing that he had a partner in Arlette, provided him with the encouragement he needed to forge ahead. She held his gaze, and then without saying a word replayed the recording. Aamir found the passion in his own voice unanticipated.

"Your words may be disputed but the truth in your tone is undeniable," Arlette said. "If you ever decide to write a story about this incident, this recording will establish your credibility."

Aamir exhaled a long sigh and quietly muttered sincere thanks. He wasn't sure if Arlette even heard it.

"Is that your source from Hayatabad?" Arlette asked while staring at Aamir's cell phone.

"Yes,' Aamir nodded. "He has a dire situation and he needs serious help. I think they all need help right away."

"Give me the details."

"Let me ask Turab to fill you in," Aamir replied and without waiting for Arlette's response, un-muted the phone. Turab was still on the other end. They could hear the noise made by stuff being moved around. Aamir yelled his name to get his attention and asked him to narrate the day's events for Arlette, which he did eagerly.

"Wow," Arlette's surprise was obvious and genuine. "And you have taped all this?"

"Yes," Turab replied.

"Are you able to forward this video?" Arlette asked.

"Yes," Turab said. "That's what I am trying to do."

"He's still having trouble uploading the video," Aamir informed her. "I told him to separate the audio from video and send it over. It will be a much smaller file and should be easy to upload."

"I don't know how to do that," Turab was heard talking. "I am afraid I might erase the whole video."

"Well, I'm no expert either," Aamir said. "But I think you will need to do it on a computer. A desktop or a laptop. I don't think you can do it on your phone."

"I am working on a computer here," Turab said. "But this is an old machine, and I'm praying to God that it works with me, and not against me."

"You keep working," Aamir said. "We're right here, staying with you. I'm going to mute on this side again."

"Okay," Turab agreed, and Aamir muted the phone again.

"You think just the audio will help?" Aamir asked Arlette.

"It will be better than nothing," Arlette said carefully. "However, the video will still be needed to corroborate the accusations based on just the audio recording."

"We need to find a way to release story and have it believed based on the audio only." Aamir agreed.

"Well, it can be put out on social media without any verification or editorial review," Arlette said. "That should get the momentum going but it will take time. And for any credible news or wire service to put it out, you will need corroborating evidence."

"Can't we use voice matching technology to assure the world that the people they hear in these recordings are really those the story claims them to be?"

"That is one way to do it," Arlette said. "If there is any other recording available which shows Sardar Timur's image and also has his undisputed audio, then that recording can be used as a standard to authenticate the video or audio from Turab."

"Let me check," Aamir said. "There should be plenty, he's appeared as a guest on many political talk shows, and besides, the man is a member of the legislative assembly. He has also been minister of some sort."

"Really?" Arlette sounded surprised.

"You didn't know that?" Aamir asked in an equally startled tone.

"No," Arlette said. "I don't follow every politician in your country. I had never heard his name before tonight."

"Well," Aamir said. "Maybe internationally he is not a known figure, but within the country and especially locally, he is very influential."

"I see. Whatever. So he is a product of your electoral system. He practices democracy or at least gives it lip service. Is that what you are telling me?"

"In a way, yes," Aamir said almost feeling guilty. "That's what I am telling you. Yes, he is a product of our democratic system of government. People elected him." He wasn't surprised by her disdainful response.

"How stupid are your people? Where the damn hell is the moral compass? How can your masses choose people like him? And when you elect such people then why do you complain about the consequences—you should know what you'll end up getting. Your people are fully aware of what you are putting in the election system."

Aamir had no rebuttal. He himself had wondered for a long time, what drove people in his native land to support candidates whose corruption was not a secret, at best. People who complained about the state of the nation the most were the same people who would support such leaders unconditionally; they would chant slogans for them, sing songs, rally for them, fight among themselves and still hope that things will turn around for the better. He wondered if they were delusional or just hopelessly optimistic. Whichever, they were defrauding themselves and compromising their future. The more he thought about it, the more he was convinced that the very people who complained and also suffered the most were the ones to blame.

He believed that people knew that this was the case, deep down, but did not, or could not, face the reality that they had helped to create. They said they wanted to solve their problems, but the reality was, they did not want the solution that would eliminate the problem, they wanted the illusion of a solution to comfort them. How could they be saved from themselves? It was just not possible until something changed in a very fundamental way. The candidates who stood for election were the same people or the same type of people each time. From what Turab had described, it did not sound as if anyone would dare run against this Sardar character anyway, and surely the situation was the same in many towns and cities. Aamir didn't see that changing anytime soon.

"Hello," he saw Arlette's hand waving right in front of his eyes. "Are you still with me?"

"Oh, yes. Yes." Aamir snapped back in the room, away from his thoughts.

"Good. Welcome back," Arlette said. "You don't have to respond to my remark. I know how you feel. How any reasonable person would feel? But we are not here to cure the social and political ills of your people. Find me an audio or video of this Sardar Timur so I can have my people conduct a voice analysis on it."

"Sure," Aamir said and then went online to find videos. It was extremely simple: as with all politicians, Sardar Timur was publicity-hungry. Aamir quickly found several videos of him appearing on political talk shows and sent a few links to Arlette, who immediately forwarded the links to wherever she needed to send them.

"What about Turab's audio? Has that come through yet?"

"Oh yes," Aamir remembered. "Let me check." He looked at his phone. Turab's blank email with a rather large attachment was still downloading.

"We should have it within a few minutes," Aamir said while staring at the screen. "There it is."

The announcement of the file's arrival drew their attention to the screen. While there was no video, they still chose to stare at the screen and see the squiggly audio lines getting crossed by a flat vertical line running across the screen. They had to concentrate to hear what was happening, as there was a lot of noise in the background and sometimes the target speaker's voice was drowned out. Aamir's facial expressions changed frequently as he listened. He paused often to translate the events for Arlette. Her countenance kept changing from inquisitive to surprise to anger and then to despair.

"That's incredible," Aamir exclaimed once the computer went quiet. "Quite an indictment."

"We will see," Arlette replied.

"What do you mean–shouldn't this be sufficient to hold them responsible for their crimes?"

"Maybe," Arlette was objective. "Maybe not. It's not our place to assess the sufficiency of evidence for criminal responsibility. But for our purposes, this should be good enough."

"Good," Aamir exhaled a sigh of relief. He felt reassured. It dawned on him that all he had to do was make the recording public through a credible source. Hopefully, that would be enough to save the lives about to be ruined. He needed to focus on that goal, not punishing the perpetrators of this tragedy.

"Do you need me to forward it to someone?" Aamir asked.

"You forward this file and other links of Sardar Timur's videos to me and I will take it from there," Arlette said. "If these files originate from my email address, they will be attended to immediately."

"Okay," Aamir said and forwarded the needed files and information.

"Let's see what happens," Arlette said and opened up her laptop. She stayed busy for a few minutes and then stood.

"It's done," she declared. "Now, we wait."

Aamir closed his eyes and let himself fall back into the soft, cushioned chair, feeling as though a huge burden had been lifted from his shoulders, even if for only a moment before apprehension would once again swoon, and doubt would once again begin to overtake. The reality was that nothing had truly changed yet. The only difference was hope that the life and honor of Badri and Gul's family might be saved. It was a monumental feat.

Little did he know, tonight was not kind to either of the two siblings. In fact, it was hell.

TWENTY THREE

G UL'S DRY, ALMOST lifeless tongue was hanging out of his mouth. His eyes were rolled backward. He looked weak, pale, lifeless, and begging for water, his prayers went unanswered. Badri, his sister, repeated his pleadings even more forcefully as she held him in her arms, rocking him back and forth while attempting to reach Sardar Timur's guard on a humane level, desperately trying to gain some sympathy, or even maybe empathy, which she knew that despite her sliver of hope, was futile.

The panchayat proceedings were suddenly paused. Badri and Gul were removed from the hall without being told what was happening. They were separated from their parents. The two siblings were brought to this hot, dirty, dark, and dingy room, away from the panchayat hall. It had been several hours since they were dumped here without any food or water.

The lone guard in the room was merciless. Badri's desperate pleas had grown stronger with Gul's waning strength, his progressively weaker and quieter whispers. She stroked his head gently while she continued to beg the unyielding guard.

"Give him some water please, otherwise he will die."

"Why do I care? People die every day, and so will he." The guard said with complete indifference. He seemed to view them as objects, not humans. His face was as impassive and disinterested as his words.

He had a low forehead, deep-set eyes, and oddly large ears. He sat on a chair near the door, watching. The room was fairly barren: a desk, some shelves. Beyond that was another room where the guards sometimes ate or slept when they were between long shifts, a neglected, dilapidated space, and stifling hot.

"Don't you have any children? Don't you have a heart?" Badri was not ready to give up.

"I do, I have both! A heart and children. But my boy's mother and his sisters are *Sharif* women. They are pious women, chaste and decent, unlike you."

"And what am I? Why would you say that?" Badri asked, offended. Her whole body tensed. Her hands, even as they tenderly held Gul, curled into tight fists.

"You…" The guard looked at her with disdain and then spat on the floor. "You are a *randi*. Just a randi. A whore, a dirty slut. Do you hear me? You are a whore." Another bullet of spit landed on the dirt floor.

Badri's eyes steeled. Her stare was locked into his and her mouth opened to let out an angry retort but she couldn't produce any sound. The guard kept staring at her and she continued to stare back. He had a scornful smile and deep resentment in his eyes. He collected saliva in his mouth–all he could–and then spat directly on her face. She recoiled.

"Shame on you. How can you say that?"

"Trust me, I'm not alone," the man replied, without hesitation. "Everyone around here says that."

"Who? So you believe what others say? I have seen you around. I'm from the same clan as you are, my word should mean more to you than the lies of others."

"From my clan?" The guard scornfully raised his eyebrows.

"Yes, from your clan, from our clan." As members of the same clan–and by extension, family– tradition dictated that he places her words in higher standing than that of an outsider.

"I know that you were born in my clan, but you don't belong. Your family members are mostly peasants. You don't deserve to be a part of my clan. You are *a randi*, a slut. Just a nothing. A zero." His voice oozed with resentment.

"You're a liar. People are lying about me, about my family," Badri tried to defend herself but sounded unconvinced of her own innocence because she simply couldn't understand what was happening. She knew men talked amongst themselves and fabricated stories and so maybe someone had lied about her. None of this made any sense. Why was this person so sure about any of it? And so vile and full of hatred?

"The only reason I've spared your life so far is because Sardar has called the Panchayat. Otherwise, I would have killed you by now. I definitely would not have waited around for the *Panchayat* to decide your fate. You and your brother have brought shame on us all."

"Even if you don't believe me, why are you making him suffer? Nothing's been proven. I know you can see how thirsty he is so please give him some water. I am begging you. For God's sake, give him some water!" Badri felt broken. Her face was forlorn and she appeared on the verge of breaking down, except that she was unable, her eyes were burning and bone dry.

The guard stared at her for a while in a sly, knowing way that Badri instinctively knew was wrong. His face was red and splotchy and he was chewing his bottom lip. He ran his fingers over his mustache, short fingers, and dirty fingernails weaved themselves through the thick facial hair. He had a strange indifference about him, and he smiled a thin, snake-like smile that felt like darkness.

"You want water?" There was an unfamiliar shine in his eyes.

"Yes. Can't you see? He's dying of thirst. He will die if he doesn't get water soon!" She pointed to the boy in her arms that she cradled like a baby.

"I see that *he* needs water," the guard replied with a snide tone. "But my question is, do *you* want it?"

Badri was dumbfounded. She was unable to understand the question or the distinction, for that matter. She had always considered herself an intelligent person, but she couldn't relate to his cryptic interrogation style.

He sat there, grinning. "I can offer you a deal?"

Badri was puzzled but willing to play this unfathomable game.

"I'll get water but you have to drink it. If you drink it, then I'll give him water too. Understand so far?"

Badri nodded in the affirmative with a puzzled look in her eyes.

"If you don't drink it then he doesn't get it either. I don't give a damn if he dies of thirst. In fact, I may just kill him to put him out of his misery."

He looked strangely thoughtful for a moment. She waited. Then as if he had a change of hearts, he murmured in a sinister tone, seeming addressed to himself but loud enough for Badri to hear as well. "I think I should let him suffer, I'll stand here and watch him die while you watch too. We'll watch it together! You're a whore. He's an animal. You can't be that different. You came from the same filthy place so I'm going to let him die like a filthy dog."

"Why do I have to drink water? I don't need it that badly, he does. Please, give it to him." None of this made any sense. She hadn't eaten in quite some time and very real fatigue was setting in. This merry-go-round was worse than any bad dream.

"Listen! It goes like this: I'll give you water first. It's simple, if you drink it then he gets to drink it too. Deal?"

"I'll drink the water, I promise, but give it to him first, I beg you." Badri was still thinking only of the boy in her arms.

"No, that's not how it goes. First, you'll drink it, then he gets it."

Badri remained quiet. She couldn't understand this "deal." The horrible guard was staring at her, waiting.

"Now." He spoke after realizing she was not going to say anything. "You leave him on the floor and step away from him."

"Why?"

"Do as I say. Don't ask questions."

"I will not leave him. You'll hurt him." Badri tightened her grip on the boy's waist and buried his head in her arms.

"If you put him down I won't hurt him. If you don't, I promise you I will. I'll hurt the both of you." The guard's eyes were narrowed and his brows appeared as one.

Badri shook her head. Disbelief and doubt were written all over her face.

"You are lying. If I let him go, you'll kill him. I know it!"

"Do you think I can't kill him now? In your arms?" the guard said with an air of indifference in his tone, while waving his gun in her face. Badri didn't respond. It made no sense. If he wanted, he could simply kill the both of them easily. Why did she need to step away from Gul? The guard seemed to know what she was thinking.

"In fact, I can kill you both," the guard said again, still waving the gun in her face. "And you can bet on it if you don't do what I'm telling you to do. If you do what I say, then I'll spare your life and his too. And you had better do it soon because I'm sick of talking to you about it!"

"How can I trust you?"

"If I tell you that I'll kill him, and then kill you, do you believe me?" The gun was now aimed at Gul again.

Badri flinched and tried to hide the boy behind her. She couldn't utter a word. She was panicking. She didn't understand why he wanted to kill either of them because to her knowledge they had done nothing to him. Gul was in trouble, she understood that, but she had done nothing wrong.

"So that's a yes, right? It means that when I say I will kill him, you believe me. But when I say I will not kill him, you don't. Why don't I just go ahead and do what you think I'll do? This has gone on far too long and I'm getting bored, you're lucky that I'm patient, but I'm beginning to lose that very patience which is keeping you alive."

"No, no. Please don't. I'll do whatever you want." Badri pleaded as she inadvertently let the boy gently roll out of her arms on the dirt floor.

"Now stand up and move. That way." The guard motioned with the barrel of his gun, pointing to the door leading out of the room. Badri started taking small, slow steps towards the door, light-headed from lack of food and water, from the stress of the day, and from sitting and holding her brother for what seemed like an infinite amount of hours. The guard walked behind her making his fearful presence known. She turned her head to look back at Gul, craning it as far back as possible until she came face to face with the now-familiar gun that he had been pointing at the base of her neck. She let out a sound that felt like a scream but sounded more like a whimper.

"Please don't shoot me." She waved her hands desperately, lost her balance, stumbled, and fell. The guard hit her once more, this time on the back of the head with the butt of his gun.

"Don't you understand? If I wanted to kill you I could have done that already. You have no say over this, you have no control here whatsoever. The sooner you understand that, the better."

Badri was now on the floor, on her hands and knees. She was mumbling prayers like rapid-fire, the guard's promises became more terrifying by the second. She choked on the dust that flew up like a cloud of smoke, it felt like sandpaper, grating, and scraping the inside of her mouth and throat.

"Now get up." The guard kicked her left thigh. She flinched and tried to get up, but he grabbed her by the scarf and pulled her up, twisting her neck at an unnatural angle. It slipped revealing her face, revealing her. He then yanked her hair while her head snapped back in order to lift her up off the ground, and onto her feet. She let out a soft scream. He let go of her hair and slapped her repeatedly leaving hand imprints on her face, and then grabbed her hair again to stop her from falling. He then shoved the gun's barrel deep into her belly, and deeper still. She cried out, bending over, falling to the ground once more while wrapping her arms around her abdomen in a self-protective hold. She gave herself a second to regain courage and then began to rise as proudly as possible. She lifted herself up from the hard dirt floor very slowly, watching the guard carefully and as she did so, never losing contact with his eyes.

"See how easily I can hurt you if I want to? I told you. Do you believe me now? I told you! He was growing more vicious by the minute and becoming empowered by this blatant act of abuse which made him feel like he ruled the world. Like the king of the jungle. Not a real jungle, but this place in which they both inhabited which was the only world they knew. "You brought this upon yourself. I didn't want to hurt you, but you didn't believe me, so I had to make you believe me." He raised his hand again to slap her.

"No! Stop. I believe you. Don't hit me."

"Good." He lowered his hand. "Don't say a word. Just do as I say and you will be fine."

Badri was barely standing, she bent over and quietly wept. She didn't know what to do, she was alone and at a loss. This was totally out of her realm of experience. She looked at Gul lying on the floor, almost lifeless but felt a brief moment of comfort when she noticed the slight movement of his torso, he was breathing. He was still alive.

"Now move!" The guard shoved her forward. She started walking and the guard as always was close behind her. The door led to another less spacious room. There was a small window high up on the dirty stone wall, and she could see through the thick iron bars and cracked glass that the ominous gray sky was darkening. It was late evening approaching sundown.

"Do you see that *matka* and the bowls?" The guard pointed to the left corner of the room. On the table in the corner, sat a big clay pot, that had a small round opening at the top, which was half-covered with a clay lid. Next to that, there were a few small bowls. "Fill those two bowls with water from this *matka* and bring them here."

Badri shifted her eyes between the clay pot and the guard's face looking for some sign of approval. Her movements were reluctant, slow, and robotic. Her entire body ached, every single muscle, and every single bone. She needed to get the water to Gul as soon as she could but without fueling the guard's anger.

"Do it. Don't try my patience," the guard barked, sensing her hesitation.

She walked cautiously towards the clay pot and reached for the dirty plastic cup sitting on the side to fill up the bowls. The water was cloudy with brown dirt, floating particles, and smelled of mud. She couldn't imagine how long it had been there, the condition of these two rooms, these makeshift jail cells were inhumane. It was better not to know.

"Bring the bowls here. Quickly damn it!" The guard cursed at her when he saw how gingerly she was handling the filthy water-filled bowls. She began walking towards him, obediently. He stepped aside and motioned for her to go back to the room where her brother lay motionless on the floor. She continued to walk holding her breath and looking straight ahead, her heart pounding, chomping on the bit to get to him.

"No. No. Stop. Not yet. Do not take the water to him yet. We talked about this. Put the bowls over there." He pointed towards the shelf on the opposite wall.

"Why, isn't this for him?"

"Be patient, he'll get the water but first our deal. Remember? You have to honor our deal. First, you need to drink water."

"Okay fine, look, I'm drinking it now!" She was about to take a sip, her dry, cracked lips longing for just a drop of water when the guard snatched the bowl from her hand.

"No, not like that. Give me your bowl, and put the other one over there." She handed her bowl to him. He placed it on the desk behind him and waved his gun toward the shelf. Badri complied.

"Now step away from there, come back here and stand in front of me."

She did as she was asked to do, but perplexed and cautious.

"Now get on your knees."

She stared at him for a moment and clumsily kneeled on the hard rocky dirt floor, little jagged points digging into her knees. Her eyes glued to his face.

"Good. Now, you will drink water from the bowl in my hand when I tell you to. If you spill even one drop or spit any out, he will die of thirst or I will kill him in front of you. I haven't decided which. Understand?"

Badri nodded in shock.

"Now you *whore* look at this?" He lifted his shirt up, exposing the upper portion of his loose baggy pants, tied with a drawstring. One end of the drawstring was hanging loose outside the pants while the other end was invisible, likely tucked inside the faded, stained pants.

"I am not a whore," Badri protested. "I am not a randi."

"If you are not a *randi* it is only because you haven't had the chance. Look at you. You're a slut and you're a woman, it's the same thing. You say you aren't a whore but I'm about to make you one and that's a deal you can keep." Badri began to involuntarily shake with ferocity as he started rooting around for the other end of the drawstring. Found it. She tilted her head down to avert his eyes.

"Look at me. This is what you're here for. If you fail, I'll do things to you, and to this boy you cannot even imagine." The guard had his hand up ready to slap her again but suddenly paused, a second of silence, then an exchange of visibly aggressive glances until he finally dropped his hand.

"See this?" He was holding the loose end of the drawstring. "When I pull this drawstring, my pants will drop, and then you're going to see exactly what kind of a man I am. You'll see something which a *Randi* likes to play with, likes to touch and kiss with her mouth and tongue. I want you to make me happy, so you'll do as I say and I'll spare your life and his. Yes? Clear?"

Badri turned her head sideways refusing to look at him. The guard grabbed her skull, digging his fingers into her head while he moved her towards him positioning her face a few inches from where he wanted it. She felt his fingers in her hair, scraping her scalp. The smell coming from him made her feel sick. Fighting waves of nausea, she lowered her eyes, refusing to look directly at what he was about to show her.

"Stop trying to move! I want your mouth on me! On this!" the guard hissed, with her head still in his grasp. Badri reared her head back, resisting.

"Do as I say!" He smashed his tightly clenched fist against the side of her head and then savagely slapped her. She dug her shins into the ground, attempting to stay balanced.

"You are an animal, a vicious animal." She said through clenched teeth.

"Yes, yes I am. I'm very vicious and you're going to tame me." A crooked smile surfaced on his face. With one swift pull of the drawstring, his pants were down. He stood exposed in front of Badri.

"I would rather die," Badri said, seriously.

"I'll kill him first, do you understand this?"

"Leave him alone."

"Your choice."

"Then I'll kill him myself before you do," Badri reached up and lunged for his gun but in her weakened state, her speed was no match for his. He jumped and came crashing down on her. She was now underneath him struggling to turn around while trying to tighten her grip on the butt of the gun. The screaming from the both of them silenced any surrounding sound and they didn't hear the outside door open.

Two men entered the room. One of them with a thick, but sculpted mustache wearing a black turban and holding a gun. Badri recognized him. He was Sardar Timur Barlas. The other considerably shorter and clean-shaven, fairly thin and appeared subservient to the other. Timur raised his weapon and shot in the air. The noise was deafening and the room was clouded in dust and smoke.

Both Badri and the guard froze in place. The shorter of the two men briskly moved towards them and wrestled the gun out of Badri's hand. The other forced the guard off Badri and kept his weapon trained on him. Gul still lay near them silent and nearly unconscious.

"What the hell is going on?" Timur yelled.

"He tried to rape me," Badri shouted. "He said he wouldn't give my brother water unless I did horrible disgusting things to him."

"Quiet down *Randi*," the guard snapped back. "She's lying. She offered herself to me so that I would let her go."

"That's not true!" Badri was loud and firm.

"Get up, both of you," Timur said.

The guard was fast and agile and jumped to his feet. While getting up, he pulled up his pants and worked the drawstring, tying a knot to keep it in place. Badri was struggling to get up but her body wasn't cooperating, it felt unnatural and awkward and her limbs were like those of a rag doll. The man reached out to pull her to her feet but she rebuffed him violently, shoving him away. He pushed her back and she landed once again on the ever-familiar hard dirt floor and her heart raced even faster.

"Is the boy dead?"

Badri crawled rushing toward Gul, desperately trying to get to her little brother, and allowed herself a small exhale of relief upon reaching him. She rolled him onto her lap once more, lifting his weighted lifeless head onto her frail, bruised legs. She began to gently tap his battered beautiful cheeks but he was unresponsive. Her breathing quickened, her panic increased and her body temperature shot up. She then shook him, kissed his soft face, continued to tap his cheeks, and prayed. Finally, a soft whimper.

Badri looked up toward Timur and nodded victoriously, chanting that he is alive. She almost dropped his head as she reached for the bowl of water, rushing, her movements impatient while she opened his mouth and poured the water in too quickly. He began choking on the excess, his eyes opening for a brief moment.

"Now get up–you, now!" Timur shouted at Badri. She no longer flinched, she steeled herself and got up. Her movements were involuntary. She attempted to cover herself with the shredded, dirty, headscarf which had been dangling over her shoulder and failed. Standing still, terror-filled her as she bravely faced the three men, almost daring them. Screams snapped her out of this trance-like state, she looked at her brother, rolling on the ground and screeching like a wounded animal. "Quiet!" Timur shouted. He quieted instantly. The guard stood in position, pistol ready, looking at Timur for direction.

"What were you doing with him?" Timur asked Badri.

"I …I…" speaking was a struggle, she felt drained and couldn't muster up enough strength to answer Timur. Her brother was alive, and a small part of her fight was indeed over, nevertheless, serious concern still consumed her. Gul was alive, but the worry of what that meant still hovered.

"Speak the truth," Timur warned her harshly. "Lying to me won't help you, I don't forgive liars."

"I'm not a liar and I'm not lying! I swear on my brother's life," Badri said. "He was thirsty to the point of being sick and almost dead, he needed water to survive. The guard–" She looked over at him with obvious disgust, "refused to give him water, and then he said that if I did certain things to him he would change his mind and give him the water that he needs, and if I refused, he would let my brother die while I watched and then kill me."

"She's lying! She's unclean and she's just a worthless randi." The guard in awe of his master, Sardar Timur, found the courage to speak, yet, without any attempt to sound convincing. He knew that there wasn't a need to convince anyone because here in his world men are always right, and women's opinions or protests were irrelevant and simply disregarded. Women were without value.

"How did he want you to please him? What did he tell you to do?"

"I don't know Sardar, I'm not a *Randi*, so I don't know about all of these things. All I can tell you is what happened." She took a quiet, shallow breath. "He removed his pants and pulled my head toward him and told me that I was to drink the dirty water, not the clean water, and if I didn't do what he said, he will kill us both."

"Hmm." Timur circled around her, never letting his eyes off her face. Then he turned towards the guard who was standing motionless, glaring at her with threatening, beady eyes.

"Is this true?" Timur asked the guard.

"She's lying, Sardar. The boy was thirsty, that part is true, but I was told that I had to keep an eye on her. She said she would do anything, anything at all to please me, anything for water! It was her idea. I swear on the life of my children."

"Stop swearing on your children," Sardar Timur raised his hand high as if to slap someone, then cocked his head to the left. "Just tell me straight. What did you ask her to do for you?"

"Nothing, I'm telling you. " The guard almost swore again but managed to shut his mouth before he could finish the sentence.

"Why were your pants down and why did you let her come so close to you?" Timur wasn't willing to go easy on the guard.

"A moment of weakness, Sardar. You can see for yourself, she's very pretty. She was ready to please me and I couldn't stop myself. I'm sorry, but don't blame me, Sardar, blame her."

Badri opened her mouth to say something but was stopped by the loud clang of Sardar Timur's unruly laughter which drowned her voice.

"I know you blame her; I know you do." Timur looked at the guard but then quickly shifted his eyes towards Badri. "You blame her, and she is pretty. Very beautiful indeed. You're right, I don't expect you to resist her." The guard was greatly relieved. The fear and tension drained from his demeanor, and he stood with newfound confidence.

Sardar Timur began circling her again, like a shark about to attack. His eyes gleaming with hunger and lust. He grabbed her headscarf, roughly pulled it off her, and threw it on the floor. She didn't breathe, she didn't move, she stayed perfectly still. "So, you think you can seduce my men?" Timur jeered at her.

"No. He's lying to you Sardar! It isn't true. I don't want to seduce anyone. Believe me, please." It was difficult to concentrate as she resisted the urge to gather her scarf and cover herself once again.

"What's your name again?"

"Badri, Badri Jamala."

"So Badri, Badri Jamala, you think I can trust you more than my man here?"

"Yes, I know you can, because I'm not the one lying to you."

"How do I know that? Do you have any witnesses?" Timur asked. The guard and the other man started smiling grimly, staring at her in an indescribable way.

"No, how can I have witnesses?" She sounded helpless. "There was nobody else here."

"That's the problem! If you want me to believe you over him, I need to hear from someone other than you in order to confirm your story." Sardar Timur was adamant.

"It was just us, and my brother was practically unconscious. He didn't see or hear anything. I don't have any witnesses it simply isn't possible."

"You are detained. You are a prisoner and he was watching you. I have to believe him over you. Your brother would not be a fit witness anyway." Timur seemed expressionless, perhaps even bored, except for a strange look in his eye.

"Why would I lie to you? Why would I make up such a story?"

"I don't know, you tell me. Why are you making up this story?" Sardar Timur now stood still with his eyes fixed on Gul, who was now trying to get up.

"Rahim Khan!" Timur turned to his companion–the short thin man–then pointed at Gul. The thin man walked toward him, stared at him for a brief moment, and then kicked him in the stomach. Gul, still struggling to sit up, let a loud scream out and fell backward. His head hit the dirt floor with a loud thud and he fell motionless. "That's unfortunate," Timur noted. "He should see this." Badri tried to run towards her fallen brother. Timur grabbed her arm and pulled her towards him.

"You are very beautiful, indeed." Lust was evident from his tone. His voice low, and thick. Badri tried to free herself from his vice-like grip but he pulled her closer, pushing his fingers deep into her arm.

"Don't even think about screaming, it only annoys me and nobody can hear you anyway so you're wasting your breath," he paused for effect. "I don't think that you want to risk upsetting me any more than you already have." He growled reveling in his dominance.

"You are a *janwar*...an animal. A violent beast."

"Curse all you want. I don't mind," Timur said, taking pleasure in her ordeal. "But remember, fighting will not help you. You need to make us your friends, allies. Not enemies. Understand?"

"I'll curse, scream and fight all I want," Badri was undeterred. "You need to let me go."

"That's out of the question," Timur said. "You will remain detained so that the Panchayat can decide your fate."

"What Panchayat, that group of idiots? They're on your payroll! A group of people that you pay to handle things and to make sure that the outcome is how you want it. They are not objective, even though they are supposed to be. I don't accept that!"

"It doesn't matter what you accept! The Panchayat has the authority to deliver justice and that's exactly what they will do."

"How can you keep us here? How is this justice? I've done nothing wrong. Nothing at all."

"You can ask all these questions when you go to the Panchayat, that's what they will be there for." Sardar Timur knelt over Gul, looked at him briefly, and then slapped him. He didn't respond. He motioned for Rahim to remove him, who did so by roughly lifting him up by his arms. He latched onto Gul's thin bruised wrists and dragged him towards the door. Badri wriggled away from Timur and leapt toward her brother, attempting to release him from Rahim's grip. The guard grabbed her, he now held Gul with his left hand and Badri with his right. She kicked and tried to free herself, unsuccessfully, the weight of the two was no match for his brute strength. He looked at Sardar Timur for direction who was standing there nonchalantly as if he was watching a typical daily event.

"Do you want her Sardar?" the guard asked. He nodded. She watched as the guard grabbed the bottom of her shirt and tore it with a quick rip. The sound of ripping fabric and cries of protest filled the room. Soon she was more than half-naked, trying to cover herself with her bare hands.

"Rahim!" Timur shouted. Rahim came running in. For a brief moment, he stopped at the sight of the unclothed girl but overcame his shock in seconds. Sardar Timur motioned to him.

"Hold her down. On the floor," Timur ordered the men. Rahim and the guard each grabbed one of her arms, threw her down on the floor, and held her down. She felt the impact vibrate all throughout her fragile, already beaten body. Timur knelt down, grabbed her struggling legs, ripped away more of her remaining clothes, separated her legs, and lowered himself on her. She tried to free herself, thrashing around, screaming as loud as she could in his right ear.

"Do something, hold her still," Sardar Timur ordered his men. Rahim slapped her on the side of the head so that Timur could continue to go about his task. She tried tensing and closing her legs to try and force him away but it was a futile attempt. He reached down, undeterred, and began to push himself inside her, pinning her with his sheer weight but she managed to lift her head and bite him on the ear. The guard elbowed her in the face.

"God," Sardar Timur's hand went to his ear, and it came away clean. He slapped her so hard that her head jerked back and slammed against the ground. Then he resumed his assault on her, even more violently than before. Now he wasn't just a savage taking advantage, he was taking action. He felt a personal affront that had to be answered. She continued to scream. He moved back a bit, got up, and looked around, his trousers falling. He noticed her scarf to his left and picked it up, rolling it into a big ball.

"You want to scream, scream now!" He started to shove the rolled-up scarf in her mouth. She bit his hand. He punched her in the face using the other hand. Another loud scream. He kept shoving the scarf in her mouth. She clenched her teeth and locked her jaw. He once again, punched her in the face while holding the balled-up scarf right up to her mouth, and pinched her nose shut. When she was finally able to open her mouth and gasp for breath, he stuffed it in further. A muffled cry.

He knelt down again between her legs, rubbed himself a couple of times, then went back to using her. As he did so, he started pinching and biting her. When she tried moving away from him he elbowed her in the ribs, and instead of stopping, he continued even more aggressively. She started choking.

"Don't kill her, Sardar." The guard grabbed his hand. Timur pushed him away.

"Let me finish! I don't care if she dies!" He was enraged and completely without control.

"If she dies, we have a bigger problem," Rahim said, looking at her face. It was turning blue. Her eyes were wide open and she was clearly struggling for air. Timur continued his act of rape, brutally thrusting into her, groaned, then moved away. He wiped himself off on his shirt tails and then put them back in his trousers. Rahim pulled the scarf out of her mouth. She sucked in all the air she could and started coughing violently.

Rahim and the guard released her arms from their grip and stood up. She was now curled up on the floor covered in mud and soil, unaware of her nakedness. She was coughing and gasping for air simultaneously which resulted in more coughing. She was unable to breathe.

The three men just stood there quietly and stared at her brutalized vulnerable body. Finally, after what seemed like an endless struggle, her cough subsided and she began to breathe somewhat normally, she lay on the floor motionless with her eyes shut. They heard her mumble for a brief moment before she went quiet. The guard knelt beside her to see if she was unconscious, playing dead, or actually dead. Sensing his breath on her face, she suddenly opened her eyes. Another loud scream.

"Stop screaming, bitch." The guard slapped her. She continued screaming. There was not much voice left, but she kept at it.

"You raped me. You, son of a bitch," Badri was pointing at Timur. "He raped me! You saw it! Both of you saw it! He raped me! Will you tell the Panchayat that he raped me? Will you?!"

The guard and Rahim shifted their stares from her to each other and then looked at Sardar Timur. They seemed to find her words amusing.

"Nobody raped you. You are–" Rahim didn't bother completing his sentence realizing that there was no reason to explain this to her. She didn't matter and so he simply shrugged.

"Yes he did, yes he did," Badri was hysterical "Look at me, see this…my clothes. They are all torn, he tore my clothes, then he raped me. You saw it! You saw it!"

"Shut her up," Timur sounded irritated.

"Shut up, you stupid girl!" The guard kicked her in the groin. She let out another shriek.

"I will not shut up. He dishonored me and I will tell the Panchayat. I'll also tell them that you two helped him. You helped him."

"Nobody raped you. You don't understand. That's not what happened." Rahim tried to reason with her.

"Yes, he did. He raped me and you two helped him. I'm going to tell the Panchayat about the two of you also. You'll pay the price, you'll see. You will."

"Shut up. Just shut up!" The guard shouted instinctively. "Nobody raped you, don't you understand anything? You are a nobody, you mean nothing. We can do as we please with you, and to you, so just be quiet and accept it. That's the way it is like it or not."

She started whimpering. Rahim and the guard looked at her, annoyed by the racket.

"Let's just kill her. Finish this up." The guard picked up the gun and pointed the barrel, ready to fire.

"Stop," Timur shouted. "Don't shoot."

The guard lowered the gun and looked at his boss who then glanced at Rahim and gestured to the floor.

"Here, help me," Rahim said, looking at the guard. He bent down and picked up the scarf from the dirty floor.

"Let's shut her up first and then the boss can decide what to do." Rahim went behind Badri and covered her mouth with the same dirty scarf, tying a very tight knot at the back of her head, which was throbbing and felt like it was in a vise. She didn't even realize that she was making any noise at all, her cries were muffled, sounding like her brother did earlier. Tortured and deflated, but she continued to try and fight-driven solely by sheer hate.

"You," Timur motioned to the guard. "You hold her and Rahim, bring my bag from the truck."

Both of them moved to obey his commands. The guard had trouble managing Badri and, seeing his difficulty in controlling her, Timur stepped towards them. He stood over her head and simply loomed, her defiant eyes met his face, and it was then that whatever fight she had left, just dissolved. Any fire that she had before was extinguished. "Good," Timur said. "I'll put you out of your misery soon."

Badri feebly began to try and get up again but was interrupted by Rahim entering the room holding a small leather bag. He put it on the floor, unzipped it, and produced a box of medical supplies, he opened it further and carefully examined the contents. Then he looked up straight in Timur's direction, nodding his head. The same gesture was returned.

"Hand it to me." Timur extended his hand. Rahim dug into the kit and quickly produced a syringe and small bottle full of colorless liquid. With practiced ease, he filled the syringe and handed it over. Timur holding the syringe upward reached for Badri.

"Flip her over," Timur ordered the guard and Rahim, and once again they complied, turning her over and trying to hold her still, gripping her arms from behind, pinning her down. Sardar Timur expertly buried the needle in Badri's exposed buttock. They heard muffled cries which quickly faded. Shortly after she lay on the floor like a rag doll, motionless and half unconscious. They left her there next to the pile of tattered clothes which were once hers.

"Now, go on," he motioned Rahim. Rahim looked at him, making sure he understood.

"Finish what I've started," Timur growled.

Rahim got up, dropped his pants, and lowered himself on Badri. His sun-darkened hands were a stark contrast to her pale skin as he pulled her hips to him and quickly guided himself in. The guard flinched slightly but kept watching. Timur reached in his pocket, took his phone out, held it up, and pointed it at Rahim.

The guard watched with a sadistic smile, staring at the motionless body of the girl. Each one of Rahim's thrusts caused her body to jerk like a clumsy marionette. Timur continued to hold his phone up, aiming the camera at them, recording this new rape. This was clearly not a novel practice, raping and assaulting women was somewhat of standard practice. Rahim continued for a few minutes and then withdrew himself from her. Bruise marks were already starting to appear on her backside and legs. Timur turned off the phone's camera.

"You, what's your name?" Sardar Timur turned towards the guard. "Oh don't bother. I don't need to know and don't care. Go on. Flip her over. Your turn now."

"Really?"

"Isn't that you wanted—you were trying to do it to her when I came in. Now finish whatever you were doing." The guard wondered why he was allowed this treat.

"You, Rahim, take this. Get everything." Sardar sighed, handed the phone to him, and motioned for him to record the guard on top of motionless Badri. Rahim complied. Sardar Timur started walking towards the door, Rahim watched as he walked away, almost strutting. He stared at the empty door for a moment, oblivious to his immediate surroundings for a brief moment until movement caught his eye. Badri's torso is what he noticed first, then the guard's head buried in her loose hair. He was breathing heavily, with occasional pleasured grunts filling up the room.

Rahim's eyes shifted between the phone screen and the real bodies performing the act. He wanted to make sure he did what he had been ordered, but it was difficult to stay focused, he felt completely drawn in, despite the circumstances. Suddenly the thunderous sound of a shot fired very close to him nearly threw him off his feet. The phone slipped out of his hand but he managed to catch it before it hit the floor. He turned towards the sound and saw Sardar Timur enter the room with his gun held high.

"What the hell are you doing?" Sardar Timur shouted, looking at the guard as he awkwardly jumped off Badri neglecting his clothing but attempting to muffle his ears from the intensity of the gunshot noise. Sardar Timur lunged towards him and threw a tightly clenched, knuckles first, punch.

"You were supposed to keep her locked in, not assault her. You mother fucker get away from her!" Sardar Timur kicked him, heavy black steel-toed boot, in the groin. The guard was still unclothed and let out a bloodcurdling scream as he folded over covering himself, attempting to block any further assaults. His face had reddened and his loud groans and cries were ongoing.

"What is this?" Sardar Timur barked at Rahim, pointing to the cell phone "What is this, Rahim? A camera? Are you filming them? You're pathetic!"

Rahim was stunned into speechlessness; he hadn't expected such an energetic interruption or major turn of events. Sardar Timur grabbed his arm and snatched the still capturing phone from his hand.

"Take care of her and the boy, both of you. Make sure they aren't hurt any further. I'm going to check again in a few hours and bring food. In the meantime, no *harami pun*...no hanky panky. Understand?" Sardar Timur sounded full of self-righteous indignation.

"Yes, Sardar Timur. Understood," Rahim said softly. The guard was still in too much pain to speak. Sardar Timur walked towards him and pinned him under his foot.

"Do you understand?" Sardar Timur asked him over his moaning and groaning "no harami pun. Just keep an eye on them. Keep them safe and locked up. Can you do that? Am I making myself clear? If the girl tries to escape, or lure you into helping her, you must tell me and not do anything without my orders. Do you understand?"

"Yes, Sardar. I understand."

"Good," he said whilst whistling a joyful tune making his way towards the door. He turned around, looked at them, and let out a malevolent laugh while closing the door behind him.

The guard's grating groans gradually diminished and soon there was a dead silence. Motionless bodies lay littered on the floor while Rahim stood there, assessing it all and dumbfounded, trying to figure what just happened. He couldn't process it. Why did Sardar Timur order them to assault her, record the assault, and then barge in as if he was surprised by it and acted to help her?

347

His comfort level was now at a sudden low point knowing that Sardar Timur had more of a hold over him than ever: saying his name on video had placed him at the scene. After all, it wasn't a crime unless someone knew that you did it. With the way contents of the video could be played, the two of them would look like the bad guys and Timur will be able to paint himself as a welcome intruder who saved the poor victim if ever such a need were to arise.

TWENTY FOUR

T URAB SPENT THE night more or less awake. Kicking, tossing, and turning in the small squeaky temporary guest bed, even though he was relieved that the audio file transfer was a success, he couldn't help feeling that it wasn't going to be enough. His conversation with Arlette seemed reassuring although he couldn't really understand much due to the language barrier. Aamir's words thankfully were encouraging, and he had no reason to doubt them but that's all he had, and it felt far from concrete. Words and faith. It did nothing to quell the anxiety about the events to come, and he kept seeing it all in his mind's eye, hearing bits of sound replay in his head. He would doze off for a few moments and then wake. Every time his eyes opened, he heard rapid movement in the home. He heard hurried whispers.

He considered getting up to talk to Mullah Aziz but kept changing his mind. What could he possibly say? He had no words to console them, there wasn't anything that he could do to solve this predicament. They just had to wait.

He stayed in bed and continued to struggle with his thoughts until the *Azan* for *Fajr* prayer was called. Relieved, he immediately jumped out of bed and spotted Mullah Aziz through the small window standing in the middle of the small apartment's private courtyard staring at the open sky above. Turab nodded his head in acknowledgment, but he was deep in thought and didn't appear to notice him.

While in the bathroom, Turab heard Mullah Aziz yell out Rauf's name, telling him to get up. He heard Rauf's rushed footsteps coming towards the bathroom and as far as he could see Mullah Aziz was still standing in the same place.

"Are you ready?" Turab asked.

Mullah Aziz nodded and turned.

They all had the intention of saying the morning's *Fajr* prayer in the mosque with the congregation, so Mullah Aziz motioned Rauf to check on the guards through the front door peephole. Rauf complied, looking for a long moment.

"There are three men," he said in a scared tone.

"Okay," Mullah Aziz said. "Let's go. They cannot stop us from praying. In fact, I'll invite them to join us."

Turab found this remark bizarre and oddly amusing. So now, Mullah Aziz was going to lead the prayer and the people falsely imprisoning him would follow him in the prayer. It seemed crazy, but then again he was crazy like a fox. He suppressed the impulse to comment and silently followed Mullah Aziz, his fearless leader, out of the house.

As expected, all three guards charged them, one seemingly in charge. He raised his hand and gestured for them to stop. They did.

"You need to go back inside," the lead guard shouted out. "You cannot step outside."

"Didn't you hear the *Azan*?" Mullah Aziz shouted right in his face.

"I did, so what?" The lead guard appeared puzzled.

"I have to lead the prayers," Aziz replied. "I am the Imam. You absolutely cannot stop me from leading the prayers."

The guard appeared to be perplexed, unaccustomed to being spoken to in such an abrupt manner by a so-called hostage. He turned around and looked at his companions. Their conversation was inaudible, and

Turab was unable to decipher the communication between them. The lead guard turned to face Turab, Mullah Aziz, and Rauf.

"Stay where you are, let me check with Shujaa."

"Okay, check with him," Mullah Aziz said. "In fact, invite him for prayers. Let him know that is what you'll be doing, praying in the mosque behind me, in fact, all of you will pray behind me. Shujaa can join us any time he wants. At least do something good to start your morning and you never know, your whole day may turn out to be better."

The guard responded with a blank stare for a moment before turning around once again to conference with his cohorts. Words were exchanged, but the volume was too low to be clearly understood, it sounded like just a bunch of harmless whispers, but their body language said otherwise. Turab was expecting a quick decision, a yes or a no, instead, it became a heated and protracted discussion. During this time, the three guards kept looking over at them and each other, waving their hands in the air, and ultimately engaging in what sounded like a series of insults.

"It's almost *iqama* time. Stop fighting and join me in the prayers. I'm moving!" Mullah Aziz shouted. The fighting stopped. He glared at them for a moment and started walking towards the mosque.

"Wait," the lead guard shouted. Mullah Aziz stopped walking.

"We'll accompany you in prayer," the guard said.

"That's what I asked you to do ages ago," Mullah Aziz replied back. "You didn't have to stop me so dramatically to announce your decision."

"I'm not sure you understand," the lead guard said. "We will stand beside you while you are praying, not behind you. All of you will have to stand in one row and we'll be next to you. Nobody else can stand beside you or next to us in the rows that we occupy. You need to make this announcement in the prayer hall so people will comply."

"I cannot do that and I will not do that!" Mullah Aziz responded, with anger. "Prayer has to be done in the way Allah and his Prophet told us. What you are suggesting is unacceptable."

"Then, you cannot go," the lead guard leapt forward and stood right in his face, blocking the way. The other guards stood to each side.

"What kind of Muslim are you?" Mullah Aziz asked, outraged. "First you interfere in my religious duties and now you want me to change the way prayer is offered, or else? What?! Or else you won't let me pray? Don't you know that there are other people whose prayers will be disturbed if I'm not in the mosque on time?"

The guards just stood silently, stone-faced, and Mullah Aziz didn't budge. Turab had a feeling that he would try to push his way past them, and he knew what might happen if he did. Turab walked toward the lead guard and motioned Rauf to move closer to his father. The other two guards walked towards Turab in a threatening manner.

"Stop," one of them shouted, pointing the barrel of his weapon in Turab's direction.

"I'm only trying to make sure there aren't any punches thrown, I mean this would become the circus, not the mosque that it actually is," Turab responded quickly with his hand held up high. "I am not trying to bolt or do anyone any harm."

"Shut up and step back," the lead guard yelled. Turab stepped back. Mullah Aziz and Rauf both stood still. By this time there were few people around them who had just entered the mosque. They saw the events unfolding and came closer to inquire.

"What is going on?" a middle-aged man asked.

"Go away," the lead guard shouted. "Go inside and pray."

"How can I pray? Mullah Aziz is the Imam and you are holding him here. How can I pray without the Imam?"

"See what you're doing?" Mullah Aziz found it an opportune time to make a point. "You're making a scene. If you had let me go to lead the prayer as I am meant to do, no one would have noticed any of this! Now, look at the mess you've created."

The guards glared at him.

Turab summoned the courage to speak as well. "You can still make it right. Just let us go and pray normally. You should join the congregation then nobody will notice what you're doing or why you're here."

The guards looked at each other, nodded their heads, and motioned for everyone to move towards the mosque. Mullah Aziz started moving immediately never looking back, knowing that they were following.

The congregation seemed confused by the prayer arrangement, while the guards did not insist that the first row of the congregation remain empty, they stood instead against the walls pointing their weapons toward Mullah Aziz. The lead guard stood all the way in the back. Turab noticed Rauf's pale face for a second and then watched as the overall anxiety and turbulence that before began to simmer, now began to boil over. Everything escalated.

Mullah Aziz was surprisingly calm. He led the prayer with no hint of duress as he recited the Holy Scripture. It seemed to Turab that the duration of the prayer was longer than usual, maybe he was stalling. Once it was over, the normal quiet and peace usually present in the hall after the prayer, was overcome by uneasy murmurs.

The man on the left of Turab whispered something in his ear, he wanted to know what was happening, and the man to his right could not contain his curiosity or his fear, perhaps both. Before Turab could answer, another person behind him spoke up.

"These are Sardar Timur's men," the person speaking sounded frantic. "Looks like Mullah Aziz is in serious trouble."

Turab considered for a second whether or not to engage in the conversation, but before he could decide, he heard the lead guard shout Mullah Aziz's name from the back of the prayer hall, ordering him to walk back to his apartment.

"You are in the house of Allah," someone exclaimed. "Be respectful. Don't shout here."

Turab saw the lead guard signal one of his companions, who moved forward and slapped the nameless man. Turab heard a loud gasp. He wasn't sure whether it was the voice of one man or many, he could barely believe what he witnessed.

"Shut up and leave," the lead guard growled. "Don't tell me what to do and do not interfere with my business."

The crowd got up and started to mill around the second guard. He raised his weapon and pointed it at the crowd. Turab felt a deep sense of doom, he knew how this whole scene could turn out. Terror. He had heard the stories of massacres in mosques in other places, especially in the war zones and conflict theaters, and hoped to never witness one. It was unspeakable to face the prospect of such an incident head-on.

Mullah Aziz's booming voice on the public announcement system snapped everyone out of the quickly deteriorating barbaric state. If even for a moment. "Stop fighting! This is all unnecessary! I am going to do as they demand so there is no need for hysteria, and there is surely no reason to show any disrespect in the house of Allah."

A small gathering of people in the prayer hall seemed to concur. There were several approving nods and some barely audible verbal acknowledgments. The guards appeared to have temporarily backed down. Mullah Aziz, after assessing the situation and the responses started moving toward the exit door. Turab and Rauf followed, the guards walking closely behind them.

The walk to the apartment was quick and quiet. The three of them entered the home together, Rauf the last one in, closed the door behind them, slid to the ground back flat to the wall, and immediately collapsed. He fell beside the door and sobbed. He seemed inconsolable. Paro ran to her son; her distress was so severe that she had forgotten to cover herself. Turab might be there and might see her and for him, that was forbidden. Turab did see her but turned towards Aziz so she would be out of his field of vision.

"What is going on here!? Why are you behaving like this? Crying like a girl. Get the hell up and get a hold of yourself!" Mullah Aziz said as he watched Rauf get up and leave the room with Paro.

"What got into you?" Turab could not resist. He had to ask Mullah Aziz why he was acting so recklessly, especially in the face of trigger-happy hired guns. His bravado could have set off a massacre.

"What am I supposed to do?" Mullah Aziz now sounded drained and almost robotic. "I am the Imam here. I cannot let them treat me like a third-class citizen."

"So you would rather get killed than act in a sane manner?"

"There was nothing insane in my behavior," Aziz replied.

"Your behavior was nothing but insane," Turab was surprisingly harsh and blunt. "Your behavior made them draw their weapons and turn them on to us. How is that not insane?"

"Well, you're still alive, aren't you? In my mind that is not the result of insane behavior."

"Stop living in your own world my friend" Turab was now truly irritated at Mullah Aziz's stubbornness. "Real people that live in the real world face matters of life and death every day. When you antagonize someone to the point where they are willing to kill you, then yes, you're acting insane. You should get that inside your thick skull."

Mullah Aziz didn't respond immediately. Turab was desperately trying to control his temper which was now on the brink of rage, Aziz and his arrogance incensed him to no end. The man had no idea when to call it quits. Finally, he spoke, his tone was calm and the flow of words deliberate. "You have known me for a long time. You should know I am a man of my own conviction. I don't relent quickly. I don't bend easily. I know how to stand my ground and I plan to do just that."

"There is no ground for you stand on," Turab countered. "You relented and bent when you decided to go along with the Sardar Timur's scheme. The conviction of your own moral standing is simply an excuse. You're just trying to fool yourself, if not others. And if you wish to continue to ride this imaginary high horse of morality, then don't drag me or your family down with it."

Aziz turned away. Obviously, he didn't consider Turab's rant worthy of a response, nor did he feel that he owed him an explanation. Turab wasn't sure how to react to this blatant condescension, it was nothing out of the ordinary and he knew that he should be used to it after all these years, but this was an extraordinary situation.

The silence in the room was broken when Rauf entered the room with a breakfast tray. In morbid silence, they began to eat but that was soon interrupted by banging and knocking. One of the guards was at their door shouting, telling them to be ready to leave in ten minutes, there wouldn't be time for food, Mullah Aziz's cup of hot tea was as good as it was going to get. Another round of insistent knocks announced that their allotted ten minutes were up. Once outside, they were led to the vehicles, no words exchanged.

Turab closed his eyes in an effort to at least dream about a desirable resolution. Deep down he knew the fateful day had begun. Realistically, there was a very slim chance of any resolution, still at least with closed eyes, it was easier to keep the hope of a blessed epilogue alive.

The vehicles carrying the three of them stopped at a distance from the hall in which the Panchayat session was to resume. They were signaled to walk towards a separate structure adjacent to the hall which seemed odd, but they complied without asking any questions. They walked into the assigned room treading softly. Sardar Timur was pacing back and forth, one of his servants was carrying his hookah base while holding the long pipe for him to suck on every few steps. He stopped when Mullah Aziz, Turab, and Rauf entered the room.

"I heard you caused quite a scene this morning," Sardar Timur came straight to the point, short of any cursory pleasantries.

"Your men were interfering in my duties," Mullah Aziz replied.

"Your only duty is to is to obey my commands," Sardar Timur hissed back. "When my men tell you to do something or stop you from doing something, you must oblige."

Mullah Aziz opened his mouth to respond, but Sardar Timur raised his hand signaling him to stay quiet.

"Don't say a word, Mullah Aziz. I don't want to hear anything you have to say. I summoned you here so I can tell you what I want you to do, so I suggest that you pay close attention, and do as I say. It will be best for you. That's a promise."

Turab was not sure how Mullah Aziz would react, given his behavior earlier, so he sighed in relief when there was no immediate or combative retort. Instead, Mullah Aziz took a deep breath and quietly looked at this malevolent giant with expectant eyes. Sardar Timur ignored him, looked around, surveyed his men's faces, and spoke.

"I'm going to find out what happened to my money," Sardar Timur's tone was measured, and words carefully chosen. "I will not be fooled or lied to, I won't tolerate it. However, all that's for another day. I don't want your ignorance or your misconduct to derail the Panchayat process today. You will announce that they will get the money they were promised for their time, effort, and service and remind them that they should not be distracted by this little drama you have unnecessarily created. This process is too important to be sidetracked, nor can it be delayed. The session needs to begin today and it should conclude today. Everything should be back to normal as soon as possible so we can move on to other things. Do you understand?"

Mullah Aziz nodded. Turab was not sure what to think.

"Okay," Sardar Timur now sounding calmer. "Now go ahead and start the proceeding, there hopefully isn't a need for you or your friend to worry. If you aren't involved in the disappearance of my money, you'll be fine, but if you are involved, you'll regret it for the rest of your life. Now go get me a conviction."

Guards escorted them out of the room and into the Panchayat hall. Turab was careful not to draw attention to his breast pocket. His phone was ready to record the proceedings. This time again he was going to try to capture the proceedings in a video. He was amazed at how poorly prepared Sardar Timur's men were, once again, nobody had bothered to frisk them at all. He sure hoped this carelessness would continue. Thankfully it did, he was able to take a seat without being checked. His phone was in place and from the slight warm feeling on his chest he could tell positively that the recording was on. He was acutely aware of his movements and the need to move naturally. It was paramount that he captured anything of significance in the hall, which required him to rotate his torso in slightly unusual angles and occasionally give it a quick and unnatural spin. His relief that he was not the focus of anyone's attention was mammoth, he wanted to keep it that way.

The Panchayat members were seated. Sardar Timur and his men arrived and visible to all. Paro and Rauf were there, but Turab didn't see the accused or his family in the room. The chairs reserved for them were empty. One of the Panchayat members asked where the boy was just as Turab was wondering if anyone else had the same question.

"He'll be here shortly," Shujaa announced. "Not just him, the whole family. But before they are brought in, Mullah Aziz has some announcements to make."

Turab saw them all turning their faces towards Mullah Aziz, always an odd sight, so many heads turning in unison. He smiled involuntarily for fraction of a second. God, he hoped the recording function of his phone was working properly.

Mullah Aziz cleared his throat, looked around, and then started speaking into the microphone, his voice calm, his tone calculated.

"As you all know Sardar Timur appreciates your service. You were promised compensation for your time. Remember, the money promised was for your time only. Not your opinion. You should deliver justice, regardless of payment and regardless of who is paying you. Unfortunately, the money provided for that purpose was stolen. While that is being sorted out, Sardar Timur has promised to provide additional funds so you can get paid as promised."

Expressions of cheer and sounds of clapping were immediate, but the zeal died down rapidly. All they really wanted to know was when they would get the money.

"At the end of the session today," Mullah Aziz replied. "We hope to conclude today. It's a simple matter. Let's all try to be fair and quick and let's be done with this."

Once again, the hall's atmosphere was filled with low murmurings and chatter. Turab could hardly resist the desire to touch the phone in his jacket pocket to ensure that the recording was on.

"We will now bring the accused and his family into the hall," Shujaa announced. "Do not be shocked."

Turab found this announcement strange. Why would they be shocked to see Gul and his family? While looking around, his eyes met with Mullah Aziz's for a brief moment, he seemed confused and definitely more concerned than before. "What could be shocking about the family?" Turab asked himself. Something was very wrong. He doubted they would look rested and refreshed, and thus different from the day before, but this didn't feel right. It was one thing if the family looked different somehow, but why make a point of mentioning it without some ulterior motive? Why point it out?

His pondering was short-lived. The family was brought in and the moment he saw the daughter, Badri, he gasped, faces around him displaying the same shock he felt. He heard inhales, and choking sounds of disgust at the condition of these people, these victims. Sardar Timur's victims. The parents were ghosts. They were hollow. Ashen.

Gul and Badri were covered head to toe in dark almost tar looking dirt. Their clothes were torn, practically shredded, worse than before, barely covering them and blood and urine stained. Both of them were gagged, their hands tied tightly behind their backs. Turab saw dried blood and so many bruises on Gul's forehead that it seemed as though the damage was irrevocable, and Badri's cheeks were scratched and bloody, and her arms bruised, one of them so swollen that it jutted out behind her back. He was ashamed that he didn't have the courage to look closer. He knew there was more that he couldn't see.

"What is this? What happened to them?" An old man could not keep quiet, the same person who questioned the money the day before.

"I told you, don't be shocked," Shujaa replied. Menacingly.

"How can you even say that?" The old man was adamant. "Look at them. What have you done to them?"

"Nothing. They were trying to run away. We had to chase and apprehend them. They had to be controlled. If they had followed orders they wouldn't look like this."

"Why didn't you give them a change of clothes?" the old man persisted. "Let the girl cover herself. Maybe let them wash themselves? Anything! This is unjust!"

"You ask too many questions," Sardar Timur intervened. "That is a bad habit old man, a very bad habit indeed. Now sit down I don't have time for your opinion. We need to go on now. Let's get moving and conclude this session and get on with our lives."

The old man remained standing for a long while, he stood in place just staring at Sardar Timur, unmoving. Eventually, he gave in and sat down without uttering another word. Turab heard himself take a sigh of relief, another potential disaster was just avoided.

"Maulana Aziz," Shujaa's commanding voice was heard throughout the hall. "You should start the proceedings now. Let's not waste any more time."

"Very well," Mullah Aziz replied softly. "But before we start, I think you should remove the gags, we'll have to question them and let the Panchayat listen to their story as well."

Shujaa looked at Sardar Timur, who denied the request.

"No. We will let them speak when it's their time to speak. First, you need to read the victim's statement."

361

"Okay, yes."

Nobody else dared to interrupt or comment. Turab felt like speaking up but decided against it. Shujaa had at least agreed to remove the gags when the time was right, a small battle won, he convinced himself that continuing to insist that the gags be removed right away, was not essential. He would intervene later during the day if need be. Now wasn't the time to take that risk.

"As I announced yesterday, the victim here is Farah, Sardar Timur's daughter. She was violated in her own house by the son of Sardar Timur's servants. To prevent her honor from being tarnished any further, she will not be presented before this Panchayat. However, my wife and I witnessed her verbal statement, which was then transcribed word for word. It will be read out for you. What you will hear are her words. If you have any questions, please withhold them until my reading of Farah's statement is over. After that, you can ask questions if you need any clarification." Mullah Aziz took a brief pause to catch his breath. The air in the hall was already oppressive.

"Questions will be entertained at our discretion," Shujaa interjected. "Keep in mind, not every question will be answered, simply because not every question may be worth asking. If we feel that the question is simply a distraction and will not aid in moving forward in the proceedings, it may be ignored." Shujaa continued. "Sorry to interrupt, but I think this clarification was necessary. Please continue, Maulana Aziz."

"All right," Mullah Aziz said softly, sitting and putting on his reading glasses. "Also keep in mind, there were witnesses. Some of your questions about this written statement may be clarified by them. As I told you yesterday, one of the witnesses is the mother of the accused."

He shifted some folders on the table before producing several sheets of white paper. He spread them in a row and started reading.

His delivery was clear and effective. When he was done reading the statement, he realized that it depicted Gul as a monster who was taking advantage of a helpless girl, a malicious boy that placed her in a situation from which she could not escape. A young growing teenage boy that was arguably stronger than her, who entered her house without permission, and without the decency to respect the homeowner's family. In this version, Gul was indeed the monster.

As a reporter, Turab's instinct was to question any story, but especially those which seemed to paint a conveniently one-sided picture. He was sure there was another side of the story—like any story—and wondered when or if they would hear it. He was anxious to hear from the witnesses and most importantly, from the accused. Unconsciously, he touched his breast pocket, felt the warmth of the battery on the phone, and felt a sense of relief. The camera was on and everything was being recorded. There was a low hum in the atmosphere. Panchayat members were whispering after Mullah Aziz completed the narration.

"Now," his voice boomed on the speaker system. "We'll hear from Zara Bibi. She can either give the statement outright, or I will question her. If you have any questions, you can ask them anytime."

Turab saw Shujaa move towards Zara Bibi, standing silently staring at the faces all around her. She balked when Shujaa grabbed her forearm but didn't seem to be really all there, she had long since shut down.

"Don't touch me, don't hurt me. I did not do anything to you."

"He will not hurt you Zara Bibi," Mullah Aziz was heard saying. Zara Bibi picked up her head and looked at him with a baffled expression as if she had never seen him before. "We just want to hear from you. Please tell us what you know and what you saw in the Haveli when your son was caught."

363

"My son was caught?" Zara Bibi spoke in a daze. "Why was he caught? What did he do?"

"That's what you are going to tell us." Mullah Aziz said, a hint of surprise in his voice. "That's why we want to hear from you. All of us."

"How can I tell you anything about it? I don't know anything about it."

"But you are the one who caught him. Don't you remember? In the Haveli. In the kitchen pantry?"

"No. I don't. What should I remember? I don't remember anything about what you are saying."

Mullah Aziz didn't answer for a long moment. The sound of a thousand whispers filled the large space. Turab's eyes were fixated on Zara Bibi's face.

"She's acting!" A loud shrill voice rose above the buzz that was filling the room, followed by two quick claps. Turab's eyes landed on Chaman. He stood up with his finger pointing towards Zara Bibi. The crowd turned its attention to him. The low hum in the room suddenly turned into pin-drop silence.

"She's good at fooling others. That's all she is doing, I'm telling you, she's a real bitch. A very wicked woman indeed."

"Sit down!" Shujaa raised his hands and addressed Chaman in a sharp tone. "We can see and hear her. We don't need your commentary."

"She's trying to trick us all!" Chaman didn't miss the chance to mutter, as he took his seat. His hands and forearms were waving in the air, ready to engage in another round of bizarre rhythmic clapping. He sat down but still kept whispering to himself.

Turab had heard of a eunuch involved in the events, but this was the first time he actually saw him in action. He had noticed him in the room before but somehow could not place him in the story. Now that he heard him speak, it was quite clear that this was an interesting

364

character whose conduct and involvement was very consequential. If nothing else, he seemed capable of drawing and holding the attention of the crowd. From his behavior, it was apparent that he was capable of saying anything without any fear, regret, or remorse.

Turab felt that Chaman's actions and loathsome, hate-filled commentary, while worthy of being mocked or dismissed, clearly had the capacity to influence opinions. He feared that Chaman's rant would influence the ultimate decision of the Panchayat, and that of any member who could be swayed. Turab took a long considered look at the eunuch's dark round face. Chaman's eyes were oozing with anger and venom. For someone fairly young, his mouth was already set in a permanent frown, even when his face was at rest. There was a strange combination of frustration, annoyance, vengeance, and sadistic pleasure in Chaman's body language. He felt a deep sense of anxiety and unease simply by laying eyes on him. Turab shifted in his seat and forced himself to look away.

Zara Bibi seemed oblivious of the verbal exchange between Shujaa and Chaman.

"Zara Bibi, do you know where you are right now?" Mullah Aziz asked and waited patiently for a response. Zara Bibi remained quiet, her face completely devoid of expression. Mullah Aziz saw Badri struggling in her chair while two men held her down. Her hands were tied behind her back, and she was shaking her head violently while trying to chew the gag off her mouth. Mullah Aziz shifted his eyes and saw Shams raising his hand.

"You want to say something?" He questioned Shams and got a nod in response.

"He was not a witness, and he isn't on the list." Shujaa quickly intervened, fearing Mullah Aziz would allow Shams to speak. "He didn't see anything, and he cannot address this Panchayat."

Before Mullah Aziz could say anything, he saw Shams lower his hand. Apparently, he lost the desire to speak.

"What a timid and cowardly man," Turab thought to himself, before turning his attention to Sardar Timur, who looked impatient.

"Maybe we should hear from the other witness at this time," Mullah Aziz said out loud. Turab wasn't sure if he was seeking permission or merely making a suggestion. He saw Sardar Timur nod. Mullah Aziz turned his gaze to Chaman and waved him forward. Chaman jumped up and almost ran towards the witness chair.

"My name is Chaman," he screeched with excitement before anyone could say a word. Mullah Aziz then asked him about the events of the afternoon in question.

"This woman, this crazy woman, she had it in for me. She was stealing from Sarah Khanum. What happened was when Sarah Khanum came to find out what all the commotion was, she got scared. Instead of telling her what actually happened, she made up stories." He took a break and surveyed the crowd with a long, sad face.

"Keep going," Mullah Aziz instructed him. The silence had gone beyond a reasonable pause.

"Very well," Chaman changed his position in the seat. "But first I need water. I am feeling very thirsty. Parched actually."

A water bottle was soon presented to him by Shujaa's men. He took his time to finish the bottle, then wiped his mouth with the back of his sleeve, and resumed his monologue.

"So, I was telling you about this woman–Zara Bibi–she lied to Sarah Khanum, your wife Sardar Timur, instead of showing respect by telling the truth about what she did to me."

"What did she do to you? Please try to speak in proper sentences you're confusing and hard to follow. Now again, what did she do?" Mullah Aziz could not help but ask.

366

"I was in the kitchen. I was hungry. Sardar Timur's kitchen is always open and welcoming to anyone who works in the Haveli. So I helped myself to some food. After I finished eating, I thought I heard some noise in the pantry so I decided to check. I opened the door and just flicked the switch thinking that the light would turn on, just the way it usually does, but there was something wrong, either with the light or with the switch. I must admit, I was careless in rushing in without first making sure that the light was on. Well anyway, I proceeded in the dark, hit something on the floor, and fell down. The door shut automatically. It has that thing installed at the top which does not let the door remain open unless you actually hold it. What do you call it? Ah, the door-closer. So obvious."

"My fall must have made some noise. I was hurting and I was crying and trying to get up when Zara Bibi started knocking on the door. Then she suddenly opened it and barged in. Instead of helping me, when I was clearly in pain, she accused me of stealing from the pantry. I kept telling her that I was hurt and that I was not stealing but she would not listen. I was so upset that I got up and tried to get away from her. But she started yelling and followed me. I kept telling her to leave me alone but again, she would not listen. I got so upset and so angry that I think I just snapped and may have punched her. I think. If I did, I am sorry for that. I truly am. But she brought it upon herself, and even after I allegedly hit her, she still would not let go of the matter. She became more and more agitated. That's when all the workers in the Haveli gathered around us. I may have said things to her which were not appropriate and again, I am sorry for my words. But listen, this woman is really annoying. Anyway, while we were screaming and yelling at each other Sarah Khanum showed up and that's when Zara Bibi went quiet."

Chaman took a break, looked around, and smiled, almost to himself. There was silence in the hall. Turab admitted to himself, Chaman had the gift to attract and hold the attention of a crowd. He looked around and found each and every soul paying full attention to the clumsy eunuch occupying the witness chair like a king.

"Then what happened?" Mullah Aziz could not control himself for long. His tone expressed the annoyance he was experiencing at all the pauses and breaks Chaman was taking.

"I'm thirsty again," Chaman said with an obnoxious grin. "Can I have some water?"

One of Shujaa's men rushed forward with several water bottles and lay them on the small table in front of him. Chaman picked up one of the bottles, took his time opening it, and then finished drinking. He cleaned his mouth with the sleeve once more, flashed a brief smile, and then started speaking again.

"Sarah Khanum asked us about our fight. This woman lied to her. I told the truth. I think Sarah Khanum believed me but she wanted to confirm my story. So she told Zara Bibi to take us back to the pantry. So we all went. I mean, me, Sarah Khanum, Zara Bibi, and all the Haveli workers. Sarah Khanum told Zara Bibi to open the pantry door and that's when we found this little rascal doing unspeakable things to Sardar Timur's daughter."

Turab heard low gasps. There was a brief round of murmuring in the hall. Chaman looked around with a victorious expression in his eyes and a satanic smile on his face. The murmur was short-lived and Chaman's voice immediately took over the tail end of it.

"I felt as though my eyes were being scorched," Chaman said. "A sight so painful and shocking involving the honor of Sardar Timur being trampled upon by a filthy animal like him." He took a break and spat on the floor while glancing scornfully at Gul.

"Enough with your theatrics." Shujaa's patience was running out. Chaman had said what he needed to say, there was no more use for him.

"He is the witness," Mullah Aziz intervened before Chaman could say anything. "He has the floor. He can say whatever he wants as long as it about the subject under discussion. You cannot dictate to him; he can say whatever he wants as long as it is not outrageous."

"You don't think this is outrageous?" Shujaa quipped back.

"Let's ask the Panchayat," Mullah Aziz deflected. Attention turned towards the Panchayat members. At first, they didn't understand what was expected of them, but after some whispering and muttering, one of them stood up.

"Do you think this witness needs to change his behavior?" Mullah Aziz asked.

"No," the man replied. "He's fine. In fact, he's more than fine. He is really quite good at narrating the events."

"Wait a minute," Mullah Aziz said, worry in his voice. "Let me remind you, you should not be carried away by his manners and charm if you can call it that. Make sure that you only hear what he says and not get tangled up in how he says it."

"Sure," the man nodded his head and looked at other members of the Panchayat, who seemed to agree with him.

"Should I let him continue?" Mullah Aziz asked Shujaa. He didn't respond verbally, just nodded, and sat back down. Mullah Aziz motioned with a hand gesture for Chaman to continue. Turab couldn't help but smile when Chaman's forearms rose up and they all heard the trademark rhythmic clap once again before Chaman's voice filled the air in the room. It seemed to grow more stifling all the time.

"So I was saying, Zara Bibi opened the door and we saw the little devil doing unspeakable things to Farah," Chaman repeated himself.

"I am sorry, Sardar Timur, that I have to talk about her in this manner. But I am telling it the way I saw it. It's all true. And for that, I feel very angry. This bum deserves no sympathy. He should be punished. You should make an example out of him."

"Like they made an example out of you," Turab could not help but whisper to himself. He could not control his amusement as he listened to Chaman and knew that later he would feel disgusted with himself. There was something compelling about Chaman, with his annoying smirk and ridiculous behavior.

Turab shifted his attention towards Zara Bibi. She still appeared completely oblivious. He then looked at Badri Jamala, still struggling to remove the gag from her mouth, while trying to free her forearms, one broken, from the armrest of the chair to which she was tied. Shujaa's men were restraining her with great difficulty. Gul stood motionless, staring at the floor. Of all the persons involved in the drama, Turab found Gul to be the most difficult to understand, his behavior strange. His face was without emotion and as far as he knew, had never spoken to declare his innocence or say a word on his own behalf. Even to prevent dire consequences to his family, he had made no move to express himself. It seemed possible that all this would take its course without one word of protest from Gul.

Turab's eyes finally shifted back to Chaman, who seemed oblivious to the pain that Gul's family was enduring, concerned only with his moment as the focus of attention. He was truly basking in glory. Suddenly, an uneasy thought popped in Turab's head: what in the world was Chaman doing in the pantry in the first place? He remembered Chaman addressing this question early on, claiming that he heard a noise coming from the pantry and decided to go in to check. However, all the events after his first entry–his encounter with Zara Bibi and then his altercation with her, leading to Sarah Khanum's discovery of Gul and Farah in the pantry—must have taken a fair amount of time. If Chaman's story was to be believed, then Farah and Gul must have been in the pantry much earlier than when Chaman went in, simply because (according to him) he ate in the kitchen and only after that was he drawn to the pantry.

Something was not sitting well with his story. Turab couldn't put his finger on it, but he was finding it hard to digest the tale. Something wasn't right. He wished someone, either Mullah Aziz or a member of Panchayat, would raise the question about the pantry, and ask Chaman to clarify. Turab didn't feel that voicing any of this was his place, but he didn't want to stay quiet either. He tried to think of a way to have the question asked, it was maddening, such a simple task and yet, he could not come up with a way to make it happen. Deep in thoughts, he didn't even realize that Chaman had started speaking again.

"Now, you would think that when Zara Bibi caught her son, right there in plain sight, she would feel terrible about it all, but instead of focusing on that she chose to attack me, and make me the culprit! She is shameless. Yes, she is shameless! Just like him. Now you get where he gets his attributes from. The apple sure doesn't fall far from the tree! He was violating Sardar's daughter and she was violating me, Sardar's trusted servant. Me! She tried to make excuses for him, she even tried to make it look like it was my fault that he was doing those shameful things to Farah. But Sarah Khanum is a wise woman. She understood exactly what was going on, and she wouldn't listen to Zara Bibi's wild stories. She had Gul dragged out of the pantry, and she told Farah to go inside the Haveli. Then, she asked Gul what was he doing in the pantry. He wouldn't answer, but his mother answered for him. As I said, she tried to make up some story. When that didn't work, she tried to apologize for her son. But Sarah Khanum was right in demanding that he should apologize. But he wouldn't. This rascal was not remorseful for what he did, not ashamed, not even a tiny bit. Sarah Khanum offered to forgive him if he would simply apologize and show some remorse. But no. His mother kept apologizing, but this one, he was made of stone. He had no shame, no remorse, and no decency."

Chaman took a break again and took another sip of water.

"This is how great Sarah Khanum is," he resumed. "She was willing to forgive him if only he would have apologized. But he wouldn't. Zara Bibi on the other hand is just wicked, she then tried to turn Sarah Khanum against her husband. She begged Sarah Khanum to not tell Sardar Timur about the incident. But Sarah Khanum is a great wife, and a great mother and she refused to do this. She made sure that Sardar Timur was aware of what happened in the Haveli that day. The rest is known to us all. We all know what happened next."

"For the most part, we also knew what you just told us," Mullah Aziz replied curtly. "The point is not what people know from other sources, the point of these proceedings is to get all witnesses to testify under oath so it can be considered truthful and official."

Turab found this remark strange. He wasn't sure if this whole—or any part— of the proceeding could be considered official. From what he could tell, this Panchayat had no legal standing at all, merely a facade of law and order.

"Well, I've told the truth," Chaman replied. He sounded puzzled.

"Do you have anything else to say?" Mullah Aziz asked.

"No," Chaman replied. "Unless you or any of these people have any questions."

"Well, I don't have any questions for you," Mullah Aziz said. Turab was hoping he would now seek information about Chaman's presence in the pantry in the first place. With Mullah Aziz's declaration that no further question was forthcoming from him, Turab surveyed the Panchayat, hoping that someone would raise a question, they all seemed equally indifferent. No one spoke. Turab found his hand rising involuntarily.

"I have a question." He heard himself but felt as though someone else was talking.

"You cannot ask questions," Shujaa addressed him directly, with anger. "You are just a spectator. You have no role."

"I just want to know what was Chaman really doing in the pantry," Turab found himself speaking again as if he had no control over himself. In the back of his mind, he knew that he was putting himself in danger, or, at the very least, inviting undesirable attention to himself when he should be edging toward the shadows. To begin with, if Shujaa and his men looked more closely at him, literally, they might recover the phone from his pocket. He would lose critical evidence against this enterprise. He knew he should have stayed quiet.

"That question has been answered," Shujaa replied back.

"You really believe his answer?" Turab spoke again.

"It's not your place to raise questions. Stop wasting everybody's time."

Turab felt the heat of angry stares coming from Mullah Aziz and Sardar Timur, along with the surprised gazes from everyone else. Before he could utter another word, Mullah Aziz dismissed Chaman, who immediately left the chair. There would be no answer.

~

For a while, there was total silence in the hall, except the sound of a continued struggle coming from Badri. She was still attempting to free herself and from what Turab could tell, trying to scream or say something. The gag was effective: no one could understand what she said. Only choked garbled sounds came through. The members of the Panchayat looked at her, Gul, Chaman, each other, and began whispering again in the pause between witnesses. Shujaa spoke quietly to Sardar Timur while Mullah Aziz watched them apprehensively.

Suddenly, the old man with the cane who was part of the Panchayat stood up, ignored Mullah Aziz's gesture to sit down, and started speaking.

"Are we going to hear from the girl or not? Why don't you remove the gag from her mouth so she can talk?" he said while looking at other members of the Panchayat. Turab saw several nodding heads, he almost felt relieved but knew better. They were a small group of compliant people, the abuse Badri was enduring seemed to have piqued their interest, but he couldn't be sure.

"I told you to sit down," Mullah Aziz addressed the old man with fury in his voice. "You are too much trouble and you don't follow instructions."

"You said we are here to deliver justice," the old man replied back. "How can we do that correctly if we don't hear from everybody involved?"

Mullah Aziz responded with an empty stare. Turab felt a bit frustrated with him once again. His friend was helpless but had made himself that way, an externally pious man too willing to be used as a hired gun. On the issue of morality, he walked a thin line, and now that line might trip him up to the point where he could not rise again.

"She was not involved in the incident," Shujaa spoke when Mullah Aziz seemed unable to decide what to do. "She cannot be allowed to speak. We might as well bring any person off the street and have them speak."

"Then why is she here?" The old man was not willing to give up. "All beaten up, covered in dry blood and urine, tied to a chair and gagged. Who knows what else has happened to her. If she is taking any punishment related to this, then she should be allowed to speak. What has she done to deserve this treatment?"

Turab finally felt a sense of respect for someone in the Panchayat. The old man had been consistent in his behavior and had been courageous in his approach. It was impressive that he had not given in to cynicism and self-interest and kept his mouth shut, as everyone seemed keen on doing. Turab promised himself that he would try to find more about this man. Despite the baleful looks and mocking comments from the other men, he was standing firm and the initial nervousness in his voice had been replaced by a firm and even defiant tone.

"I think I explained it earlier," Mullah Aziz intervened. "If the boy is convicted, the punishment is already decided for him. He will be castrated. But he is the only male child in the family. Therefore, Sardar Timur gave his parents an option. His sister can take the punishment for him so their lineage can continue. That is why she is here."

"That is such a travesty," the old man spoke again. "The boy hasn't been convicted yet, so why is she in is such a state? How can you condone this type of injustice when you are supposed to be a religious, honorable person? You know she is innocent. How can you force her to take the punishment for something her brother may or may not have done? And even before any guilt has been decided?"

"Well, he did what he is accused of, that is pretty much established. Isn't it? Didn't you hear what Chaman had to say?" Mullah Aziz blurted, then suddenly went quiet. He probably remembered that he was supposed to act as though there had not been a decision made.

"I heard what Chaman said," the old man retorted. "But it is for the Panchayat to decide if his story is true and correct. You cannot make such an announcement. It is as if you assume the verdict will be guilty. You have already decided on his punishment and you have already arranged for his sister to accept punishment for him. So what do you need this Panchayat for, then?"

Mullah Aziz stared at the old man's face. Turab knew that look, his mind apparently had gone blank and for some strange reason, Turab hoped he wouldn't be able to come up with an answer. At that moment, more than anything, Turab wanted Aziz to fail.

Mullah Aziz recovered his composure and started speaking. "That was just my opinion," he said softly. "And my opinion means nothing in this respect, it is the Panchayat's opinion and the verdict which matters. My own aside, if the Panchayat decides that he is not guilty, then he will be considered innocent and will be set free."

"Well, then let us do our job," the old man spoke back. "We need to hear from everybody involved. Let us hear from the girl."

"Once again," Shujaa intervened, "The girl was not involved in the incident. She has nothing to say."

"But we want to hear her. If she has to accept a punishment she should be allowed to speak." The old man was stubborn. He turned towards the other members of the Panchayat who were sitting quietly, listening intently to the conversation. "We all agree right?"

The old man's hope that the other members would support his position, turned to despair when no one else raised a voice in agreement.

"I think not," Mullah Aziz said. "You are alone in this demand. Nobody else wants to hear from her. It's decided, then: the girl will not be allowed to speak."

"What about the boy?" The old man asked. His tone was full of disappointment and frustration. "We should hear from him."

"Uh, yes," Mullah Aziz replied with obvious reluctance, which Turab found surprising. Apparently, Mullah Aziz was not convinced that the accused should be heard or even have the opportunity to confront the allegations against him. That seemed strange, he kept switching his strategy. Turab didn't get an opportunity to ponder this too much because, without warning, Shujaa's loud voice took over.

"Even that may not be necessary. What do you want to know? What do you want him to say?"

"Whatever he has to say," the old man declared. "We should hear his side of the story as well."

"There is no *his* side of the story," Shujaa replied with anger. "There is only one side of the story. You have already heard that side of the story. There is nothing more to it."

Turab heard several surprised gasps. A low but rising hum in the air rose in intensity very quickly. Suddenly the Panchayat members found something to express concern about.

"This is strange," the old man said. "How can you say that we have heard all we needed to hear when the accused has not spoken a word yet? From the looks of it, he appears to have been mistreated—really badly—and his sister is clearly struggling to be heard. How can you say that there is no other side to the story? Chaman was there. He spoke. Farah spoke through her testimony. From their stories, the boy was there too, so why should he not speak? How can we deliver justice correctly if we do not hear from them, especially when you present them in front of us in this battered condition?"

Shujaa stared at the old man for a long moment without uttering a word. The crowd's hum died down quickly as the tension increased. Without shifting his eyes or speaking, Shujaa waved his men forward. They came close and surrounded the old man in a circle.

Turab was sure that he was not the only person to sense that this was a serious threat to the old man. Not just the old man, but for that matter every member of the Panchayat and everyone else in the hall. The facade of due process and proper procedure, even in an illegal proceeding, was crumbling. From the beginning, Turab had questioned in his mind the viability and sustainability of this charade, and it was almost comical, almost. All it took was one non-compliant character in this otherwise sheepish group of "yes men" to blow the whistle.

"Mullah Aziz," the old man addressed in a defiant tone with a very slight shake in his voice. "What is this, am I being threatened?"

Turab's eyes landed on Mullah Aziz who was glaring at Sardar Timur. Turab saw Sardar Timur ignore him and instead shot Shujaa a very off-putting look, then nodded in a deliberate way.

"No, you are not," Shujaa's voice rose above the hum in the room. "In fact, we are here to protect you."

"I felt perfectly protected before you began circling me like this." the man responded. "Go back to where you were standing before and take your men with you."

"We know exactly where to stand to protect you upstanding citizens. We are the best judges, not you. Don't worry yourself about it. Now sit down. If you want to hear from the boy, fine. He will speak. But before he does that, I have another story to tell you, since you are so curious about stories. Not just you, but everybody who is sitting here, anyone who really wants to hear from the boy."

"What do you mean?" The old man asked. "What kind of story? Does it have any connection to this matter or is it just another threat?"

"You can always make a connection," Shujaa spoke casually. "The question is not whether there is a connection, the question is how do you make the connection. If you cannot make the connection, somebody else will. Someone here who is saner than you."

The old man didn't reply. Turab surveyed the hall. There were Panchayat members in the central area of the hall. Sardar Timur's men, under the command of Shujaa, were scattered all over the place. Gul's family was placed in one corner, and there were many spectators in another portion of the hall, including those who served in Sardar Timur's Haveli.

Turab noted Sardar Timur's face, his expression, for a moment it seemed as though he was smiling, then his expression switched back to his usual poker face. Mullah Aziz seemed perplexed but visibly afraid. Something he never was. Members of the Panchayat, spectators, and even men under Shujaa's command, looked unsure.

"Are you addressing just the Panchayat members or everybody present here?" Turab found himself throwing a direct question towards Shujaa.

"If you can hear me, then my address is directed towards you. That goes for everybody."

"What story do you wish to tell us?" Turab asked. "And for what purpose?"

"To make a connection to the situation at hand," Shujaa said.

"I am not following you," Turab replied. "What connection?"

"Just listen to the story and you'll surely figure it out," Shujaa said. "You're a journalist. You should be able to make the connection. But first, you have to listen."

"Okay," Turab almost whispered to himself. The room was completely quiet now. Shujaa heard his whisper, nodded his head, and then turned towards the Panchayat. He spoke slowly and carefully.

"The event I am about to narrate happened a few years ago in a place that was much like this one, a situation very much like this one. When one's honor is attacked, one is bound to react. The reaction depends on the strength of the victim. When the victim is strong and has the ability and desire to act in a way that can be harmful to the perpetrator, there is really nothing that can stop him from acting upon it, except the control and discipline which come only from the goodness of one's heart. Just like Sardar Timur here.

"In this other situation, some members in that Panchayat started acting irresponsibly. Before going in, they had taken the oath that they would not come out of the Panchayat hall without a verdict, one way or the other. But because of the stubbornness of some of the people involved, they could not finish the job at hand in time. Since they had taken a pledge to stay in the hall till the time they reached a verdict, they ended up spending the night in the hall.

"That's when the most unfortunate event occurred. While they were sleeping, something went wrong and the hall caught on fire. Before any help could arrive, the entire building, with all members of the Panchayat and the accused inside it, was totally consumed by the raging fire whose origin was never discovered. It was a tragedy. But a tragedy which could have been avoided–had the Panchayat acted responsibly. Well, history cannot be changed. However, a repeat of history can certainly be avoided. You will be well advised to do just that."

Shujaa went silent for a long moment. There was a complete hush. Turab suddenly had a sinking, sick feeling. Was this a real story or something Shujaa just made up. Was it even a story? It felt more like a prediction. A story about the past, with comments about not repeating the history–this was not a history lesson, it was a threat.

Turab's eyes wandered around the room, jumping from one face to another, his gaze moving as quickly as his heartbeat. He did not have the presence of mind to interpret the variations of expressions on each face but there was a common theme: disquiet. For a long, painful moment, there was total silence.

Suddenly there was a movement where Sardar Timur was seated. Turab saw him get up and walk towards the door leading out of the hall, his men followed. He did not look back. Turab, along with others, caught a glimpse of the outside for the first time since morning, when the heavy wooden door of the Panchayat hall closed behind them. He was struck by the fact that the day had almost passed. The sunlight of the morning had given way to the almost dark of the evening. He checked his wristwatch, it was not that late, not late enough to justify the inky almost midnight looking sky. He looked through the two windows, high on the wall, almost touching the ceiling. The sky definitely looked dark and cloudy through the iron bars.

The gate was clamped shut after Sardar Timur and his entourage left the hall. Turab's attention was drawn back to Shujaa and his men, who were circling the Panchayat. Shujaa spoke again.

"You want to hear from this boy?" he asked, looking directly into the old man's eyes. He stayed quiet. "You will have plenty of opportunities to hear from him. You can listen to his side of the story, as many times as you'd like."

"Where did Sardar Timur go?"

"Sardar is a busy man," Shujaa replied with arrogance and indifference. "He has many things to take care of, a lot of responsibilities."

"In the middle of the proceedings?" The old man asked with surprise and suspicion evident in his voice.

"There are more important things," Shujaa spoke after a brief pause. He then motioned his men to walk towards the door. They complied, Shujaa following at the end. As his men left the hall, he then turned around and spoke out loud.

"We'll leave you alone with this boy. You can hear every word, his whole story."

He turned around and left. The door was shut behind him. It closed so hard that it made a loud bang which almost threw Turab off his chair. He started to reach for his phone.

Once again he caught a glimpse of dark growing even darker outside. His eyes shifted towards the windows again. The sun could not be setting that quickly. This time, he recognized the dark, as black smoke rising. His heart sank. He heard himself scream. At precisely the same moment, the bright lights in the hall went out. Sudden darkness enveloped everything. The resulting loud gasps from those around him drowned his scream.

The black smoke outside was thickening rapidly, and there was no air, only smoke, no light, only darkness.

END OF BOOK ONE

AUTHOR'S NOTE

SAIFUL MULUK IS a mountainous lake located at the northern end of the Kaghan Valley, near the town of Naran in the Saiful Muluk National Park. At an elevation of 3,224 m (10,578 feet) above sea level, the lake is located above the tree line and is one of the highest lakes in Pakistan.

Saiful Muluk was formed by glacial moraines that blocked the water of the stream passing through the valley. The Kaghan Valley was formed in the greater Pleistocene Period dating back almost 300,000 years when the area was covered with ice. Rising temperatures and receding glaciers left a large depression where glaciers once stood. Melting water was collected into the lake.

The Lake Saiful Muluk is named after a legendary prince. A fairy tale called Saif-ul-Muluk, written by the Sufi poet Mian Muhammad Bakhsh talks of the lake. It tells the story of the prince of Persia named Prince Saiful Malook who fell in love with a fairy princess named Princess Badri-ul-Jamala at the lake. (Wikipedia 2020).

CPSIA information can be obtained
at www.ICGtesting.com
Printed in the USA
LVHW092041310821
696583LV00001B/1/J

9 781735 453507